PROWLER

a novel by

Marion Campbell

Banksiamen scramble in the shadows beyond the picture window. A grieving woman struggles to recover a voice for herself from the notebooks left behind by her lifelong friend. The black-eyed Spider stalks and mesmerises, feeding on the desires of her acolytes. These are prowlers that haunt the narrative of Tom-Tom O'Shea.

On the surface *Prowler* is about the anguish of 'growing up', but out of this Marion Campbell creates a profound and often savagely funny and satirical exploration of the personal hazards of separation and engagement, exile and belonging. *Prowler* is also a deeply affecting novel about the erotics of memory, desire and obsession.

Prowler confirms Marion Campbell as an inventive, linguistically impressive and politically important writer.

Cover image: Memnuna Vila-Bogdanich, Big Banksia *(detail), 1973, etching, artist's proof, 620 x 470mm. Reproduced courtesy of the artist. Photographed by Victor France.*

Marion Campbell was born in Sydney in 1948. She has published two novels, *Lines of Flight* (1985) and *Not Being Miriam* (1988), both with Fremantle Arts Centre Press. She has also written two works for performance at the Perth Institute of Contemporary Art: *Dr Memory in the Dream House* (musical theatre in collaboration with composer Stuart Davies Slate, 1990) and *Ariadne's Understudies* (an adaption of *Not Being Miriam*, with director Noelle Janaczewska, 1991). She now lives and works in Melbourne.

Photograph by Margaret Campbell.

To dear Barbara

PROWLER

a novel by

Marion Campbell

*whose work is
a wonderful revelation
with affectionate admiration
Marion*

FREMANTLE ARTS CENTRE PRESS

First published 1999 by
FREMANTLE ARTS CENTRE PRESS
PO Box 320, South Fremantle
Western Australia 6162.
http://www.facp.iinet.net.au

Consultant Editor B R Coffey.
Cover Designer Marion Duke.
Production Coordinator Cate Sutherland.

Typeset by Fremantle Arts Centre Press
and printed by Australian Print Group, Maryborough.

National Library of Australia
Cataloguing-in-publication data

Campbell, Marion, 1948– .
  Prowler

  ISBN 1 86368 251 1.

  I. Title.

A823.3

The State of Western Australia has made an investment in this
project through ArtsWA in association with the Lotteries Commission.

Publication of this title was assisted by the Commonwealth Government
through the Australia Council, its arts funding and advisory body.

to the memory

of Marie Maclean

*for the inspiration of her work
and of the friendship extended*

I am a little girl and there's a prowler outside my picture window. The prowler watches me watch. I paint what I want to watch in my picture window. Sometimes I paint the prowler myself. The prowler looks like me in some of these pictures. But I'm stuck in my spot and the prowler prowls. The prowler is sniggering in the labyrinth of my ear; he is the marauder in the margins of my notebooks. The prowler says: Arrest that contour, fix that line. This is what she means if she's writing for anyone beyond her own little circle. The prowler is my intimate framer. The prowler is my right hand. He says: What are you looking at, girl; wouldn't you like one too? This is what the little girl wants. The prowler says I'll be your dealer if you'll stay behind that picture window. Sometimes the prowler is God. Sometimes, returning in this shape, he is the voice of the mothers I invent. The prowler's feverishly flicking eye and side-shuffle are my own imposture returning in the dark. I write sometimes like a straight guy. What I dredge up in my draglines, you'd be surprised. The prowler returns to haunt me. He's an old hand at cross-dressing. He finds me out when I sneak into his baggy pants, iron shiny serge, low at the crotch, his twisted belt. The prowler knows the protocols. He whispers at my ear: they'll say you're mad, self-indulgent, illiterate ... You a rebel? Watch your words clot with your fear ... You'll never have the guts to be lawless like me, to be a real iconoclast — that means image-breaker, sweetheart.

I'm trained to think with an alien brain. I'm in constant dialogue with it. I make a nice couple; I make a nuclear family all by myself. The prowler says: You will never shatter the glass. Obedience gives style and panache to your revolts. Kick open a door, you'd make sure your foot described an arabesque. The prowler incites and rebukes.

The prowler wrote this on his visiting card.

I

She Chose Venus

It's as if he's always been there, as if he'll always be at it, twisting the white cloth into the glass, watching with his Byzantine eyes. He will remain young, as icons remain young. I like his long fingers; they'd look good in a mosaic, poised over a flute. He pours out the chardonnay carefully, twisting it tight and yellow between the bottleneck and glass. He gives the bottleneck a last emphatic turn, unfurls the napkin and slings it back over his shoulder in one continuous movement. Stylish gestures are almost enough now. His hair is cropped close to the skull. I nod to him; he comes; he goes. Only minimal signals are necessary. The underwater time he establishes suits me perfectly: day fusing with day.

The name of the place suits me too — they didn't look far for it: The Corner Bar. Perhaps death is only this, an exile from proper naming. The regulars call the barman Tony but he could just as well be Mimesis; it's the way his name came in that dream. He turned from the glass-washer and said, without moving his lips, as if through voice-over: I'll shape it for you, if you need me to. You know ... As if that afforded comfort. I have to take my clues from somewhere. Otherwise the numbness will win.

So, that's why I've been coming back; the dream insisted. It's as if he could maintain this stillness until it becomes some sort of liminal dance, letting me cross over, as if when he speaks it will be only to shape silence, nothing more. His presence laps at the edges of the ... feel it remotely as if through someone else's nervous system ... Strange, it's not emptiness. No, it's full, full, and dense as basalt. Against this basaltic heaviness I feel his presence like the hush of dream waves, sound cut, rhythm visual, before any colour. I need this austerity of black and white.

His delicate hovering lets me move into Tom-Tom's death — and again it's the fitful dozing on the apricot leather sofas in the waiting room with Maurice, Karim and Isidore, the pastel flower prints blurring as they are meant to, along with the twilight flickerings under the door, the faint humming of intensive care, and through the porthole, the spectral shapes of nurses and doctors. The beeps, the stuttering beeps, are the worst because they've become pattern too, a climate, as night fades into the drizzling light of morning.

Once or twice Tom-Tom's eyelids part but the capillary-crazed whites roll back. No signal can get through her thickening dreams. I could swear — as Mother used to say, By Jove, it was vivid — that more than once the irises have darted their black flame through the lids right into mine. Maurice takes my elbow as I rise to give the bedside chair to him: No, no, please, Lou. Please stay. It's better you're here too. Besides, and he dips his chin into little Isidore's tangled hair and presses his lips into the plump arm around his neck. But Tom-Tom is ebbing — each time we look across at her steady profile, her still hands, it's we who are further stranded.

Isidore is in the grubby lemon and lime fairy costume she refuses to give up to the wash. The leotard is bobbled, the netted tutu gashed, the star of the wand whirling dangerously close to the tubes and the monitor knobs. If only her magic could work. Her little hand, calloused from days on the monkey bars, grips mine like life itself and down we go, day after day, to the lift, stopping at the drink machine for her to laugh as the Fanta can clunks into the serving window. Now in her mother's dying time, we retreat into the fairy's balancing act, all along the limestone walls outside the ugly brick hospital. I think each time: if Isidore gets through that shrub without losing her foothold on the wall, Tom-Tom will live. Our concentration is fierce and wonderful and each time I have to take hold of myself to go back to Level 5, where there's all that grim concentration and waiting, waiting, for the unbearable to happen or to retreat. I just want this suspension, to be weaving with the dark-eyed fairy through the shadows and light, with her wand waving, wanting, wanting, more and more of this.

Sometimes I brought Isi here at Happy Hour for the chunky chips that Tony puts in baskets along the bar. The drinkers in the place suited me straightaway: small battered veterans who ask for little beyond the drink in front of them.

Then the clot wipes out what is left. Maurice crouches and buries his face against his little daughter's chest, against that tight round tummy, letting his sobs break while she stands, the wand immobile, and stares ahead. Her sorrow will come later. The monumental absence, an implacable statute nailed at the centre of her life, there in every scene. Sometimes I find myself thinking that she's our daughter, hers and mine. In any case Maurice won't be there for her; he'll be too abstract in his loss. Already he's asking too much of the little one, for her to disappear as Isidore, for her to become what has eluded him in her mother. As if he wants to curl up in some nursing space inside his little girl. She puts her finger to her face and holds it out. Look, Lou Barb, I've got tears, I'm crying! This shocks her, and she begins to sob really until I think she will rupture something. There's no space for me to howl. Of course I couldn't begin. I would be lock-jawed, obscene.

We leave Maurice there, with Tom-Tom, and go down into the night — the street is deserted — just a few frosty residents' cars in front of the little houses and above, there's a dazzle of stars. Somewhere I heard a hospice nurse say to a little girl: look for the brightest star, and think of Granny's spirit going up to it. This is what we must do now, Isidore and I. She points to the knot of light close to the moon: Venus. Clichés grow enormous with the weight of what really happens.

Now Tom-Tom will never leave me. How many times a day do I turn to speak to her or to phone? Or is it continuous? Already I find her in every crowd, in every room I drift through in my dreams. Those black eyes plead, then reproach me before she turns away. And in the street, the thousands of faces affront me with their refusal to be that face, clamped down on their own factuality, with their own moving, alive eyes, taking their own business into account. I need Isidore now, to look into her black eyes to make them hold my look. Here I am doing it too. Isidore must be Isidore; not a reliquary for what escaped either of us in Tom-Tom. And Karim! How did Maurice break the news to him? Giving way to Maurice, Karim, her own son, had gone down for a smoke and missed the moment when the spikes flattened out on the monitor.

Perhaps it's always just a matter of bad timing. The obvious rolls down so heavy, there's no room. I want to ask Tony, whose quiet gestures lock him in a temporal loop: Do you have a … life beyond here? This is what Tom-Tom might have called imperialist reasoning, a failure of imagination become class habit. Yet I need to have him suspended at the bar. I don't want the details of his life beyond; don't want his anecdotes to impinge, any more than a therapist's client wants to hear her problems, her mucky appetites. Perhaps he doesn't have any. His face says back to me: *Of course I live alone. I withdraw to my room in the Fremantle Hotel. I read the Shorter Oxford Dictionary. It has everything I need.* He smiles at me, recognising something. He could be my son.

What would he have read? Woman shot in Theatrical Bid to stop the Inevitable. Alongside the TV coverage of flood, famine, law and order marches, freeway pile-ups and kidnappings, maybe he's seen a shot or two of the aftermath, photo-journalists trying to recover drama from the still life: a plinth, a trampled zamia palm and then, a passing shot of the empty bottles near the back door as a hint that this is the sort of lifestyle the woman was trying to defend. Tom-Tom holed up in the closed verandah at the side of the old house, slides a length of pipe between the louvres. In 'self-defence' the cops fire. There'll be, of course, an internal police inquiry, and then, whatever the findings, nothing. That's always the way here. For twelve days it was: 'Condition serious but stable ...'

Police meant something different to me then, just a childish cartoon because of Mother's little slogans. She'd say: You've got to look after the little things, Lou, or they mount up and sooner or later you find a policeman on the mat. Well, I have tried to keep my life in order, answer memos, pay my fines.

And then, there he was, a few days after the funeral, the man in a faded blue shirt on the front doormat. Thought: Oh God, of course, I've begun to slip — those envelopes with windows left unopened on the mantelpiece. But it wasn't a cop; it was Maurice all right, tan faded, face crumpled. Simply hadn't recognised him through the flywire. The voice too was crumpled, as if from lack of use. He said: I couldn't think of who I could talk to apart from you, hope you don't mind. I swallowed that, chose not to take offence.

Isi?

Isi's with Josie, you know, at Banksiafold.

Why didn't you bring her round? I'd love to see her.

I know, I know. But ...

Yes. They'll know how to help her through all this.

I can't cope with her around. When I look at her ...

He began to sob, falling back into the sofa.

Under the light I saw that his cuffs and collar were a little grubby, frayed. He'd come on some sort of a mission, though. After one or two wines he mentioned that he had in the car some notebooks of Tom-Tom's, a few computer print-outs and even a little exercise book recording those last hours. He said: To be frank, Lou, it's left me quite distraught. It's like she felt the average Martian to be closer than me.

It's as if he wants me to recover something for him, to bring it back close and negotiable, or simply to continue the unpredictable of her life. What he has read shuts him out. The thing is, I can't see how I'm meant to let Maurice into Tom-Tom's story, at least not in the way he seems to hope. What does he want or need in the afterlife of her words? Oh, I suppose there'll be some shocks in store for me as well. I can see at a glance her old motifs: the banksias and the picture windows, the charged stuff of her childhood. There's Tony quietly watching me scan the pages for traces of myself even where I'm clearly wiped out.

I don't think that I can face a class again. It's as if I'm full of buzzing minuses, as if they will hear it through the words: performance, practice, spatiality. Buzz words! They stick and choke now. I can see their faces already, the way they make them moony, blank, to deflect questions. I still have three months' leave.

At work they gathered in little huddles in the corridors, trying out their pleasure on their palettes, like a moral delicacy. It's as if they were consuming her death avidly, as the ending she chose to give her story. I felt them studying my face for closet knowledge as they said how sorry they were; they gathered we two were close. Close! What did they want: a scene from adolescence, clothed but experimentally close, or naked, deliriously so? Her extravagance, my constraint. Our composure, finally, despite the pitch of singing blood. How close did we get? Have I buried that too, along with Mother, that old terror of her walking in and saying: What on earth's going on in there? I was so afraid of Mother reading on my skin, in my voice, my walk, the fever I had caught that I would avoid Tom-Tom for days. The fear closed my throat, snagging every second syllable when I tried to answer Mother neutrally if she mentioned Tom-Tom's name. I skirted the phone as if it were the most dangerously addictive device. I was perhaps also afraid that if Tom-Tom got any closer to me she would be quickly bored. At least it saved me from becoming one of her discards like so many others, people, art forms, causes.

I wonder with how many she practised her intimacies. At the funeral 'bereaved' took on so many shapes, so many expressions. Was this multiplication for each of us a betrayal? How many of them came close to throwing their hearts to her — beyond simple physical infatuation? A number of solitary women were there, come to think of it, on the edge somehow, outside the normal social circuits, oddly dressed as well, as if for years they'd drifted from any notion of fashion and at times fluked something like its anticipation. There were a few nose-studs, a few tattoos, none as indiscreet as Tom-Tom's banksia. What Mother would have called Bohemian Lasses, and Mutton

Dressed as Lamb: velvet and leather miniskirts, bodices in patchwork cutting into the loosened skin of breasts. A few power dressers I recognised from the Arts, a few ferals. Well, good on them. And there was Millie and her family — Millie who simply said: She should've stayed with us. It was losing touch that did it. I didn't like to pursue that just then.

His level gaze is on me. Sweet Tony. In the corner alcove he couldn't say I take up much room and anyhow, an empty cafe's not much attraction to anyone. I order my share of coffees before moving on to lunch and the wine. It's good having these notebooks of hers as a prop.

Running Writing

People from the highway see late into the night Grandma Maeve lit like a black and white negative under the old hurricane lamp hanging from the ironlace and through the sprawling shadows, they see us, those kids running wild.

Josie, Zak and I race around the bonfire whooping to my gobbledygook chant. The ceremony peaks with our tossing our underpants to the flames, as we wave our sizzling sparklers. It's running writing we're doing. There's a message in the sparklers' looping trace, but we won't translate it. That'd kill the magic. Around us we can hear the old banksia cobs mumble words without saliva, catching, tearing them on their horny lips as our hot piss shoots into the firelight.

Maeve calls: Whoa there! from the verandah but it's not about the aerial pissing. Her eyes are almost transparent and her hair's like spun glass through the hurricane lamp. Her big smile floats across like the Cheshire Cat's. She tells us about spiders pitched between the branches, to watch out that we don't collide. We say nothing but stop the ceremony as suddenly as we started it. We've got giddy with our own rhythm, still racing inside.

Then I can move into a slow place. I watch for hours the banksia's cobs knocking at the glass, glamorous, gold, their glistening styles held captive, close. Against the picture window I trace with my tongue the unfurling of the styles until they tip at the glass and write back, nectar-sticky. I see my own eyes seeing and my mouth parted, fogging the glass with my breath. The styles, becoming me, unfurl like chameleons' tongues.

Maeve adds a wing onto her house for me. This is my *wing*, I say. I can take off into this other space. It has big picture windows for the prowlers. It's in jarrah weatherboard; it's oblong. As it weathers it goes the same as the grey of the banksia bark, rough, like fossilised moss. I can multiply mothers, and fathers here. I call up the debbilwomen, the wolves, and Banksiamen, and witches, all the bogeymen. They press their urgent faces to the glass.

Between my wing and the main part of the house there's a draughty, closed-in verandah, painted ultramarine, filled with ferns. Fishbone ferns, tree ferns, and maidenhair ferns rustle in the lace of their shadows. From here, my room is Somewhere Else. I can make any day crawl back into darkness where the Wild Things outdo one another at the windows. The stories I tell are just a lure, to dare them to fog the glass with their breath.

The Golden Book has a centrefold. I tape it to the outside of the window so that it looks in. Backed by the melaleucas and grasstrees and banksias and zamia palms is the Big Bad Wolf. The mouth opens. What a cave. The redness fills the room. The long tongue lolls and drips saliva just for me. I am Big Bad's food. Then I make my screams sound, climbing to the highest. I wrap my arms around my shoulders and dance. I can feel the wolf's rough fur grazing my lips. Grandma Maeve walks in. I just turn down the sound and hold my pose. There's nothing to say. We can switch things around later: I can cut open the wolf's belly and let Grandma out like a Caesar birth, like in the encyclopedia. The wolf lives here; he's part of the household.

Sometimes at night if I listen through the wolf's panting, and the scratchy noise of the scrambling Banksiamen I can hear Maeve groaning in her sleep. Where does this come from? What's this she keeps apart from me? Mostly she just gives me Strong and Bright. This moaning isn't mine. Then sometimes I can make out Mummy's voice through the crunching of leaves on the metal roof. Maybe I can make her meet me. Get to her through Maeve's moaning, move through that tunnel. All the hairs on my arm stick up. I make myself brave, make myself get to the toilet without light. Why can't I have a bottom like the Gumnut Babies, a little slit always clean and no hole anyhow? I've got to do it without Maeve calling out: Is that you, is that you Thomasina? It's as if she always expects someone else. The hallway is full of ladders, paint tins and roller trays. She dresses in old striped pyjamas to do the painting, making it whiter, day after day. And I get caught amongst the painter's gear in the hall. I can't go forwards or backwards without making a clatter.

Is that you, Thomasina, Thom-as-ina? She puts this fake man thing into her voice. She's been drinking whisky again. It is horrible and I can't reply. She makes me a prowler in her house. I can't say anything. She was moaning and now she is the stern man's voice. The gravelly boom comes again: Who is it? Who is it? Whowhowhooo? I am this Thing in the black hall amongst the White Prowler's clutter.

The light switch is thrown. The brushes, roller trays and tins with their white drips down the side, the ladder barring the wall with its shadows, and amongst it all, me shaking. In the black and white I go red: and this fear stuck like an egg in my throat. I screw the crotch of my pyjamas, but the wee-puddle spreads at my feet; it counts my toes warmly, one to ten. She has shrunk me back. I fold up tiny, warm-wet. She takes me in her big arms. I smell the whisky on her breath all right.

But we've met here now; this is different. I will be brave next time I meet her like this with the growling man's voice, and me in the dark, still the prowler, coming towards her fake fearlessness.

Lou Barb

The Attractions of Extinction

Immediately the screen of myth comes down. Inaugurate me now, we say to the past; give me a founding story. There's no equivalent ever for this scene. It's condemned by its prestige to the fatigue of endless substitution.

There was the wail of another ambulance. I saw a poor woman on the other side of the glass twisting and craning her neck to the sound; the skin corkscrewing, the mouth loosened. I wondered what ghosts were disturbed for her. It was only as she mimicked my movements that I realised. All I could think was: *so, that was my face, my ageing skin, my bereft lost look — too bloody bad.* This, in a way, is what I hold in reserve now as I read her, Tom-Tom young. I come to feast on impossibility, our coming together, younger, intact, gloriously alive; yes, and I have to admit that I need to maintain this barrier and how much easier it is with letters from the dead; it's a museum space, casting me in a different time. Reading, do I disturb this or am I simply repeating the habits of this sick culture, promoting the attractions of extinction? Now she's dead I can receive the heat of her life. It's just like fogging the glass as one gapes at skulls and stuffed animals in display cases. As a four-year-old I knew more about the Pterodactyl than any living species; I could still draw it more readily than the Mountain Devil, sacred to the Wongar people because of his wisdom, because he has survived. Oh and what of my own survival? Have I survived her? As my eyes travel down the page, I can even love myself as something that might return on the other side of the glass, getting the habit of the oblique gaze; why not: the prowler's sidestep? The past conditional: *that's where I could have lived and there, there, there!*

In the Wheatbelt

I guess my mother thought it would be easy. The mirror would sing back her sweet, high dreams to her. *The world's your oyster, Evie.* The wide-set almond eyes, the finely arched eyebrows, the black bob, and between the lips parted on the span of teeth, the voice held in a long note. Just looking at the photo you can almost hear the soprano voice: to be in its transport, to resonate with it, you'd be inside rapture, not yearning for it. The breasts rise and fall against the stiff, strapless bra cups.

I reckon I was too laid-back about it all, Maeve says. Always thought talent would advertise itself, but there you go, what happened is her beautiful voice got buried in the wheatbelt. He fell in love with her for that voice. You know she designed, produced, directed and sang in you know that thing with that ...

She hums 'I'm gonna wash that man right out of my hair ...'

South Pacific?

Yep, that's it, *South Pacific*. He would've heard about it at the Bruce Rock General Store, and he thought himself a bit of a specialist in the voice department, just like he could tell the sort of speed he could get out of a horse by looking at its chest and rump. So he went along. And of course all the boys were gaping, ready to throw themselves at her feet. He'd remember that. You know she wrote home about this grey-eyed farmer with his delicate manners, and because time teaching in the country made her feel marooned, far away from any sort of future and because he worshipped her gift, or so she thought, she married him. Talk about the caged bird she became. He thought all the time of those gaping farmer boys. There was no more being out rehearsing at nights sharing herself about. No way. He wanted to keep it for himself. Well, even there, in the farmhouse if he walked in and she was singing, it would be: G*lad someone's happy, don't reckon you'd have anything to sing about if you were out on the harvester in this heat.* There was nothing really vicious — he was just a sad sort of sack. I'd get this stream of comments he'd served her. She was a brilliant mimic, so she had me killing myself laughing. I didn't see how depressed she was getting. No more question of even teaching. It was something he let her do occasionally, relief teaching, to keep her hand in, in case they needed it in hard times. Even that was a comparative joy. She should've got out. But then she had you, and you were tongue-tied, I mean, literally. They should've snipped that flap of skin from the start. So, you screamed and screamed. The more you sucked the more air you got. But if he could be real mean, and I don't think he ever realised it, he would happily take you in his arms, so she could take a bath or sit on the verandah for five minutes away from your crying. Come to think of it, it might have been postnatal what's it? We didn't think like that back then.

I didn't read him right anyhow, so why should've she? He always made a fuss of us older women, practically had us believing we were young belles. Manners, he had manners. Everyone said: What a gentleman he is, that son-in-law of yours, Maeve. No reason then to see it as anything less than genuine. And you never saw him get ruffled. Like a duck, he was — everything just trickled off, even those sharp replies she'd send him at times, were just met with: Well, if that's the way you see it, Evie. To the point where she became the bitch in everyone's eyes. She's found a real pearl there, and three thousand acres of good land, they'd say. Reckon he's got a pearl in her, I'd say back, defiant, you know, of their tone, of what they wouldn't say.

Your mum, well, she was always another kettle of fish, highly strung, what we used to call the Artistic Temperament. I was glad she was highly strung. Too many floppy people about. At least she's got passion, she's tenacious, I thought. She rages in the troughs but then when she peaks she goes higher than most, too. As a child she threw some awesome tantrums. Thank goodness there were no supermarkets back then, I would've lost her a million times. And she'd reverse things, claim it was me who was disobeying her. Why did you go and lose me? she'd say. It was a bit of a laugh when you think about it.

Don't, I'd say, leave the door open, this was winter, mind, you'll let all the warm air out.

Good, she'd say, she must've been five then, warm outside is good, that's what I want.

So the way she finished things looked like a spoiled girl's tantrum to anyone who didn't know her. There was some party coming up, people from neighbouring farms. Suddenly it was important to him that she had clothes. He was proud of her beauty. He said he'd wheel you around in the pram while she chose something smart. Stuffed some cash into her hand as he dropped her off at the store. He said: I gave her money for a nice dress, and God knows, I thought she'd be pleased. It wasn't as if we could really afford it.

She'd spent such long periods isolated except for the fencers or shearers who'd come in for tea, she panicked at the idea of mixing, I'd say. Maybe what got to her was the idea of choosing when there was only a choice between the ugly and the boring. Maybe what was on the racks in that store hit her: this was her life. I don't know. She'd found some floral numbers and a thing with navy spots — you can imagine the range they had — and hooked them on the dressing-room rail. When he came back to see how she was going, she'd shot through. She'd tried nothing on, apparently. She'd just bolted out of there. The shop girl said: Reckon your ladyship's too fancy for us. There wasn't far to look in the town, of course. They found her soon enough down the track leading to the council dump. She'd used her belt to hang herself from a white gum. It was the first time she'd had half-an-hour away from you.

Modals

One still, one photograph, one scene lit with the dressing-room bulbs. Looking at the lit scenes why always do I let so much, so many, who should have been there, who were there, yet not caught in the light of my need, slip into the shadows? Between the bra cups and the moving breasts, I become. That powder puff there. That stick of grease-paint. The lipstick she will never have finished applying will write my own lips in.

Lou Barb has always played the grown-up. You force me into it, she says, the grown-up.

Lou Barb says this is what I do, splitting, that I keep splitting off because of Evie.

Well, I say, if you'll excuse me, it was some split. But what did she call it — severance? Severance needn't be your way. You don't need to take it as a foundation story. You're not just the little girl whose mother killed herself. You play out your life in this sort of nostalgia as if you want to remain some kind of ... incandescent orphan.

Whoa! I say. I like that. Can the *incandescent orphan* get a kiss then?

No, darling she says, well, yes of course, she can, but she's trying to distract me. You're more than that. You keep abandoning out of fear others will do it to you. And really, all you're doing is repeating.

It wasn't so long ago that we were tearing with our grasstree spears, hurling them like javelins. Josie, Zak, and I hammered in the slats to make the ladder up the giant melaleuca, then slung the rope to haul up the planks to make the cubby floor.

Now, remembering Odette coming home for a weekend from Caedmon College, I can't see where they are. Maybe they're helping Millie and Maeve with the food or watching 'Home and Away' on the old black-and-white TV. They must've seen it as a betrayal, the way I let Odette cut them out, not actively, but by regarding them as curiosities. She would study them with a brief, blinking fascination, as if they were bit players to be accounted for and quickly dismissed: I thought you were quite stunning, Tom-Tom, but Josie outclasses even you. *She* could be a mannequin if ...

If what? Last thing she'd want to be. She wants to be a singer. Blues and Country and Western.

Oh surely not!

Not everyone has to sing arias. Oh no, Josie's got her own style.

Well, I expect that's true, she says. When I hear them talk, I realise where you get your style from. I thought your sort of storytelling was original but I suppose you picked it up from them. The way you act out, the direct speech?

Them. So now you think I'm a pale copy.

I didn't say that, she goes, and opens her *German for Advanced Students.* I can see where you come from, that's all. We've got to do these modals.

We're revising for the final exams. It's modals on the menu and I go: *Ich hätte das Fleisch nicht essen mögen. Es darf keinen Dritten Weltkrieg geben* and she goes: *Ich hätte ein solches Wunderkind sein mögen.* It's as if we've been up here for ever, above the midge haze on the melaleuca platform, with the birds' song against the frogs.

That's a Mud Lark, the bright-voiced one. That harsh squawk, Noisy Wattle Bird.

She prises away the paperbark. Examining the under-layer, she says: Like baby's flesh! Baby pink, baby tender, she goes, giving each vowel a tweak, like she's distributing umlauts everywhere.

There are insect eggs under it. She presses her cheek to it voluptuously. She's a bit like Hermione in *Women in Love*, demonstrating Magnified Rapture.

See that, I say, that's a Red-Eyed Coot, down there, wading into the mud, Eurasian Red-Eyed Coot.

Oh, she says, with another umlaut. She watches it flexing, retracting its blue-lobed toes. Now in the gathering dusk, all the melaleucas are hung with cormorants, Sacred Ibises, Great Egrets. Watching, watching the water for fish signs. Oh the pelican, Odette says, just look at the carry bag! So serious, parading it across the water, all plumped out. Doesn't know she looks ridiculous.

Ridiculous? Come off it! She'll have the last laugh. Look at that eye.

Pied Cormorant plunges vertically in. Pacific Black Duck flashes its under-wing, emerald, then violet. The water is gold now, with green-bronze tucks in the V-wake of the scudding birds.

You don't need to be so grave about nature, Odette says.

Well, you're grave about bloody grammar.

I should've worked harder. *Ich hätte tüchtiger arbeiten müssen*, she says.

Hey, just listen.

I watch her lips moving. I'd swallow all those umlauts.

Just listen to it. Calm down. I'll have to ask Joe if he'll play his didge for you. The way he channels the swamp music.

It's like I've got a beeper implanted in my brain, she says. Daddy's Girl has got Daddy's Beeper, like he's trying to get me even here.

I take her head in my hands. I soothe her forehead, *there, there*! I make out I'm smoothing away the beeper bump.

She jerks her head away. How come, she says, you get to come to Caedmon when, you know, well, Maeve and that are so ...

So what?

Well, poor ... Like everything's been thrown up in the air and left where it landed, and sort of ... just sort of patched together? So how come she can afford to send you to Caedmon?

The voice falls flat out of me: My father pays the fees. He sold the farm after my mother ... He's in Queensland now. Maeve says we may as well accept it since it's the only thing he does for me. I'd rather go to Yangebup High with Josie and Zak, but there you go.

I wanted to deliver that to Odette like a cold slap, wiping her out. I want to make her feel bad now. *Thrown in the air, patched together!*

I lower my feet to the first rung, start climbing down. Her voice continues, in pursuit.

No, I envy you, in a way. At least they don't pester you. Maybe this sort of hit-and-miss place is what you need. Maybe it's what makes you so confident. Maeve and Millie and that. Maybe you owe it all to them, finally. What we think is ... unusual about you.

It's true that I find myself in any story I like, pinch a brain from here, powerful legs from there, energy from somewhere else. I can slip into any hero or heroine. Hubris is a word we learned at school, like with Antigone standing up to Creon. If that's hubris, Antigone's is a midget thing compared with mine. I've got a certainty in my muscles, in my nerves, in the way I crave, in the pulse I pick up from things, that what you know is nothing if you can't dance your knowledge. Dance your own story, Daughtergirl. Otherwise they'll stick you in their story in ways that hurt. It's Millie who's told me that. Never apologise for who you are, Maeve says. Sound your own true note, and to hell with anyone who finds it jarring.

It's probably because Maeve just lets you float around doing your own thing. She's casual ... Or maybe she just couldn't care less?

Oh, no, I reckon ...

But, you know, when she puffs on her pipe and with those ... mismatched eyes, one brown, one hazel ... don't take this the wrong way but, I almost expect her to go into a trance, like some sort of ... witch. I don't think she likes me very much, actually. Well, she ignores me. I suppose I'm used to Mummy and Daddy interviewing everyone who comes to the house. She seems to have no curiosity.

It's not that. She goes into daydreams, that's all.

I hope Odette won't start on Maeve's drinking. I think with dread, she will have emptied her first beer bottle by now. It'll already be there on the red Laminex table next to the saucer with her pipe. After tea, it'll be the whisky.

She's been through a lot, I suppose, Odette says. You seem surprised at all this. Like you never examine yourself?

What is this? I look back at her glazed eyes and her silky blonde-tipped lashes. She funnels her lips. They're pale, bluish, like all her blood has retreated to the little thought nesting in her brain. She's not really talking to me but to some piping voice in there. She's about to give me another serve. Pick-pick-pick — what is examination anyway, self-examination? What am I lined with that she'd unpick?

Odette doesn't like me much, I realise now. Why did she come? Maybe so she can just tell the others what it's like.

Hey youse! Josie shouts. Tea's ready! S'lamb and eggfruit!

Eggfruit!

Yep. It's Moroccan. It's got eggfruit and maybe dates. Just eat what you can.

I want to say: When we eat it's not acres of charred steak, a mountain of mash and a scattering of water-logged peas and carrots. It's not *thrown up in the air and left where it landed.*

Oh-debt Blues

Who *was* that picked up O-dette? Zak makes it sound like Oh-debt.

That was Oh-debt's daddy, in Oh-debt's daddy's Jag-u-ar.

Phew, he whistles, watching with me from the verandah. The Jag's bumper gives a last flash before the trees swallow it.

I feel the tension easing out, all the knots unravelling, and then I'm boneless, sinking down, through the jagged gap she has left. It will take time for space to be smooth and elastic again. Zak's presence swims around me, rising to distinct focus as I look up from the beanbag on the verandah: his cinnamon skin, his brown eyes with their shot of jade. He has a smudge of dark down over his lip; he's a man-child now. The smile eases as he looks into my face, lifting my hair.

Whoa, Tom-Tom!

His voice is a bit cracked at the edges; there's almost a soreness to it. Keeping his eyes on me, moving softly, he picks the guitar up by the neck and tries out a few notes, adjusting, listening, tuning, as if it too is listening for signs of where this mood is taking me. Ol' Marvin, he calls his guitar.

Hey, Marvin, he says, plucking out a chord, our Tom-Tom's gone to that Oh-debt place.

She gets to you, that hard girl.

I take grim satisfaction in the summary.

You know, you start talking like her, when she's around.

I do not.

Do so. Even on the phone, when you're about to talk to her, you sort of arrange your voice?

Oh, lay off why doncha, I say.

He tightens the strings, plucks and strokes.

> Tom-Tom got the Oh-debt blues again,

he tries.

Josie has come out, towelling her hair. She bends at the waist and drapes the towel around the back of her head, catching the dripping hair, twisting the towel into a turban, then rises, flinging back her head. She stands there, quiet, attentive, her nostrils flared, latent amusement in those dimples.

Zak goes again:

> Tom-Tom's got them Oh-debt blues again

He tilts his jaw towards Josie, opening the space. Her stillness takes me to a calmer zone.

> I can tell it by the way she hangs her chin
> Can tell it by the way those black eyes glaze
> She'll be havin' Oh-debt blues for days and days.
> I say ol' Tom-Tom what's the use
> Strange friendship if it always leaves you … bruised.

Zak laughs at the way his soft growl breaks like a spreading bruise.

Maybe all you're lookin' for is pain
Tom-Tom's got them Oh-debt blues again.

But she needs me. She sort of chose me once, I bleat.

She needs you because no one else would put up with talking them into a corner all the time, that's what I reckon, Josie says.

She said now she knows where I get all my ideas. From here.

What's wrong with that?

Yeah, what's wrong with that? Zak goes.

Nothing, it was just like she was saying I made out I was original when I wasn't.

Tom-Tom got them Oh-debt blues, Zak's voice hovers, then shifting up into a drawn out nasal whine, he drags out the 'again'.

Josie crouches at my side. I put my fingertips to her cool skin.

You know what I reckon flows in Oh-debt's veins? It's not blood, it's something colourless, more like acid?

They both laugh quietly.

Sometimes I think so too, I say, surprised it's so easy, but knowing I'll be back there, under her spell, taking it all again. Being talked into a corner, like Josie said.

I wish I could leave now. The school and all that.

But what about Miss Hoffman? Josie teases. Miss Proud-as-a-Camel Hoffman?

Once I was Fou Roux's Lover

Or I loved Loopy Red as I like to call Vincent van Gogh. Not Fou Roux as the Arlesian children chanted after the ear episode. Not mad. But not straight either. Loopy.

At my first meeting with Vincent it happened. There was no question of a return. I wanted to laugh with the boom in my blood, the ricochet of trouble through my world. Nothing would stay put anymore. My vision was jolted. I'd got supreme, slow sight. It was like my eyes had grown fingers. Shadows hummed with colour. Things processed me as they grew. Give me any sound I could dance it. I was seeing so close-up it was like blindness was the new kind of vision.

After this I could never be straight, see straight. So there, Odette. Maybe this is what I'm lined with.

I was Loopy Red's lover.

I was twelve when I first found him in Maeve's lounge room, on the rack of the blondwood table, under the glass. He was sleeping there with the calmer, coolly sumptuous Gauguin. I knew straightaway why Gauguin didn't stay on at Arles in the Yellow House. Gauguin was a good housekeeper, kept his palette in order. Loopy Red had always been too much. As he looked at a plane tree he could feel the sap rising under his own bark. As he looked at a lopped plane tree, he bled and sprouted again through his wounds. The sky was a whorled dance-for-joy in his head. With him I danced-for-joy: I was bride and I was groom outside their churches, under the vault of Starry Night.

Maeve had put a single gardenia in a shallow white bowl on the glass. She was careless and mucky in some ways, but she could clear a space for a simple, beautiful thing like no one else. The quiet circle of the white flower floating in the white bowl made a scandal of my noisy heart. As I went into the gardenia's perfumed flesh I found the white sky with the gold beating behind it. I was sunstruck in my straw hat. I walked straight out of my picture window, along convulsive walls, though the flamboyant grass. Flowers flickered their little tongues at the palm of my hand. I felt the weight and the acid dampness of a clod of clay. I let my fingers bog and glue with it. I was Loopy Red's lover. I could stay for ever in this ploughed field, between the almond trees. I rolled and opened: I was greedy for every kind of contact. I was all finger footsole palm and tongue. I thought: *my skin has developed a genius.* I could feel each petal-fall acutely, as if it could last and last in the depths of the moment. I was kissed and kissing, I was inside out.

For years I'd been tracking him back from Arles to the grey mute town in Belgium. I came to the little miner's hut where he used to practise his martyrdom as a young pastor. Already I could hear the Arlesian children chanting *Fou Roux Fou Roux*, which means Mad Red. I put my cheek to the stone, feeling in each pore the syringe of the wind and on my tongue the sour taste of coal dust. There, with his face to the wall I saw my Red, his body blue with the cold. I saw how gaunt his buttocks were and then wondered if gaunt were only for faces. He had no clothes left because he'd flung them to the miners. The oil lamp flickered blue back onto his skin. He turned his face to me: it was like The Potato Eaters were starting inside him. The peasants with their sunken cheekbones didn't waste words. Right then I could see them glancing from behind his eyelids. He carried the Potato Eaters protectively although they don't want his charity either. He was shivering in his litter bed. I took some lumps of coal from my apron pocket and I stoked the fire. We didn't need to talk. I lay down next to him and fingered his rib cage, wishing I could play the instrument. He accepted me, under-age or not, a century too late. Loopy Red and I cradled one another. We warmed the black room with our unevenly shared breath. We found all the colours in the darkness. I felt the closeness of his God as my fingers explored his shoulder and his ignited my hair.

I take this book of Loopy Red's pictures down to Millie's house.

Hey, what do you think of this fella's painting? Vincent van Gogh? Don't you think it's a bit like what you ... I mean the feeling of it. You know, not the actual ... They say he was crazy, called him Fou Roux, Loopy Red.

— Oh, oh, that's one troubled man, Daughtergirl.

She sighs, as she turns the pages, then goes very quiet. Still, we look at the irises and walls and wheat fields and almond trees and the patients doing their round and round in the exercise yard and the crows circling and circling and he brings us back to where we are. Millie, Josie and I put our boards on the ground and dip into our pots of acrylic. Millie helps me do the swamp and all the waterholes. We do the numbat tracks under the echoing stars. We do the frog song and the cicada song.

Millie says, Your Vincent, I reckon he's better with us, eh! We tack the paintings onto her wall and watch them a long time.

Engineers of Betrayal

It's seven o'clock. This is the bus taking Odette and me to the literature exam. She's blue-white. This bloodlessness never struck me before Josie said it. After being with Millie and Joe and even Maeve who's milk coffee, I can't believe such whiteness. I'm relieved in a way; it helps me not want the tenderness she can't give. Her hands are wrapped around her marbled ankles.

Just look at these men, would you? she says

I look, yeah. Like they're unused, like all their orifices have fused. For how long has anything gone out, come into them? Like they're full of boiled eggs.

They've not even had their morning poop, she says.

This is Odette's kind of daring, not like the girls who say they fuck with boys, who drink bourbon, and smoke cigarettes behind the gym. I like the way she can use a kindergarten vocabulary to make out she's got a sort of stark and primitive knowledge.

They're full of poop, she says again. It has an authority

which stops me from wondering how anyone else might see her body. Like it refuses to have anything to do with organs and food and shit. As if she's never seen these grave, suited workers before. Maybe she despises them for their lunch boxes, for the briefcases perched on their laps.

She's like Virginia Woolf with her pinched nostrils repelled at the vigour of the Verlgah Classes. I try to chase this away. We're not trapped in class, I tell myself. Anyhow, I'm not. And I don't want to cast around for a word to defend these serious men. I find lurking in me something like disgust for all of this too but like a future that's unthinkable. I like this shiver of wickedness. And at least she's off the topic of Maeve and everyone at our place. Maybe she's thinking of her father again.

He's a Public Servant in Mines and Energy, advises the Minister or something. He's vigorous all right and voluble. I like the way his boom manufactures big spaces. There are vast steppes in his voice when it sounds from that big chest. I see bears loping through the volume of his talk, knuckle-grazing and frightening. Siberian wolves prowl, and huge skies open up. Amongst the antiques in their living room it's something all right. When I stay over I'm amazed at the way he makes you notice his retreats too. You'd think it was Ulysses going off. He retreats with the newspaper to the toilet or to the lavatory, as they call it in Odette's family, just as they say napkin quite deliberately after I say serviette. Like the word toilet has got a mock grain veneer, or gives off an embarrassing, cheap perfume. They feel a sort of pity for people who use these words. Come to think of it, Odette's snobbish like this too. It's like a kind of hygiene they practise in their talk. Still, I get my own back and check out lavatory in the dictionary. I say, hey, that's a euphemism too. Odette's dad doesn't take it too well.

He comes back from the lavatory whistling anyhow, full of news after his half-hour session. This is what fathers do, I think. He's so jovial that I find it hard to resist even when he shakes out the giant pages of the newspaper back at the table. Yuk, I think, that's air straight from the toilet, sorry, lavatory. Odette focuses on other things. It's like she's scanning the place, tracking him down to feed her nausea.

She says the sight of his hairy wrist toying with the breakfast napkin makes her gag. Or his crumpled handkerchief on the sofa.

She warns me, like I'll get contaminated if I get into little talks with her dad, or what she calls intimate. He likes to get into the daily confessional bit with her but she's playing hard to get.

If you dare let him seduce you into that sort of conversation, and he'll try to ask his dirty little questions about me, about us, I'll never talk to you again. He thrives on *intimacy*. Odette seizes the word, as if she'll never finish throttling it. He wants me to open up all of that to him. Let him think what he likes, she whispers furiously, let him have his disgusting thoughts. I'm not going to play his game. He wouldn't understand anything beyond his slimy idea of *intimacy*.

I don't let on that I don't know what she's talking about. If I go to put an arm around her, she shrugs it off, shudders. Disgusting thoughts, she said. The problem with you is that you come on too strong to everyone.

Then Cruelty Enters her Life. I am stuck by the epic grandeur of this phrase which she uses afterwards.

I reckon it's to get her escape from Daddy's Beeper that

she sees so much in Hjelmslev, a postgrad exchange student from Oslo. Like Vincent but the opposite, he is literally too much. He has forged a personal discipline out of excess. He stands at the bar and studiously drains the whole bottle of vodka, maintaining all the time some argument which I don't follow. He uses words like History and Dialectic and Ethics and Becoming as if they're characters in a morality play. He manages to make even Being utterly incomprehensible. But she nods like he's a hero. His drinking is as remote from pleasure as you can get. Well, against her family, she gives herself to the abyss he seems to be staring at. There's no stopping her. She sees any warning I try to give as jealousy. He's a good-looking man, I guess, but there's something outside my jealousy that worries me in his face. It's a bit Supermannish, almost a Chesty Bond tilt to it, too based on the set square. His eyes are a blazing blue. Anyway it's into that blue that she launches herself away from her family.

Odette's dad comes into her bedroom one night after Hjelmslev's departure. Rather than doing her study, she's slept through the afternoon. For days she has lain there, letting the cyclone die down. Hjelmslev has stirred this up in her almost despite himself, it seems. Maybe it's just *autoerotic* she says, like she's picking up the word with tweezers from a specimen jar. Maybe he's just a catalyst for that. She has this new technical vocabulary for sex. I make out I understand and nod. For those days of lovemaking her body has lost that marble-cold sort of definition and I see real blood blooming through her skin. But she says there's never anything to suggest in his attitude afterwards that they've been together sexually. He keeps cool, formal, aesthetically appreciative. It might be the nausea before that full-blown expressive stuff of her dad's that makes it difficult for her to want anything more than his kind of minimalist lovemaking. Come to think of it, if his lovemaking painted or sculpted it would make something like Ben Nicolson's bas-reliefs.

I can see it now. The father enters the room. Her mother manoeuvres herself behind him. She's gymnastically honed, into push-ups and infra-red ray lamps. Garth tries to engage Odette in conversation, sweetly at first, wondering if she hadn't better take a shower, come and eat a meal with the family, think about the approaching exams and if there isn't an essay overdue. For this father she's still as mute and cold as marble despite the cyclone in her blood. He tugs, like he wants to rouse her, the hem of the tartan nightie which hasn't left her all these days since Hjelmslev's departure. It's now that she hisses, and she rarely swears, fuckin' get lost!

Yes, do it, do it, Garth, her mum cries. The child needs a jolly good spanking. This is what you should have done years ago.

This is what Odette hears her mother say coolly, from the doorway. She can't stand Daddy's fixation on me, Odette says later. I let him continue. He thrashes me on my bottom. See how base he can be. Let him go to the limit. When he has finished, and I can hear his breath cut out, and my mother tiptoe off, I creep out the front door, over the verandah. I will embarrass them in our Leafy Suburb with its tasteful Federation houses in which Mummy and Daddy rate as Very Acceptable Neighbours.

At dawn but there has been no time, the police find me crouching behind bushes next to the golf clubroom in my wet-hemmed nightie.

Go on, go on, Garth. This is what you should have done years ago.

It's now she starts siphoning off money from her dad who's careless about the banknotes he leaves in his suit jackets. Anyhow, for a half-smile from his daughter I'd bet he'd quite happily sign away a fortune. She sleepwalks through the exams and miraculously comes through as if she's caught my techniques by some sort of osmosis up on the melaleuca platform. Some time before I take off for Marseille she leaves for Oslo where her Hjelmslev has returned to present his doctorate.

She turns up at my flat in Marseille. Her face is a blank flag hoisted above the black coat. I can't see the body. The coat's hem grazes laced boots on heroically stacked heels. It's crazy footwear for this city full of stairs and steep rises anyhow. So, at my door I've got this tragedian who won't let her composure crack. Oh dear, I think a bit guiltily, this isn't going to be fun. She wears this blankness so resolutely I don't dare let the honking traffic and waves of fish smells rising from the restaurants challenge her hieratic nobility. How has she looked, ghost-walking through the sunlit squalor of these streets? Her boots, come to think of it, are of the type the pros wear, more festively, in white. There is no way of getting into her face. It's a final sort of mould. Even hours later in my room it's a wax abstraction.

After days she begins to speak. Her engineer, he's done the work.

He didn't turn from the shaving mirror, in the bathroom, at the end of the hall. Oh, I saw a tension there, she says. Like a little tourniquet working in him which he resisted with his filial discipline. I saw his ankles twist, his hips sketch a tiny movement towards me. He would have heard my voice. I said: I am Hjelmslev's friend from Australia, I have come to see him.

His back stayed where it was, blocking the sightlines.

The hall stretched and that tiny disk of the shaving mirror had swallowed all the blue.

Odette says she chose Hjelmslev because of the cornflower eyes. Her mother's dictum was: Never trust a man with blue eyes. Hjelmslev's mother barked: the Antipodean Girl is here. I have told her that you want nothing to do with her.

He's a traitor and I hope life engineers for him a terrible betrayal when he most needs solidarity, I say.

We are all traitors, all engineers of betrayal, she says. Even you, Tom-Tom, although I know you entertain other fictions. Like that Molly you're talking about, like that Asif. You sleep with a theme, and when something seductive puts that under pressure, you will betray it. You will convince yourself that you're saving your integrity, but others will read it as a betrayal. I've copped it from you in small doses, myself. The way you used to flirt with my father, for instance.

What? I say. What?

Oh, she says irritably, you wouldn't know how you come across. I suppose it's your upbringing, so unused to dealing with men. Anyhow, she says, I know my limits now. I know my disappearance point.

She sleeps in her maxi-coat, a seventies vestige bought in some flea market, her little boots with optimistic heels, poised on her suitcase. Her back is still propped by the Tunisian cushions, the glass I put in her hands, remains after hours half-full of red wine.

This blackness is quite a denial. Her regular style is in levity and surprise, believe it or not. She went for combinations painters have always known about but which so-called good taste won't hear of. Violet and tan, lime green and a tiny note of cobalt. Even ox blood and ochre.

Now she is this diminutive, mute thing, cloaked in black. As I watch and listen and feed her, I can't locate her in her features; in this waxen mould the eyes are ringed and embryonically lidded. They brood on the dark corridor, on the retreat of blueness from her world. Her loss, just like her first intoxication, leaves me out. I feel saintly in this composition: I am a Sister of Mercy but she doesn't want comfort from me. I feel as if she's come to test the scale of her own sort of martyrdom.

Later, when she is established with Guillaume in Lyon, she writes that she has given up any Grand Hopes and has No Regrets. Simple lines in furniture and carefully placed flowers are a consolation. Experiences are basically equivalent, she says. What matter are elegance and restraint. She thinks that one day she might join a madrigal group. Guillaume is a quiet, intelligent man who provides what is necessary. She says she is a gracious entertainer of his colleagues, that she serves them impeccable meals. Of course I flirt a little with his colleagues but only enough for them to envy him. In France you learn that there must be measure in everything. If you'll forgive me, Tom-Tom, your life might be easier if you learned a little self-policing. But … then your experience of France was hardly representative. Those actors, those lesbians and gays.

Lou Barb

Necrophilically Feeding

Tony has cleared the counter; stacked the glasses in the machine, and now sits down next to me. He has brought a tray: dark chocolates in a bowl, a bottle of Southern Comfort, two glasses.

Compliments of the house!

Oh, Tony! His mere half-smile makes dimples; his eyes dance with questions but don't impose.

How's she emerging?

He reaches for one of my cigarettes.

Love, I think, is always an unfinished reading. A regard for what remains below the other's horizon. Maybe what makes parents inconsolable with the death of a child is bound up with this. In the excess of loss you're brought up against the penury of your imagination. You will never imagine enough to compensate. With death, there's the arrest of the future, of the story to come. The future's now a wound in the field of the past. You thought you were one step ahead of your child in that particular story.

Now you see it's what escaped your plotting and planning that you most cherished. Oh, and the child's bedroom becomes a mausoleum. The bedroom never to be messed up again. The arrangements in museums of the intimate are always obscene. They cannot speak of the living person. They can only speak of the will-to-preserve-in-formaldehyde of those left behind. And now, with the pull of his gaze tugging on Tom-Tom's lines, I blush for this. As if I'm caught necrophilically feeding. As if once again it's merely my own lying silences I give between the lines I feed upon, never even knowing what my own truth might be … I blush because I couldn't even explain if I took all night why I'm parasitising the remnants of her story, nor to what unspeakable of my own I'd have it gesture.

Only in this oscillation, only in this hovering, not to collapse back into her, not to draw once and for all the line of separation, can I rescue something from her words. Why, she once asked, did I deride the material of my own life, cherishing the prisons I secreted without ever counting them as experience that mattered?

On one hand there's Mother who found it so hard to receive my truth; on the other, there's Tom-Tom whose cues I never had the nerve to act on. I thought I'd packed it away, what they routinely call grief. Yet months after Mother's death, when the little white Mazda in which I used to chauffeur her filled my rear-vision mirror, I was seized by dread. Was it sorrow or shame that flickered over the bitumen at the traffic lights, always these lights next to the triple-facaded oatmeal brick hotel, like a crude kid's pop-up? I would do anything to avoid this intersection, wouldn't you? Mother would say. It is irretrievably ugly! Even in such a pathetic thing I felt a failure. Oh sorry, Mother, sorry about that hotel!

I've been prolonging the hiatus of Tom-Tom's dying to … Can't even say that. What if I were to front up, show my passport, try the runway into my own story and if there were nothing, nothing, to lift me into it? This is the fear. Have I waited all my life for a fantasy without contents; have I just made of Mother my excuse through my own moral sloth or cowardice?

I'm going dancing when I close this joint. Feel like it?

Can Tony mean this? I can dismiss my reflex excuses as they present themselves. Roly's long since in bed anyhow. He wouldn't mind, in any case.

A nightclub? But look at me.

He shakes his head. You look fine. A turbaned *femme fatale*. He said fem-fey-tale.

And crumpled pants?

No one looks for crumples.

As long as they don't take me for your mother.

He shakes his head, exasperated.

All right, why not? I say to this stranger. Mimesis! If I told him!

Let's go dancing!

Lou Barb

If She could be My Mother

At first Tom-Tom was so quiet, it seemed she wanted absorption to the point where she disappeared into the rituals, the uniforms and the choreographed etiquette of Caedmon College. But whatever her efforts, she was always missing buttons, somehow got her clothes stained the first day after drycleaning, let her hair dry tangled and had her tights screwed at her ankles. She cut a figure all right against the beautifully mown lawns and trim petunia and pansy beds of the school grounds. The detention points which her untidiness heaped up for her left her quite unmoved.

If there had been a chameleon need, of course her grandmother would have frustrated it, turning up in her battered, smoking ute, leaving it askew, driver's door open. She came, in her canvas shoes, sweater, and jeans, into the boarding school to make her deliveries to the kitchen: vegetables the resolutely Anglo cooks didn't know how to deal with: capsicum, zucchini, eggfruit, okra. The school spent a lot of time encouraging Caring for Those Less Fortunate. We wrote letters for Amnesty International, donated our lunch money for famine victims and queued for high protein four-by-two biscuits so that the Anglican press could photograph our sacrifice, but there were a number, I can tell you, who found their liberalism hard to apply when Maeve O'Shea arrived with her ute packed with her friends from Banksiafold. We'd see the Principal arranging her smile before she crossed the courtyard to give them A Grand Reception.

She had done all her primary schoolwork by correspondence. Public transport was inadequate, and besides, Maeve had wanted to keep her home for as long as possible. She had acquired a kind of thinking from Millie, Joe and the kids which always took classroom exercises in unexpected directions. Where we wrote little telescoped scenes with description alternating with action, Tom-Tom always spoke from the scene, letting the writing conjure the land acting with the characters. It wasn't something she wanted to explain. Banksia, flannel flower, egg and bacon, numbat, and bandicoot were there on the same level as the people, all speakers in her story. Because I piously applied the rules, she always took me by surprise. I felt slightly ashamed of my own cramped efforts. She would use the humming of the electric cables and the great pylons strutting across her grandma's place as the sinister part of the bush music, or the spinning tread of a four-wheel drive in close-up to announce an arrival. A motif like that became a shorthand for a particular kind of menace. Tom-Tom got her culture from the stories the Banksiafold people told her and she applied it literally, fervently. It had a force no one could deny but when it came to history, white 'Discovery' and 'Exploration', there were confrontations which awed us. Even in the year eight history class, Tom-Tom stubbornly refused to learn the names of those she called the invaders. I didn't question then how she thought she could escape that category herself, that in any case she owed her being here to those invaders. She didn't 'give a stuff' for marks or for assignment deadlines: if something interested her, she did it straightaway. If not, she just ignored it and happily took a zero. Maeve had let her structure her day as she liked. If she wanted to write all day or grow crystals, it was okay. Mainly she wrote stories or painted, I think. She read promiscuously and had devoured all the grandmother's obsolete encyclopedia.

With Tom-Tom every friendship became fierce and narcissistic. Back in the schoolyard, she and I were still chalking out the hopscotch while the others were already in clusters talking about boys and socials. I watched that thick ponytail flashing its blue-black, her brown legs hop, stomp and turn. Each time I caught her eye as she swung around. The frank acceptance of the great open smile was enough. With her you felt the sun in your blood. That was enough. I remember her dark blush, stooping over the taw: Lou, I saw a sort of white smear on my pants. Have I got an infection or something?

Oh, I get that too, I said. It's normal, I think.

She had stopped, stock-still. Odette's dad's burgundy Jaguar had swung into the car park. She could not take her eyes off Odette as she slid out and slammed the door. I was not enough. Odette would tell her more about that smear. I was now just a flicker in her peripheral vision. I was left to the shadows. Voice stopped in my aching throat. *Normal,* I was sure now that she loathed the word. I would think of better things to say days later, when the heat had faded, sleepless in bed, while Father gave his loud commentary on late night soccer matches and Mother prepared for her reading group, marking novels, as she'd once marked assignments, questioning the grammar, psychology, historical accuracy, scanning for redundancy, contradiction.

The boarders used to get around in a boisterous mob and they stuck pretty much to themselves. They'd line up behind the buckets of fruit and biscuits and consume these together at recess but she'd back up against a tree and eat hers alone. She took on a kind of regal distinction in her solitude. At times I'd glimpse something that looked like the ravages of homesickness, but she would make a quick retreat if you tried to quiz her on this. That unfocused gaze of hers was an insult-proof perspex the others took for arrogance. One day I left the day kids I was with, on a dare to check out what was going on. I simply sat beside her. It was one of the times when she and Odette were not speaking: I think Odette had joined the biggest mob of day girls and Tom-Tom was holding out on her own. She performed her resistance with an attention to detail which made me hesitate. She kept her breathing perfectly regular, her eyes abstracted. It called for an explanation from me which I couldn't give. I'd stuck my legs out alongside hers, my spine catching the knobby skin of the salmon gum. I couldn't withdraw with poise. She had monopolised poise, silence, obduracy.

I said. I guess. I suppose. I ...

Then she laughed: It's okay. You don't have to talk. I don't mind being left out of it. Not *normal*, you know. I know that's what your mother thinks.

Oh, come on, that's crazy. She doesn't, I lied. Well, anyhow, who gives a stuff about *normal*. Your painting today with the bits of broken mirror. It was …

I didn't want her to think I was sucking up but I said, swallowing, It was fantastic.

She said: No it wasn't — it was real.

Funny, but I think this was the first time I realised the connection between fantastic and fantasy.

I just do the connection lines between the bodies and where they are: here it's Old Joe and Millie, and Josie and Maeve and me talking on the verandah, and there are the zamia palms and the hovea and the banksia, and the frogs from the swamps. I just stick it in, that's all.

But what about the bits of broken mirror with the Banksiamen?

I don't know, she said. It's just what came to me. Why would I put it there if I could say it?

Now, of course, I can see the pride in the way she wore it: *dumb as a painter.*

Our art teacher, Eva Hoffman, had us to her house. We all found her exciting, but Tom-Tom! Eva was big-breasted and small-hipped, and the way she carried her head even imposed its irregularities as somehow ordained in a blueprint for aesthetics. She wore, transgressing the school rules for teachers, but maybe the principal liked to incorporate a delinquent or two, tight black jeans, bikers' tall black boots, red or black leather jackets with surprisingly feminine floral blouses, often unbuttoned to the breast cleft, so you got a glimpse of black lace bra. She wore a Star of David on a chain. It swung as she bent over our work so she'd clasp it between her big white teeth.

Swarthy, and in the summer a deep brown, she could have just as easily been taken for Arab as Jewish, and her broad Australian accent was just another edgy ingredient in this high-flavoured hybridity. Her forehead was beautiful, sloping back to the frayed hairline, which she emphasised dragging the henna-rinsed, self-ringleting hair backwards. It cascaded down her back and then fell forward on our drawings as she made her suggestions. Never straight, always through questions. Have you thought about the jagged line? she'd say. And we'd look, and see that yes, there was too much continence and elegance in our contained forms. Her black eyebrows were emphatic. Her eyes registered a concentrated vitality and an ardour that even Tom-Tom's couldn't rival. Tom-Tom said she wanted to curl up and purr, just basking in their fire. The nose in profile had a certain hieratic quality; she bore its great curve with the confidence of a camel. Miss Proud-as-a-Camel-Hoffman, Tom-Tom would say. We used her studio overlooking the river in an old Claremont mansion marked for demolition. She knocked up marvellous meals for us. Eggfruit casseroles, tandoori chicken, pasta with pine nuts, basil, romano, and garlic while she maintained the stream of talk and laughter. We were all seduced; we all basked, but Tom-Tom! She was the favourite and we were a little jealous because Eva would muster us summarily with her glance and as she stoked her talk, her gaze would lock into Tom-Tom's, to whom she'd dedicate the after-resonance of the full period.

I remember Tom-Tom looking through a Lucien Freud book, lying on her stomach on a floral floor rug among the scattered pasta bowls. How come, she said, all these people have dead flesh? Like they've always lived in a laboratory under fluorescent lights, like they've never breathed real air? I wouldn't have dared ask this since Freud was one of the painters Hoffman seemed to admire. Still, the way Tom-Tom used ignorance to unsettle what seemed natural made it hard for anyone to sidestep her. Eva sank down on her hands and knees behind her; threaded a lock of Tom-Tom's tangled hair between her fingers; placed a hand over hers. What struck me was the utter naturalness with which Tom-Tom sank backwards, offering her head to Eva's lap. Like a mother cat, without any trace of embarrassment, any sense of impropriety, Eva continued to stroke her hair. Tom-Tom's eyes were closed. Afterwards I said to her: You'd better be careful; you'll have everyone talking. Eva will be sacked and then what'll we do?

She stared at me and chose not to engage.

Tom-Tom confessed later that it had become an obsession, a disease, that she couldn't stop thinking about Eva, longing for those arms, for that embrace again; that she contrived walks to the local deli to coincide with Hoffman's routines; that she had them mapped out even for the weekend.

I told her to recognise it for what it was: some image of her own talent she loved in Eva. The talent that was drawn out more by Millie than by Eva, in any case.

So why does she do this to me?

I was struck by the raw plaintiveness of this question but I went: Well, she could be your mother.

She didn't say that this is what she wanted.

She lost weight, was so distracted in Eva's company that she botched drawing after drawing and screwed them all up. One Friday afternoon, when she'd asked me to

Banksiafold for the weekend, we were waiting in the schoolyard for Maeve to pick us up, I saw that the anxiety has reached its pitch. She was tearing at her fingernails, her eyes unseeing. As she began to speak her teeth were chattering. I noticed how diminutive she looked in the school uniform which hung straight down. You've got to tell me what it is, I told her. For Christ's sake. I can't spend a weekend with you if you're going to lock tight like that.

It's nothing. I've …

What? What? Her speech jumped in little staccato riffs between her chattering teeth.

My heart clenched. What could she have done now?

I've done a stupid thing. You know how I've been dodging art. Been telling myself I must give up on this crazy fixation, mustn't linger on the drive shivering, shaking, hoping to see her. It's pathetic; it's humiliating. And then when she drifts past so casual or makes out she's busy with some other teacher or treats me with such coolness in class, I can't bear it. So, yeah, well that's why I stopped going. Then I get called up, not by Eva but by Blackie.

Blackie was Deputy Head and Queen of Counsellors: good at the confessional bit, she drew out confessions from the most skilfully resistant amongst us.

So what'd you end up telling her?

Nothing much. Told her some bullshit about being miserable with what I was producing at the moment and so on. She acted like she'd swallowed it. But I felt so betrayed by Hoffman who's got to know what's going on. Well, she started it, for Christ's sake. I left her a letter under the art room door.

60

Oh no. Oh, tell me you didn't. Any one could find it! What about Guy Abbott or Liz Stephens? Anyone of them could pick it up. It wasn't a love letter, was it? Don't tell me you did that?

I don't know how she'll read it. Yeah, I guess so. She'll have to read it like that.

Did you put it in an envelope at least?

No. I'd run out. I just folded it.

I suddenly felt very strong and practical.

What we'll have to do is get it back. Pretend to the cleaners you've left your wallet or folio there or something. Say you've got to work on it for the weekend.

But what if Hoffman comes to the staffroom door? They're having some sort of happy hour in there.

We've got to take the risk. I'll go. It's more believable since I was in art yesterday.

Maeve drove in, her little ute smoking furiously. I could hear her hailing us, wrenching the handbrake as I was running across the quadrangle to the staffroom. It was a rather flushed and giggly Blackie who came to the door. Her breath smelt of cigarettes.

And what can I do for you, my dee-ah?

Can I borrow the master key, Mrs Black? I left my folio in the art ...

Lou Barb, you're what? Year 11? And you don't know that rule by now? I'm sorry my dear, but not possible, not possible at all. All the University Entrance folios are in there awaiting examination and no one is allowed access.

She must have read dejection on my face because she touched my shoulder: I know you're a dedicated student but I'm sure, this little hiccup will help you generate a whole lot of new work. Oh, I'll tell you what. It's … How silly. It's just occurred to me. No one would worry if I accompanied you there. Just a mo.

I couldn't believe I planned it all so badly.

When we got there, I'd have to step on the letter first. How could I guarantee I'd see it first? And then, what would she say when she saw my folio wasn't there at all?

There I was already climbing the art room stairs behind her. Maybe I could trip over the lintel. I paused on the steps to undo my shoelace. That was it: I'd sprawl over the threshold and somehow gather the letter under my jumper.

She must have been a bit pissed because she had one long cat-and-mouse game with the lock. When the door gave way she was the one who nearly went flying across the room.

Ah, goodness, what have we here? Must give that to Miss Hoffman.

Now my dear, where did you leave your folio?

I made as if I was searching the pile on Hoffman's desk.

No, dear, surely. Those are all Year 12. See, Miss Hoffman has tied them and labelled them.

But I could've sworn.

Perhaps you left it in your classroom? In your locker?

It wouldn't fit.

No, it wouldn't fit.

Look over there, there's some folios leaning …

No luck? Well then, my dear Lou, looks as if you've a little work cut out for you this weekend. When are your folios due?

I'm sorry. Next Wednesday, Mrs Black.

Well then, what's the panic, my dear girl? Miss Hoffman will help you find it on Monday. So don't worry! Goodbye now!

Tom-Tom was leaning against Maeve's ute. She was making a half-smile anticipating victory.

It wasn't there, I lied.

What?

She must've got it already.

Come on. I've been watching those stairs for the last five minutes.

Well, I don't know.

You went up there with Blackie.

Okay. It was there but it isn't now. Blackie's got it.

She's going to put it straight into Eva's hot little hand. Buggerbumshitfuck. I want to die. I'm not going back to that …

Maeve raised her eyebrows, licked her cigarette paper: Something up, Tom-Tom?

Oh nothing. Just lost something, that's all.

Maeve had an unquestioning respect for Tom-Tom. She never pressed her out of this silence, as my mother would try to do. Tom-Tom nestled into her misery and as the minutes ticked by, seemed to luxuriate in it. I felt that she was imagining now a closet reconciliation scene with Eva. What could Tom-Tom hope to get out of it? Maeve just let her take her retreat, even from me. As soon as the ute swung in next to the house at Banksiafold, Tom-Tom, without a word, attached the ancient farrow to the tractor, turned over the weeds in the orchard, set the fruit-fly traps, and fed the chooks. She took it for granted that I would work at her side, which I did. By now she was whistling and laughing. I thought there was something about Maeve that held back from Tom-Tom. She laughingly would brush her aside when she went to kiss her or to take hold of her hand.

We've got to stick our work experience applications in next week, I said.

Oh yeah, Maeve, said. Well, guess it's up to you. Do you want to, Tom-Tom?

With my parents there was never any choice.

Lou Barb

The Factory of Your Eyes

Something happened last night. Dancing together Tony and I moved soon enough into the mesh of gazes under the fluctuating lights. Somewhere I saw something Tom-Tom wrote about the attraction of the stranger, letting the sexual charge arc before tepid familiarity ever has a chance to settle. The woman I danced with later had something about her, which frightened me as it attracted me, a kind of intransigent demand. The eyes dragged a pang through me but I was carried by our dancing, a dual control beyond us. *Some machine we become*, Tom-Tom's voice said. Afterwards, I had drinks with Tony, for once on the same side of the bar. He'd found a compact man about my age — intelligent, green eyes, a grey stubble on his skull. His thumb was hooked in Tony's back pocket all the time we talked.

I went home to lie next to Roly, still pulsing from all of that.

Had a bit of a liquid workout? he said, jovial enough, as

he caught the fumes of unmetabolised alcohol.

Well, yes, I said. Had a few drinks with the barman. He's a lovely boy.

Satisfied, Roly kissed me. Well I hope it doesn't catch up with you tomorrow, he said.

Now Tony's eyes come back to me from between the mirrored bottles. Lou, he says, guess what?

The one last night? You've fallen for him?

Mmm, he hums. Mmm. Something like that. Eric. My first Eric, ever. He's coming round here later.

No, it is not envy I feel. He is radiant, frankly transfigured. I know I can't meet my desire clear-eyed like that the next day.

My passions were secret even back then, working up their composted heat, like abscesses festering in nocturnal pockets, lanced by the order of the day. Where does this all start? Look at Tom-Tom. The adult doesn't simply emerge from the motifs the child speaks of. The adult emerges from whatever ravels away from the spoken stories. Why in the mother's absence or the grandmother's distraction should I read her future oscillation between men and women? Why should oscillation be a drama? Perhaps these are my questions anyhow, rather than hers. Or why should desiring one sex rather than the other give a sense of sad relinquishment? Why does a dance with a woman I do not know make me feel my own situation as forlorn?

Tony is at ease. His body speaks clearly. His movements are economical, but with each gesture, something more expansive is drafted in the air. Watching his hands I wonder at how little I use mine. His curve and flex, fingers enmeshing, loosening, flowering forth. The fridges are humming. His smile stretches. He is irradiated with Eric's arrival.

Do I ever open to a smile? Why even this fear of writing it? Words are little marks on paper. They can be erased, these papers torn up. No one need ever read this. Why then this fear clutching at my throat? Is it the fear of miscarrying or of mothering these fragments?

I must stop staring at them. Eric wants more than sex from Tony. I feel pleased as the mother I might have been.

At the Institute there's a lovely man who's fashioned himself a little like Andy Warhol: he's set off his sharp blue eyes with a thatch of hair bleached albino white. I see him nursing his knees, crouching at somebody or other's desk, always intent and intimate, working in consultation, smoothing over misunderstandings, with that irreverent merriment of gossip.

How do you see your job, I asked, which was fair enough because nobody's brief is very clear these days.

And he said: Oh, I see myself as an unreliable narrator of this place. I'll get ditched I guess when you guys learn to speak in the first person. Perhaps that's why I dreamed up Tony as Mimesis. My first person!

I saw a fragment in one of Tom-Tom's notebooks:

> In the desert of my spotlight
> I build the factory of your eyes.

Did she write me in as her reader? Am I simply manufacturing a mode of seeing, framing her, to counter the desert of my own making? So Eric and Tony are transporting one another and here I am in T-shirt, and underpants, letting the parade of Roly's fingers stir my blood, yet catching their dance, arresting it in my clasp, signalling no, tonight, perhaps not, because the surveillance helicopter's also stroking me with its beam and as the throbbing recedes it's as if I can hear the cries of all the deletions, all the abortions from which some sort of truth might have been born.

As I drift off, I find myself in her arms again, within the demented architecture of that hotel where we all farewelled her, before she went to France on her fellowship. We are sitting under translucent canopies and beyond, in the dream, the tower pursues its logic, a wild relay of interlocking planes, and if there is something web-like in it, it is in numberless dimensions, a kind of galactic cartwheeling, the eye performing cosmic acrobatics just to trace it. Just to trace it is ecstasy. What we could aerially draw together, I murmur back in sleep with her again. I think, while we meld, this architect has expressed our ardour in these spaces: this is space-age baroque, baroque in seductions like Piranesi's prisons, but with endless possibilities of escape.

Lou Barb

DNA

At that farewell lunch we gave Tom-Tom after her short term in the Department of Cultural Affairs, she and the others had their go.

Suspended from one hundred metres above us the metal-strut and plastic distortion of the DNA molecule performed its rotations. With the long-range spotlights pitched at intervals up the cylindrical wall to the top of the tower, the sculpture moved a spectral net of shadows across their faces. There they all were from the Department of Housing and Roly from the Ministry of Health, Tom-Tom of course, and a couple of other Cultural Affairs friends who had joined them. The Vita Nuova Restaurant in the Blue Sky Hotel.

I still had ringing in my ears Mother's words: Oh well if some people want to blow their pay on such extravagance I suppose it's their choice. I've never seen the attractions of smorgasbord myself. Don't roll your eyes, Lou, no, I know my opinion doesn't count for much these days but I find this invitation to unlimited consumerism quite offensive: all you can eat for twenty-five dollars. I'm surprised at you, actually.

My father comes in here: Really Bea, leave off your moralising for once. Give the lass a go. Surely she earns her own money.

At least I had seen to his daily correspondence, which he attended to with manic intensity as if the world depended on it. This comment for the *Herald*, that for the *Guardian*, that for the *Tribune*. As a reporter and later, as a sub-editor, he had tried to go too far to the left, meeting with increasing censorship until he was axed. Mother would take any opportunity to reproach him for his flagrant knocking of the establishment. Yet I think she would have fiercely defended him to outsiders, those she called Strangers. You could have played it more subtly, Bob, and saved your skin. You had to see yourself as one of those Great Crusaders. Practically every week she served me this line over the lamentably 'unanalytical' news: If he'd kept his head in, he'd still be respectably employed at the Paper now. He hangs around me like a clammy plastic mac these days, I heard her complaining to her friends. In this retirement, in this *solitude à deux*, something had festered between them. Because he'd blacked out on low blood sugar and run his automatic into a wall, Father had surrendered his driving licence. Mother had always seen herself as requiring by birthright a chauffeur. I had become that chauffeur. At times to get a break from her small bickering, and I can tell you her tongue wasn't slowed by age, I'd propose taking Tycho for a walk. Father's voice would ring out youthfully loud behind me as I was linking leash to collar. Eh, I'll come with yer lass, need some air myself.

So increasingly Mother saw us as conspiratorial,

especially with the morning letter writing sessions — he dictated while my fingers hovered and tapped at the keyboard — and for some reason I found the ritual an easy entry into the day.

I suppose we'll walk to the shops then, if you're going for a prolonged booze up. Perhaps you should book a taxi, by the way.

I'll do that, Mother. I'll leave my car at work and catch a bus in tomorrow.

Why don't you have the groceries delivered? I said over my shoulder.

Agh. You know what I think of supermarket meat, she called.

Going meatless for once wouldn't hurt, I wanted to say.

Anyhow, as I entered the shifting web of shadow in the Vita Nuova, I was gripped by that old fear. I could talk to any of these colleagues about issues, about policy, about political philosophy, but if they got into what I was doing with my life, trying to matchmake me as they often did, I knew I wouldn't be able to handle it. On that level I didn't think I could even trust Tom-Tom. She seemed to think herself a privileged commentator on what she called the 'family romance'. She always got it wrong, but that's another issue: she worked creatively by getting everything wrong. I've got my ticket, she'd laugh, mine's a necromance. And then her curiosity knew such charming turns, I would always tell her more than I had meant to. I noticed as I sat down that several of the women had by magic slithered into evening mode. I felt instantly inhibited in my office clothes, by my boring haircut, my sensible, low-heeled shoes. Still, creased or not, the bronze linen suit, which Tom-Tom had helped me buy, picked up the gold of my skin, she assured me, and made my hair more flamboyant. I tried to hoist my ego with the reminder that she saw some sort of 'slow grace' in me.

There was Roly, stuttering and earnest, telling them how he left medicine. I only saw later that he resorted to this anecdote when he was with strangers, nervous and drinking too quickly. His face was lean and shadowy and gave him a look of bruised vulnerability. His charcoal grey eyes smouldered and smarted in turn; the pink, fluted lips looked too tender to be exposed. His whole face seemed over-sensitised.

Laura from Housing enlisted me to his story: Should listen to this one, Lou, she said. He has us all pissing ourselves.

Roly looked bewildered: Nnn-o, I tell you it was awful. You see, Lou, when I came in the old woman said: He's out the back. You'll find him there. In the chook pen, I couldn't believe it. There she was turning her face into the antimacassar, and saying through her teeth: Why don't you just let the poor old bastard die?

Perhaps she didn't want him to be left a vegetable, June said.

A vegetable scrap for the chooks? Stop being so sentimental, Junie, Laura said. This is real life not a ...

Anyway, it was some time before I spotted him even in the chookyard. Itself in a disgusting state. Water full of green slime, chookshit and feathers and a stench! All the food meshed in with the straw and shit. The wheat had germinated into a nightmare carpet full of dank puddles. There was an old wardrobe on its side with the mirrored

72

door ajar — to serve as a shelter to the chooks, I guess. I first saw the back of his head, his old grey cardigan in that cracked feathery mirror. And then I looked closer. I'll never forget it. He was literally being hen-pecked.

Je-sus, that's poetic justice for you, Laura said.

Ss-orry, don't get you. What's the justice in that? The chooks were pecking at him in some kind of frenzy, at his hand where the papery skin had torn as he fell on the chicken wire, at the side of his face, tap-tapping at his glasses which were awry but still on his nose. It was just, well — unspeakably ghastly. I tried to feel his pulse but I had no idea whether it was there or not. I mean I was just out of m-m-medical school then. I tried resuscitation, massage, and my head was spinning. All the chooks were pecking, at my stethoscope, at my bag. His arm was smeared with shit, broken eggshell and yolk. And behind all that there was the voice of his wife from the darkness of the front room: Why don't you just let the poor old bastard die? I don't know how long it took me to recognise that he was dead. I remember closing his eyelids. I was sure my own heart was going to burst. And all the time the hens were pecking.

Still how'd you like that old woman, eh? Tom-Tom said. I've seen it a bit. A kind of dedication to the habits, the little daily fascinations of loathing. It's used by old couples I've been around as some sort of disguise for affection. I guess I just don't understand couples. I don't really know what people see in them. I'd rather live in a group, that way there's always someone to run to, some one to placate. You'd probably understand that relationship, Lou, what couples can do to one another and to their kids?

Come again?

Well. She looked right into my eyes.

Oh, come off it, I said. I might send my parents up from time to time but it's not that bad.

She raised her eyebrows and forked an oyster.

No, I guess it isn't.

I took refuge in the smorgasbord queue in the hope that the topic would shift by the time I returned.

Poor Roly's voice was swallowed by their orgiastic pleasure in the horrible little vignette.

Phew, I said, that white burgundy tastes good.

Better than sherries with Daddy, eh? Mona said.

I was stunned. What had they been talking about while I was in the queue?

Seriously though, Tom-Tom came, her eyes intent, you really owe it to yourself, Lube, to break out of that prison. It irritated me the way she used the nickname as if to invoke inviolable friendship at the very moment she was betraying me with others.

It always came to me afterwards that I could make that reproach to her, living in Woop Woop with her grandmother. Because she seemed so unquestionably bohemian in those days one never thought to reproach her with any kind of homeliness — not that it would have occurred to me to do so. I knew what her answer would be, should any one have pointed out her situation: That's not Nuclear Family.

The meal was a blur after that. I was aware that they were making plans, for the exotic thrill of it, to go and watch some drag queens in a run-down pub in North Perth. It was not just the DNA sculpture that was spinning now.

Their faces multiplied like those early time-lapse movement photos; their mouths left a trail of ghosted teeth and bloody lips, like Bacon's screaming Pope, and there was the carnage of the table itself: the forest of empty bottles, the lobster shells and fish heads, the ham fats, the spilled noodle salads, the half-eaten bread rolls, the overflowing ashtrays, all profligate breeders of themselves. Only with the greatest willpower could I stop this happening. I used my hand palm-down on the napkin as anchorage and brought it into focus: it was a pinned, extinct specimen, its tan retreating as if through extreme cold. It was covered in dry, silvery scales like the remains of the rainbow trout next to it. They were spooning up their cappuccino foam at this stage and some were ordering brandies. Tom-Tom crossed to my side, putting her hand on my shoulder.

Hey, sorry if I went too far. I just think, sweetheart, they're siphoning off your lifeblood, she said. And I happen to care a hell of a lot about you. Surely you know that.

I couldn't answer her.

Beyond the many faces of Tom-Tom with the wide mouth and span of teeth and those dancing black eyes, I saw a travelling glitter on the cobalt violet of the water, close to the jacaranda bloom outside my bedroom window. The light had persisted. It was early summer and I had the heart-cramping feeling now that I would forever live death in small doses, life in small sips.

People were making moves to go.

Aren't you coming, Lou? Mona called.

I was about to say, look I'll make my way back home, won't I? Mummy and Daddy's little girl can't have them worrying, can she? My throat closed over.

I'll skip the drag queens, sorry. Not my scene, I managed. I even managed a smile.

Tom-Tom and Roly gestured that they were hanging back.

There was panic now, a seizure of black dread.

In the toilet I threw up. Not that I'd drunk anything much.

I gargled some eau de cologne and tried to coax my face back into a contour, to touch up the make-up. Then there I was at the counter inquiring about a room.

I've tried to replay this scene and always it jumps. It was a vertical impulse; it projected me right out of one sequence into another. It flashed in my mind that I might call out to Tom-Tom, and propose it to her since she'd hardly want to make her way back to Banksiafold at this hour, but then I felt there would be much more attractive proposals put to her, by Roly for instance. There they were, leaning into one another across the table, cradling the space between them. Again I felt I was the shadow, left out.

When the receptionist handed me the key, the hush of his voice and the soft light falling were a benediction. Once I was in the sweetly humming lift with its black marble floor and its mirrored walls, I realised there was no reversing out of this one.

I looked at the cars crawling on the freeway loops below and the superb cumulus in the night sky. I thought of the slow curve my body would make, spinning, spiralling, cartwheeling into some midget event far below, into another day and there, making a tiny splash like Brueghel's Icarus, while on the foreshore freeway, business ploughed and drilled, seeding the vacuum.

I thought about the run I needed to propel myself through the thick glass. Would it be possible? Laughter grabbed me as I peeled off my shoes in preparation. I think I was weeping at the same time.

There was a knock at the door. I heard solicitous murmuring. The voices set me shivering now: it was Roly and Tom-Tom.

I was plunged into winter; ice set inside me. Inside my head it was loud, loud. Absurdly I hid behind the bed. It struck me then that my command of logic was not what it might have been. If I gave no answer, they would seek help. I called out as well as I could through the chattering of my teeth that I was all right and simply needed to be alone. Tom-Tom persisted: Please, please, Lou. I know we … Well, I for one was grossly insensitive. I'm sorry.

It's perfectly okay, I said. I'm thinking things through.

Their voices died on the carpeted walkway that spiralled around the perimeter of the hollow tower, around the suspended dream of Life. The sole function of this tower was to signify space at high cost, the dreadful academic in me thought. Oh all that expensive fall, inside, outside of the tower. I surprised myself in thinking that the academic might be just a version of my mother's Puritanism. I longed for the company of Tom-Tom and Roly but the last thing I wanted was to be a tear-stained beggar for sympathy.

I was nothing but a regressive little girl. I was an under-achieving twenty-three-year-old infant in ill-chosen clothes, I thought. Sensible, responsible girl. The tantrums that should have played themselves out so long ago, still there, nearly two and a half decades of mini-storms suppressed. If I charged at that window, I'd simply knock myself out.

I knew I should ring Mother but I could hear in advance her voice crackling its reflections on my decision to stay out, whatever I cooked up. I pulled out the phone. I would think more clearly in the morning.

In the morning the panic was worse. Along with the newspapers, I found several memos from Reception under the door, phone calls from my mother. I would have to brave the streets to … find clothes. Oh I felt terribly trapped and stupid. I called for Room Service to supply me with an iron so that I might press myself, crumpled suit and all, into some kind of shape. For the moment I wrapped myself in the floor-length luxury of the Christian Dior bathrobe. The ironing rhythm helped me restore some calm. I swallowed the fizzy red vitamin B drink greedily and surveyed the face in the mirror for damage. It seemed to be cleared of something but I couldn't identify it.

In the hotel dining room, I saw Tom-Tom and Roly at breakfast, their faces lapped by reflected river water. They were bright-eyed, unabashed about their presence or mine for that matter, and like parents bestowing grace in some eternal spring, they rose to kiss me on both cheeks.

Weren't the bathrobes something? Hey, did you check out the bar fridge? We decided to copycat since we couldn't join you, you dag, Tom-Tom laughed. She put her arms around my neck then and kissed my forehead, my cheeks, my mouth. Roly looked on sweet, discreet, and then turned his eyes to the river.

II

Beautiful Thief

This is Marseille then and these are the St Charles steps where Simone de Beauvoir once stood, with her head still in Paris, and this is the city rising with its untouched futures and the huge weight of its past, murderous brigands and traders and disseminators of plague, its resistance fighters and its collaborators, its Armenians and Greeks and Jews and Romanies and Madagascans and Malians and Ethiopians and Tunisians and Moroccans and Algerians and *Pieds Noirs* and Corsicans and its turbaned traders of carved artefacts and its sippers of mint and orange blossom-scented teas and downers of pastis and Côtes de Provençe and its overstatements in voice and colour and passion and corruption and violence. This is something to hang on to, never forget: this kind of pause, night washing down the city's gutters and a timorous awakening of colour in everything, the icy wind waking the full curve of eyeball to extreme sensitivity. Think my gaze is lucid, like Millie would say: my whole skin is looking.

After the hours on the prickly carpet at Hong Kong and the cruel metal of the benches at Rome sleeplessness itself gives me the raw nerve to meet this like something newborn. Have spoken to no one except to buy food for forty-eight hours. Like I left all power of speech back with Maeve, Millie, Joe, Josie, and Zak at Perth airport. I've left speech in those hearts, that treasury. Whatever I make of this they will be there: they don't clock up my absence like a debt. Be an actor for life, for them. Perform. Could dance Marseille even now before I have moved my body through its spaces, plying my particular trade with it, do it just on the ride from Marignane to this, with the limestone vertebrae vaulting into the *calanques* as the bus hurtled us along, the jade water ruffled by the mistral, and now with the city pouring its cries and colour onto the pavements, it's like my repatterning has begun.

No such thing as a stranger here: from the Phoenician beginnings, this town has been built and fuelled by strangers, exile is its domicile: these are Armenian faces, Algerian, Vietnamese, Madagascan. Triangular, oblong, oval, huge cheekbone spans, riven by vertical lines, dazzling smiles which punctuate the talk of some of these Africans who know the grace of immobility as well as movement and the shadows slanting across them in the early morning pick out a hand, the glint in an eye, a bead of saliva. There's garish dressing with heavy eye make-up, concerted elegance, somehow on the edge of what Parisians would call bad taste because here it's marked as display; there's an excess in the attention it calls to the cut, or some baroque deviance that has made for more cloth to be used on the bias than is necessary for a statement about a curve or cowl. There's excess even in the adornment of the street kids, whether Arabs or French or Romanies. Buttons are missing from the waistband but there's a multiplication of bangles. Here's a group of kids who've raided an army surplus store, all in brocade-festooned peaked caps and oversized ceremonial coats, which flap open. The girls have high-pitched breasts and their superbly erect nipples pierce through their light T-shirts and mock the severity of the flapping military jackets.

Before I work up the courage to phone, to produce a new voice and send it along the line, must have cigarette. Before cigarette, must go to toilet. For that need *jeton*, but for *jeton* need to consume in bar. For that need local currency, of course. The crisp virgin notes convert me, step closer to future. Not to spend, the only way of holding it all at bay. Gradual starvation, negative induction. For this pathetic series of gestures I seem to take half a day. In the Bar Tabac quiet groups of Tunisians are playing cards over minuscule cups of dense black coffee. Their eyes are intent on the table. I let the hush of throaty Arabic rise around me with the coffee steam and the Turkish tobacco and catch the smile of the young woman at the tobacco counter and I'd like to pivot on one ringing syllable of affirmation, on the crown of Notre Dame de la Garde, like Molly Bloom remembering that first acceptance of Leo in Gibraltar from the sweet hotness of her Dublin bed and go 'YES' to all of this. I'll phone before I freeze with fear. Stab out the wrong number. Repeat process.

Without her body as distraction, Xavière's voice comes over as posh, la-di-da as Maeve would say. This voice has nothing whatsoever to do with the street talk around here. In Australia she was merely an accented foreigner.

She was a motor-mouthed artistic despot, chic and warm, then lacerating with her ironies, always unpredictable and all that was part of her sway.

Yes I'm calling from a bar near the station.

You've got my office number, she says, and I'll not be back until around seven. But yes my dear, you go to the apartment as soon as you like, you must be exhausted. I've told Clémantine you're coming. Yes, our housekeeper. Just speak through the intercom at the door. She'll let you in. *A ce soir alors.*

Well, of course. What did she say his name was? Jean-Etienne … Jean-Hippolyte? A mouthful anyhow. Maybe should've kept things long-distance. Out of the Perth context she'll see me as an encumbrance, a messy eruption from the past. She must keep her schedules intact. Giving the invitation she must have thought there'd be no risk of my actually surfacing. Could back out. Ask around for a cheap hotel instead.

Burning cheeks. Mustn't react like this. What was I wanting? She's a professional. She's married. It's a bourgeois household. What was I expecting? Well, of course, she can't cancel the whole day. I would for her. She won't for me. Why should she on the basis of a couple of dinners, fired-up talks? I don't want to be one of these beggars for contacts. Saw them at Marignane with their unshaven faces, their hungry eyes and crumpled suits, holding up placards for distant relatives, long unseen. Waiting for hope to arrive. Well, Xavière and her man live composed lives. Why should she clear the day for my arrival? Could find a room and call them from there, say, no just wanted to say hello, last thing I want is to be an encumbrance. Invasive. Which word to use? *Envahissante*? Tip thesaurus down telephone. *Dictionnaire des synonymes*. Then no, it'd be like playing the tease, hard to get, coy, disingenuous.

Will simply walk; working out bus routes too hard. The weight of my pack. Crushed and dusty. Eyes lacquered with sleeplessness, now gritty and spiked by the sun. Shower and change.

Worth the money. The jet of water, each rose-hole spurt discreet, drilling into the skin. Body awake again. Nipples attention! Turn from the shower and am in full frontal dialogue with another woman. Her narrowed eyes and dark olive make me swoon. Eye-drift downward and up. Each salient point magnetised. Talk about the old cyclone Odette marvelled at. Cyclone in the blood, cyclone in the bone. This woman strange and dark and wet stands naked ten feet away and I'm in this unknown city and I'm blazing for this unknown. I pick up the towel from the bench and enrobe myself as they say here, slipping into her gaze. She is towelling, dressing, and still holds me with her eyes.

Get into my jeans wet. Struggle to pull the rough stretch denim up. She is already dressed. Reaches, maintaining her half-smile, for my leather jacket. You wear this bit of dead animal, she laughs? I move to defend it, to arrest this. She slides her arm into the sleeve, zips up. I'm in suspense. She is not; she is gone, out the door in my jacket. My wallet, my wallet, was it in there? Adrenalin of panic — for flight or fight. Grab pack run, run in pursuit of this thief. There is the imperturbably milling crowd on the three hundred steps, surging, pausing to talk, to bask, to eat, or to doze. My black jacket and wallet gone. It had to happen. Three hours here and stripped of papers. This is the reverse baptism. Call yourself up a name as you will now, girl. I will have to check out this housekeeper of Xavière's and what's-his-name's. It's happening before I know it. Map, a street map of the city under glass. How good is your memory? Without money you have to have a memory. I'll just follow the map on foot. Now in the shadowed street it's decidedly damp and the wind is lifting. Idiot that I am for leaving my jacket on a public bench. What better opportunity for a thief after all, when the owner's half-naked. Half-naked, half-seduced and naive. No papers either — no laughing matter. Can get arrested for less. Vagrancy.

Rue Breteuil: the Théâtre des Marges is somewhere around here. No, better sit quiet; collect, calm myself down. This pillared imposture is called the Palais de Justice. Perhaps it's the effect of the shower, or the theft of the jacket but it is, as they say, unseasonably cold for late October. All the same, the trees have not begun to lose their leaves, uncertain about being deciduous, as in Perth. See on a marble bench in the grey light a woman, hair grease-strung, face hidden, a man dark-stubbled, and a ruffian dog, their eyes trained ahead in some pact to observe their privation with austerity. The dog holds its gaze unswervingly. They have what they have between them in a knotted cluster of Casino supermarket bags. An empty wine bottle lies between the dog's front paws. The fountains arc and dribble according to some design which escapes reflection in the shallow blue-green tiled pools. Gilded trio of cherubs, the bronze breaking through green in places, strikes a fiesta against the blue-struck coldness. Shadows are indeterminate and I wade through the rising damp, making out, in case they think I'm feasting on their spectacle, that I'm shifting to the last sunlit corner on the other side of the park. What would it be like dragging old blue arthritic pain through these spaces, from metro bench to hot air vent?

Like they're agents of inscrutable transactions, suited men with attaché cases trip precisely up and down the stairs of the Palais de Justice. Boys contemplate their knees through slashed jeans, at the edge of the balustrade. The next time I look at the bench of the homeless couple, a third, his gestures wide, moustache theatrical, has arrived with three half-filled garbage bags, and slowly, almost didactically like a laboratory demonstrator, begins his conjuring. Out of the black plastic proceed plastic boats and glasses full of food and drink: salads, hot dogs, fries, coffee and cokes, bread, cheese, yoghurts, in such profusion you might just as well expect all Marseille to follow: apartment blocks in a rush of half-glimpsed anecdote, roaring autoroutes, high revving one-way streets, and then the harbour with all its clamouring metal masts like some sort of auditory Giacometti. The three celebrants are bound in the force-field of this performance, by its tenacious intensity. The shifting of weight from one foot to the other of the conjurer is as serious as any ritual movement of priesthood.

To think I was worried about the theft of a jacket and a few replaceable papers.

It takes two hours, three hours to get to the main artery traversing their quarter. Prado, Cantini, Michelet. Mazargues. Few remnants of the old village swallowed up. Select apartments here, three storeys only, not like the ten or more of HLM State Housing towers. Increasingly tree-lined streets and marble-facaded apartment blocks. Some romance of the artist, hey, that I imagined her to live in a done-up slum, still tatty on the edges.

Xavière's voice speaks through the intercom. Yes, my dear Thomasina? Yes, we were starting to get anxious. Come straight up!

This is better. She is her warm self when she opens the door. Hair chic and short, new peroxide, eyes aquatic green. And she turns to include the suited soft-eyed man next to her. He is pale and spindly, hair an electrocuted crew cut, like Beckett's, but rather English in his lit-up pallor. We like one another, I can tell. And the 'we' Xavière uses this time is an embrace. I'll accept it.

Ah, but here she is, as superb as ever!

Bisou bisou bisou; bisou bisou bisou. She hugs me tenaciously. The last thing I want to talk or think about is that wallet but for some reason I launch it in the space of intimacy, as if a distancing vocabulary were needed.

I've just been fleeced. In the showers at St Charles. Money, papers, jacket.

Like some sort of tandem machine Jean-Hippolyte and Xavière set off a round of exclamations and then move into soothing reassurance, as if they played all of the world's bureaucracies on their home computer. Look, we'll go through that with you later and work out what we have to do to replace them. Remember, alas, it's the most banal thing to happen to travellers anywhere. For the moment, relax, put down your bags, and refresh yourself.

This is Clémantine.

Clémantine has short, coarse black hair, and wonderful, emphatic eyebrows. Her lips are thin and sinuous, but not unsensual. They look naturally burgundy. Her skin is like parchment, stained with olive oil, giving a dark glow you mistake for translucence. She meets my gaze with an effrontery I like. Hello, hello.

Handshake strong. She retreats into the kitchen.

Look, Jean-Hippolyte is to go up to Paris; he's driving there next week. You can go up with him to your embassy perhaps? Report the loss, get a new …

In the meantime, make yourself …

Xavière shows me my room. I splash about again to gratify them.

I grope into my pack for the book of landscape photography I've brought them. There is the rolled up acrylic on cotton I painted. It's the giant melaleucas at the swamp. No, that I'll bring out if the moment's right. In any case their décor is long since decided; there is a rigour in the arrangement of objects it might upset. A gesture at dressing for the meal: I pull out the diamond patchwork jumper in teal blue and ochre. To hell with the papers; I must accept their welcome. Now here, wrapped inside the coiled jumper, under my fingers, I have the sweat-moulded shape of the wallet.

Love the beautiful thief now for getting it wrong.

So what's a leather jacket. Dead animal, like the thief said. Oh well, she can wear it.

Well, your identity caught up with you! Let's have a drink to that!

Xavière tells me you're accepted into the master class with the Théâtre des Marges.

But it's thanks to her recommendation that they accepted me.

I'll drop you off there tomorrow. May as well let them know you're ready to start.

Wait a minute, wait a minute. Give her a chance to catch her breath. Jean-Hippolyte is like that, doesn't like the thought of anyone hanging out free for a moment. Let her get into things in her own time, J-H.

Of course, of course. But I'll bet she'd like to get all those things in place. She's come here to work after all.

J-H doesn't like a hiatus in anyone's life any more than nature likes the proverbial vacuum. You do things at your own pace, Tom-Tom, and don't take any notice of him.

Except when he would offer you a drink, he laughs.

The badinage of this couple.

He takes ice cubes in the claws of the silver prongs, drops in lemon, pours Campari, pours vermouth, pours himself pastis and *sirop d'orgeat*. Very Marseillais drink we call a Mauresque. Thees sirup ees made from almond? he says, sounding the 'l' like a Scot. He offers me a pistachio in a hand-glazed pink bowl. He uncorks some wine to air.

I swim up-current in the stream of talk, the play of eyes on plates, glasses, hands, breaking bread and pressing serviettes to mouths between words, and bask in the yellow light on the rough-rendered wall. I scale through the wine the rearing female form in charcoal behind the rubber plant. We begin with a *salade aux épinards avec des oeufs pochés*, left warming by Clémantine who has vanished, I now realise. Guess they give themselves the usual rationale for having a servant, whatever they call it. *Too much work — why not share it out? She is better at cooking than we are and without her, this household wouldn't function …*

I am held for now in the spell of their warmth, in the mesh of their looks, in the tune of his soft baritone and her higher melodic improvisations. Harbour within the harbour, her green eyes launch me, his amber eyes buoy me with their acquiescence. Being childless, perhaps they hope I might stay. The theatre stuff frightens me now. The way I strutted my global fearlessness in front of Roly and Lube comes back to shame me.

They talk about a welcome lunch, about an Ariane, a philosopher 'between teaching jobs' with whom I'm sure to hit it off. She'll want to show you around — any excuse to get into her new Golf convertible. She blew all her father left her on that. And besides, we've already inflamed her interest, Xavière says, smiling. Not sure what she thinks she knows, but she knows it.

The modalities of desire can be imagined around ideas of traction, fast manoeuvres, and balance. I could fall in love with a ringed hand, palm resting coolly but sure on the gearstick, the foot rarely going for the brake, the high revs of the little motor, my hand folding over hers as the singing motor pitches: it is Ariane in a car doing the climb behind the Panier quarter, because it's where I've just been, mounting the kerb as if balance on two wheels were the future register of love, and plunging then into one-way streets, finding the passage blocked by a film in progress, reversing back to the crest of the hill, now a three-point turn, and doing the climb again. It is especially the lightning quick play of side-glances with the facades fusing past the windows. The woman is taking me to an unknown assignation, in the past: it is assigned, of course, but in whose consciousness is this lodged? There is a shot-reverse-shot from my eyes to those of the driver caught in the rear-vision mirror: I recognise that thief.

Not Talking Banksia

From the moment Simone Choiseuil moved into action I could see she was going to be some sort of dominatrix. The whip will come down on flab or fuss. She wanted our work lean, she said, perched on the stool; she wanted it spare. I felt that black eye on me, felt myself striking a resistance to its charge, but already as if she were daring me to carry it, to convert it under the cover of performance. She's dark, with high, broad, Mongolian cheekbones, accentuated by the turquoise and purple turban. Under the eyebrows, so radically plucked they could have been drawn on, the black eyes darted away and returned. It's hard to pin an age on her; could be in her late forties. As they say here, she is of a *certain age*. Hard to tell when it was a flare of recognition from those eyes or withering contempt. She's got what they call *du chien*, style. She was wearing an ornate, brocade jacket, black, with shards of purple and turquoise, whose raglan sleeves were caught in tight cuffs at the wrists. The knobby, ring-laden fingers flared out, sliced, and clawed. It was like she set her own scale as a standard. As she approached, I could see that she was quite short, one metre sixty-three at the most, but perched on her stool, she gave the illusion of height through the thinness and relative length of the thighs in the tight black pants. Then she was on the prowl again. She was like those autocratic ballet mistresses stranded in outer-suburban Australia with White Russian nostalgia in their voices. She looked as if she'd brook little debate. She made it clear that we were to experiment strictly within her parameters.

As you will have understood, she said, we'll be dealing with exile here, singly and together. She made the scene; she drew its horizon, keeping us magnetised with those eyes. You will keep a performance notebook. If you have any interaction after class, it will be through these images you establish here, now, in this first workshop. This is so that you will first of all feel exile as a loss of language.

There were four of us in the group today but extras will be brought in when necessary, Choiseuil said. We'll shoot the process in various locations, here, in the studio, out in the streets, on work sites. You lay down some motifs now and watch them clash, fuse, bounce off one another, she said. You'll start striking some sort of pattern. The rest of your material will follow from here. Up to you to find the rules of proliferation. There'll be no way you can say *rub that out; I didn't say it.* You'll be bound by these first improvisations. Let's see if you can find something productive in the tangle of starts, even something dangerous to trip you in new directions. Now for introductions, she said, nodding into the far corner.

There was a young woman staking out her own space,

already sketching out a slow, contained little dance, chewing on gum, or making like she was. She looked up and gave a broad, gap-toothed smile. Stocky, compact and muscular. Good legs, high calf muscle, like she'd done more than a bit of dance in her time. Her hair was dyed mulberry with a darker under-layer, cut in a bristling flat-top. She wore a diamond nose-stud, and two or three rings in the left upper ear. Her skin looked pale, slightly jaundiced in that light and a few acne scars amongst the whacky ornamentation looked part of the design, advertised as part of the deal. The nose was curved towards the tip but slightly flattened on the bridge like a boxer's. The upper lip had a sharp bow, which she accentuated with black-burgundy lipstick. It was like she wanted us to think that, with a flick of the wand, she could turn cruel, a Wicked Disney Queen.

Oui, d'accord, she said, chewing, *je m'appelle Molly*. The accent was American. Confident, perhaps nonchalant. New York Jewish, I'd guess.

Eh vous, Monsieur? Oui, vous. Choiseuil nodded to the boy who turned from the window. With his Titian hair, hazel eyes, and light olive skin, he could be Northern Italian. He was watching the dark guy closer to me. Basilio, he answered, though more to the dark guy than to Choiseuil. The twitch around his eyes rescued his regular looks from blandness. Maybe the name's a pseudonym; it suits him too well. His voice resounded *basso profundo*; cause or effect of the big Adam's apple? He had on tight, faded blue Levis, an olive-green cotton skivvy, and brown moccasins. Didn't seem to be claiming anything beyond his glowing presence.

Moi? J'suis Asif, the dark one practically hissed. He looked like he'd play his cards close. Like straightaway he was trying to be interesting by maintaining that retreat, at least from all but Basilio. When he spoke it was more the push of silence that I felt, like the words were tuned in silence, turned in it, resisting release. There was the glare of something non-negotiable in his eyes. His teeth looked even, almost like orthodontistry enamels but for the chipped canine. There was the sense of darkness massing inside his clothes, of force available, but in harness for the moment. That's what he wanted us to think. Oh, he gave something; he let a faint smile travel around the group.

Je m'appelle Thomasina, I said. Their eyes popped; eyebrows shot up.

Migration … exile, Simone said; she was on the move, nimble and angular. She'd somehow mustered us into a smaller circle and spoke from behind us. Right! An image from your own place, your own repertoire, take it on, move through it. Make it speak in the new context. Ah, you'll find out how it sticks. *Comme tout cela va vous coller.*

Already I'd forgotten where we were. The studio returned, in a disaffected *Menuiserie*, a carpenter's workshop, scarcely renovated. Maybe the floor had been re-tiled; that was all. On a balcony framed by our high window a woman was beating out doonas to some funky disco music. She was pleasured by her own exertions and her form wavered with each puff of dust. She was in a black lace bodice. With each doona beat I saw the golden domes of the breasts shake slightly.

Make it stick, wear it, Choiseuil said; you'll be wearing it, or something that grows out of it, for the next three months. Negotiate the scenario through each other's images. Thomasina, what is yours? Her voice was a plangent wave-slap. The place was rebounding in echoes; hard to tell where speech started.

What's my image? Is that what you mean?

She gave me an impatient nod. I hadn't begun well. The worst thing would be for her to catch a whiff of my fear. That she'd despise.

I am ... Banksia, I said.

I couldn't resort to showing them the tattoo; that would've been too cheap. I don't know how long my silence lasted but I rehearsed in a quick scan all the possibilities. With the weight of those first words she had me on trial already.

I am a banksia tree, I said, and am covered in great golden cones —

I tried to mime the honeyed styles unfurling —

but they like to depict me as dead, a brown-grey cylinder, bristling with livewire hairs. A speaking thing held mute. I'm covered in lips, and when the fires come, each mouth can pop a seed, a syllable more potent for being long held back. They say that it's gibberish, my savage speech. But I can dance my way through the words they use for me.

Asif said his was a battered cardboard suitcase. I came to this country for work, he said, because our place was invaded, raided, ransacked, ruled in then ruled out to feed French bellies, he said. But do you think they left us industries or educated managers amongst our people? No way. Okay, you might say that exile means nothing to me because you see me as some sort of nomad who can't stay put. Call me Kabyle, Berber, *Maghrébin*, *Beur*, it's all the same to you. I have to produce my identity card a dozen times a day because I don't look right, sound right. *Jeune Beur*? Perhaps, perhaps. The people here read me like I'm the battered suitcase on the metro. Don't park that too close to me, man. Might ladder my stockings.

His vehemence outdid mine.

Cut the narrative, Choiseuil said. Concentrate on physicalising the image.

I bet he has had the best of middle-class education. I bet his family has a cellar full of prestigious wines. I bet this is a brief vertigo of revolt, produced just for this fancy little class. Sure he's dark and could be partly Arab but so many in Marseille could be from either side of the Mediterranean. Bet he's doing his rebellion while dining on Carte Bleu. His shoes looked hand-sewn.

Eyes drifted to the mulberry-haired punk. Maybe she didn't have too much riding on this or she was an old hand. It was hard to tell.

What she trotted out was a bit clichéd, a bit slick, but then mine meant nothing to anyone, so who was I to say? I'm an aerialist, she said, her palms floating upwards. I'm an aerialist. I've had to be. My place, my base has always been somewhere else. I hover, float, or drift on what's available. I use the thermals and the cracks and the fissures. Give me a cliff-face, I can scale the rock slides. Ah, tumbleweed, I'm a bit of a tumbleweed.

Et vous, Basilio? Simone asked.

His voice came slow, soft, coasting in like a glider: I am a shadow. My body has been stolen. I was raised in the barbed-wire school. Somewhere in a terrain of grey cement and broken glass, I found my poisoned pickings. Fuck the 'green paradise of childhood loves'. Until my body's broken, they sell me for my labour. I was thrashed, fed scraps, thrashed and fucked and left for dead. I am a shadow asking for my body back. I play pool and I'm looking out for a ride on any body, any life that comes up to the table. See my shadow across the green pool table. That's as close as I've got to nature.

La Simone came in, in a new kind of voice, with a slight Turkish accent, her arms wavering: *Moi, j'suis l'Araignée.* I am the Spider.

I watched their faces. It took everyone by surprise.

Mine is the sideways mode, she said, each and every time my web is torn, I secrete another dragline, drop into another place.

Her gestures were economical, choreographed. The hands were so convincing I expected to see Arachne materialise in a dew-strung web.

I can give you temporary accommodation, in this web of mine. My abdomen is fat and glistening. For the moment you feed me well. Because you know. I am a leader, because you hang me in the space of devastation where once you might have built altars.

She snapped out of it to resume her Mistress of Ceremonies mode. *Alors,* she took in all our eyes. Those are our elements. We are flung together just as life flings us together in our various states of exile.

Basilio, the Shadow, padded up to me, smile gentle as if to offset the Spider: And you, tell me more ... Bank-sia?

I knew my voice was going to be caught, muffled before I spoke. Wished I hadn't started this Banksia stuff — no way I could make it work. I felt stupid. I wanted to go home. He was smiling patiently.

I am the monster at the window, the demon of the invader's histories. Only told by them or reduced to their unspeakable. I am the 'savage' they would slaughter. I'm jangling with barbaric tongues.

I began to dance around him, bringing the foot down with slow, flat emphasis. Look, I have many stages but in the pictures they make of me, my lips crack open on nothing decipherable, I am stopped in this mute multiplication. I will dance my stuff at their windows. I'm here to remind you that all the cosy stories depend on my exclusion.

The Spider comes up. Well, I no longer knew if it was as Spider or teacher.

You have too much to say, Banksia. Hmm. Mutism is too eloquent.

I half expected her to slap me across the face. I'll have to send you all to an image clinic! Get rid of discourse!

I can't move into your tongue, *Madame*. Only speak Banksia.

At least she met my look. Yes! she said.

Now Asif moved to her side and broke in. What's that meant to mean? He said to me, Think again if you expect me to read you, Mute. You've tried to snatch some kind of privilege of the outside. But there are outsides and outsides …

Yeah, well who do you think you are? You with your battered suitcase? It was Molly who came to my side and delivered this close to Asif's face.

I am Algerian, Moroccan, Tunisian? What's it to you what I am? I've watched too many guys in *bidonvilles* all over

Europe. I'm going to stir things up for the xenophobes here, screw their codes.

Okay, Mr Cardboard Suitcase, Molly came, decide where you're from. Can't accommodate all that in our little heads.

She gave me a look that was very pleased, conspiratorial and sexy at once.

Asif shrugged: Oran? Okay? Don't fix me in an address — that's the whole point. Got none, get it?

I wasn't going to be pushed into the mute victim corner: Where I come from we understand a bit of that, I went, ignoring the narrowed eyes and their message: *Who are you, Sister, to presume to identify*? I come from No-man's Land — it's what the invaders wrote all over my place ...

Well, Babe, this Asif goes, if you're from No-man's Land, you've stumbled into *Bidonville*. You're with us now.

Molly was chewing gum again. She seemed to have an endless supply. She was sketching out a dance-step too. So what's a *Bidon*, anyway?

What's a *Bidon*? A *Bidon*'s a bit of shit on the urban scrap heap, a tenant of any old *bidonville*, see? Fringe dweller makes it sound too pretty. I live on the smell of hope, the hope they throw to the dogs sniffing around here. I tell you for those like me it's life on appro. We squat under the sign of Here Soon. Here Soon luxury apartments, even for you *Bidons*. Dream shopping centres, bright classrooms. We'll take your culture into account. Champion chances will be extended to the children of all migrant workers. He looks across to Basilio: yes, fuck their 'green paradises'. In my quarter anything like a tree is muzzled in metal mesh, roots snagged in the rubble. We're suckled on the poison of their promises. He makes out he's spitting. You can practically see the great gob, airborne.

I thought: It's now or never. I had to claim some of the scene, draw it before they did. So what's that you got in there? I nodded to the space behind them.

Ah, that's our arsenal. He hoped his effrontery would make me faint. See this here, he said, this is my Shadow, he'll do anything I say, won't you, man?

Molly comes: You're kidding, that's no arsenal.

Too right it is, Basilio says.

Asif, gathering the Shadow behind him: And you better get quick smart out of here before your butts get burnt.

All right. Molly and I could take them both on if this was the kind of division they wanted. Hey, I say, to Asif, who do you think you're talking to? Back home there are a few who'd list me as dangerous.

Congratulations, Sister. Tough talk, whoa! Should've seen that fear ripple through you as soon as we talked of guns. So what earned you that Glamorous Badge?

Well … I … we intend handing our land back to some of our Nyoongar friends.

Come again, he went. Nyoongar?

The South-West Aboriginal people, where I come from. Many tribal groups, many names. Before … Invasion.

So, you, how come you're not an invader yourself? So radical, Banskiasister. How come you say you gave them back *your* land then? Eh? Eh? Tripped you on that one! … You give us that as if it carries some sort of cachet. Should've seen yourself blush. *Our land*! I bet you've been travelling on the surplus you stole.

I could see little pearls of sweat on his forehead. His gaze did not let mine go. Cocky bastard.

What? It was shorthand, for Christ's sake.

I reckon that veneer's starting to crack little, Radical Friend. Your Radical Chic cosmetic's cracking.

I'm considered as a threat to Progress. A traitor.

I blushed for shame at the facility of this.

Whoa! Savage Miss Banksia!

I slowly pulled up my sleeve. The tattoo rose on the muscle, big and potent.

Here's my tattoo, see; the lips are creaking open. I intend to wear this to the end. You say I'm savage, let me be savage. I'm not going to be docile. Even in your alternative scenario, Brother.

He showed a glimmer of respect. I walked back to Molly, hooked arms with her: Sister? See these lips: you say not a pretty sight, I say it's just a matter of where your Beauty's coming from. We've got to learn to live with the deaths they've dealt us. Let the bodies of our dead sisters speak too. Okay. Look at this. On the other arm a whole series, on the one branch, the many dead and the blazingly alive. See the Banksia knows how to live with its own death; it wears its skeleton on its sleeve. I might be Banksiawoman. But you know, I can be a mime when necessary; a hairy menace given to cradle-snatching. That's how I was first written into their children's books. They reckon we kidnap the pale-skinned Gumnut babies. This is their own lie that terrifies them. We haunt them because we operate together and speak in many tongues.

Basilio, voice muted, says to Asif: What do you think? Can we trust her?

This is more or less how we started, circling one another

over the immense floor. We were all defending our separate territories. And the Spider, by saying nothing, subtended our performance. Not a joker this one; she wanted to keep some power in reserve, as if all her movements were variations on immobility: at once fluid and restrained. I realised that we'd all left a space which the Spider claimed; that each of her manoeuvres kept us peripheral: You're all wondering what my function is; you're loath to admit it, but I'm Mistress of the Network. We are not crude terrorists but there is a cache of guns to back us up. I'm Minister for Culture in our Provisional Government. We are all *Bidons* inhabiting their unthinkable. Our town is the *Bidonville* in any of their cities. But I operate in the *colon* world. I operate as a burovirus; I descend along my draglines into the bureaucratic maze. I put pressure on Housing, on Social Security and on Health for all *Bidons*: first, second, third generation *Bidons* whose labour, black or white, carries this place. You boys are indebted to me. What were you before? I'll have you recall that for a moment. She was speaking to Basilio, the Shadow.

I was nothing man, nothing. He hangs his head: I was a dropout and I was dealing some drugs. I was bullying my little sister to let me be her pimp. I was ready to get me some dogs, go vigilante against my people ... I wanted to swagger in the neighbourhood. I didn't care if it was coke or smack or cunt I dealt in.

She seized his arm: You will not utter that word around me or away from me, boy! Clean your act! And you ... Battered Suitcase?

Asif, this time was docile, almost humble. As if this were ritual worship but with a bit of a yawn to it: I thought I was pretty cool. I was the only one ever in my family to get a degree. But what's the use of theory? What's theory un-applied? Wank, I guess. I guess I was wanking, before I joined. What you taught me is to disturb the system from within. Tunnelling under.

I wasn't going to have him seize this imagery all for himself.

That's like me, I said, that's like how I see it with … the Tumbleweed here. We work like that too, tunnelling under? Alices in *Bidonville*?

Simone's movements are now more staccato, brisk. So, she says, slapping one palm against the other. You see yourselves as a cell of militants, do you? *Bidon* Liberation? Mmm. That's the easy part. We must work through this for a few sessions and, later, try it out on the street. Think about movement. Words, words, words, and for exiles with little communicable between them, this is very strange. I want you to continue with what has been established but cut the sound. You are now moving mutes. Go on, do it!

As Spider again she assumed a weaving mode like she was gathering all our different dances in her web. Molly turned her back on me, folded into her own space. Slowly she raised one thigh, pointed the foot in its pump to the floor. Good relationship with gravity. Offering herself to the Spider? Draglines and parachutes — some sort of dialogue here? Perhaps they'd already got things scripted and I was the only one improvising. The Spider had settled an ironic eye on me.

Close eyes, raise leg, suspend thigh at right angles to pelvis, keep it for a long time, bring it sharply down and repeat with the left leg, slowly, slowly progress, backwards at first, move backwards into the breathing shadows, bearing my arms up, at shoulder level; feel the slow growth of the whole tree, feel the weight of all the dead, the skeleton cobs and the blazing new ones, the pale new leaf growth, soft-downed at first, serrated, getting stronger, darker, harder, each saw-edged leaf catching at the light, moving backwards still, through the ripple of blue shadow over gold, movement quickens with the honeyeaters burrowing into my cobs, feel the intoxication of that siphoning beak and do the dance of the whole banksia forest moving ...

Right, Simone said. Break it. Enough for one day. You'll have to refine and simplify the vocabulary of your movements.

Already this loneliness was invading, emptying me of all possibility of communicating beyond this scenario. The impoverishment of it all.

Coming out into the six o'clock animation of Rue Breteuil, its bumper-to-bumper traffic roaring and honking in the steep ascent from the Vieux Port, picking my way amongst the purposeful pedestrians on the narrow footpaths, past butchers and grocers and craft shops and galleries and bars, I wondered what I thought I was doing. Like the dance stayed inside me, cocooned metamorphosis. Snagged in the rubble of language, language, like Asif's muzzled tree. In the down-draft of fierce November air, I tasted toxic night. What was most real to me was turning fake. There was nothing I could report to Xavière and Jean-Hippolyte that they'd believe. Simone Choiseuil wanted us struck mute in the poverty of our repertoire. She had me feeling I could never speak again. How could I muster up a croak to ask for a drink? There was the Bar L'Unic, its walls plastered with theatre posters, photographs of a dark-lipsticked peroxide blonde with various actors, musicians. A little terrier in a scarf was being fondled by two young women, one feeding him peanuts from her cupped palm. The ease of their laughter made me realise my teeth were chattering. I took my draught beer to a window table.

Banksia *Bidon*. It was indefensible, ridiculous. Maeve said any coupling could be made to rhyme. It was up to you to find the connections. If it was what your life had served you, up to you to make something of it. She pointed to the pylons strutting across our place. They get into my bag of images, these cheeky pylons, she said.

Hey, you move fast, Banksiagirl!

It was Molly, the Tumbleweed.

What do you make of it all, hey?

It's like some silly game of animal, vegetable or mineral.

At least we're in the same category.

Yeah, like we could be Vegetables in revolt! Outside the images, no relation? I laughed.

She leaned forward to give the triple *bisou*, kiss-kiss-kiss in defiance or affirmation, I couldn't tell. Then she made her jaunty exit.

I could see from the beautiful peroxide blonde behind the counter that whatever this relation, it was approved.

For a brief moment I descended into my shape, felt that I was occupying it.

Exile

I am an orphan in this thin language rain, in this alphabetic drizzle; I must find the leeched substance of my old sky within your chilled busy days where there are words to spare for everything. My mind has become thin and mean. When I walk amongst you, my loneliness outlines me. Your talk, your gestures, your knowing where you're going give you concerted solidarity. I am at once utterly alone and represent utterly my community. With my tongue stuck for words, I start to feel dumb through and through. What a nightmare for you if I had others to identify with! Sometimes if you glimpse in me something like singularity, you have to call it rule, and evacuate my particular humanity with words like 'intriguing custom', 'Antipodean inventiveness'; you'd call the fringed cloth I fling over my rickety table 'fringe dweller' style. My half-dozen photos tacked on the wall are documents to you. This is how you people live, you say.

I do not have to rehearse language loss. Of course I have

French but when I see myself heading straight for a lexical hole, I reroute, say something I never intended, throw out images false to me, that pop up as available clichés in the alien repertoire.

But all of this is just a game to me, Asif would say. I can pick myself up at any moment and leave but those he identifies with live inside the smell of misery. They can't walk away.

His vehemence, or his venom, I taste it alive on my tongue.

I look at myself as he wants me to identify.

I remember the one o'clock glare in St Georges Terrace back in Perth. I see the suits manoeuvring in this wind tunnel, their ties flapping over their shoulders, selling vertical space, doing mining deals, quarrying the country out, sending off the old forests as carton fodder; see them shuffling shares and trading off the city spaces, see the moonscapes left by their greed.

For him I take on the puckered beige, tan, and strawberry faces rising from these suits, I graft on the skin of these people who call themselves white, these people Asif makes me identify with and I remember that I am travelling on the surplus I stole, like he said. I can't find it within me to protest. *How come I'm not an invader myself?*

Look at all those empty high-rises there! On our horizon, on the horizon that all our freeways lead to. Of course we're loath to squat, because squatting reminds us of the squatters' disease. That we squatted and snatched, and fenced and chased. And killed.

We mortgage our horizons. We buy our plots in the urban squeeze and yes, we're endlessly inventive as far as walls and fences are concerned: we know how to pave, reticulate, renovate. Sure we're nice, open people, but often out of neglectfulness. We forget to hate: too much moral energy goes into that. We forget to hate anything beyond the odd burglar rustling through our Babylon of indoor plants. We've got our interiors. We build around our atriums.

In the name of property we even throw privacy to the wind, literally, listen. Hear the sky beating black? This is the nightly sound of helicopter surveillance in the suburbs with names like Balga and Lockridge and Willagee, its beam stroking like a perverse finger, the parks and backstreets where the cops think the Nyoongar kids hang out. See, as the helicopter beam strikes straight through my bedroom window onto my pillow. Feel our collective fear kick over with that beating rotary blade.

Lou Barb

Choosing Black

For us of course she was an exotic kind of fringe dweller by association — by her knowledge borrowed from Millie and Joe and their family, by her relative orphanage along with her range of surrogate parents. *Did you get to go to Banksiafold?* The question ran amongst us, hissing along the fuse. Had to wait a long time for the chance and then it was a matter of dodging Mother's questions. Soon enough she ran me through the gauntlet.

Her grandmother has that drinker's skin. That broken capillaried look. Coarsening of the face. And a smoker's wheeze. I'm not too sure if I should let you. I saw her outside the Principal's office. And Lou, it's nothing to do with prejudice, that would be very wrong, because it's her, who's meant to be white, that I'm worried about. Not her Aboriginal friends. And what does this Maeve O'Shea do?

What does she do? She runs a sort of farm. She grows vegies and stuff.

Oh, Lou, don't say stuff.

Well, they … fruit, vegetables and that.

What could anyone produce in that sandpit?

What sandpit? You've never seen it.

I beg your pardon; I know that Yangebup area very well. In any case all this coastal plain is the same. It's a sandpit. Your father and I have not established this garden without a lot of work, you know.

Well, then, okay. What if Maeve's done a lot of work too?

Across the darkness with the jostling of branches on metal, and then the muted roar of the rain, I could feel Tom-Tom breathing, like the pulse of another climate.

Lou?

Yeah, Tom-Tom?

Lou, you … I can't sleep.

I can't either.

Then she was standing there, in her pyjamas.

Can I come in? So's we can talk, she said, muffling a low laugh into the pillow.

We lay still and breathed so close that I could feel each hair wavering, every follicle alive to her. I could smell the Colgate mint on her teeth; I could see her smile gleaming, a mirage floating on darkness, I could hear it in her, like cell-division, like an incubation held in suspense, something she didn't want externalised. It was just a breathing darkness, a heated chastity. I felt her calf slide over mine, the coarseness of the hair. There was a kind of levitas, as if air were up-draughting our fingers, wrists, freeing us of agency, but it was only an impetus towards the arrest of this or any other story. There was none of the pitching intensity she made her theme later. It was as if a rapture from way beyond had claimed us. There was no sense of this ever needing an ending. Then she was sobbing. I held her in my arms. I realised that her face was wet. I slept in that wetness, but as on a beach, with no knowledge of the tides. Towards morning she spoke.

You know, Lou?

Yes, darling?

You know why Millie calls me Daughtergirl, like she does with Josie. She says I'm a bit like the girl she was made to give up ... by a terrible trick. She had twins. She was sixteen. She wasn't with the guy for long. An orderly from the hospital where she was training, a white guy. And these nurses came to her hospital bed with papers which they said it was, like, just a formality to sign. She thought it was for registering the births or something, and she was that tired, she didn't look too hard; she just signed it. Almost in minutes, she realised she'd been made to sign over Josie's sister for adoption. When she tried to undo it, saying her mum would look after the twins while she worked and did her nurse's training, this matron tells her she's done it of her own free will, that she's known perfectly well what was coming down. In any case, that it was for the good of her child. How could she possibly look after two kids at her age? Now we'll have the social worker look out for you, watch how you're managing. We have to look after the child's interests, you see, my dear. So Millie was never sure if they wouldn't come and take Josie away too. Living in terror. Say if she'd go off on an early shift and the washing-up mightn't be done, or her mum didn't have all the nappies pegged and bright on the line and the kitchen floor scrubbed, she expected those Social Workers to move in and take Josie. And now there's always this awful, empty shape, like a wound cut out next to Josie. The other twin was called Billie, after Billie Holiday, I think. One day she reckons if she's ever strong enough, she'll try to find her. But she said she'd tried once, and it made her feel like Billie was dying on her: the paper maze you go into and never find the way out, the closed faces, the people who walk away from the counter for files and never come back. But I wish ... I can never make up for ... but ... There's no way Josie feels she can measure up to Billie either. Billie's become so huge in not being there.

You know I guess that it's only when I turned twelve that I realised I wasn't going to become black. That you can't choose black. That I can never move into that shape Billie left.

No matter, I wanted to say, how close you come to your Nyoongar family, you can't occupy that space. Your loss, your grief, are not the same.

I thought it was like going into a corner shop. You could choose black.

If I could only be like Josie's twin. It would give Millie back to her too. Josie's a bit jealous of me, you know with Millie and that. But tell you what, Lou, I'd like to lie there, just like us, now, and be that twin, only here, alive.

She's not dead, but adopted.

Well, it's like she's dead.

Webstruck

I say to Xavière: Okay I'll give it a few more days. The whole thing seems increasingly cooked. Can't see where it's taking me as a performer except into Choiseuil's control. And the aggression, the competitiveness they all put into their actual roles, I mean, the made-up ones.

She shrugs her shoulders as if such tensions were inevitable.

You can't make performance out of sweet beds of roses, she says.

Xavière and J-H don't like any dropping out. Not in their repertoire. I should go to the limit, seize the opportunities as they come. I'm probably reacting to a major dose of cultural shock. Do I realise how privileged I am to have a place in the workshop? I think, Jesus, they're worse than poor old Lube's mum. Yet, I owe it to Xavière, of course.

During the break I watch Asif in the square, near the sandwich kiosk. He's there against the plane tree.

113

Smirking. The role is sticking to him. He's playing it cool, leaning, his feet crossed. A great slab of shade comes across his face, so that his eyes are in darkness and his teeth glint. He's turning a matchstick between them. I look right into that slab of shadow for some sort of response and there is shoulder movement, a twitch rather; he kicks up some chalky dust with his runner and that's it.

His withdrawal makes mangy dogs of us, begging for titbits, of me and Shadow who's just a chalky shape in this light, see, sketched out on the ground behind me, like a police marking after homicide. Waiting does this to people, Asif, in Real Life, remember, you are so used to Style, to the restraint the rich can afford, you can't stop practising it here. To show eagerness, hunger, any need at all, would be seriously uncool.

We all jump at the Spider's voice, except Asif, who would have seen her coming: Now, she says, you're getting yourselves into something a little tangled. So there's a meeting at my place? Eight o'clock. I'll have extras on line. The Shadow will be recording, of course. *Bidons*, 20h, my place, okay? 64 Rue des Grands Carmes. I'm perched under the roof. So, 5th floor, got that?

This is a transformation all right. Of course you are seductive: I want, like all the others, to donate my story for you to re-spin it as you need. Who would suspect that you're any more than someone's fantasy lounging in that alcove? You're immobile. Only your eyes move underneath the black netting, the lovely spiderveil, attached to the turban. Cursive eyes! Eyeliner looks tattooed on. Because of the prickling fear that rises with the need to curl up in your lap I take revenge and imagine you bald under the indigo turban. I give you straight-away the prestige of indigo, not blue. Your look says that you are dispensing with our sentimental investments, that you want the truth hard and raw. You want us to confront the bankruptcy of our knowledge; you want to tear our agitated speech apart. You want us to re-invent ourselves. Well, I need you to remain remote but always to have that potential for coming into close, soft focus. You are lean enough in those coral pants. Silk! I wonder at your flexibility. Do you make off to a gym when they imagine you working? Your thighs are crossed and the calves folded above the ankle but it makes me think of threading, of coiling like snakes that can't have enough of each other. Your back is plunged into an avalanche of cushions, the alcove draped with some sort of brocade baldaquin. I wonder what kind of parody this is? You've got to be joking. You're beckoning me now ...

As I kneel down to be presented, almost as if you're blind and you have to touch to certify your suitor, you encircle my hips with your hands, encumbered with rings. You whisper through the Spiderguise, lovely little hips. Boys hips! Cruel. I cannot respond and stay in my role.

I want to know how I can help with ... in terms of ... a proj ... cultural work for ... We've got a proposal just about ...

I just about choke on the inadequacy of any line.

Like one of these, my dear? you say. There is laughter in your voice. It is a slice of marzipan log, covered in pine-nuts, in cross-section white, pink and pale green. I pop in a slice, my eyes still caught in yours. We have to come up with a viable program. The mayor has funds available. It's got to look like after-school care, aimed at social integration, curbing delinquency, mopping up the violent elements, cleaning the state housing basements of addicts. A gym, theatre, martial arts, literacy catch-up programs.

I say: We have drafted a performance script that we'd like to workshop with some kids.

Your look is an inspection of my skin, in no way a show of interest in anything I am saying.

Yes, why not, you say, but don't jump the gun. We can do nothing without money. I don't want to throw cold water on your project. Quite the contrary. And these children here could benefit, I'm sure.

But ... there's a warehouse behind St Charles, Belsunce. They'll let us use it for 2000 francs a month. We've already ...

First things first, you say. Write out a proposal. You can submit it to us at our next meeting and if it meets the criteria, I'm sure funds can be released.

I wonder about the behaviour of my mouth, if a pine nut isn't stuck to my chin. I see a spark of malice light up and soften in your eyes.

A calendar and a budget. First course first.

I have hated marzipan but I am finding this deeply vivid, reaching from burning sweetness into something else. I take another.

Who ... are all these people? There seem to be kids everywhere, mostly young boys. They stand around in clusters, awkward, indolent.

Ah, those are some of the younger *Bidon* recruits. We'll have time for names later.

I follow your look: they're materialising from the front

door, coming out of walk-in robes ... A cloud of boys, some could be Malian, Madagascan, Arab, Berber, gathers around you, a nebula with a nice range, from caramel to coffee. You look at them as if they are all edible. Do you want me to imagine they're your foot soldiers, code-troublers or simply toy boys?

Basilio comes up fingers curled around his glass of Baume de Venise. He eyes Molly perched up on the mezzanine platform. At first, he says, I thought you two were a bit of a joke.

Molly takes it up from on high: Maybe we saw ourselves as a joke?

No, it's this sort of lurching way you talk? Always with that rising intonation? As if everything's a question?

Maybe we're just always ready to be wrong? To be counted out?

Yes, Basilio, laughs, like you've even got our names wrong? Shadow? You say, Spider?

Yeah, ask the right questions maybe we can fall through to another space? Like Alice down that burrow?

Yeah, Molly goes, neo-Alices, how's that, Shadow? Free-falling through the cracks. Hey! Dykes in the cracks! She laughs.

Speak for yourself. I'm still sussing out the cracks in the dyke, I say, giving her face close scrutiny. Here I am travelling on her pun, broadcasting what she'd have us become before I even know it. This is Simone's trick of course. She has us never knowing the boundaries of performance. Is it Molly or Tumbleweed who wears her preference like the colour of her eyes?

The Spider's asking how come you girls can't decide who

you are, he says. Out of synch with yourselves as well as each other.

So what, Molly says, through a mouthful of nuts, we can couple tactically, take the mickey out of the malestream, out of the *monsieurs*? That a problem for you? That a problem for the Spider?

Well, he laughs, she says it's like you can't make a statement. Like as I said, everything's interrogative with you? Even your bodies?

Mmm, seeding space with questions. That's cool if that's what we're doing. So, we hazard she's accepted us as Webworkers?

He laughs sweetly, quietly now and smiles from Molly back to me. Well, the Spider's still trying to suss you guys out.

We're not *guys*, Molly says and falls back into the mezzanine cushions.

Oh-ho. So-rry. So the Spider says, and he takes up her precise enunciation and rapid delivery: *Under all the imagery, the harlequin stuff, it's hard to see what those two are aiming at in their tandem act. Maybe they're just two spoilt hippies who've strayed into the wrong scene, wrong decade? I wonder if we can accommodate such frivolity.*

He lowers his voice as our eyes beam in on her: She is holding court, mustering the strays with her gaze. I'll give you that, the Shadow says, she's got a kind of cradle-snatching charisma, especially over those kids, the new recruits. She sets one up in front of the others. She comes out with some pretty withering formulae. You should hear her: *This is a pretty knotty bit of plantation pine, but we can make a temporary ladder out of him, what d'ya think, fellas?* Then she'll feast on the round of automatic laughter. *Now I always say you need a bit of stodge in any revolutionary diet, and this one is a raisin bread if ever.*

What's this new turn? Is this the way they're trying to move the plot on, through gossip? Is it improvised? Is he clued into some bigger story? Has she sent him to mesh us into it?

Look, Banksia, of course she uses the struggle as a kind of self-extension. Narcissism is not to be excluded. Obviously. But what the hell. It's academic whether she's fake or not. We do our stuff for her. And does it matter whether we're fake or not? She gets us to do her work, framing the National Front in the Press, infiltrating their meetings. We offer it to her as a kind of gift. Her appetite's monstrous. We get addicted to feeding her … it's that we've got to watch. That's why we've got to keep check on one another.

I do take time to think how generous the Shadow is, always watching, aware of the life in contradictions, keeping definitions tentative, alert to the dangers of set roles. I find myself envying his fluidity, annoyed with our strident clowning.

I climb onto the mezzanine. On the wall opposite there's a costume display, Kabuki masks, Balinese ritual horse costumes, Noh robes. The wall is honeycombed with niches for these, their glass flush with the stone. They dim and begin to fuse. I stretch out next to Molly half-thinking that if she's going to make a move then she'd risk it up here out of the Spider's sightlines. I know she's immobile but I feel her touch hovering over me, dredging the causeways of blood, banking it tidally, this way, that … I wake up on an echo of a cry, as if that's my voice wailing in the farthest crease of space, I am afloat in the wake of that wail but the hand slipping away from the top ladder rung is ringed, fortyish, the nails not squared like Molly's. And the music is a Turkish song, endlessly looping. Lights have dimmed. I must climb down. Am I the last one here? Am I bitten?

But, no. There are the Shadow and the Tumbleweed, on their cushions, quietly talking.

Time for you to enter the Spider language, Sister, he says, cocking the camera view-finder to his eye.

So the Shadow is chosen as Cameraman. What then do I say about this manipulator, hiding behind all the Mistress of the Network stuff? What do I make of my intoxication?

I look into the lens and speak Spider to it.

She'll have us doing all the work, all the scaffolding, which she'll remove once the structure's there so we'll have to say the web is hers. We're agents of her eccentricity; dance attendance on her phantom pregnancies. We can even manufacture Spider clones for her. Sure we'll work. With our pedipalps we'll service her all right: puncture, probe, crochet. We tick-tack dance on livewire legs but she's our choreographer. We digest her food for her, so she eats outside herself. We're her kitchen and her stomach. We dangle from our draglines, decoys in relay. Need be she'll expend us all. We know the risk and love her for it: at any time any one of us can become her food. Caught plucking out our amorous code, when she's in that mood, we're lover-tucker, running, webstruck, all of us.

And the Shadow picks up the words and runs. He delivers with the camera trained on the Spider.

Yeah. Well I'm caught too. Webstruck like you say. If you've felt trapped in her gaze, you'd understand. And watch out, sometimes she fakes she's blind but she's one walking panopticon, man. Seriously, she's covered in eyes. Those black eyes of hers, they're writing us into their ink.

The spots multiply Basilio's dancing shadow on the walls, wrapping tentacles around the ceiling. His voice comes in hard, bitten spurts. As Shadow he imitates the Spider's side-scrambling; he moves fast and keeps his eyes gleaming towards a spectator, which he seems to see at every turn, as if the threat is in n dimensions and his dance is ready to tell all our stories of resistance — shoulder, elbow, footsole, palm. He sings and snarls, his breath chopping the words:

We think we're speaking, we think we're moving, we think we're pacing ourselves but we're in, caught up already with running for the Spider. Beware of her tongue. It's good spectator sport, you know, and that's the danger. I've watched a whole gathering getting blissed out on that whiplash tongue of hers. She can make a table of twelve disappear into her anecdote, too. One time it's about her getaway from her German doctor-lover. She tells us how she broke into his Marberg surgery and, putting on her best Turkish-German imitation, told him where to go. She pointed to his crotch: *you call that a toolkit, she jeered. Take away your prescription pad, you're nothing!* She boasts she served him that in front of all the patients. Then it'll be about her diversion of funds for the *Bidon* cause when she's working in the Cultural Affairs Bureau. The rorts, the scams, the junkets, the *magouilles*. We can't pass judgement. We're intoxicated with the drug she deals. Her arbitrary power. Well, before her, we were nothing, man. Nothing. Nor were you, as far as I can see. And he winks.

Crossing

At the terminus I saw her arranging herself. She rotated slowly with palms outstretched to catch the warm air from the idling bus engine. She needed to toast herself; the mistral was cutting, especially for someone in a mini-skirt and skimpy T-shirt. The great height and the broad shoulders argued against the female fat distribution, the small, wide breasts and the relative softness of the buttocks. Despite the radical waxing, phantom male eyebrows persisted under the make-up. The skin around the wide-set eyes had the sheen of scar tissue. A light, silvery scar also crossed the lip at an angle; an old fight when she was still a bullied boy, or cleft lip repair, hard to tell. Like she was exploring her face for the first time from inside she slid her tongue over the teeth, a travelling bulge, while she kept the full, fluted lips closed. As she turned to face me, her hands fanning out behind while she offered the backs of her thighs to the heat, she experimented with a smile which showed the braces on upper and lower teeth. Like this was too much, too painful an exposure, she quickly drew the lips shut, and made the focus of the amber eyes indeterminate. I could feel the tension between shyness and exhibitionism. I knew it exactly. Her hair was short, feathery, softly waved and tinted apricot blonde. Her legs were as long as a basketballer's, but silkily smooth and with some blue varicose veins sketched in filigree. She wore black flat pumps with discreet little bows. The fingers wrapped around the patent leather purse wore wedding and engagement rings, opalescent varnish on manicured, rectangular nails. She had achieved the miracle of making those huge hands look infinitely delicate — weightless, almost. Again, as the upper lip shrugged away, I could feel the catch of the braces against my own skin. I gave back a half-smile; didn't want to make it look like some frontal offensive. On the bus she sat obliquely on the bench opposite, Egyptian profile, so that the immense length of her thighs was accommodated. The skirt was deeply creased across the hips, molding the crotch closely where she crossed her thighs. I tried these out as I reviewed them: a pocket fashioned as the vagina, phantom testicular pressure as her thighs crossed; something like a clitoris surgically rescued from the penis. Did past organs persist just like once the fantasy body shared the contours of the real? Had she kept the dialogue going or was she now blocked in regret? I dropped my notebook. It slid, disgorging loose pages, towards her feet on the bus floor. We were nearing the Place Castellane. It was behaving like a triumphal carousel, spinning its traffic, lane braiding with lane. She stretched her immense arm and plucked up my book, sliding back the loose pages, offering it across to me, the eyebrow arching, puckering the strange scar-zone.

Merci, Mademoiselle, I sounded, regretting for a moment I'd not said *Madame*. But no, she was not into matronly dignity.

Je vous en prie, Mademoiselle, she returned.

There was gravity and tenderness in her recognition. Did she see that we had crossed, for a moment?

Asif He'd been There

It's time for Asif, the Cardboard Suitcase, and he plays it straight to the camera for what it is. His voice is clear, full of glassy water. As he talks he becomes increasingly vivid; his intensity has an authority, I've got to admit. He has chosen a single spotlight and throws his voice straight into the darkness. He's tense, seriously tense.

I've been with them through the decades on the battered buses, and ferries, and stinking third class compartments. We didn't speak. We refused the smell of hopelessness of the others, of the shiny, flea market suits, the frayed shirt collars, the obscene need in the private focus of the eyes. The battered cardboard suitcases. It said: I'm only appearing for the moment to be one of you. For each of us, our luck made an invisible line around us, a tripwire. Don't come closer, man. I'm cut out for a winner's story. I'll use these French fuckers and show them.

I go back there in my head, through those journeys of miserable hope, because hope for us migrant beggars was low-grade, miserable, and I can feel my anger rising again. As I travel with them, I can feel my stride working itself up. Never need to look like a sloucher with time on his hands, cause he's a loser. Winner's time!

So, okay. We measured up; we fitted. All the same, it was hard to see how some of us guys did. All over Europe they'd measured our biceps, heights, weights, cocks; they'd dipped tapes into urine samples, peered down our holes, up our holes, pinched scrotum, cupped balls. Just testing, they laughed. We all felt pink and glistening then. No secrets. But the cement of that inspection set inside, made us hard and grim. I told myself I had other certificates. I was certified as not one of the losers. I was written into European law, its codes and local rules with the right style through those certificates. I had connections. I knew the tricksters to avoid. I wouldn't end up paying my first wages to an agent. I had practice on the machines. Licences. Wouldn't be fazed like some I can tell you who had missing fingers to show for it. I could read their language. I could do a ratio sum. I wanted to puke at their inwardness. That cowering inwardness, I could read defeat all over it: it had them barracks-bound, sucked into the tunnels, the work without earmuffs, the pain in phantom limbs, and always, no-compensation-because-no-papers. That pathetic inwardness was what stopped them from coalescing. Coalescing, massing: we had to amass all our labour in reserve. We would withdraw, be reserved, and watch their cities choke on their shit without us.

I could've made my way blindfolded anywhere in Marseille like I'd swallowed and metabolised the map. I knew how to feed the ringroads and the freeways from the cul-de-sacs and one-way *Bidon* streets. It was for the taking. My confidence aroused me. My blood didn't flow;

it *drilled* through my veins. I was pumping for the *Bidons*. Of course the *Bidonvilles*, caught in their ratty-treed terrain between the freeways and the Supertrain lines, they were my material. I had to start with the cement high-rises twenty k's and three hours in traffic jams from the centre. There were chunks of countryside still caught in their fire escapes like old food between the teeth. I had it all on the tip of my tongue — it was my stuff. Like one of their sociologists, you could say I was something of a student of graffiti. The stairwells were my memo pads. The messages were grafted into me. I'd connect with all our people who whispered and swallowed and make *Bidonlingo* with the thick spit of their angry children. I'd line them up and give them super-Joe-cool cocksureness: back erect, head still with the slight rear-tilt, expression impassive, pelvis easy, all movement from below, fluid, fluid, flexing only in the legs. All we needed was a bit of ruse and a few guts. We'd turn the *Colons'* language inside out so that their own tongue would terrify them. That was what aroused me, if you want to know.

Of course you want to know about her.

I get it: he's speaking to the video as if he's being interviewed in some future time about the Spider. Bit arrogant, I think, to project things ahead like that, outside the shared performance time.

Why in the hell, I asked, was this woman who calls herself the Banksia, looking for a cause here when she had one stinking cause back in her own country?

He glances into the darkness, alongside the camera, towards me: he needn't labour the point — realisation creeps under my clothes.

I was amused at the thought of leading her on, feeding

that infuriating glossy humility those middle-class women try out when they look at the losers. They watch us with smiling indulgence: fascinating culture, they say, inventive *bricolage* of the oppressed, they say, like they're looking through their little glasses at the Opera, when we trick them with shit we've made up that moment. I massaged something in her head into a hot ready-mix, which she took for my lust I guess. Then I saw how I could use her misery, her need for a theme and a sequence that would make her a champion, a minor one maybe, but a champion all the same, of the Cause. I could see how to get her into our imagery and then to feed it. We needed Webworkers, whatever their motivation. In a way the more deluded they were, the better.

He's fired up and he goes on and they are all transfixed by his performance. I slip away.

Outside our play, Simone is always there, watching. Poised, ironic. She nods to me and smiles. What's happened to the Banksia? she asks. Her voice is almost caressive. I see you've lost sight of your own material. With one sideswipe he has you out of it. You must find a way to return.

My stuff doesn't … translate.

Make yourself the disturbance then. Remember: *mute.* What you did at the beginning was not bad at all. As Banksia he has to take you into account. Think about it.

Her voice is mellifluous, still low, her look weighted. If you find a mode that resists his expulsion you will have succeeded. Perhaps … Why not? Why not come around to my place this evening, try it out? You and she — she nods in Molly's direction — should join forces. She has some experience with costumes, I gather. I can release a little money for her to knock something up. Perhaps you can sketch for us what you have in mind. You should insist on the Banksia, make us believe in it.

I do it in big ink sketches on watercolour paper, the banksia seedpods cracking open on blackness. We'll have the head and torso fused. Leotards on legs, maybe some sort of hair attached. All afternoon I work feverishly. The pen is excited in its cross-hatchings, febrile in its dance. Two of the mouths I enlarge into great carbuncular mouldings, a dual carapace for our breasts. The Banksiasisters. We will have mikes hidden below the speaking lips, so when our voices come, it will be as if they issue from any one of them. My donation to the Spider. I catch myself in Xavière's hall mirror, an oval, baroque gilt-framed thing, oddly dissonant with the functionalist leather furniture. I see the Spider's face, receiving mine. Already my look is there in her almond eyes, caught in their black onyx. I recognise the rising flush as mine. The old adolescent thing that tugs and inflames. At least with Eva Hoffman there was a basis. This time it is more like fear. When she summoned me and offered mild recognition, I felt tiny, weak. Simone Choiseuil could be my mother. Again I can hear Lou Barb saying it. If she tries anything on me I wouldn't know how to resist. I wouldn't find the will to. I know that if slowly, carefully, she began to undress me, talking with that musical intonation I would be gone, every nerve tweaked to a pitch. I see that I am rehearsing my part as utterly docile. In any case this is not to be a seduction scene: she has asked Molly to come as well. Still, I have avoided arranging to walk to the Rue des Grands Carmes with

Molly, hoping to arrive a little earlier. She will answer through the intercom with an exclamation mark in her voice: *Montez donc!* I want to give myself over to the will of this woman who could eliminate me with a sideswipe, just as she said Asif did. I feel it in my muscles as I strike out along the cafe terraces on the Vieux Port, with the mistral keening my skin. The Fort St Jean is pink ochre in the dying light, the limestone of the cliff face glowing a paler pink. The sea is ruffled, inkily rocking the mast reflections. Going towards her! Fluidly finding my level, I move through the plateaus of light, the drops into shadow. The faces in the cafe are lit with anticipation: rendezvous, assignation. The waiter in his black apron catches my glance, smiles. Marseille runs on desire for the stranger. I will present myself wordless, breathless from the stairs and she will usher me in wordlessly. She will delay letting go of my hand as she accepts the orchids — why not? — the spider orchids — which I will have bought in the Rue St Ferréole behind the Vieux Port, and leads me to the kitchen where she will carefully arrange the waxy, spotted blooms in a clear crystal vase. It will be subtly fluted and her fingers will pause on the frill to which the vase neck trumpets. And you would like? No I insist, you must have something. To please her I will have Turkish coffee. Again I will eat marzipan. I will say, I hope my intuition wasn't wrong — that you like Spider Orchids? I will be pleased to say *ochidée araignée* whether or not this is what they call them here. As reply she will stretch out those long fingers with their burgundy nails and knobbly knuckles, displaying the rectangular ruby amongst the gold rings and she will trace the contours of my face. My dear, she will say, you have judged right. When Molly arrives she will delay replying through the intercom. Her hand will linger a little longer on my upper arm. *Oui, montez, la Banksia est déjà là.* In her eyes kisses will proliferate. We will take our coffee into the baldaquin-draped alcove and she will invite me to take up one of her cushions. She will seat me beside her this time and gesture for Molly to take up the cushion opposite. Tacitly we will already be in league. Yet the Spider's talk, less mellifluous now, practical, tolerant of our youth, will come in clean riffs. The spurt, suspense, and fall of that cool music will play my nerves until the web becomes fluorescently obvious in the space between us. I will stay a little longer to ask about money available for the mikes, just to settle some technical questions. I will accept Baume de Venise this time. I will tell her of my unease vis-à-vis Asif. She will not enter into gossip but will imply solidarity with me. As I move to leave she will stop me, cup my chin in her fingers. You must speak to me as Spider, Banksia. You know I've noticed that you clone your movements on mine. I will laugh. I donate my story to you as best I can, I will say, making it as clearly an avowal as possible. I am happy to be in your net, my look will say. With her arms enfolding me, my mouth opening to hers, our finding ourselves back on the cushions, her fingers in one movement clearing the stud of my jeans fly, and unzipping it I will receive as inevitable the lips grazing my skin, and know that summarily I will sign myself away for this moment. That I will accept readily, even hungrily, evil consequences for it.

Yet it is Molly she sends to the door to let me in. You got those sketches? She gives me a frankly, openly fresh *bisou*. I blush for my anticipation.

Unreachable Cartoon

Being endlessly fugitive, the beloved of dream passages is pervasive, and somehow everywhere caught, commingled with her stalker in a fantastic osmosis. As if a slight fatigue has occurred in her psychic texture, she can recognise that the stuff of her life has been borrowed, and altered by its transition through the world of the other; she can see it in the lean of gestures towards inappropriate intimacy. Why Tom-Tom did not record what happened between Choiseuil and her — I nearly wrote *transpired*, or *came to pass* — because of the solemnity of her confession, I can only guess. She said she'd wanted to stay on, that night when they were discussing costumes. Against Molly's imperative stare that said, *I'm leaving and I want your company, for safety as much as for friendship*, she longed to stay there, to see if her dream could materialise. Instead she accompanied Molly home and then found herself retracing the route to Choiseuil's apartment. It was not too late, she said, as if she had ever respected protocol. At the intercom, all the same, she was seized by panic, found only a tiny, infantile voice within her.

C'est ... encore moi. Me again, Thomasina, I ...

Oh. Well, my child, I suppose you'll have to come up then, won't you?

So, Tom-Tom said, you can imagine how I felt then, so transparently an inopportune child.

She had no turban. He hair was short, tufted, greying at the roots. She was in a black silk *peignoire* and as she leaned forward, the skin between her thin breasts made a sharp fold, like a scar. I wondered if this was designed to put me off.

She said: You know this is inappropriate and yet you have come. You had to allow yourself this little transgression.

I'm sorry, Tom-Tom blurted.

I think I know what has brought you and, well, since you are here, and shivering, sit down, make yourself warm at least. I do not want to talk about your motivation; perhaps that will be possible, later. I would like to think it might be. I will only talk about you as it affects your performance. What is getting in your way is sentimentality. Oh! You are surprised? You want my benediction and I will not give you that. It would ruin everything, and besides, I would be culpable. You are only a student and you have yet a lot to learn. Your singularity, which I sometimes glimpse in your performance at those moments when you forget your audience, is that you are capable of violence, even capable of murder, I think. But then you are appalled and you cloak this capability in aesthetic lies. Your gestures, your looks, secrete a dream of mergings, of reconciliations, of folding all your sharp and cruel edges into a blanket of understanding. Exile is for a purpose; of maintaining radical separations; of

133

exploring a certain horror in differences entrenched.

Remember your difference, your untranslatable, is a cutting edge. Respect it. The vigilance of insomnia! Do not yearn for sleep in me, or, for that matter, in any of your classmates. Exile must be played out relentlessly, vertically. Do not aim at horizontal connections. What do you think, she said. I'm right, am I not? I want your separation to work for you. I expect a lot of it. But it is up to you to find the discipline.

Tom-Tom made her mumbled withdrawal. Of course she ran through the melodramatic rosary of Wanting to Die, to Hurl Herself into the Old Port, to Leap on the First Plane Home. Instead, she returned to the workshops, intent, I suppose, on finding other ways to find succour, or benediction, as Choiseuil called it. Choiseuil was right: Tom-Tom needed her to remain the hieratic, unreachable cartoon of the artistic dominatrix. Her whole childish desire resided in that.

What Passes for Us

Molly catches a lift on anyone's number and takes it to unexpected places, while Asif and I repeat, repeat, dig our heels in, get locked into the mirrors of antagonised structures. A strange heat builds between our warring mirrors.

There is another hiatus in the play. We are all in body-stockings in order to cut out cheap differentiation: these must come from the active image only, the force of the word, not the word itself, rather, its translation into music and movement. Choiseuil has said nothing about the Banksiasuit agreement. In this pause, and caught in the net of her glances, I let these lines hover less for the elusive Spider of our play than for the one Molly calls the Metaspider.

    We crochet the lines between us
    as we change to see us
    pass one another by

Play lean, stop all that fuss, she says.

It might be just a masque for Molly but she plays lean. It's there in the directed muscularity of gestures: a certain spatial genius which would make you watch whether she's dancing, driving, or slicing vegetables. And the steadiness of her look. Becoming Tumbleweed she moves liquidly into a series of back somersaults. Cardboard Suitcase shoots up an eyebrow in approbation. Cartwheeling I am hurtled on, seed-cases ransacked by cockatoo beaks, rattling dry husky lips on hard earth. Now we are moving along the fault line between the Spider and Asif: we pluck and pick at space, weaving, weaving the tissue of commands we fancy we'll receive, that get us irremediably into her game: my fingers all nerve-tips issuing this connective silk with which we play each other out.

> We crochet the lines between us
> as we change to see us
> pass each other by
> we make our negative passes
> mismatching what passes
> for us
> and now our web
> is this draft
> of where we might well be
> a messy thing
> this need to make a Spider
> from the sticky stuff
> of little deeds

The Spider smiles, bleakly, recognising my donation.

I go to the threshold to take a smoke. I feel the force-field intensify rather than weaken: I am dizzied, shaken. It is Molly who wraps her arm around my neck. The gesture is relaxed, easy. I can smell the sharp salt of her sweat. The grocery shop opposite comes back into focus.

We're not bad, hey.

I return the gesture. We laugh frankly, freely. We pull apart as Choiseuil's recitative drifts towards us, reminded of the dictum: *outside the performance repertoire, no relation.* Molly's smile is slow and deliberate. Her lips are huge in the black-burgundy lipstick, so close to my cheek it makes me gasp. Two women in the shadowy garage opposite are admiring a bonneted baby, padded and trussed against the mistral. The women's eyes flash their pleasure. The fruit display impacts tangibly: red, green and yellow peppers, bulbous and gleaming, golden apples, round and perfectly satisfactory as breasts could be, oranges, so bright the colour clangs like cymbals, tomatoes whose vermilion would turn a white world pink, and Chardin and Vermeer and Cézanne juggle their versions behind my eyes as if I had held, weighed, and bitten each colour, snapped onto and sucked into each texture. The lights change and the traffic roars across the field of vision. This is the best, this connection through work becoming simply a climate that buoys desire. Forget the Spider delirium. Could be my mother, etc. Still, that cupid's bow lip of Molly's could send some poisoned arrows too. There is malice in the French sense of cunning and wit in the eyes. Perhaps also in the English sense. Am I scared of her strength, of the way she takes my imagery up and away through the rhythms she imposes? Does she read me too well?

We can seriously beat the shit out of that Asif bastard, she says.

I peg out a smile between affirmation and denial. Dark flame, Asif. His vehemence is commanding. It comes from a deep spring, which escapes her mockery.

I receive a kiss on the cheek and an emphatic caress down the neck. She adds a peal of laughter as cautionary note: I have made these moves, she seems to be saying, but don't go taking them seriously.

Within the space of the performance I feel myself hollowed out, weak, weak from this constant bickering, this rivalry in performed alienation. And I never question his authenticity out loud.

Lou Barb

Stanley Spencer

When Father retired prematurely and drifted into depression, Mother persuaded him to use the accumulated long-service leave and take off for a few months in Europe. She decided that I could board once, feigning declining interest, I managed to dispel her fears about the Influence of that O'Shea Child. For me the Caedmon regime offered intoxicating freedom after Mother's surveillance. Tom-Tom persuaded me to accompany her to a little op-shop on Stirling Highway, to get something less *boring* to wear. She coaxed me into a $2.00 number that I knew then I wouldn't have the courage to step out in. It was a maxi-length thirties black crepe-wool coat with leg-of-mutton sleeves and oblique, wooden buttoning across the chest to the shoulder, somewhat Russian style, so that a single lapel flapped down. To carry it off, I would have had to affect high heels with peekaboo toe and ankle strap and a tiny hat secured at a cocky angle with a pin. I bought it because Tom-Tom *saw me in it*. But what Tom-Tom brought back in

139

the little white plastic bag was even less likely for her. However unconsciously, she used to wrench her school uniform from its subjugating purpose into a display of unruliness. Then on weekends she was the down-dressed tomboy in jeans or shorts, so in the little sixties number she picked up, an empire-line lime-yellow mini-dress with a coy little bow beneath each breast, she looked as if she was in drag. The coarse dark hair on her brown legs added to the effect. And the shoes! Boat-like, white, winklepicker, sling-back numbers with squashed heels. She was probably the only one amongst us who went bra-less; and when she tried on the little dress and strutted laughing around the dorm, I could see the dark nipples trembling through the cotton. One weekend when Maeve couldn't make it to the school to pick her up, she covered disappointment with defiance and announced she'd take a bus to Perth.

I guess you wouldn't want to come, would you, Lou?

I wanted very much to go, but didn't dare risk it; I could already anticipate Mother's phone call from Europe, every moralising parenthesis, every rhetorical question, every oratory pause: *Of course it's not* enough, *is it, for us to be paying those* fees? *No, you have to* disgrace, *not just yourself, but your* parents, *by this* delinquent *behaviour. What is most* disappointing *is that you betray our* trust *like this.*

I lied, pointing to *Women in Love* before me on my bed. I made my voice sound tentative, interrogative, as if it were all negotiable, as if it were fine either way. I'm really into this? I'd rather just hang around here?

Her tone flattened me: Let them serve me a detention, she said. I'm going into the Art Gallery. She would check out the Stanley Spencer show, she said. She was going to write something on it for Eva Hoffman. Every assignment was performed like an oblation to Eva, for whom, despite everything, she fuelled her infatuation with any material that came her way.

She said she got off near the Cloisters and took her empire-line and little boat-like shoes up Barrack Street, all the way to the Horseshoe Bridge. On the bridge she noticed a restored '60s white-finned Valiant, cruising close, so close that the white-wall tyres rubbed the kerb. She was good on cars, something she'd picked up from Maeve. He was maybe thirty, maybe more, she said, with a rocker's crest to his black hair. He had that narrow-eyed feline look, as he pulled on his smoke, trying to be the cool cat. Somehow, though, she fell for it, and looked into the car. There was a crucifix hanging from the rear-vision mirror, and a couple of red and white velvet dice. The dash was covered in a sort of spiky, white fleece. He was in a black shirt with white stitching.

Hot day for a girl to be walking.

Oh, she said, I dunno. Haven't got far.

Can't give you a ride?

Nah, she said. I'll be fine. See ya.

She shouldn't have said that, she realised. It was already like an invitation. Sure enough, there was the Valiant parked in a No Standing bay, engine idling, ringed hand with cigarette dangling out, waiting.

She tripped up the Gallery steps and partly to prolong her visit, sought out one of the curators to get his number on the Spencer. Oniric, I remember she came back with that word. She was quite funny parodying the pedantic guy afterwards but seemed to have enjoyed the audience with him all the same. He even lent her a box of Spencer slides to show at the school. In turn she bought for herself a postcard of Stanley's self-portrait. It occurs to me now that Asif, with his rather brutal good looks, was already there, in the thrall of that image. It was around five when she came out, parched, realising if she bought a drink she would blow her bus fare back to the school.

The winged Valiant was still there, the guy leaning against it, planting his lips on a can of Coke.

I just wanted a sip of that Coke, she said. He had Marvin Gaye's 'Grapevine' playing on the radio. She said she sort of went into the space of that music. When he held out the can to her, she felt: Oh, well, it's happened now, as if their meeting had happened a decade or more before, through their choice of retro gear. A minute later she was gripping the dash, watching the dice do their mad jig while he whipped her through the streets of Mount Lawley, plunging finally down into a car park under huge Moreton Bays on the riverside — Maylands, or East Perth, she wasn't even sure where she was now. She said the river flashed cruelly like beaten metal there and beyond she could see the huge WACA lights, like gigantic, rearing insects, all compound eye. She wished she'd brought her shades. She closed her eyes against the glare but the insect shapes persisted as his hand plunged and rifled. She opened her eyes on the dice as he directed her hand to his crotch.

The first I knew about it, apart from her tear-congested face, was the yell she gave when she realised she'd left the slides in his car. Oh, Lou and I'm meant to take them back. Shit! Then she laughed: in her hand, creased, but all the more precious for having survived it, was Stanley Spencer. I must've held onto him all the time, she said.

Just then Miss Thurtell, our House Mistress came in, wanting to know why Tom-Tom hadn't been in for tea. I had to wait for the story of the car and the slides, while this one-woman tribunal launched on the routine if-you-persist-in-carrying-on-like-this-you'll-find-yourself-out-on-your-ear-my-girl, then delivered the terms of detention and grounding. You could tell Miss Thurtell's heart wasn't in it; she was fragile, and milky-eyed in her pleated, baby blue, crimplene dress. She was tremulous with the violence the ventriloquy of the rules did to her. Tom-Tom attempted no excuse, offered no extenuating circumstances.

Later, she said, well, at least it was decent of him to drive me back. And he didn't shoot his stuff all over me. He had tissues! He must always go around prepared!

Then she began shaking. If I hadn't been so cowardly none of this would have happened, of course, but I'm certain it didn't occur to her to reach for recrimination. I think it was more to comfort me than herself that she forsook her bravado to let me fold my arms around her. Later, perhaps in defiance of the contamination, she pinned the Stanley up next to her bed, and delivered a marvellous little exposé on the Oniric in Stanley Spencer to Eva's class.

Those Femraps

I have a rendezvous with Basilio at the Cintra down on the Quai des Belges to see the rushes of the Banksia rap. There installed on the terrace, is the Spider, an Eau Perrier before her. Well, she says, stretching out her hand, I am listening. She leans back into the plastic-coated raffia chair. She marks out a space between the jostling masts of the fishing boats and yachts. Tell me what you think about what I said. About refusing those horizontal connections? The lures of sentimentality?

I play remote, I play cold.

I don't think anyone's going to understand the first thing about it, I say, watching the masts. You know, reclaiming the racist insults to hurl them back, where we're coming from in all that. As … as women.

Keeping her eyes on me she sips her Perrier. Touches the back of my hand lightly.

Forget polemics. Leave your Banksia country dark. Let it remain savage, claim it as savage, as rebarbative. The insurrection of a monster from … ah whence they need not know. Make your bodies suggest it. Well, I trust that you have. Ah, there's the Shadow. I'll leave you both to it.

She withdraws. Black today, scarlet and black turban. Black, calf-length overcoat. She could almost pass for a Redback, an un-French spider. A pithy glance my way as she pays the waiter and her profile is carried off. Confident as a camel, I think and again, the Hoffman comes back to me.

This is getting me confused, the Shadow says. You been talking to the Spider or Simone Choiseuil? It's a hell of a spin-out. You know, like who's writing who into whose story? Anyway this is what I'm trying to show with the camera work. Like the idea that it might be the enemy dictating our scenario. What I'll do later is get some footage of me shooting you picking up the Spider's look as she slips back into Choiseuil. I've already got the confounded looks of the passers-by, and workers, carrying on with their gestures in a space totally alien to yours. And always, beyond all of them there'll be the cops, watching, watching.

The cops ignored us, of course. That's all it's going to amount to, the whole bit, a little pocket of carnival. We're dismissed as innocuous clowns.

Stop being so cynical. Have a look. He hands me the video camera. Take a look at your femrap. No, through that, that's the view-finder!

At first I think what a pathetic space we've been in, working it off, fogging up our own warped mirrors with our hothouse breath. Hothouse Banksias! Basilio gets a great shot of a crane operator watching the show in bemused indulgence of our madness: it's at best a distraction. In the silence of the miniature video rushes I can supply the jeers coming from I don't know where, along with the power hammers and the muted roar of traffic beyond the site. In the middle ground there are workers continuing oblivious. I'm pleased with the job Molly and I did on the costumes though. We are fully metamorphosed: the Banksia suits make their own claim. Undeniably, whatever they are, they are there, covered in huge horny lips from which they speak and growl and cry. At times a high gibbering came from our lips Basilio says, which made his own hair stand on end. Our stockings are worked through with mesh to which we have stuck horsehair, as are our arms, extended by stick-form fingers, webbed together with a waxy vinyl skin Molly found in remnants. The hidden mikes give a weird amplification above all the workplace cacophony, which we use as grounding for the musical structure.

>we're the Banksia
>*Bidons*
>scurrying through your *Bidon-*
>*ville*
>hairy big fat violent
>we're polylabial through
>and through
>our horny lips
>but songs come honeyed too
>or oyster-luscious
>ding-dong uvular moist
>we ring for you
>we're softies hard in the middle
>we're what you need
>to make of us
>soft-heads with hard-ons

we're peeled almonds
at the centre should you care to lick
we've got our biceps up
on your machines
with our single battery cerebral lights
we redden the workplace
we bloody it up
we're the catch
in your safety regulations
we're the spanner in the works
we're working it up
working it off
we dance with the chainsaw
the sledge the jackhammer the bobcat
we're all ditch-witches
we cream and we spout both
asbestos fibre, battery acid, you name
the poison we give it back
recycling your batteries and brakes
we make you go and not go
materially we're the basest
we're building little shrines
to what you admire in us
to microcephalia and hirsutism
singing polylabially, we make
our polyglossaries erupt
in your monolingo
we're the banksia cobs
come back to haunt you
we wear our skeletons on our sleeve
we're capable of glistening styles
we dance with the bones
your machines have crunched

send up the stench your hygiene
bestows upon us
toss our foetal and fecal detritus
down to your restaurant courtyards
we splatter your demographic tables
with our discreetly dead babies

Nursing Landscapes

The chasm widens between us. Asif is entrenched in his own kind of untranslatable and if Choiseuil really has a bigger picture hanging in some space in her head she's not letting on when the viewing time might be. She seems to have chosen to suspend any seductive manoeuvres, or did I imagine them? Has she seen the odd caress and play of looks between Banksia and Tumbleweed? She is severe, removed, now. Again you're hamming, she says, as if this charge has already been made, which it hasn't. Hamming isn't the same as exaggerated play. Start again.

There is always the refuge with Xavière and Jean-Hippolyte but I know parasitising on their intimacy must end. They need evidence of progress from me daily, want assurances that not only work but relationships are firming up into more autonomous orbits for me. Rising later, since workshops only start at 10, I find a trail of little attentions: my bread set out, my ringed serviette in place, the coffee machine ready to go, a note in Xavière's beautiful hand: Hope your monologue is well received, *ma belle*. I know J-H delays his departure for the Faculté to offer me a lift. If I mention an item I must procure I find it on my table on return: tissues, tweezers. They are too kind and I cannot tell them of this building dread, that the whole workshop is a bad mistake. Can't explain it, it's at once entirely sham and so real I feel it like a bodily sickness. I am becoming addicted to this round of feint and barb, of thrust and parry, of multiplied simulations taking on the density and randomness of the real. I can't say how lonely this constant erotic inflammation makes me feel, this infinite solicitation which can't deliver except in the gestures of dance. Maybe that's the point. Exile is having your dancing met with incomprehension. I don't know whether I can go through with it, I tell them. I see the exasperated look he gives to Xavière.

Look, I say, I won't throw it in yet. I'll take it as far as I can. Besides, you two have been so good to me. And I've been parasitising off you for too long. Molly, one of the women in the workshop says there's a studio free, you know, *coin cuisine, cabinet de toilette* and all, where she lives in the Panier — Rue des Muettes. Same landlord as hers. I might check it out.

You suit yourself entirely there, my dear, he says, fatigue invading his voice. We are delighted to have you here as long as it suits you.

He breaks his coiled waffle cylinder into the raspberry ice-cream. I have noticed that he always seeks distraction in the available props if there's a risk of naked emotion.

I really think we'd better think twice before buying our ice-cream through Félix Grenier. He of course procures them from The Glacier de la Rue Sainte, you know, Tom-

Tom, once the most highly reputed Glacier of Marseille. Ah, well timed. Curse the phone: it's the utter imperiousness of its demand I object to.

He carries the phone back to us. Likes to perform his side of the phone calls to an audience. It's ... for you my dear. It is your Molly, judging by the accent.

They both watch me intently for reaction. I keep it neutral.

Hey. Tom-Tom, Molly says. You're not cutting loose are you? Something tells me you want to pull out. Look. What about coming over my place tonight, grab a meal with me, talk it through? Maybe take a look at the studio I told you about?

This is the first time she's spoken in English to me. The voice coming through the holes is so loud it will send the ice-cream into instant meltdown. I try to stop it leaking by pressing it securely against my face.

Yes, yes. I'd like that. Eight?

I withdraw to my bedroom, let the siesta swallow the waiting time. Leave all the rest in suspense until then.

Her face is a nursing landscape, features blurred but can be called up at will. I can find other worlds through her eyes, the Chateau d'If, the St Jean fortress at the harbour opening. She is absent-minded. She is Evie but doesn't know it. She says: these might be for you, whatever you're called. You can make your name; but first you've got to take a chance. We fill the car with the silver presents she has brought me. Moonstruck. Silent. We are back in Australia. The car eats the blue road between the wheat fields from horizon to horizon coming in waves. We ache — I feel her ache too — at the beauty of blue and ochre and silver. We drive and yet are still. Then we're overtaken, just like that, with hilarity. Something makes a draught in the air. I cannot read its message. I just know it's a new kind of banditry, holding us up. We see the joke when the Farmer harvesting his ochre wheat carves a curve between the waves and waves a silver hand. Good-bye!

I dream of them all, Evie, Maeve, Molly, the Spider, separately, inter-fused and superimposed; I dream of trancing between them, losing Maeve to find her real affection in a decoy smiling like a young woman. I dream of the betrayal, a passing shadow in performance tells me is for real: of Maeve, of Millie, of everyone at Banksiafold.

Now out of Maeve's country I am looking urgently for the sea between the Maritime pines. Behind the jagged horizontals of their black-green foliage I see the mountains. Their limestone outcrops shine wet-blue, oysterish, in the shadows. The bleaching light on the biscuit buildings lets their pink speak only in subterfuge. I need to find for Maeve a last residence whose windows will be filled with the violet of the distant sea. We must rise up improbable slopes, where tall pink-ochre houses look promising: I am a wheeler-dealer, manoeuvring the gears to reach the house, which, I am told, is vacant. I have my chequebook ready on my lap. I keep coaxing her up towards this new life in my struggling car, saying: Let's try this one, Maeve, this might well be it. This is a sad time where I become her mother, incline her towards my decisions, summon up practicality in the retreat of hers. I consult her as my financial partner but feel treacherous in the knowledge that her failing breath blurs any process of decision making. It is definitely a question of looking after her now. The villa is modest, a replica of many others sighted but it seems unclear now whether they figure other than in children's drawings: it's tower-shaped and simple with its rust and pink ochre tiles and its long narrow windows. Our bodies are drawn upwards by the pull of the purchase and it's during the climb of the last rutted limestone track that I lose her from sight and feeling.

Inside is another world: the volumes are arranged horizontally in defiance of the tower impression. It is another time in which I both see the woman and enter the first, sinuously beautiful paragraph she is writing, attentive to texture. The house, whose inspection does not matter because it's done in a blink, is schematic as in someone else's dream, or as if hurried on by the imperatives of sexual attraction. On the horizon, where Maeve has dissolved, there flickers an anxiety, fugitive. I cannot pause for pain to name itself.

Her Semitic features superbly moulded, her skin swarthy, her eyes black, her hands in black fish-net gloves, the woman moves endlessly towards me. It is the glassy night ocean I want to remember even as I look into her eyes. I write on the pad before me: *I will believe in it even when I can't say yet what it means*. This is an act of faith we are engaged in, I must bear the risk of betrayal. I write this, confident that it speak for itself. It's like I've got all the sums of the world on my nursery abacus. I mark my truth with a sure contour: my force is in this fierce belief that the truth of the child can be told. My writing is as certain as the blood sucked from my own wound. My immediate need is to enter her written world and to have her receive my untranslatable fact. I am aware of how big the script is as it unravels behind her eyes. I kiss her and, rising through the first cool of saliva surf, passing through closer croppings, see the texture huge, like magnified Conté crayon on textured drawing paper. Her power is established through the clarity of her face and the defiant presence of her writing: I accept this as my climate, swimming through the night swell, breaking through the lace, roaring for breath, crashing back through her surf. In this time we occupy the world.

There is an arrival. The room returns with violent suddenness. I am left at the table and because our exchange is too precious, fragile and desperate for continuity, I duck below the level of the frosted mirror, which is also a sliding servery window between the two rooms.

The woman's father, who is Jean-Hippolyte and isn't, has been here all the time in an armchair turned away from the window. Without examining him, the visitor says she is worried that he has had a relapse and that his daughter should stop entertaining illusions that he will recover: she has her own life to claim. Something is said about a nursing home. In the meantime, no, she wouldn't resort to enema suppositories. Just maintain the vegetable and fruit intake and hope for the best. She lifts the red and white cloth from the Red Riding Hood basket she has brought: incontinence pads, new dressings for wounds, disposable syringes, a blood pressure kit and a tangle of complex medical devices I cannot name.

The father has dark, long eyes. His face only suffers from lack of dentures; despite the liver spots and broken capillaries, the skin has kept the tautness of youth. He is trapped in their third person accounts, as if the non-compass verdict were long since established. No, they are saying. He's often in these grumpy moods in the morning. Then he'll break out of it and be Sweetness Itself, as if nothing has happened. Also forgotten by their talk, I travel with my smile into the penumbra to which he has been relegated and he smiles beautifully, back to me, flooding my heart with light and says in medieval courtesy: *Et comment allez-vous, ma chère Madame?* From now on the sweetness of the lapsed seduction is sharpened by a fear of our cruelty confounded: theirs through ignorance; mine through my distraction. The thought comes like a child's wail from a neighbouring valley, already engulfed in the shadows: this man in his sad exile has screened me from Maeve. My Maeve has slipped down the limestone face into oblivion. I forgot to find a place for her!

I awake, my pillow soaked, tears still streaming.

In the shower the water ravels around my brown nipples, laces on my belly, coils around my pubes. I recall her mouth, her dark lips and that black surf. Somewhere, beyond this, a hand in a black netted glove retreats. Drying, I leave an electric zone, crackling around me.

Rue des Muettes

Molly is in a tiny medieval lane, Rue des Muettes, within the Panier behind the Vieux Port. This is where I fancied driving with the mysterious Ariane who so far has never figured beyond the talk of Xavière and Jean-Hippolyte. She doesn't hide her pleasure at my arrival but bellows it from the third floor. Hi! Come on up! Her shutters are the only ones still open. She doesn't recognise their function: to economise heat in winter, coolness in summer. It would be hard to have anything like a discreet relationship with a woman like this. She is a broadcaster. Well, I think, why should I have a problem with that?

The lounge has been furnished by forays into the *foire à la brocante*: two sofas face to face in faded floral brocade, stacked with a variety of cushions, some bold, geometric, some with elaborate Moroccan motifs. On the walls are black-and-white blow-ups of dancers, other productions. Opposite the sofa is a huge still of Molly and me, dressing for the Banksia work site performance. Basilio has caught her as she eased her breasts into the carbuncled carapace.

He has caught my eyes on this spectacle.

Yeah, she says. A still from Basilio's video. I like metamorphosis, hey. If someone asked me to sum up what I'm about I'd say it was that. Those moments slipping out of one skin into another. I have a *porto* in my hand. We are on the sofa before a buffet feast: *brandade de morue*, anchovies, salamis, *salade de mâche*, bread. Let's talk about your idea for the kids' show. Here's to us. Here's to the femrap. Banksiasister! Glasses clink. The hand is on mine. I realise only now why we have this odd mirror symmetry in our performances: she is left-handed.

Miles Davis' trumpet soars, ebbs and giddies along that line of Cyndi Lauper's 'Time after Time'. I think Molly's somewhere between Midler and Lauper and that I am pleased to be in this location. We are both smiling as we dance, liking it, admiring one another, fast, sure-footed. My body mimics her steps. She likes the devotion of my mirror; even when I trick her with displacements, she receives them as variations on hers, a homage to her attractions. She laughs, a long throaty gurgle, throwing back her beautiful throat: *You're moving mutes; do it*! Ah, Choiseuil! The Chateauneuf du Pape is taking. I try to tell her about my dream, about those netted gloves Choiseuil was wearing which must have triggered it, but something quite different comes back to me as we lurch together on this particular deck. I say: *it was like I was lurching on this cruise ship, I crossed the immense parquet, diamonds within squares, I liked the geometry, I was smiling at the dancers, turning circles within squares; below us and above were chandeliers, diamonds within squares, I sang, going tiptoe,* pianissimo. *I opened the grand piano and my fingers prowled and picked. Then, note by note, it came to me, a Lied about a yearning for a Turkish song, I thought, a German song of* Sehnsucht *for a Turkish song, and I made myself a leather larynx and launched myself after it and sang that it was a cruise to Turkey, that I was singing the cruise ship in, that I was cruising for the Spider's word, and then she came to me, her netted hands, beckoning with her knife; the edge she said, remember the cutting edge, lend me your ear,* while with Molly my fingers prowl and pick and my breath finds her ear. *This wasn't what my Lied expected, I thought, as her blade came down. Here's for radical separation, the Spider said, watching the gush; or you'll be stuck with those pathetic dancers, circles within squares! You must endure your own Walpurgisnight, your witching Sabbath.* Sehnsucht! *Can't believe you fell for that! I'd lost voice and ear and face; like I was watching figureless as my blood spread,* Walpurgisdunkel, *on the sea.*

Can't you ever stop performing? Molly says. Let's give the Spider a break, eh? Can't we have this space alone?

The hard lines of her face dissolve; her tone is meant to be endearing. I accept it and we are on the sofa, slip-sliding away before Miles' dancing trumpet has swooned out its last with Cyndi's song. In the ebb of the music I think that I have dreamed this as well, but the difference eludes me, as poignant as love. I try also to warn myself not to fall into the trap of calling love the giddiness of attraction, but already I'm moving into a sumptuously irrigated chamber.

Out of One Web

Asif feigns boredom when the Spider convokes him for one of her briefings yet he maintains lip-service. At the quarry near la Sainte Baume designated as a corner of the studio, they decide to show me the real basis of their power. I see the arsenal glittering in their eyes. I see the peach tones of the rock and begin to wonder whether all of this is really at base a more serious game than I've imagined. There is mirth dancing in Asif's eyes as he looks from Molly to me. Perhaps the whole studio thing is a front to get recruits and they are laughing, laughing at me. What better cover for a suicide mission for Maghrébin power after all than a first world feminist from a well-heeled school, and Molly with her Jewish background! Goose bumps come at the thought. I'm not sure either whether the fear of their ridicule isn't greater than the creeping suspicion that I've been otherwise framed. Basilio, Basilio is different. Fervent: wants to do 'valid things' with his life, doesn't want to use up his talent selfishly. Can I class myself with him? He's not a threat, in any case, because kindness is a value he keeps alive. Yet the way even he talks about Asif tightens my throat. Don't, he said, do not mention to him that you have primarily a feminist agenda. Well, I know that they were very sensitive about the way feminists have crashed into their world, lumping them all together as sexist bastards who treat women as beasts of burden. I know in France how they've outlawed or tried to all the practices of female mutilation, clitorectomy, labiaectomy, infibulation and all. The Tchador, the veils ripped off. Somehow, because Asif after all was a product of French education, and one of the top few percent in their University admission exams, I thought he would be beyond those investments. Oh, I try to remain discreet; say my agenda will be limited to challenging the way their macho strutting operates against them in the workplace.

Somewhere between devotion and the discipline of radical separation, between addiction and the need for the total break, there are the seductions of betrayal.

Choiseuil turns up at the workshop which Molly and I have decided to conduct in the warehouse without waiting for her go-ahead. Asif must have told her, must be in collusion with her. This, we are really doing, we tell ourselves. We are also a little guilty about using it as fieldwork, hoping to get a close look at these kids. It uses rap, skateboarding, a lot of tricky dancing and we pinch from Genet's *Screens* (banned here) the gestures of graffitists to write our world in. When things explode it's in the war of graffitists, hurling punning projectiles and painting caricatures of one another. There is a gang confrontation with skinheads in which the laughter of the *Bidon* kids ransacks the high seriousness of the skinhead gangs. Things are jubilant, untidy, almost chaotic. The *Front National* guys come in and rip off the scarves of the young *Bidon* girls to find beneath them tattooed skinheads. They peel off their mock skins revealing beneath new scarves …

Choiseuil has brought her retinue of toy boys, mustered from those 'extras' we saw in her apartment. I wonder where I've seen this before and it comes to me: it's Winnie Mandela and her United Football Club. One of the kids says: O-Oh, the Queen is here.

I feel it in my blood like a rearing breaker but I know I'll lose everything with these kids if I let it show. Okay, I think, I'll retreat behind the director bit like she does.

Whoa there, come on you guys, the skateboarding sequence, let's get it up. The cops are coming down. They're going to rip the scarves off the girls. Underneath, they'll find a bunch of skinheads, remember? That's right. Slowly, slowly peel off the plastic skinheads …

Molly says: That's looking wicked, man.

Choiseuil nods to me. The kids proceed in dumbshow. She drapes an arm around my shoulder. I have to suppress the *frisson*. Intriguing, she says. But tell me what you have in mind … I'm sure it must be more than *divertissement*, more than entertainment. You recall our talk?

Molly comes in on my stupid silence. Well, this kind of slippery metamorphosis, like their graffiti, writing on the run, the hip-hop which sends up what the cops are saying, that's their mode of resistance, survival … and, well, I guess they're having fun too.

Choiseuil delivers back to me, the ring-laden hand still resting on my shoulder. Mmm. Fun. I admire your … optimism, my dears, but resistance is not just a matter of disguise; you'd be the first to know that, of course. She drapes her other arm around Molly. You don't think that so much 'play' might distract a little from what you two are trying to do?

It's a collective thing …

Yes, of course it is. But I start to wonder what your message is. At the moment it's rather too busy, I think.

It's not *our* message, I say, keeping a steady measure. They're the ones who've evolved it. We only gave them the broad outlines.

We are not about documenting. Nor can we instigate revolution. We are opposing our images to theirs in a provocation, which might cause some interesting friction, that is all. Forget those flabby dreams of *théâtre engagé*, please. The most we can do is disrupt their imagery; create perhaps a rip in the fabric of their reason.

The roar of the skateboards persists through the hip-hop. The kids get air from ramps and vault over the heads of cops. The knocking and grinding silence Choiseuil. She beckons us away, clasping her ears.

You mean it's, like you said, sentimental … ? Give us time. You'll see …

A word with you, my dear. She draws me aside. Think *a certain gravity*, think *ritual*. You are dispersing your energies here. The American has more gravity, intentional gravity, for you than for your work together. For her, this is a comic mask, no more, something to do while she spends Daddy's money. I suggest that the only way to make this work is to let your attraction remain virtual. Harness that. Like a tidal force. If you maintain that vertigo, it will weight every gesture. But perhaps it is too late? She smiles curiously at this.

She draws me back to Molly's hearing range, as if the little pep-talk is now over and she's poised to broadcast the results. She secures their attention, half-veiling her eyes, moving into her Spiderguise. She rakes my hair. I can't believe the gestures she arrogates in this role. Don't be so prickly, Banksiagirl. It's hardly sentimental. She cups my chin and purrs: Ah, this is an incorrigibly prickly one.

She says, more to Molly than to me, We will talk further about this later.

Prickly One! Molly laughs. Her brazen laughter is nerve-jangling. No, *we* won't *talk about this later*. What we're doing is fuckin' good. She's just jealous. When it's staged in the fringe theatre thing, I bet she'll claim it like it was her idea from the beginning. Shit, now the kids have shot through.

Even these wild kids have obeyed some sense of curfew or else they've just picked up on our dismay.

Yeah, they don't like the Spider's vibes, Molly says.

You mind if I join you guys. It's Asif. His tone is flatly declarative; it is not a question.

Molly raises an eyebrow at *guys* but says nothing this time.

She thinks we're wankers, Asif.

Not what she just said to me. She says what you are doing is a tad … busy. With a bit of analysis of what you're trying to do … it should work.

A bit of analysis! Molly says. Her fuckin' analysis. Tell her all analysis does is take … Alice out of Wonderland.

He laughs.

We've got ten hours of work out of those kids today. I nearly lost it with her fuckin' Queenly queries. You're strangely silent, Tom-Tom. She got you having second thoughts?

Molly's owning this thing now. I feel like bolting. Say nothing. At the same time I feel running through me a current of betrayal. For Molly, for Choiseuil. I feel it as burgundy, rich, triumphant. My cutting edges! And yet, like The Shadow, I think: Without her where would I be? Still they are talking and I'm complicit and the Spider's the sacrifice fuelling our talk.

I've gotten real close a few times, Molly says, to losing it with her, I mean. Look, what d'ya expect? She's just one monstrous fat ego, stuffed full of her own self-perpetuating eggs. Well, I'm making off. The glance she gives me is sort of imperative. She wants to resume intimacy. Like she wants me to get rid of Asif, right now. You coming, Banksiagirl?

Mind if I tag along for a bit? he goes.

Molly hooks my arm. *Aïe*, feel that wind! I'm meant to read in her look scandal at Asif's presumption. I let my return glance query her right to be scandalised. She unhooks her arm from mine and walks ahead.

Asif catches up. Is it okay by you if I come along for a bit? Don't feel too warm a welcome somehow … from a certain quarter.

So, he tags along. We pick our way home between the garbage bags. A strong sea breeze balloons our shirts.

Asif takes a crumpled netted hat from a bin of cast-off clothes and perches it on his head. The breeze snatches it away. Molly fumbles for her key to the big front door.

Do you mind if I come up for a bit? He stares at a pyramid of honey and almond pastries in the shop window below my flat.

Repeat that Kiss

I withhold my answer. Molly is already halfway up the first flight. Her back is eloquent: *do your own fuckin' thing then*, it says. The time-switch will give out.

Sure, why not? I say, as if I'm indifferent.

Is something wrong there? Have you and Molly ...

I know what he wants to ask but I'm not going to gratify him. I say: as you saw, we've been working closely together. She might have hoped to talk a few things through tonight.

I'm not talking about work sessions.

Oh, feel free to speculate. Anyhow what about you and ...

He nods to the door which has closed in our faces.

Who? You mean Simone Choiseuil?

Yeah. Well, no, I was going to ask about you and Basilio. But surely n ... tell me about Choiseuil if that's where it's at.

What's it to you?

If I've got to work with all of you, I reckon I've got a

right to know what's going down.

She'll make us her sexual servants as she likes, he says. You can see she's a chronic consumer of new talent. It's in the character. I'm trying to ease out of that.

What? Out of what? The character or the woman?

Come off it, no one's been playing by Simone's rules.

And that accent she's manufactured for the Spider, where does that come from?

Maybe from her days of establishment mimicry. It's just become part of her. She couldn't fake her own natural voice now if she tried.

For once I see him laughing. It strikes me that he's quite lacking in the humour department. Christ, I think, this man is a time bomb. My body goes into alert at the very moment I am feeling a wave of attraction. No, there have been moments of humour, if you can call it that, but it's of a kind that rolls on predictable ironies, understatements or exaggeration, puns so well rehearsed they're embarrassing.

Sometimes, he says, I find myself dreaming of going back to the Polytechnic and doing a few months of pure research. I know that's heresy.

Oh yeah? Shit, I say, the switch has given out. I stab it on again at the landing. It lights up the whites of his eyes. Eerily.

Just about there. Is he the Spider's probe, amorous or punitive? Just play along. At least he's not giving me that aggro sarcasm.

Well, I say, whatever we're meant to be, I reckon we're entitled to some time out. Take a break, a holiday from all of that … We're just about there.

I pull out my key.

It could well be that he's been sent by Choiseuil to check me out. It's strange the way he's clung to my company. I'll go with the impulse to change tunes. I'll tone down the rebelliousness, stop being so *prickly*, let departures come from him. More levity. Just act tired, unappreciated child …

He is leaning on the bench next to the gas cooker.

Well, I mean, can exiles or performance revolutionaries take holidays?

She fuckin' does. Have you seen the way she plays the bourgeois press?

Who? Choiseuil or the Spider?

I'm talking about her, Simone Choiseuil.

You know what Molly calls her? The Meta-Spider.

Well, of course. The Spider didn't come from nowhere. I mean, like that's her fantasy, man.

How well does he know her? Surely he's not Choiseuil's lover?

Are you saying. I mean … Have you …

Sure. She's hooked on my persona. She likes me to take her to task, chastise her. Make love to me, she says, as you would to the Spider.

I'm shocked that I'm shocked. How could I have been so naive to think all this wasn't going on?

She's heavily into stardom, old Simone. I nailed her the other day. She's on the phone arranging an interview with a young dude for *The Left Eye*. Full Marlene Dietrich treatment.

If we dropped out, where'd she be?

You mean? The performance? If we went, it'd be a bit shaky, but not for long. We're all replaceable. She's pretty well-connected, like she says. In touch with a whole network of organisations. You know she's got a whopping big Municipality grant. No one, but no one has checked out that it's not *Maghrébins* getting the benefit.

And …

And?

And what about Basilio? How do you and he …

Could be. Like you and Molly, I'd guess.

This is crazy.

Well, he shrugs, it seems to be life.

Seems, seems …

What else?

Bread? Any bread around? I pass him the loaf, baton-hard by now.

Shopping suffers, you know, when we're getting a show together.

This is fine … whoa! You're the last girl I'd expect to hear apologising for housekeeping.

He drinks some mineral water straight from the bottle.

Turns on the TV. It's an old Jeanne Moreau: *Mademoiselle*. Black-and-white, an alpine scene. Huge black pines tower above. Moonlight sprawls on the icy grass. Moreau lies down, slowly, ceremonially in the distended shadow of a tree, no, of a man …

I used to be in love with her, he says. And her patent-leather shoes! She gets her erotic flare out of persecuting him. Genet wrote the scenario. You know Genet?

He takes my neck in the crook of his arm. Brings my mouth to his. I taste the bread through the water and feel the force of the lip, gum-hardened. There is a concerted display of strength. I wonder if what brings this on is his picture of Molly and me.

I use the wine as an excuse to wander, take out two glasses.

I'll pass on the wine, he says. Time we threw in all the *Bidon* stuff. It's taken me twenty years to put misery and anger behind me and now I'm choking on it again.

Tell me … where it comes from.

Do you really want to know?

We fling open the windows, climb out onto the balcony. The night is fading. The street-sweeper truck has left the gutters running in clean streams. The ochres of the tiles are starting to ignite with the first light. A tramp stirs in the doorway of our building. A couple of cats start to wail. Some thugs in an open car, radio blaring, rip down a street nearby, maybe along the quays but it's violently loud. Don't ask me to go back there. The performance stuff is escapist bullshit compared to the banality of … well, what I grew up in. Man, it's nearly morning. See, down there, a whole family on cardboard. Interspersed with long intervals of silence, there are sounds of sirens, a few gunshots. You can hear yelling now but it's hard to see where it's coming from.

Go back home, Arab Shit!

I don't want to think about the *Front National*. He steps back, closes the windows.

I'd like to repeat that kiss.

This formal reference startles me, makes me think *performance*. I wonder where Molly is at, if she's out on her balcony above listening to this.

I strain away as he tries to swivel my jaw into alignment with his.

You're very wary of me, aren't you? You think I'm going to rape you or something.

Don't give me that.

I kiss him quickly. It's approximate, somewhere between the lower lip and chin.

Now the imperious weight of his hand at my nape comes down like the end of levity. Intoxication of improvisation! This is like one great big name-tag. The constriction of something like a plotted future cuts my circulation. What have I got into? Molly and now Asif. I don't even know who they are. And I'm too pathetically proud to let them know this. That I should have such a bourgeois concern for their official identity. But then I don't want to know them. I struggle, clowning, from the weight of his hand. His desire is serious. This is not a man to tease. I have a wild hope that Molly will find herself pacing about in her apartment upstairs and come down with some tapes and half a bottle of red.

I am already straining for the vibrations of her footsteps.

Why do you and Molly look at me with such suspicion?

Again, it's as if he's plucked the name from my brain.

Eh, Asif. It's not like you've gone out of your way to applaud our feminism or our inventiveness.

Surely you don't want or need my applause. Anyway, not true. I admire your guts. I don't know how effective it is finally. And they've gagged you now, haven't they?

What, the cops? Did Molly tell you? The visa people? Oh they threaten my visa. They're checking out with my supervisor whether this can be treated as a bona fide performance class. I've got people who can stick up for me, if necessary. I mean if Choiseuil is discredited as actually running a serious class. I can put in some real work at the faculty, reactivate my phantom enrolment. The people who put me up before I moved in here, Xavière and Jean-Hippolyte. Jean-Hippolyte is a professor. Even I'm not quite an alien as far as that world is concerned. I can knock something up, get a 'supervisor' on my side. Come to think of it I could even present what I've been doing as material for some sort of paper. That should shut them up. Call it field research for a personal performance project. No politics intended.

A cynic too!

I don't have the same respect for official learning as you seem to, Asif.

Science is different.

What?

Well, I won't go into that.

You can make anything real if you can sell it.

I do not sell my knowledge. I apply it, which is regrettable, you might say. I'm ready, like one of your not-whiter-than-white philosophers said, to get my hands dirty. But are *you*?

Maybe I'm already in the muck.

Now we are undressing one another, with some delicacy. Our eyes are intent on eyes only. The rest is trance, perfect coordination. Hard to tell to what degree he's performing. His body still feels dangerous in its tension. He slides under the doona and I roll onto him. His love-making is slow, almost pedantic in its attention to detail. It's like he's addressing every nerve-end, like he's trying to re-map me.

You and Choiseuil, you didn't really?

No, he laughs. Of course not. I was just checking you out, wanted to test a theory about …

What?

Oh, forget it.

And then …

Sorry.

He is up, zipping up.

I can't do it. You've overwhelmed me. It's … I need time.

It's …

I can't talk about it. I need time to think about … this.

I am your idea then, Asif? It sounds like I'm an idea you've decided to shelve.

I'm sorry.

It's …

What?

It's all right, I mean, if that's what you're talking about. I'm quite happy to be on the edge. On the what's it, cusp.

Bring yourself …

No, I can't with you here.

Well, then.

He is gone. I do not want pleasure at any cost, I whisper to the shut door.

Cruising the Alternatives

I wander tiny within an immense bodyscape, my little miner's headlight flickering uselessly. My battery flat. The heart pulses out images whose tenor I cannot catch … towards you; it's you who are conjured by that image-drive. You go snap in my synapses. You fizz in the rods and cones behind my eyes. I slip, forget my purpose and see that you are the locus of my deviation. This world of flesh and pulsing organs seems lit by some painter's palette too quickly composed according to the reflex of bristle, dab dab; our interchange is only half thought through by the painter-dreamer: there is a mind behind all this that is not reducible to your will or even that delirious painter's hand. We are trapped in a dead-end draft, a brief trial of a cartoon. That hill, for instance, with its white trees along side the dense foliage gives me delight where it shouldn't have. Something suggests there's dieback here and I like the contrast of skeleton to plenitude and eye-mocking complexity … I need to escape from the glare of scrutiny … The mind behind the mind behind the mindless painter might cast out this draft in which we try to live: I am headed for the undergrowth rooting around like a nuzzling marsupial foetus for the nipple, the happily erectile nipple ... Again the waking sorrow, the humiliation in the reduction: I wanted something like a mother, that's all.

Re-reading this I see the fuse running insidious: it's effected in little advances, little retreats. There's no saying when I lose sight of an Asif beyond the performed ones. Beyond the Spider, there is always another. We are addicted now to what has bound us: I find meshing in these tentative notes, these little improvisations, the net of our entrapment: we seize glimpses of our phantom selves at the frontiers of our image-logic and make these into visions of growth; finding a searing need at the tips of our tongues, we stake out the zone of our joint unspeakable, calling this passion, calling this attraction.

I can't get him out of my head. More than anything, what weaves the charm are the pliant fingers, a trickster's fingers, the fingers of a prestidigitator, flexing, arching and plaiting like those of a Balinese dancer; oh and the power of the neck, rising from the yoke of the sailor-style shirts he often wears. Come to think of it the gait too, managing the tilt with the swell. A tilting swell. He is naturally perfumed, this man, as the fur of some cats is, musky. It's the thighs, the way they arch against the fabric in those tight pants; it's the management of his gestures, the measure of his voice. He is as fervent as he's remote: I know him in the paucity of our tongue-tied delivery.

But while we watch and circle one another, Asif and I, there is Molly too. The looks she shoots to me! She catches my gesture in flight and takes me again and again into the undertow of needing her, elsewhere, her place or mine, away from these roles. And then I think of her mastery over me. Mastery is the word because she can be hard, and a bossy bloke to boot. Now she thinks she's got a right to me and I want to slip, she targets me with some tongue-lashings. Even uses the cover of improvisation to put me on the spot. I wonder whether the others pick up the change. And always it seems she's stalking me, at the studio at least. At every break, she shadows me. I'm not ready for her to write her signature into me. I want to be unwritten for a while, not depth-tattooed by this woman. I want to cry out: I want to improvise in life too. Why do you want to impose your will on me? What contract did we sign?

My nerves snap electrically at random turns. I find Fou Roux swinging in the bulb over the desperate green of the billiard table. I want to cruise. I want to lose myself in the shadows around solitary drinkers. Hands wedged between thighs or disappearing into pockets excite me. I don't want to get fixed. Don't fix me up with anything. I will keep wandering from bar to bar. I will carry a little oriental cat draped on my shoulder, and send her, tail wavering from table to table and those who caress her, in the Bar l'Unic for instance, will at times engage with me. I will be blatant about the ploy, about the cat as emissary of my desire. I will be free of *Bidon* Romances and their high seriousness, I will be anyone, and will talk about, well, cats and sometimes, I'll end up in an apartment high above the pollution cloud that always hangs over the city, pinnacled high on the hand of Notre Dame de la Garde and will stretch out my satin stomach for the caress of a woman's gaze. I will maintain the austerity of sex without romantic investment; at other times it will be the quicksilver of someone lonely for Africa; I'll sip some alcoholic ginger drink, exchange an anecdote, fall into bed with her or him, or not, but it will be the approach to the repose of namelessness that I'll be addicted to. I might have caught the eye of a waitress and swoon under the boldness of the stare. It will be the touch of the encounter that will set me free into the muff of night. I will slip from the bed, go home through the pre-dawn streets and write it in or write it out.

I need not be trapped. I write this in the early hours of the day I say yes again to Asif. I miss the performance. I can't face Molly. I sleep, wanting to burrow deep into the dark, and never be stripped by the light again. I hate the way I keep turning fake when I'm trying to find the right tune. As if only in fakery I can be true to some idea of freedom. Missing the rehearsal makes it worse. I've drifted from Xavière and Jean-Hippolyte who gave me so much. I am sometimes ashamed of what I've become. I need a Confessor. I will ring them up. I'll tell them what I've got into. Instead I do nothing; I burrow. I dream.

Don't throw in a good thing for an illusion.

Molly has brought her jug of coffee down to share with me. Is she here to check out whether once again Asif stayed through the night?

She pours the bowls and carries hers to the window. You guys make it again last night?

I'd like to say: What's it to you? We've negotiated no pact, no deal. Yet was it I who whispered love in her ear, or did I? Was it I who, afraid of her naked lust, rehearsed these words in my mouth? A voice within me says: *As soon as you manage to separate lust and love, living them along different lines, through different lives, always preserving the discipline of naming your desire, your appreciation, but not putting it into the bonbon wrappers of love love love, then you'll start to be authentic.*

We might have but we didn't. The room was crowded, if you know what I mean.

The bed?

The bed was crowded.

Did you tell him about us or did you keep that little secret to yourself?

I told him, but not as if it should prevent me being with him.

Hm. Is that how you see it? Well, I guess only your desire can prevent that, sweetheart. Do you desire him?

I don't know.

Shit! You don't know? Isn't it a dangerous trip if you don't even know that?

Shit, I want to shout, what right have you to cross-examine so soon?

Perhaps, perhaps, I say, instead, and smile. My eyes burn backwards into my brain. She directs my face to receive a kiss. I cannot resist it. The thing is honesty. If I reserve the right to improvise, I must be honest. But honest to what: the raw state of my nerves? Continuity might be the fiction. To be consistent, to come across as *authentic* in the moral retrospective, that means a predictable fiction: authenticity is conferred at Death's Door. So goes the vicious circle in my head.

Where does this compulsion to invoke love come from in this or any context? I don't know what it is but it's something waiting for a costume, a set of gestures, a style of delivery. I can't resist rehearsing it, trying on its clichés. When I find a particular fit, whether it's a stretch, sag, or distortion, somewhere in that set of clichés, I undergo a transformation, like I was customising it, making this worn-out thing close and new and tender, like a miraculous new graft on the skin, on this skin alive now with desire for this person still a stranger, still standing for infinity, because the limits have not come down to be lived in. I try on all the clichés while the distances that burn desire into ache are maintained between us.

I decide to say nothing of this. Molly is right to give almost nothing of her past. Why marry our stories?
In the dying light, with the doubts that anything has or will happen with Asif, we are together again.

Proposition

I am a door
& offer
not the room expected
but sudden prairie
when you thought you'd found
a sofa, earth for the blue
idea of lightning

I can be a verb for you
vaulting blue
verb me briefly in return
fire? let small fires run
reciprocal in muscle
in our slow approach

I'll never frame you
but ripple you perhaps
in watery relations

make with you if there's a hint
of structure

catscradling for a scaffold
I'll be devotee of demolition
where prepositions
are concerned
no fixatives you understand

music? you ask for music?
I'll be song you'll invent
pegging sound shards on a line
drawn for laundry mornings after

I refuse to leave you like a forlorn
Lorca woman wondering
if hate struck first to cause
such numbness in the wake

I'll be glad
satin sheath for your emigré
appearances
I'll do the fugitive line
be nomad thief of name-tags
ruin of directories

still I'll baby you
nuzzling trackless
and have you unashamed

by mothering
as debtless I desert you

Disputed Zone

If only I'd spoken to Maeve about these things. How do you avoid possession in love? Was there ever anyone for her or did I simply occupy that place? Grandpa and she split up after Evie's death. We poisoned one another with blame, resentment, she said, decided it better if we went our separate ways. He remarried, an American woman, Florida tourist agency; he shifted there, outside of Miami. Susan, her name was Susan. Then, no men. Millie and Joe were the closest to her. She must have had desires. Was there ever another woman? She was so vividly Maeve I never thought of her in any category sexually. Or was it just that she wiped out the body? For her it was like the body was to be pleasured and punished at once by the rigours of hard work, hard liquor, smoking, little sleep. Maybe pleasure simply became block-out: anaesthesia, amnesia. It was quite a systematic denial, really. Maybe she has lived her own life as a kind of afterlife, a scandalous survival of her daughter's. What was I then; what am I to her? I remember, no, it's not even memory, it's a whole climate I lived in and still carry with me, her removal, her abstraction from Odette or Lube if they came to stay. Was she jealous? Was I meant to be for her alone? But still, she stood apart and quietly watched. When I go back I'll talk all this through. In any case she never judged.

I can hear Molly's breathing coming hard. Let her pleasure be enough; let it release me from the bargain that mine should also happen. Her nipples are purply brown, beautiful on the olive skin. There is no fat on Molly, except for the surprisingly ample statement of these breasts. They're like the breasts of Modigliani's lover, Jeanne Hubertine.

It's okay, I say, I'm not really there. Just the stage of the month, state of the nerves or something.

You needn't tell me that, sweetheart. Is it him, Asif?

It's not. You're quite wrong there.

Her hand pursues its course but the phone is shrieking. The voice is faltering, distant recognition takes my breath away: I think madly that Maeve must be my real lover to have this unerring synchronicity. And that dream! Maybe I should just give myself up to this fatality. Is she the only love I can really accommodate? Is she really so big? Is there no room left?

I am as pained by her failing breath as I am to be dragged into wakefulness away from the tepid voluptuousness with Molly.

But as I think how I'd paint Molly's body stretched out on my coiled sheets, her hand grappling for one of my cigarettes, Maeve's deep old voice goes through the rosary of practical concerns. I think of those vocal cords like ancient cables, weighted with their load of tar.

When will this masters class be over and have you got enough money, love, and did the bond set you back, and are you looking after yourself, eating enough fruit and vegies? The people around here are putting pressure on me to accept subdivision. All they care about is bloody appreciation of their property values. Millie and Joe have gone off to another funeral, one of their Guildford friends, the cops chucked him in a cell and made him go cold turkey from the grog. He was real depressed to start with because he'd just lost one of his little grannies with pneumonia. You know what that does to your system. Well, they never learn. So many of us dying and things aren't getting any easier. She stops.

I hear the slow surf of her breathing. It's hard from here to come back to her world with the immediacy she needs. She needs me physically there. She seems to be saying that she's getting too old to fight for all we cherish at Banksiafold. She wants to ask, I know, how I can put this performance of exile ahead of what really counts. I could tell her that I'm seriously wondering what I'm doing and that I've copped this sort of criticism even at this end, but then, yes, I've lost the sense of where the performance ends and shame silences me. I wonder if she doesn't suspect some other sort of agenda which has betrayed her.

You keeping healthy, eating fruit, and all that? she asks again. I wonder about her short-term memory. Has the grog taken its toll finally? Avoid eating too much of that industrial bread, she says. I think, I've left Molly in the lurch to talk long-distance about my diet. For the moment the mulberry smile is tolerant. The hair under her armpits is totally, seriously black, something I hadn't noticed before. I think the French expression suits her well: *elle est bien dans sa peau*. She's at ease in her skin.

Maeve has the authority of being firmly who she is. I've never questioned it or any of her habits. Like I've never even asked: you stopped smoking that pipe? The pipe she took up instead of roll-y'r-owns and which always these days hangs from her lip. I can hear her sucking on it now.

You eating enough protein?

Sure, Maeve, not just fish fingers, I tell her, mine hooked into the coils of the phone cord.

Well, there's some protein in that I suppose, as long as it's not that petrochemical seafood, you know the stuff grown on plastic or somethink.

No Maeve, really. Look, you're ringing long-distance. Don't waste ... Do we have to talk about what I'm eating?

And how's that what's his name, he behaving, not treating you bad, I hope?

I wonder what I wrote in that letter. I can't remember mentioning Asif.

Molly is listening in. Amused, for the moment, she has her green eyes on me. She doesn't like Maeve's intimacy with me invading ours. Maeve is telling me that Odette's dad was on TV the other night, promoting deals between the mining companies and traditional land owners. For a moment I feel guilty with the Odette connection, but then ...

That's his version of reconciliation, Maeve says. No bets on where that's going to take us.

But now it comes back to me and I'm shocked that I could have buried the memory so quickly. When Odette moved to Europe for that failed assignation with her blue-eyed engineer, she warned me not to have anything to do with her dad, as if she suspected that he would make a move on me as soon as she was out of sight, like some sort of more accessible daughter. Sure enough, not long after she left, Maeve passed me the receiver with an exasperated look, miming pain from her ear. From the kitchen door I could hear the monologue pouring out: Ah Mrs O'Shea, and how *are* you, he said, without pausing for an answer, I was just wanting a word with your *delightful* granddaughter, there's a package we'd like her to take to our Odette when they meet up in Europe, if she could spare just a *moment* of her time, I would be *most* indebted. Oh, Thomasina, yes I was saying, yes, a little package, it will barely take any room in your luggage, and we'd *love* to catch up with you, anyway, Jill and I and thought why not ask you over, for old times' sake, we are *so* missing Odette. That earned me an interrogation from his daughter.

Maeve is giving me the full run-down on this turn in politics because, with Millie and Joe away, she's lonely. I feel Molly lean into my back and my brain starts to slide. I feel like I'm swelling huge like that cheeky frog that drank up all the water and left the country in drought …

Things are getting ugly here, love. The backlash against land rights. It only takes a few rabblerousers to work up hysteria … I fear for the worst when I'm gone.

Don't you worry, Maeve. You know I'll honour your promise for Banksiafold. But don't talk about … It's not as if you won't be around for a long time yet.

But Molly is twisting my hand and skewing my answers. I inch away from her reach.

Now Maeve gets to the point: Look dear, some tests I had

done, don't want to alarm you, don't show up too good. So I'll be in hospital to follow it up for a while. Nothing to worry about, but you know how these doctors get you trapped.

Molly laughs at something and Maeve says: Oh you've got company? Sorry then, love, why didn't you say? Go back to him. Molly's zipping up her pants over her naked crotch.

Her, Maeve, her, but it doesn't matter.

Molly says: I don't *believe* this. I'm out of here. She threads her arms through the shirt sleeves as she moves to the door.

The door bangs. I can't hang up. I need to find out about these tests without making Maeve name what is wrong; I need to give her time. Yet, while I fuel her talk with questions, the panic intermittently flashes: I'm throwing away something that could be so good. Maeve has managed, despite everything, to do a whole lot more planting of the banksias, zamias and near the swamps, of melaleucas where the fires went through last year. My eyes wander to the delphiniums and stocks which Molly arranged in my vases. I can hear the street door clang and stretch the phone cord to the window. Molly has just said: I don't *believe* this. I'm out of here. Now she's hit the freezing street in just her shirt to walk out her rage. I watch below for her reappearance from the grocery awning and on my finger I collect a pine nut from the little Arlesian cakes I bought for our dessert. Down in the little square they're playing *pétanque*. P-tank, p-tank, I can hear the dull thud, even from here. The white dust rises, hangs in the air as one ball lands, rolls and clicks, glancing off the other. The old man curves his finger around it, and straightening his arm, lines it up, like death is an algebra he's coding into his body. P-tank, p-tank.

The outrage subsides; I am shivering with a deep chill now. Why do I have to be a Disputed Zone? Molly's departure, Maeve's illness, rip-winkle in my veins. I hurl myself onto the bed. Goodbye, goodbye. In this apartment, scattered with the remnants of our little feast together, that's what hits, Evie leaving me. I cannot find her, not in Molly, anyhow. I will never find her in Molly, who is a bargainer. She wants me undivided. But must I carry that division, wear the split? *Cackle, cackle, Mother Goose, have you any feathers loose?*

Lou Barb

Incubation

You know Lube, Tom-Tom said, I reckon that for as long as you're an academic you'll avoid really putting yourself on the line; you can be a relay for other people, sure, a ventriloquist, but you won't have to put yourself on the line.

But surely, I protested, thinking of the endless time spent coddling my students' work and yet too fatigued to leap to my own defence, you can contribute something of value by being a relay, an incubator, for other people's words.

Within my dream last night the words presented themselves as if in an audition for my own story, but as I tried to read them they refused to stabilise. Trying to fit my tongue around them I realised I was again an infantile stutterer and the panic took hold. Each word opened in a kind of vertiginous cross-section, a catacocoon, the dream guide told me, communicating in pupal form the disease from one etymological layer to the next, a sort of recursive spread of corruption which, as I looked, liquefied the body of the word into a seething, semic flux. I realised that I was pregnant with these diseased meanings; I was incubating at every level words with baby words nestling inside them, and already, in the uteruses of these babies, there were more pop-eyed word-foetuses, words lip-reading one another, words with digestive tracts in which remnants of other words were visible. It's not as if I never speak myself, I wanted to argue back, but now it was too late. I woke up in a sweat next to Roly who switched on the lamp, checked his watch and blinked his concern into my face.

Really, darling, I think you've been living with that stuff for too long. You have your own life. Remember? he said, his eyes sad and clouded.

Sometimes, I croaked to him, sometimes I tried to tell her where I was at. She said I kept my silence as a sort of power. So many times I wanted to pick up the receiver and deliver it straight to her. Once I did it, Roly. Why don't you listen to anything I say? I said. If you did, you'd see how I expose myself just as much as you do. Put myself on the line.

I do, Lube. I listen, I hang out for it, she said. But it's so tidy, what you say. You bring it out so formalised, I find myself just hanging out for a hiccup in the flow. See, there you are, a mixed metaphor. I'd never catch you doing that. Your idea of eloquence is so precious that you won't let your talk catch your mind undressed and, well, that's what interests me, the mind before it's made up. So, as much as I care for you and love you and in many ways admire you, I mean my life might have been easier if I'd taken your path, but listening to your silky eloquence, well, sometimes my attention strays. You've got a beautiful word list for all the moral delicacies but where it's a matter of calling the brutal truth by its name, I wonder if you can.

This froze my voice in my throat.

Roly, I realised, had been asleep for some time.

But could Tom-Tom face the brutal truth herself, call it by its name? Even in the situations she chose, running Molly against Asif, it was as if she wanted more than anything that ruinous oscillation between them. She played with their need for attachment, and called this 'darkness' or 'possessiveness' on their account.

I dreamed I was Mulberry Molly and feeling the heat in my fleece, walked down to a strangely silent *Calanque*. Its emerald and aquamarine waters opened out between the limestone flanks, which I felt immediately, as if they were my own thighs. On one of the promontories, a figure stood, stocky and permanent, looking out to sea. His coarse black hair was closely cropped. Two lean boxer bitches on leash also had their eyes trained on the horizon, now a powdery blue crease between sky and sea. I liked the wedge of the hand in the back pocket of his jeans disturbing the line of the leather jacket. The man turned his head briefly my way. There was an ironic twist to the mouth. It was Tony, from the restaurant.

The breeze lifted. The sea unfolded in choppy lines like a million cocked eyebrows. It was as if the sea had taken face, Asif said, for it was Asif with me, his arm hooked into mine. Winedark, I said. *Walpurgis*dark, he said, yet the sun was drawing our blood. Ah that lustrous pet, he said. I saw that I had come undressed and in fact I had a large, glossy pubic fleece, black in defiance of my mulberry hair. He slipped in a finger, then two. The sea, the sea, always the same, but always different he said, tasting. Let's swim, seaweed delicious one! I discerned his penis, aubergine-dark, profiled under the white *burnous* he was wearing. I said: You know, Tom-Tom is not who you think. Not at all. She wants fugitive sex, dream sex, not the living relation. You know what she used to say? She had recurrent dreams of the Spider. She could bring them on at will. She said it was grave and wonderful, making love to the Spider. But afterwards they would laugh and eat marzipan in bed watching television. I was near to swooning, to falling mouth-to-mouth with him but retained my composure. I blinked at the little sharp-bladed wave-crests riding into shore. The shell rubble cut into my hot legs. Kiss me, then, Spider, Asif said.

III

Le Pen is Real

There's loud banging at my door. It's Molly, intent, serious, as if last night left not a ripple. She hugs me, holding me tight. But she's grim, urgent.

Have you seen it? she croaks, as if her own breath jags her throat. She is clutching the *Marseillaise*. She opens the newspaper wide. It's Saïd, and Mustapha! They were on their way home to the Aygalades quarter in the North, Saïd told the reporter. After the rehearsal. They were recording some street sounds for our show! Suddenly they see this big Peugeot with tinted windows cruising. Some middle-aged guys get out with brushes and pots of glue plastering Le Pen 6th Republic posters on the walls, Rue Le Châtelier. They start to run with their cassette. Saïd could see the bus coming. Buses are rare up there. So the guys from the *Front National* see these young blacks running and spray them with bullets. Just like that. Saïd's not too badly injured but Mustapha's dead. He's … He was seventeen. And we drag them into a fucking performance and that's what they were living, lives on the line for those racists seething with hatred.

I can't speak. I don't know for how long we are there clutching our faces on the unmade bed. Perhaps it's not them. There are tons of Mustaphas and Saïds.

Of course it's them.

Look.

On the next page is a family shot of Mustapha. Smiling into the camera in that hat with earmuffs. His wide beautiful smile. As if the future is his.

The F N guys say these kids were threatening them. Running. They were sure they were armed. Some kids a few minutes earlier had been throwing rocks. These are good fathers, it says. *De bons pères de famille*. One of them migrated from Algeria in '62. Used to be a communist. Two years ago he was still active in the dockers' union. On the basic wage when he wasn't on the dole, he became obsessed with getting the Arabs out, any one dark out. The Arabs working black, the *Maghrébins* choking up social security. He's not a racist, he says. He gets on very well with the Tunisian family next-door. These kids were making savage squeals like Sioux as they ran. If they hadn't fired, Jean-Marie Le Pen says to the reporters, death would have been on the side of the French. Of these F N murderers, one is from Algeria, one from Tunis and one from Italy. These kids were clearly dangerous, and in the dark, the cassette player looked like a machine-gun. And anyway, why were they running?

We look at one another. So much for exiles.

Back at the workshop we don't refer to it directly.

I think we've got to give one hard look at what we think

we're doing, Molly says. All of us.

Don't you think, *mec*, Molly says to Asif, the whole bit about us all being *Bidons* is a bit close to the romance the Spider accuses us of? She uses *mec* as she would dude or man. Her face is bright and open, but the eyes are serious in their shadowless attention. The glare of her scrutiny has no hint of irony. Despite the gappy teeth and great Luna Park Entry burgundy lips, there's no jest here. She gives it to Asif's face at fifteen centimetres' distance. How come some of us get shot then, eh? And some of us keep on performing? You're no more a *Bidon* than I am.

Asif keeps his frank gaze on her throughout this. Molly is not sure how to take it.

Of course, he says. Don't you see? I've been waiting for someone to come out with it. Finally!

And then the whole Banksia *Bidon* bit.

She's turned to me. She's served him and now she's turned to me. There's racism and racism, she is saying. It's not a dialogue of mutes pointing to their dumb cooked images.

Throat cramps. The way she's tipping her own shame back onto me. But then, it sticks like a terrible, hot oil.

Well, of course she's right, Asif says. I wondered when you'd wake up. In this kind of deal you always think authenticity is just round the corner. Go behind the next mirror and you'll be involved in valid action. Check out the Belsunce Centre Social, why don't you? One of you? You might start to understand, where all of this … fits in. He gestures wide, hopelessly, to include all of us. Choiseuil, I realise, is in her office on the phone. Wonder what she's shaping up, how she's going to claim or disclaim our stuff with the street kids now, after what's happened to Mustapha and Saïd.

I'll go, I say. Who do I ask for?

Nadia. You ask for Nadia Buchared.

Aren't We Sweet?

Nadia Buchared is on the phone. As she listens she taps her foot and lights a cigarette. The glance she gives me says: *bourgeois chick doing a thesis on us, I'll bet*. She says across the receiver, Be with you in a moment. Yes, yes Asif. I'll send her with Claudie. She'll give her a slice of what it's really like.

She hangs up and blows smoke over to me. Her long, high-bridged nose is serious. Her eyes are deeply set, keen in their focus. Her hair is short and rippling. Long, it would be frizzy. She keeps her eyes on me as she stubs the butt into a saucer. She rises from the chair. She's wearing Levis and a simple sailor's jumper, unbuttoned at the shoulder. So you're one of Choiseuil's students! Asif's given me the run-down. We've suspected her some time so we sent him along to check out what's going down there.

So. He's one of your workers?

You could put it like that. You should go out with Claudie

on her house visits, see a bit for yourself. Where you from? Australia.

Ummm. Not quite the touristic stuff they'd expect you to bring back? No, Claudie's not into performance. Nor social work of the bandaiding kind. *Une tête dure qui ne veut rien à faire avec tout ça.* Yeah, for what it's worth I can tell you a bit of what our network knows. Choiseuil, well I guess, you've started to suss it out. Simone Choiseuil is a prima donna and some of us would say, a crook, and what's more her rorting the system is pushing us out of any possibility of keeping our work going. Why, by the way, do you think she's going to give Asif Badaoni top billing?

This is news to me but I say nothing. In my docility towards Choiseuil, it's never struck me that he might have a family name. I cool a few degrees. I'll have to examine this later.

No, I didn't. Why?

He is the token, of course. The convenient Arab token. I guess you know by now her so-called *Théâtre des Marges* is hardly for the benefit of the *Maghrébin* community here?

Well, no. I thought there might be some indirect flow-on. Some raising of … ?

Consciousness? Consciousness? Aren't we sweet? Eh? You know the sort of audience it attracts. The well-heeled bourgeoisie who fancy themselves as progressive. Couple of academics. Aren't we sweet!

I could almost hit her for that phrase.

What we need is fucking flats, excuse me, but that's where it's at. Not fancy little metaphors of exile. And do you know who still gets the flats here, all the good state housing blocks? All the F-4's and 5's? The friends of the councillors, that's who. The bourgeoisie of Marseille or Montpellier or Lyon, you name it. People like your Simone Choiseuil with her theatre of provocation! *Théâtre des Marges*, my foot.

But, at least she's been backing the show Molly Schor and I are putting together with some of the kids from the Centre ... I wince. Stop in my tracks. I see Mustapha's face, its confident smile from the *Marseillaise*. Saïd airborne over the ramp.

She raises her eyebrows. Lights another Gitane.

But of course she would've wanted to put her name to that. The time was ripe. Oh and she'll see Saïd and Mustapha as quite dispensable. The next round of funding applications is due. We're so busy here with next to no funding and a permanent staff of two trying to keep people from starvation and putting a roof over their heads even to get our applications finished. You can trust that Choiseuil will claim a show you're doing with the kids as proof she's authentic.

I see on the office partition: *Collectivité des femmes. Permanence pour les Droits de la Femme.* Women's Collective, Women's Rights Service ...

I gesture to the posters. Does some sense of solidarity amongst the women come out of ...

This is so pretty! She winks at the guy at the other desk. Look, I'd recommend you check out the situation of some of these people. And what people in those conditions think of your nice notions of solidarity.

Underground Women's Army

Claudie whisks her little Fiat into the bus station in front of St Charles station. She is talking in a continuous stream even as I crouch low to slide in and the car takes off before I've closed the door. The glances she sends me are practical, contact glances, nothing like scrutiny. She's frank, impersonal. No place for ambiguities. Straight hair in a bob, no fuss. Puce and cobalt floral dress, something viscose like a million others you'd buy at Casino. Claudie's shoes are canvas and rubber. Greasy sweat marks outline the toes. There is no advertisement of sexuality here. She is austere, clear-featured. The last thing she would think of is being noticed. I am glad that the dye is growing out of my own hair and that I have on boring jeans instead of the harlequin pants.

Today it's around St Charles, Claudie says. I have a Tunisian woman to check on. I hope she'll end up being an animator, an educator, to speak to people in her sort of situation. It's a delicate operation. For her children's sake she sees the only way of climbing out of the hole she's in is not to identify with the others. So you can't expect her to manifest anything like solidarity with her neighbours in the tower.

Solidarity.

I got a serving from Nadia. I made the mistake of asking about solidarity, you know, amongst the women in the neighbourhood.

Her smile is like limpid water.

Well, yes, that'd be her, but you've got to understand why she gets angry. A lot of do-gooders expect a romance of solidarity amongst the migrants which no host population would find amongst its own people.

Of course, of course, I say.

Her lane-changes seem to be dictated by some magnetic field. Screaming of brakes and toots leave her unruffled. She seems to be doing a bit of tailgating. What a quick tongue, never snagged. She's producing a thousand words a minute.

I'm glad you haven't come in high heels because what you're going to see is not very beautiful, not at all. They are not just slums where she lives, they're utterly dysfunctional. No hygiene. They should be blown up. Some of the flats have been condemned already. They've given up on them. Walled in.

We undertake the old port through the tunnel. Postcard Marseille dead, buried. The manoeuvres through overpasses and bypasses and swoops through one-way climbing and descending streets leave behind the Marseille I know by foot. Coming out between the blackened facades I long for a strong liqueur to sear my blood and let this retreat into soft focus. The car swoops in between two high-rise clusters. These, Claudie says, you'll understand, are privately run. By a nice irony, they're referred to as Le Parc. People like to distinguish between the right and the left sides. I'm on the right, they say, as if this makes them high class. She chuckles, bleakly.

Here the rain camouflages nothing: squalor is fixed under its veneer. No lyricism can reclaim this. This is the triumphant banality of misery. Between the two high-rises there is a relatively bright ochre-rendered building.

That's the school, she says. Pre-primary and primary. Nice escape for the kids, isn't it?

In the square, covered with patchy bitumen, rubbish floats in puddles. The buildings themselves are what we used to call taupe, *torp*, we'd say, back in Perth, torp. Mole-coloured. But it's the death of all senses, not just sight. It hesitates between grey absence and contaminated earth except where the soot has made blackheads of the stucco bubbles. There are cyclone fences topped with barbed wire, backed by a crumbling limestone wall, grey-rendered with glass embedded at the top. Even as a prison it's dysfunctional. The buildings were once, I guess, called brute functionalism.

Here nothing wants to remain. You'd have to become abstract to survive. Limit yourself to line, find the acid poetry of detritus. No curves except those described by the odd bit of laundry flapping on balcony lines. The washing has long since abdicated colour too, become *torp*. The squall agitates it. The wind itself is a moaning variation that always delivers the same. Delivers no one anywhere else. Just stirring the shit. The grey-brown bog is glittering with glass shards, flattened cans, studded with polystyrene pellets. Plastic, plastic.

Well, she says, most of the tenants have been working on this but the minority who've lost it, who've had enough long ago of being the rubbish, get their own back on the place by hurling their own shit down.

Ah, here she is. *Salut!* Isabelle to show us the way.

A girl, somewhere between ten and twelve, smiles at us. Her anorak is zipped against the drizzle and she has a floral umbrella ready to guide us between the puddles and broken glass. Her black wavy hair is in a French plait. Her bands glitter as she flashes a smile. Somehow her mother has found the cash to supplement the state dentistry costs.

Bad news! she says. The lift's out of action again. Maman was in tears yesterday: she had to lug the weeks' shopping up the five flights. And me everyday, four times a day with the school books because at school, there's no place to store them.

Even inside the walls are the colour of burnt toast. The graffiti's knocked back by pollution into a general gangrene. We gasp out our words up the stairs. Clods of hardened cement are everywhere. The dim light in here and the trimphant smell of piss and something rank, impossible to name, bring me near to gagging. Strange moulds. Bad conversations trapped in the air, deals made out of virulent hopelessness. Nowhere to go in this column of trapped air.

This place is a scandal, Claudie whispers, it should be bulldozed. One of the flats we pass is bricked in.

What happened there? I ask Isabelle.

Oh there, the vandals, squatters, addicts, you know. They

seriously messed it up. Well, the owners just sealed it off. That's the only stuff they do around here, bricking up doorways. You should've seen Maman when, you know the candidate for the Mayoral elections comes around? He was doing the garbage, picking up the garbage so's he could be photographed? With all the cameras on him, you know? He came back on five different days to pick up garbage. Maman said to him she'd be his campaign partner if he liked. That threw him. She said, why not? *Hasni for Rosny* is not a bad slogan. She said they could use some shots of her cleaning. Some shots of him stuffing garbage in bags. *No Shit with Rosny*! She reckoned she could say that cleaning toilets, or: *Make a Clean Slate with Rosny*, as she's wiping desk tops in the office block.

Bonjour, bonjour, I've brought along a friend, Claudie says. Madame Hasni smiles quickly at us. I'll be right with you, if you'll excuse me a moment, I have to deal with this … *monsieur* first. There is a guy who looks as if he's acting out some sort of authority role in a shoddy school production. Too young for the part. The reefer jacket is too broad on the shoulders; the fabric falls where the shoulder pads begin. He has a bunch of keys, a clipboard, and a pocket full of biros.

Madame Hasni shows us to the mattress next to the coffee table. Make yourselves at home. It's the owner's son, she whispers. I'm going to show him where it's at for us.

He looks nervously over his shoulder. He plucks a receipt book from the clipboard and puts it on the table in front of her. He fingers his clipboard and snaps the clamp over the papers several times.

Madame Hasni hands him a cheque: That's for the rent,

she says. For the services I'll give you ten francs instead of the hundred and sixty. Ten francs for the trouble you had climbing the ten flights of stairs because once again the lift is not working. As for the rest — we are getting shocks from the tap in the kitchen; you still haven't earthed our electricity and there's a gas leak in the water heater, the water heater you'd said you'd replace four years ago.

He says, you must understand, this is for upkeep so that the repairs can be done for you, Madame.

Young man, your father has been feeding me that line since I came here. He'd have to think me pretty naive to be swallowing it now. When the repairs are done, the lift, the gas, the …

He looks at the cheque in his hand: Well, then, I'll pass on what you said to my father.

Claudie says: Bravo, you did brilliantly, Fatima.

I'm rather pleased with myself. I was … quite nervous. But something made me bristle this time. I'm not taking that stuff any more.

I see now that the coffee table is a door on bricks. But it is draped with an embroidered cloth in emerald, purple and black. The mattresses are also festooned with woven shawls and scattered with cushions. Think how the Spider weaves her picturesque out of these elements. A wall unit in black wood-grain plastic. The calendar nailed to the shelf face starts at thirteen hundred and something.

Fatima follows my eyes. Mohammed's flight from Mecca, that was year zero, you see, she says. Yes! Yanif, he's my eldest, says that's why I'm backward, stuck in the old time. But you know there's a sense in all of our rites. Like fasting, in what you'd call our Lent. It is to understand in our bodies what it's like for the starving, it's for the sense of compassion. Oh well the *Islamistes*, the *Intégristes* in Algeria are giving all this a bad name. We had our times too but in Tunisia the government cracked down. Sure it was pretty savage, and pretty repressive but it was a brief tyranny instead of a long one.

What's the writing on the wall? Claudie asks.

I wonder what kind of fatality she's suddenly referring to. But it's there in huge letters. *C et F*, it says.

Fatima says: They traced it with a lit cigarette into the lace curtains too. *C et F*. They told me it means *Casseurs et Fonceurs*. They break in and shoot through. Wit, eh! You know, last year we go back to Tunis, my father's not looking as if he'll last long. There was no choice about it so I collect my kids before term's end and borrow the money from my brother.

My eyes take in the calendar featuring cats. She says yes, I stuck that over their obscenities. When we came back — you see, he didn't last until my arrival, my father — we find this, the lock broken and the writing on the wall and everything strewn on the floor. Yanif has taken just shorts for Tunisia, you imagine, it was summer, and we come back to no linen, no proper shoes, no jeans for the kids and I saved and saved for those 501's so they wouldn't look as if I dressed them in the Arab quarter. Nothing!

I say: Did they take the books?

Books, you're joking, *Mademoiselle. Pensez-vous*? They are not intelligent, they have no use for being intelligent. Do you think that kids who write their tag into the curtains with cigarettes would take books, what do they want with books? Well with my father's death and then the brother, the one who always helped us after my husband's death, he is killed on his motorbike and I come back to this. I lost it. I lost my head. The kids, lucky they were with me, they didn't lose theirs. They are good kids. They had to make the statement to the police. Of course they knew not to tell them who we thought it was. Since then we've seen our sheets hanging from one or two of the balconies around here. If we said anything, they'd turn on the kids. I'd be frightened for their lives. You've just got to keep your mouth shut.

Yes, their school work suffered. I'm making them repeat this year. They've never repeated before, so that's what they're doing. It's going well.

I look at them. They have respect for their mother. They are quiet and attentive. They watch from under their dark curling lashes. They are well fed, slightly on the fleshy side, and they watch her every movement. In her blue and purple-fringed shawl and her lilac pants and gold earrings she manages to look optimistic. Her eyes sparkle with pleasure through the standing tears. She holds her daughter close to her. Isabelle's hand rests lightly on her mother's.

Eh Maman! It is the big brother, Yanif, with a black down starting on his lip. Me and Cheb are going out.

Where?

You know? Over there, behind the school, not far.

Don't come back late.

Oh we won't be late.

Don't be after eight.

Eight's too early.

All right, a bit after eight then.

They all smile. Isabelle snuggles into her mother.

Have you thought about the job I was talking about, Fatima?

Claudie is tentative, not wanting to push some sort of intrusive line.

Oh. I don't think ... she says. You see, I would feel very awkward talking to the women around here at the school. We prefer to have nothing to do with them. How else can we get out of this hole? I do not want to talk about hygiene. Some of the people here are peasants, you know, not like us, from the towns. I don't want to have to preach to them.

She smiles straight at me as if a little laser has searched out my romance of solidarity.

Yes, I understand perfectly well, Claudie says, her eyes sad.

Isabelle brings in a tray with orange blossom tea, bowls of fruit salad, cakes.

So you'll stay with the office cleaning?

I'll stay with the office cleaning. It's regular. It means setting out at four and being through at eleven-thirty, so that I can be home to give the kids a good lunch.

What? You hit the metro before four? Isn't that dangerous? Does it make you nervous? I ask.

Nervous? Who do you think it is in the metro at four? Men? No way! It's us women, an army of us women, the ones who keep this city clean. Your underground women's army!

A Pause on the Stairs

At the bottom of the stairs there is a shape that jolts me. I can see by the carriage of the head that it is Asif. He flashes a smile.

Salut Claudie, Thomasina! Nadia told me I'd find you here.

Would you like a lift anywhere? I'm heading back to the *Centre*, Claudie says.

Not me. I thought you two might come for a coffee with me.

Sorry, I can't. I have another visit to make.

Well, maybe. I've encumbered Claudie enough.

You had enough of real slums?

Cut it out, Asif.

We wave as Claudie takes off, the car slithering onto the road.

I thought it was about time you came home, met my

family. You might see where I'm coming from ...

I can't have heard properly. Maybe he means in the sense of understanding. Like I'm his student. Like he's supervising my Masters in Misery.

Well, what do you say?

I don't know what to say. I should feel alarmed but I feel like every emotion is muted now. I'm still in that apartment with Fatima, thinking about having been lured so far in by Choiseuil, about these weeks spent beguiled in a lie.

Asif Badaoni is saying carefully: I told Maman I'd only bring home a girl I was serious about.

This takes my breath away. Perhaps he wants to reassure her that he likes girls. And what, I say, what about your ... other attractions?

It makes no difference. Like I'm sure it won't make any difference to you with your ... other attractions, as you so nicely put it. We have that understanding. I don't want to lose sight of you now.

He is grave, suddenly older. He is almost noble. This annoys me for some reason. Everything around us seems fugitive or in a state of dissolve. The bodies of pedestrians ripple in their reflected continuum; the colours of the cars are awash in the patisserie window; tiny raindrops tremble on his thick lashes; his lids blink rapidly but his gaze is steady in its direction, in its resolve. I might close the door on it now but like a stray dog which sees you put down some milk before shutting it out, this moment will be waiting for me in the morning. Of course, I realise, he has decided that he will accept nothing but a yes.

Yes. I say looking back to the St Charles steps. Yes, I would like to meet your parents. But, please, not yet.

It's probably not the squalor you'd imagine from … well the way I carried on. But Les Valentines is a far cry from what I grew up with in the Aygalades quarter.

He's carrying on as if I've said nothing.

The Aygalades, that's where Mustapha …

Yeah, that's where so many of us have lived, been fucked over, fought it out, got out or died. You know Maman was brought in the hull of a boat. She said coming out of the darkness onto the quay at the Joliettes was like a second birth. But Marseille, she says, has to be one of the most terrible cities. Still, she wouldn't survive anywhere else; she wouldn't transplant now. She's part of the place. You'd take her for an average Marseillaise. We are weaving through the little streets of the Arab merchant quarter. She still does housework for the bourgeoisie. Got a good situation now. Keeps house for a professor of medicine. The job lets her get home on time for my little sisters. Papa is retired now. Emphysema. He's pretty silent. Don't let it throw you. But when he talks you've got to listen.

Asif, you didn't hear me. I said: Not yet, it's too early. Sorry, I don't know where you're coming from. This is way too quick. We don't even know if we've got anything real between us. Don't worry, I wouldn't misbehave if I came. I mean, when it's time.

He is the downcast child now. Disappointment congests his face. He blinks in the drizzle. He slides his hands into my hair, raking it back from both sides of my face, grazing the nerve-ends. His face approaches so slowly, it is disconcerting. For a flash I think there's a kind of intransigent glare in his eyes. He blinks too much, too quickly. Up close, though, it's more like simple confusion. He looks around to see if anyone is watching; he draws me into a doorway. His mouth engulfs mine. I feel his gums, the clash of his teeth, taste the freshness of his saliva.

We have something so important between us. We have a connection you can't deny. I saw it in the performance, even if you chose the way of antagonism.

Me! What about you!

He laughs softly.

Opposite is an all-purpose luggage and haberdashery store stacked with great bolts of gold- and silver-shot fabrics, piles of backpacks and umbrellas, desert scenes on velvet with black fringes.

Even your leaning towards women, you know I understand that.

I will tell him later that I am returning home; that I've had enough disenchantment; that the idea of really knowing him frightens me; that it is the unfathomable beneath the role which has had me in its thrall. Then it comes to me as I withdraw unsteadily from him and see in a tumble of details the extent of my not-knowing, of being hooked on not-knowing, on absence or disappearance, so much more elastic than presence. Like my mother and father. I remember the daydream where I'd have them both bouncing on that rusted trampoline of Maeve's. I'd send him up and bring her down. They'd blow kisses or float talk bubbles towards me as they came into the frame of my picture window. Knowing that Asif has a bag of biographical details to unpack comes to me in a wave of nausea. I foresee my knowing him settling with time into a becalming ennui. Yet right now I tell myself: This is an illumination. It is asking to be treated. The moment is pulled out like the drawer of scarves in the shop, denouncing by contrast the shadowy confusion and pastness of everything else. Les Aygalades, Les Valentines, Professor of Medicine, emphysema, man of silence. I don't want these wares; I don't want to see his aftershave in the bathroom or to know that he uses a nasal spray.

On the threshold of passing from not-knowing I wonder what this addiction to not-knowing might be. I don't want to know him, to find his limits. This moment with its lurid beckoning and its tinselly shine makes a crude demand — it would retell my whole life so far. I have to resist that smug reduction. The bolt of fabric unfurls in the light: *Oh that was all it was!* As if to be held in the sway of something, someone, is not to know, but to prolong wonder, and the sense of endlessness, enfolded. Perhaps I simply want this suspension, fancying that there could be captivation on either side, if we so wanted, even while I dream of the Spider, real or not, toxic or not, enmeshing me and in turn captivated by me. Intoxication ends with real poisoning. As long as I am in the not-resolved, I'm not trapped in any story. My gestures as Banksiagirl will be at best recorded in an orphaned piece of the jigsaw puzzle. What was Simone Choiseuil's *Exiles* to be? Am I deserting it too so it can endure in some shadowy alcove? Do I care only for the web I have torn, the dragline I have severed? Am I turning from Molly, relieved to see her cruel, insensitive to my own relation with Maeve because … Her imperative is for me to look the present in the eye?

Asif and I enter a darkened bar. He wants to phone his mother, to tell her that we will not be coming for a meal tonight. I am shocked and saddened by his assumption. I am also flattered. I ask for a red wine. He asks for a *citron pressé*.

In my home we do not drink.

But you drink wine sometimes.

This is true. A little is enough for me. I notice that you gulp it down. Why do you drink so quick, like it's medicine, like it's punishment?

I don't know what to say. I am tongue-tied. *I was tongue-tied as a baby*, how'd that be for a cheap excuse? I don't know what to serve him. None of my stories is suitable. Maeve behind the wheel of the tractor drawing her little flask of scotch from her shirt pocket. Can't give him that.

Am I addicted to slivers of memory, terrified of the coherent picture, loving only in advance or retreat, only in partial knowledge?

I watch him talking to his mother on the bar phone; he is earnest, speaking very fast. I think he loves her. Suddenly I regret it. I want to be loved by her too. He is speaking in French to her, which is something I hadn't expected. I notice the clock — the workshop! It was meant to resume at four and it's four-thirty already. Asif's eyebrows shoot up as he walks back to the table.

Well, what is the problem now?

The workshop. I must go, explain at least why I can't continue.

But who's to say there's any crediblity in Asif Badaoni's or in Buchared's version of Choiseuil? Is Molly really going to drop out? How could she and Basilio continue if we defected? What are any of them going to make of the abdication?

Choiseuil will take our dual absence as meaning one thing: that we're together.

Well?

Maybe that we've ganged up against … I don't want to draw lines so fast; I don't want to condemn her so quickly. She might have some very genuine commitments to … migrant people here.

Putain! … So? She might have a tiny part of a cosy corner of her little brain that fondles such thoughts. You know I can do without knowing that a Nazi plays Schubert nicely, feeds his dog well and loves his grandchildren or even saved the life of one Jewish woman because she looked like his nanny. What Choiseuil has been doing is getting the lion's share of funds for her precious little performance groups while the kids are deprived of cultural centres and eighty percent of the *Maghrébin* youth are unemployed. And that's just the start of it, as you know very well. Choiseuil probably does have something of value to offer the good burghers of Marseille and even to the odd *Beur*. But what in the final analysis does it amount to?

I feel like saying: well, what does anything we do amount to? I feel like yelling: Fuck it, brother, we all end up in the great festering heap of deadness. And I want to add, slowly, so that he can hear in my voice the ever-so-slow whip-crack against the blue sky: *We all will go that way. We all have limits, petty vanities, pathetic contradictions, which in your wonderful final analysis make failures of us.* But he is resuming.

I'd much rather see what your Saïd and Mustapha and the gang had come up with. I think it's a great shame you cancelled that.

It would've been obscene to replace Mustapha.

I think not. You could've dedicated the show to him and raised money at least to pay for his funeral, and to fight the *Front National* bastards.

Asif, can I tell you something? That I've been wanting to say? That I need to tell you.

And? Well?

I'm going to tell Simone Choiseuil the simple truth, which is that my grandmother is ill and I'm going to have to return to Australia pretty soon. I mean I'm not going to invoke her fraudulence or whatever to explain my defection.

Oh my God, you have a way of delivering your shots! Now you tell me! That you're leaving.

I'm not saying anything is finished. I've just got this feeling, that if I don't go home soon something really bad will happen.

You're not just using it as an excuse, an escape hatch?

No, I'm not. I smile to him as best I can.

Perhaps you're right. Maybe it was too early to ask you home. But I know this place, a restaurant on the old fisherman's wharf at the Goudes, that ... I want to take you to. Maybe we can talk through this ... departure of yours. Tonight? Or am I pushing my luck?

No? I mean, yes. Why not? Sounds good. But I've got to see Simone first.

I have to seize my courage. I walk towards her slowly. It's true that this tiny autocrat manages monumental beauty. And it's still true that I could still risk everything for the lightest touch from her; a mere breath on my skin might do it. I know I can't relay to her the versions of Choiseuil I've heard. Molly and Basilio don't seem to be here. Basilio must be shooting a sequence of her Tumbleweed dance.

J'suis désolée, Madame, mais, j'suis obligée de partir, de quitter la performance. Vous voyez, c'est à cause de ma grande mère, qui m'a élevée. Il paraît qu'elle est gravement malade. I've said this in a rush without any reference to the tensions between us: I'm so sorry but I have to leave because of my grandmother. Who brought me up. She's very ill, it seems.

Simone Choiseuil says: Is this the woman you told me about? Who brought you up, in that banksia country you speak of? My dear, well ... Of course, you must go to her.

This is the rorter speaking, the woman who diverts funds her way ...

She holds my hand for a long time. The performance will suffer without the prickly Banksia, but of course, she is irreplaceable. This leaves us quite bereft, but I understand. You must go. I think you have learned something?

Yes. Thankyou, Madame. I am sorry. Goodbye, then.

And Asif? Has he not something to do with this?

Asif?

Oh, my dear. I am not blind. I see something is going on there. Not content with the American, you've made your contact there. You are both prickly, both wear your *farouche*, like it's a vocation. I said *no relation outside the performance* for a reason. I think he is too much in love with sabotage for its own sake. Still, it's too late now. And you say your grandmother ... *Mais vous pleurez!* Surely you're not crying? She wipes the tear away and folds her arms around me. You will write? Tell me how your work goes? Of course, like all of them, you promise ...

I am numb, shake my head. I stupidly place a platonic kiss on her cheek.

When I stumble out into the Rue Breteuil, I think: Thank

God, he's gone away. Asif must have chickened out, shot through. There is a stained but empty pavement in front of the art-framer's shop opposite. Maybe he's liquefied, having performed his function. Maybe he was just one of those they call donors, like in a fairytale. Inside the shop, behind a still life of fruit in an oak frame, I see the man who exercised his boxer bitches on the Prado beach. He zips up the black leather jacket, whistling. Now he's rubbing his hands against the chill. He has come out to pull down the metal security blind. He looks across, meeting my gaze in recognition, still whistling. It sounds like the overture to *The Marriage of Figaro*. I feel such trust for him that I am almost ready to climb into the bashed up little Auverland on whose front seat the boxer bitches wait, panting, their chests thrust out. But there is Asif pacing in front of the patisserie. *On va dans les Goudes, alors?* Do you still feel like that, going down to the fishing village, a meal, walk on the beach?

I've got a friend who says we can sleep in his apartment, if … you know, that's what we want to do. I mean if it gets too late to catch a bus …

Oh dear, I think, it's like one of those pauses on the stairs in a '40s movie. The encounter has taken place, the love-making consists of a kiss and the next shot will see me knitting booties.

Home

Am some bulb banking time, more vegetable than animal, turning season into season, composting me into not-me, printing tattoo upon tattoo, graft upon graft, this other beating in me.

Am bulb hoarding heat. At a switch of nerve, recall slithers of frozen dread. How not to let the idea of cancer in. Proliferation in stagnation, seething in a crawling time. Slow as glaciers, am shrinking backwards into a future where the lava of a birth, the grinding moraines of death, loop into one another and hold this life, whatever it is, enfolded beginnings and endings, in abeyance.

Whole body peels open and raw as an eye: nerve-ends sprout like wicks and fizz incandescent. The colours are drawn out of the cardboard suitcase, back to Banksiafold, here where, becoming mother, am motherless child again.

Maeve's name seems as if it's always been prepared for

this; a body whose only word is wound. Should have gone straight to the hospital and slept in a chair in her room.

The air is loud with magpies, honeyeaters crazy for grevillea nectar, noisy wattle birds sideswiping one another, swooping and squabbling, landing heavy on flexing twigs, clouds of silver-eyes rising, floating, resettling. The undergrowth crackles with reptiles and the cicada pulse quickens. Frantic stagnation. The heat throbs and now in the banksia, sheoak and marri stands, the pinks and violets hum along one ramifying optic nerve. The French windows fly open. The easterly breathes like a lusting animal on my sweat.

Now it's good to be on the old cane lounge with Millie, Joe, Josie and Zak on the verandah listening to the raucous bush. They don't make me talk. The vulgarity of questions, questions, the intrusive surgery of that western mode. How was your trip? Sum it up, do it in, encapsulate it, get it over. They know I will tell them when the pictures have had time to develop. The hush will come as the sun climbs of course. I think, coming back to this, no sex could beat this bush tuning its blood song on your skin.

Millie and Joe and I have jammed ourselves into the cab of the ute. Joe's taken the wheel. Zak saunters ahead to haul open the gate. He's sticking to that horticulture course, you know, Tom-Tom, Millie says. Bit of a run-in with the cops for a while but he's settled down real good now. What was that about, I wonder. I remember when he'd just got his licence going to a Fremantle bottle shop with him in his Falcon after Josie's gig. We wanted to pick up some wine to take back home. The guy behind the counter asked for his ID card or driver's licence. He had neither on him. I said: It's for me, I'm getting it. The guy didn't ask me to produce a card. Well, that's different then, he said. I paid up for the Jacob's Creek or Carrawarra claret or whatever cheap stuff it was, and as we left, I passed the bottle to Zak and let my fingers slide down to pluck a twenty dollar one, a Vasse Felix, from the stand to the left of the counter. Thanks. Seeya! I said and as I turned, I swung the bottle close to my thigh and kept it there until we were on the pavement. To my dismay, Zak was shocked. What the hell didya go and do that for?

This old Indian skirt is the only summer thing I could find at the bottom of the wardrobe.

You know, we should check out that sale in Myer's, Millie says, and get you a couple of smart outfits. That would make you feel better, hey.

Acid mounts as we move out of Banksiafold onto the wide spread of bitumen. Peeled raw, inside out, by the intensity of the glare. There are new gated estates everywhere: soon the suburbs will be fused right to the hills.

As we take the road swooping into the coastal dunes and rise away again, a reminder tugs that I can't place. Then I see it's that never ending hill-climb I dreamed about, trying to get Maeve up to the house with the view. Why didn't I act on those messages then? Silenced all those voices for the sake of a performance. It's been a long time since someone cared like this. The ache of desire was the closest to poignancy I got. My throat tightens. Now we've hit the built-up roads the heat is something else. I need to close my eyes away from the glare, dragging my nerves raw into its incineration. The dress sticks like plastic. On the high ute seat these thighs look immense in their spread. It's only Millie's body that seems to limit them.

Those French people give you the diploma you were looking for?

Oh, I got a bit of paper. Don't think it'll count for much.

The motor roars in second gear. Joe depresses the clutch again.

How far is this Southern Cross Hospital? Is that clutch going to seize up on us?

Don't you worry about that. We'll get you there. I've got to put a new one in for Maeve, he says. I had no idea it had got so bad. You know, we've been using the Commodore. Don't know why Maeve is so slow in asking. Hurts her pride, I reckon, that she hasn't got the strength anymore to work on the ute herself. You know, since she's been so breathless, she tends to ride the clutch for too long.

Yeah, Millie says, I miss seeing that black grease in her fingers. When we see that again we'll know she's on the mend.

Here are aprons of lawn, rose beds, yellow pencil pines and cotton palms dwarfed by the white cement colonnades and the sentinel lions at the balustrades, the steep blue-tiled roofs of the pale-brick '50s and '60s houses. Here's a letterbox built like a church with red twin spires. Love it, love it, Millie laughs. It's as if these features were geared to make the stretch of sea all the more unreal: that searing blue with dancing violets. Millie's hand is on mine.

The hospital is in a concave terrain next to the railway. It's in chocolate brick, its wide cream eaves settled flush with the aluminium window frames. It's a series of single-storeyed oblongs built around courtyards with sheltered walkways and ramps, looking more like one of those nursing homes they build as low, cramped, wandering euphemisms, antechambers to Happy Valley, Sunset, Mon Repos, Tranquil, Everlasting Retreat.

Wonder who dreamed up this place, Joe says. Enough to make you crook. I'll just wait down here in the foyer. Give you women some time together.

He hates hospitals.

Yeah.

We walk the endless arcade with its zigzag following the ramshackle additions. Feel my thighs slip and sweat against one another.

Jesus, what kind of ward is this?

Dunno. Looks like it might be some sort of rehab ward for people who've had strokes.

Ah, they've got a real sad look as if they've been trapped here for ever.

They are thin, these pale-eyed men in their striped pyjamas, edging towards something on their walking frames.

I think, once she's had this bout of chemo, they'll let her out for sure. Maeve reckons she'll be in remission no time at all once she gets home.

If she's got this parade of sad people lurching past on their walking frames all day it can't help her spirits.

How long are they going to take, those embassy people, to let that man of yours in? Well, if you're only a couple of months gone, that gives a bit of time. They looking into his politics, eh? Might be worthwhile giving them a bit of a nudge, though.

She nurses my arm and pats it as we walk. Yeah, Daughtergirl. You've got to keep strong, think strong. Don't let it get you down. It'll work out.

I don't say I'm afraid he'll never meet the Maeve I've loved and so never understand where I'm earthed. My home space is where he'll have to meet me now. I wonder whether his coming puts all of it under threat, anyhow. I have to give my guarantee to the migration people that I will marry this stranger. What have I done?

I have glimpsed this man as real through the inter-shock of his performance and what escapes it. And what about my performance? And Jesus, I think, what is this we've conceived together?

Another green vinyl corridor with high-gloss dove-grey walls, another walkway. Another chocolate brick arcade.

At least she's got those grevilleas to look at, Millie says. And there's a little courtyard where we can wheel her out, have a cuppa together.

The nurse at the station peers over her glasses and glances at a chart.

Mrs O'Shea? Yes 23a. But she's only allowed family, she says, looking from Millie back to me.

We're family, all right, if you mean … Millie says to the flickering eyes above the half-moon glasses. Hey, I've been coming tons of times …

Well, she says, that must've been on another shift. I'll check that it's all right with her. She tires quickly, you know. The nurse makes her face blank so you can write something like weary resignation onto it.

I say nothing; mustn't blow Maeve's relationship with these nurses. Swallow the acid anger.

Maeve's voice comes through the surf of troubled breathing, faint, for all its effort: Oh, I thought I'd told every nurse on every shift these people are my kin. And this young one here she's my grand-daughter come all the way back from France to be with me, to bring me home.

Tom-Tom, this is Judy.

The nurse has a tag with a picture of Sturt Peas and Judy written below.

Hello, Judy.

Judy nods and pads out on her rubber soles.

Old Sturt Pea Judy, I call her the Belsen Bovine, Maeve wheezes.

Millie says, ah, Maeve, you're wicked.

I can't see Maeve for the flowers on the trolley. They are variegated purple and pink supermarket carnations, lemon-white chrysanthemums with bedraggled leaves.

They don't survive too well in the air-conditioning, she says.

I mustn't register the shock. The blanket, smoothed out with the overlap of sheet, is flat except for the sharp knee hillocks. This is what has happened to big, powerful

Maeve while I've been gone. Her body's been stolen; this remnant left behind.

While I was intoxicated with Molly, with Asif, and the Spider, I kept shutting out those images from my dreams. I move, leaden, and know it's more than jet-lag that's taken up residence in my muscles, in my bones. It's this feeling I can't recall her. I can't call her back. Already she's retreated. The joke's exhausted her. Her eyes are glazed. Your eyes, dearest one, I want to shout, are shutting us out. Let it not be tears. If it's tears standing in her eyes and blinding her to my return, I'll never get her back. And an awful performer wants to let my own roll down to show her, to earn her return, but I arrest them. Again, let ambiguity stand. I type these words in my head and am appalled to be detached from this moment that wrenches my life from life, her life from life, that makes me want to scream and run. Down the shiny hall of my falseness I see that nothing can excuse the sequence of non-actions leading to this: I am resolutely too late. But I have to muster a smile.

She puts all the force she can in the hand that folds over mine. She hasn't got the strength though to twist her head to include Millie.

Why don't I change the flower water for you, Maeve?

From another space she says quietly: Yeah, Tom-Tom, we've got the vase room sussed out by now. We know where to go or otherwise, if you wait, they die on you. Anyway, these've got some life left in 'em.

Her cheekbones push their alabaster through the skin. In the sags and folds the skin is tea-coloured. The shadows under her eyes are yellow like urine. Maybe it's kidney failure? And the nicotine-stained gappy teeth are kind of whacky and wrong in the collapsed face. Her shoulder bones are big and unruly under the sleeveless nightie, but the skin hangs, withered, and there are bruises everywhere, mulberry and grey. Her hair is still coarse, with vigorous black amongst the white. She has taped to the side of the metal cabinet the photo which Joe took of Millie, Josie, her and me on the verandah. We look smiling from the photo space into this hospital bed.

Darling, she gasps in the old gravelly voice.

I can't recall her calling me darling before. She closes her eyes.

I dunno why they're so obsessed with my lungs, she wheezes. They've taken I don't know how many X-rays. If you ask me I think they're stabbing in the dark. It's the bloody treatment, you know the chemo, that makes me feel so bad. If they'd just leave me be I'd be much better off.

There's a long silence, so long we think she's gone to sleep.

You've got to get me out of here. I've got to get home. I'll die in this place. I'll start to get better once I'm back with you and Millie and Joe and the kids. And Millie tells me you've got your little one coming …

Give me time, Maeve! It's only been a few weeks.

I'm appalled again at what I missed in all my forecasts. How can Asif fit into all this, or rather, he can't. He won't. He won't understand the hold all of this has on me. Dread takes me up in a tight fist.

I'm going home, just tell them that, Tom-Tom, Maeve says again.

Tom-Tom O'Shea Notebook III

Against their Advice

At the counter there is a blond nurse with a skinny moustache talking to a little girl perched on a stool in front of him. But he turns, like a method actor.

I'm Maeve O'Shea's grand-daughter.

Ah. So you've finally come. She talks a lot about you.

She needs more than anything to get back home. She's really low, being in here, away from everybody she loves, the place she loves. We've got to get her out.

You've got to get her out.

I'm not criticising the treatment she's getting here but she just wants to get home.

Well, if you'll excuse me for saying, you're hardly in a position to know what's best having just turned up …

Yeah, sure. I've just turned up … I'm listening to her.

If you take her home right now, you know what'll happen? Away from all the support systems, the drug monitoring, the drip? You know she can't digest anything much. You take her away right now, she won't last the weekend.

She will die, that's what she reckons if she stays in here one day more.

Look, it's understandable. She's into denial. She's being kept alive here. Do you know how much trouble we've been taking with her pain control?

Can't we administer that? Millie, her friend in there, she's a trained nurse. A … registered nurse.

He rolls his eyes.

I feel my blood boiling in my face and the adrenalin surge. I want to yell: you snivelling little racist prick. I saw you roll your eyes. And then I think: what if Maeve really needs to be in here. What if we can't cope at home? What if we do kill her?

What's in the drip then?

Her digestive system has broken down, that … It's her food-line.

Why doesn't he give me the technical name?

You could give us the scripts. I know that what she needs more than anything is to be back home with her family.

The doctor won't be back here until Tuesday and the Pharmacy is closed for the weekend in any case. You'd be taking her home without anything written up.

Maybe I could ring the hospice people. Anyway, she's got her own doctor who could prescribe what she needs.

Well then, she'd have no continuity of treatment.

There are other ways of dying.

Look, you, if you'll excuse me, have been away, haven't you? I'm just suggesting you can't possibly have a realistic assessment of the situation. You've just fronted up … She needs twenty-four hour nursing, you know. The doctor from RPH does his rounds on Tuesday. You can talk to him then. Or, if you like, I can link you up to the resident.

He taps out the number. Look, Dr Richards, I've got the … grand-daughter? Yes, the grand-daughter of Mrs O'Shea here. She wants to take her grandmother home. We've tried to explain that it's against all our advice …

Yes, Miss?

O'Shea.

Miss O'Shea. If you want to precipitate your grandmother's death, go ahead. You'd be taking her off without her drugs.

She reckons being in here is killing her.

Being in the hospital is keeping her alive, and just as importantly, her pain under control.

My voice dies in my throat.

Well, when this doctor comes on Tuesday, can I see her?

Him. The oncologist, Professor Yu.

I expect that can be arranged. Now, I beg you to do what's best for her and to let us balance her drugs to insure the best relief.

I hand the receiver back to the nurse.

Well, Maeve says. Can I go? Can you ring up the ambulance? I'm in the fund, we may as well use it.

Maeve, they won't let you go at least until Tuesday. Well, after the oncologist sees you again. They can't write up the drugs until then. The pharmacy …

Her look calls me Judas.

Rubbish. All they need to do is give us the scripts. Dr Morgan could do it anyhow. What's happened to you? A couple of nurses and doctors reduce our Tom-Tom to a little yes-girl.

They say it's too dangerous, Maeve.

Now my tears are coming. A little yes-girl.

What's the use of having all my drugs nicely written up on my way to the morgue? That's the next stop if I stay another minute in here. Do you take their word over mine, now?

On Tuesday, Maeve. I promise.

Tuesday will be too late.

Okay. I'll ring the ambulance. Millie, you got some twenty cent pieces for the phone?

Get my purse, love. Maeve points to the drawer in the bedside chest. Her fingers are shaking.

It's just the Ventolin, for the breathing. It does that to me.

What about the oxygen?

Oh she's got that machine at home.

But on the way?

The ambulance would have it.

That's what they're bloody for.

Now Millie, can you get those nighties out, while she's phoning?

I walk past the nursing station clutching the coins. Tear-blind little yes-girl.

The nurse calls out quietly. He's in a huddle with the Belsen Bovine. Where are you off to?

I go to say: *What's it to fuckin' you?*

I'm calling the ambulance. She insists on going home and

I have to respect her wishes.

Look, I gather you've just come on a long plane flight. I don't think you're in any state to make this decision. Sit down here and have a cup of coffee. Don't go back in there. I'll have a word with her. She listens to me.

Yes, says the Belsen Bovine. She's a tough old bird but she fancies Simon. She'll listen to him.

I sip at the insipid grey coffee. Judas, little yes-girl on a stool.

He is in there for an eternity. What will Millie say? Maybe Millie will stand up for Maeve.

He comes out beaming. Like he and Belsen have had a bet. I did it, he says. She'll stay.

Maeve's face is turned to the window, away from me.

I'll come out Tuesday, then.

Her voice has gone flat. Got a bit of an ache in the old chest, can you get the nurse?

She doesn't name me any more.

Simon draws the curtain. We wait outside.

I'll ring through to see if we can get some extra morphine. She is in a lot of discomfort.

Phew, that's starting to work. Just close me eyes for a moment.

The lids are parted slightly. The whites roll away.

Better leave her to it.

We'll be back tomorrow, Maeve, and then we'll get you out Tuesday, whatever, Millie says.

Maeve gives no sign.

Joe walks towards us. He can see it's no use asking. The heat outside is infernal.

We couldn't bring her out into this in any case.

How much morphine did they give?

I don't know. It worries me. She didn't look like she was just falling asleep. More like she was going far, far off.

Shit. I should stay with her.

Look, you've got to get some sleep for your own sake and for that baby.

We'll come back tonight, if you like.

The tiredness presses down with such bulk that even the suffocating stagnancy of air is a temptation. I give myself to it.

Wake in the darkness. All lights are out.

Millie's voice comes, like it's days later. Some sleep, she says. It's Monday, hey Daughtergirl.

Feel my blood banking like a huge breaker, ride in its trough through the air, onto the verandah. Hell. Maeve!

Take a shower and we'll go as soon as you're ready. Millie and I went yesterday. She was asleep. Wasn't aware of us.

That morphine? Did they give her more?

Couldn't get anything out of them. You know, different shift.

Awful stillness in the room. Maeve's in the same nightie.

They've made her unconscious, that's what they done.

Look, I'm ringing the ambulance. I don't care what they fuckin' well say. We've got to get her home now.

I tell the nurse over my shoulder as I head for the phone. We're taking her home. I wish I'd done it Saturday.

You know it's against our advice if you're doing it? If you'd just wait a few hours, we'd have everything written up.

The ambulance guy is a red toad. Grumpy in the heat. The drip comes with her, at least that.

They push the trolley through the walkways, and ramps, the chocolate brick arcades, in and out of the heat, back into the air-conditioning. If you ask me, you're mad trying to get this woman home in this weather.

She is dying.

Yes, she is dying and this is going to kill her real quick.

We can't reply.

I'll get in the back.

We'll go ahead, Millie says. She's got a tangled mass of hangers and nighties looped over her arm. Joe is carrying Maeve's little blue case. We have left the flowers. We can't tell one another why we've done this.

Hey Maeve, I breathe, into her ear, we're going home, the voice is strangled. Her eyes roll as if … Is she trying to open them? Was that a faint pressure on my hand? Please God, I find myself saying. Please God, if there's anything like your energy available, give it to her now, let it flow from me to her, let her not be in coma, let her know we're getting her home.

Jesus, the Driver Toad calls, as I lead him off Armadale Road, you people need your heads read doing this to a dying woman.

If I had a gun right now I could shoot this man.

The ambulance slips on the limestone gravel of the drive-way. We feel each jolt magnified.

Banksiafold, well I'll be damned.

There's Zak and Josie coming out. Their eyes are wide with the unspeakable. Where the limestone gravel gives way to a narrower path he stops the ambulance. The second guy opens the back doors.

But what about the sun. There's …

They carry her through the blaze. I can see her blood heating through the skin.

They have caught her arm on something. I run to hold the flyscreen but Joe's already set it open.

Fuck, they've tore her skin, Zak says.

He's just about crying. I take his arm. We walk slowly together.

It's true: they've snagged her skin, tearing away an ugly triangle. The skin is already bruised. Bright blood trickles.

The Toad and his workmate are grim and sweating. The mate says, well at least it's cool in here.

You got her oxygen ready?

Yeah, and I've set the bed on bricks like you said, Joe says.

What's this for?

So we can tend to her more easily.

One of the bricks has a snail still stuck to it. For years those bricks have lain there, growing moss, a settled border to Maeve's herb garden. What must he have been thinking as he pulled them up, leaving the little indentations in the earth, scraping off the slugs.

Someone has knocked the wind chimes.

I'll go, says Millie. That'll be the hospice nurse.

Joe and I ease Maeve onto the bed.

She needs sponging, I say. She's awfully hot.

Maeve, Maeve, you're back home with all of us now.

Maeve, Millie and Joe and Josie and Tom-Tom and Zak, we're all here.

I want to lie next to her.

Got a fan?

Joe nods. I listen to the retreat of the creaking boards. He returns unlooping the cord from the fan in a slow fluid motion. Everything has taken on the pace of a ceremony.

Millie comes back. This is Shirley from the Red Cross Hospice, she says.

Shirley puts her hand on my shoulder. She helps the ambulance guys out with the trolley bed.

She sits down next to me at Maeve's side.

My dear, you did the right thing bringing her back. She hasn't got long, she says.

I did it too late. And they gave her that morphine.

By the look of her, Tom-Tom, she wouldn't have had much longer without it.

But she begged to come home Saturday. And the staff wouldn't let me. I shouldn't have listened. I thought she'd …

You have done it for her now. You have brought her home. Look, she will know she's back, even if she's not conscious. She'll know. She'll hear your voices. Have you been talking to her? Music, that can be important. Did she have some special music?

I can't get my voice out this time.

The noises from the swamp, those birds. That was the music she loved most. That and Joe's didge, Millie says.

No, I think, this is too much. This is like sending her off.

She has held on, till she got back, Shirley says.

Again Joe walks slowly, slowly away.

We watch. Her lids flicker. Shirley is wrong. Maeve will open her eyes soon. This will bring her back, just the quietness here. Joe's put more grevilleas in the vases with the purple Geraldton wax she loved and the enamel-white Rhicinocarpus flowers. The room looks very beautiful with its bare jarrah boards and its simple lace. Millie's and my paintings are on the walls. There's that photo of Evie at the dressing-room mirror. All the sorrow Maeve has survived.

Now, as the darkness is settling, and the coolness breathes in, lifting the lace at the windows, we hear it, almost like a whale moaning, channelling the night in, so the didgeridoo comes in subtle as Maeve's own pulse, with the insect sounds. It rises now like some glorious, grave bird, deeper than cathedral organs into the room. Joe is giving his rhythmic breath to Maeve.

I rest my forehead on the pillow next to her.

She is beautiful, Shirley says.

Yes, comes Millie's voice.

You lie down with her for a while, Shirley says. It won't hurt.

Can you hear that, Maeve? It's Joe, playing for you.

She's going now.

Shirley's fingers are on the pulse.

A howl rises. I don't know where it's coming from. Is it the didgeridoo setting off one of the dogs?

The howling space between us.

IV

Lou Barb

An Offering to Morpheus

After Maeve's funeral, Tom-Tom came to stay for a while with Roly and me. She simply said: I need to be with you and Roly for a bit. I don't know what's better, being there where everything is her, or away, because everything reproaches me for denying her what she needed most, for not getting her back in time.

How to live through someone else's grief? She paced through the same questions, the same lacerating self-accusations. It was an almost voluptuous abandonment to masochism. *I should never have gone away. I should've come back earlier. I would have seen what they were doing to her. I should have brought her home. We should have tried naturopathy.*

I said again and again: by everything you said, darling, she was riddled with metastases. No naturopathy could've helped.

Fight is everything. I should ...

All I could do was rock her in my arms as she wept and

wept. At the same time I thought of marking I should be doing, of that lecture on Artaud. I also felt guilt at my boredom with these circles that the grieving cling to, the way they will accept no consolation, no attenuating circumstances for their own inadequacies. Oh Black Swan! Nina Simone wailed from the lounge room. Here again Tom-Tom showed no measure. If we listened to *Black Swan*, we listened to it a hundred times that month.

She lived her pregnancy in grief and anxiety. By night Asif tended to incarnate her worst fears. Tom-Tom was just a vehicle for him to escape France. He didn't love or desire her — all that had been an act. By day he was transfigured in her talk as this wondrous person, some dark saviour. But it seemed as if the Immigration people at the embassy were never going to clear him. Roly tried pulling strings through friends in the Department of Immigration. Fatigue and frustration crept into Asif's letters which Tom-Tom knew by heart.

Maybe I'm just a fading cartoon to him, barely a contour left, she said. Maybe I've become bourgeois whitey again for him. Maybe he's really got no intention of coming and just making up this stuff about embassy delays.

Tom-Tom, I said, why then do you think he would write these detailed, laborious letters?

Do you think he's laborious?

Then she caught my smile and she laughed too. She veered from irrational despair to paranoia and back to laughter within minutes.

She said: You know, Lube, sometimes I think when I'm dozing off that it's not from him at all, that it's Molly's baby and I dream it too, that it comes out grinning with the Luna Park smile and mulberry hair and the flattened boxer's nose. Sometimes I dream it's the Spider, you know, and her skin is crazed, with wet web stuck to it. Sometimes it's Molly and Asif that come together in a dangerous, dancing thing that scurries away from me at birth. I watch from my bed as it looks over its shoulder and sends back an artillery blast from its black eyes. Sometimes too the baby is a miniature Maeve, alabaster bones through the tea-stained skin, cold, cancer-struck.

I would lie awake listening to Tom-Tom's panting through these nightmares, then the throat-clearing of awakening and later the sobbing into the pillow. If I went in to comfort her I glimpsed something disturbing, like a glint of childish satisfaction in her eyes. She'd drag my face towards her own streaming face to receive a kiss. It crossed my mind that this suffering might be at least in part a seductive ploy, designed to bring forth, under the guise of the maternal, the amorous in me. But then, immediately I'd thought that, I'd dismiss it. She was a child in need. Bereft. After her mother, whose loss she relived in Maeve's death, she seemed to live her own pregnancy as an orphanage. I wish I'd had it in me to cradle her more.

Her belly was a tight mound, as much an expression of muscularity as pregnancy, almost, I remember thinking, a boyish disavowal of her maternal body. With the big coarse cotton shirts and jeans Tom-Tom chose you could easily forget that she was pregnant. While I marked essays, groaning at the insipid stream of banalities and fashionable formulations, reading out the howlers, and Roly listened to Bach, or read Pynchon, I'd catch Tom-

242

Tom watching us with burning eyes from the sofa. If say, Roly passed me a gin and tonic as I stirred the sauce, we'd find Tom-Tom had moved behind us, enlacing us both at the waist. Her lips brushed my cheek, then Roly's. I flipped the wooden spoon and a shower of tomato sauce came down on the stove. You're both so gorgeous, she said.

She wants us to be her parents, I thought, with a ripple of fascination and dread. There was something about her wanting to squeeze in between us that I didn't like at all. For her to be in my arms, that was one thing, with its own problems, of course, but I could imagine, even cherish the image. But she as our child! Roly was a bit of a sucker for this. He'd always liked Tom-Tom's infantile fierceness and they went back a long way.

You know, he said, his hands folded under his head, his dog-eared copy of *V* across his chest, I wouldn't be surprised if she wanted to get into bed with us both.

His calm surmising, his bemusement left me speechless. I could only reject it with an oh!

It's hard living with a couple, you know. She's so vulnerable.

I wanted to ask him if this is what he wanted, if in his mind he was already rehearsing something.

Well, there'd be nothing so very strange about it. You and she after all, I gather.

Come off it, Roly, I said, glad of the penumbra on my side of the bed. It wasn't just Tom-Tom's pregnancy, it was the outrage that he presumed to embroider, let alone participate in whatever had been between us.

Then I felt for her desolation. I withdrew to the kitchen

for a glass of water, creaking past Tom-Tom's room. The door was open. She was leaning back on the pillow, attentive, yet without any pretence, either of reading or of trying to sleep. She had her right arm cocked behind her head, the hand to the nape so that the armpit was exposed. The gesture shocked me somehow, that in conjunction with the smile she suddenly gave me. There was something so overtly animal about it. I thought: Mother would find that obscene. As I mouthed good night, Tom-Tom, immobile, mouthed it back. I felt weak at the knees. I stumbled on down the hall. Returning with the glass, I realised that my hand was trembling. Little waves kicked across the surface of the water. I placed the glass at the door, padded across to Tom-Tom who was grave now, with expectation. She is a child, after all, I thought. She wants her goodnight kiss, that assurance before the light is turned out.

Again as I bent, Tom-Tom strained towards me, but more insistently this time, pulling me down. It was no maternal peck she wanted. Her lips were insistent. Felt this concerted pull as if I'd become the raw abyss into which she was being drawn. I veered my mouth towards her forehead.

Oh, you are so very sweet and chaste, Lube, Tom-Tom said. Her voice had a hard, bitter edge to it, this time.

I stroked the child's hair in reply. I returned, on fire to the bedroom. I ignored Roly's interrogative look. I realised I'd left the water at Tom-Tom's door.

And if I were to give myself to that child, I would be vaporised by the heat of her need. We were just two of the many that Tom-Tom wanted as fuel to keep her own furnace firing. It's true. Her passion was intransitive. She wanted love through and beyond, not in the person. She wanted to borrow what there was between Roly and me to turn our quiet relationship into a blaze for her own consumption, and then of course, she would move on, leaving us with the taste of our own ashes.

What demented things she had me thinking. Roly snapped *V* shut. Since Tom-Tom came to stay we had both become distracted. We were seduced into the abeyance of her waiting, her pregnancy. We were doing too little work in the evenings, drinking too much. And especially Tom-Tom who should be thinking about that baby, for goodness' sake.

The next morning Roly said: What strange custom has Tom-Tom acquired in France that makes her leave a glass of water at her bedroom door? Is it a propitiatory offering to Morpheus?

You know, he said, why don't you ask Maurice if there's not some opening for Tom-Tom's Asif in engineering. Tom-Tom's got his CV; why don't you stick a copy in an envelope? There might just be a little job on line. Didn't you say Maurice collected a research grant?

Well, yeah, why not? It might work, especially if this Asif of hers is willing to enrol in a postgraduate program of some kind.

Eet ees Scondalose

Give them that dazzling smile, include them in your first greeting, I want to say to him. He is thinner than I thought; his cheekbones are raw, his eyes reddened and he's biting the inside of his cheek. He shakes his hair back; it's longer, coarser than I recall. Looks as if he's cut it himself. It's a pretty artless, basin sort of cut and for some reason this makes me cross. Under his darkness, his skin is a bit jaundiced. Something I don't recall. It was Molly who was a bit yellow. His look is not one of searching intensity; rather it is distracted, impatient.

Asif, this is Millie; Joe, this is Asif.

His look travels quickly over to them and back, searching my face for some sort of confirmation.

Well, well! And this baby of ours?

He holds me tight and then stands back, awkward, as if the embrace has been some sort of transgression.

You've put on weight, he says.

We'd be pretty worried if she hadn't. It's what has to happen, eh? Millie laughs.

I do not know these things, he says stiffly.

I swallow. I can't have heard right. My heart will shut down. Don't let him have said that.

He resumes French. He is shutting them out, but of course his English is insecure.

We've been waiting and waiting for you to come, eh.

What's this job you've lined up for me, he says. Will I be able to bear it?

Look it's Lou Barb, my friend, who arranged it through a guy called Maurice, a mate of hers, a colleague. He'll talk to you about it when you've got over the jet-lag.

Of course he is not a sweetly mannered middle-class boy, a docile citizen. What was I thinking? Yet I am chilled. This man will be touching me soon. Or will go through those movements. Will he recoil? He liked me when I looked like a boy, that's it. And since I left Marseille, he's probably been with boys more than anything.

We watch the suitcases burst through the plastic straps. He's as scared as I am of what we've committed ourselves to.

His suitcases, leather-trimmed in a sombre floral brocade, are really quite chic. Cardboard suitcases, whose romance was that? But he is laughing as he hauls them onto the trolley. He threads his fingers through my hair. I like it longer!

Didn't have the money to have it cut!

Nor did I. How are you with scissors? Do you reckon you can rescue mine?

In the car he puts his ear to the mound of my belly.

Can you feel the kick?

Ah! There's a strong baby in there.

He is present now, returning to me with the sharpness of his sweat, the hard thigh next to mine. I trace the snaking vein on the back of the beautiful, brown hand. He brings the hand palm down on mine, then wedges it between my legs.

Can't wait to be with you.

We swing out of the car park into the long avenue lined with young river gums. I hold my breath. How is he going to receive the flatness? How is he going to receive the suburbs? Suddenly I feel dismay at not having prepared him for all this. I talk extra fast to distract him. He must know that approaches to airports in any city are pretty grim. We pass the new estates on Armadale Road. A bulldozer is working, raising its shovel load high over a pile of uprooted banksias.

What is this?

They are clearing, to build more big houses for little families. This is what I tried to tell you about.

Mais c'est scandaleux. Eet ees scondalose.

Joe eyes the rear-vision mirror. You're going to like our place but, Asif.

This is not the time to say it, in front of Joe and Millie. That we might have to move closer to the city if Asif is going to take that job at the Institute. Public transport is hopeless out here.

See it's banksia time. You've come for the banksia season, they're all decked out for you, Asif! Millie says as we swing into the gravel drive.

He laughs. His laughter frees my blood. Realise how knotted I've got with his tension.

As the ute draws up next to Maeve's house, the *Banksia menziesii* cones blaze through the dripping blue grey leaves.

In the murmuring softness, with the light drizzle on the roof, his tentative hand moves over my belly. He listens for the baby. I feel his eyes translating through the dark.

Now over breakfast, as he pours his coffee into a huge white mixing bowl and dunks bread, jam and all, slurps it up, we feel it in his silence, in his absorption. He has written us into his knot, his ganglion of tangled nerves. He spreads his own strain about. Our brains throb with his headache. When we talk, if we dare, our voices walk on eggshells. He blinks fast. He is going to talk. He says it in French. Oh, again, he is excluding Millie and Joe.

I'll never understand this Australian. I was good at English but this is not like English.

You'll start to pick out the words. *Ca te viendra vite*, I say.

But they fuse them all together, in one long nasal drone.

He's in a bad mood, your man? Doesn't like it here?

Nah. I mean. Yes. It's just all strange to him.

Reckon, he's in shock. Give him time.

Jet lag. Jet lag more like it.

It strikes me that Asif might not be nice at all. I have never viewed him in this way. Of course, he is clearly not very *nice*. Niceness is moral sponginess or something to him. He is Not Very Nice.

But today he's a sunny child. Reborn! It's only sleep he needed. Why do I doubt so quickly? He stretches like a gloriously innocent animal at the muslin curtains. He draws them and flings out the French doors. He strokes the sparse fur on his belly, and then wedges his hand under the elastic at the back of the silk boxer underdaks, so I can see the triangular tuft of fur above the coccyx. He likes himself in this glittering morning. Coolness breathes into the room. In the bed I know with my belly's taut arc that I can shoot myself arrow-sure into the future. He opens his mouth, teeth glancing with white light. He yawns voluptuously until I wonder if his jaws will lock — an awakening of the man-child never quite completed. But he comes back to the bed, burrowing under the doona. He kisses me laughing into my mouth, and then he watches me, reads my face close, and I see that tears are rolling down his face. He buries his face in my neck. His hand moves downward, delicate, interrogative, full of awe this time. The three of us! To think we have already done this together, he laughs. His voice is melodious, richer, more baritone than I remembered it, more like Basilio's. I know that this is the moment to which I'll have to return when I wonder how or if I ever loved him.

Lou Barb

Free-Range Chook

I offered them the wedding meal as my gift, since they were both strapped for cash. It was all thrown together at the last minute because they'd had no way of knowing when Asif's passage would be cleared by Immigration. With the cool weather we thought we could risk shopping on the way to Cannington, of all places, where the only available celebrant happened to be located. So there we were in my car, Asif alongside me, Tom-Tom behind. It struck me as odd that she yield the seat next to me but I guessed she was trying to manage his moods. He looked as if he'd like to take the wheel. What a long ache for the eyes Albany Highway is: car dealers and wall-to-wall carpet empires and all the cubes with red pyramid roofs selling fast food. Still, I told myself, those French have made a mess of some of their landscapes too. Why are we so ridiculously defensive of aspects of the place we despise? He was mocking me gently for my new Celica but he liked the gadgetry and was studying the specifications booklet from the glove box.

Putain, he said, *c'est pas mal ça.*

He could obviously read English far better than he could follow it in speech.

We decided on the Carousel. *C'est tout à fait comme les Géants Casino à Marseille*, he said.

Did you know, Lube, that the Casino at Les Valentines is so immense they've all the checkers on roller blades?

I wondered whether he'd ever really shopped before; he seemed to take so much delight in it. Of course it was my money they were spending. His childlike pranks with the trolley, turning it sharply, making it rear or jerking it into rapid reverse, were part of a concerted clowning which made me uneasy at first. As I placed a jar of New Zealand asparagus into the trolley I looked up into his face: in his eyes there was no trace of the grim glitter I expected. Rather, he gave me a smile of flooding candour. There was a radiance about him, I thought, a simple exuberance at that moment which was utterly endearing. I thought: oh you gorgeous, glossy boy! It would be all right for Tom-Tom. His hair swung blue-black. He had on a cinnamon pullover of silkily fine wool, a green corduroy jacket with an elongated '70s collar, and a belt buckled at the back. Around his neck, improbably, because it was crisp rather than cold, he had a heavy cream woollen scarf in moss stitch. He was wearing big heavy cowboy boots, of the type I suppose they wear on the Camargue. He towered over Tom-Tom in those stacked wooden heels. Her russet gloss answered his: the fake chinchilla jacket continued in its crimped patchwork the foxiness of her hair, cut now to a stubble, a henna haze over the black roots. She still sported a few ear-studs and rings, jade, fake ruby, fake diamond, and from the lobe on the left ear, jauntily dangling, a magpie tail feather. She was wearing, perhaps for old times' sake, her purple and green harlequin pants. The boots were floppy, flat-soled, in emerald suede. The Carousel shoppers froze in their tracks and stared frankly. One woman placed a jar of dill cucumbers in mid-air. With the fat cucumbers in their puddles of dill at her feet, she was still transfixed. Well, they were behaving like joyous children who'd strayed from some carnival out of the *Grand Meaulnes* — Tom-Tom the fey spirit; he, the mysterious woodsman she had danced with. There was no way you could tell she was seven months' pregnant under the bulky fur.

Smoked salmon? To start with?

Why not?

We'll need more than one, I suggested.

Asif plucked two packs of Tasmanian from the refrigerator shelf and launched them into the trolley, laughing at his extravagance.

We'll need capers.

Why?

People usually have capers with smoked salmon, and white onion. And Italian bread.

Ah bon? Asif looked puzzled.

Some dip?

Oh, dip, I dunno.

Brandade de morue, doo yooh ev thet?

Not too sure.

Avocado dip.

Free-range chooks. Three? We can do them in the big outdoor oven.

What eez chook, eet sound vairry strunge.

Tom-Tom tucked her hands in her armpits to make wing stumps, clucked and waddled, jerking her neck.

Thees ees whort we call ze police in Fraunce. *Les poulets*.

Yeah, Tom-Tom said, we'll eat roast cops.

Asif's face froze in puzzlement. We had left him behind in our laughter. I saw temper flash across his face. He pulled at his fingers to crack the knuckles. I'd thought men only did that in movies.

J'ai dit, she said soothingly, *qu'on allait manger des agents rôtis*. Tom-Tom gave him a widely indulgent smile.

And I'll do beans in almonds. I only know that and eggfruit. I can do eggfruit. You baste it with olive oil and grill it and then layer it with tomato sauce that you make with garlic and basil and chuck in some mozzarella, stick it in the oven and it works. Well it did for Maeve, anyway. But Lou, she laughed, Lou is very domesticated.

I felt mildly put down by their bohemian alliance. I thought, well, my car and my wallet are all right in the driving and the buying and so will my domesticity be when it comes to the eating. If it were up to what they could afford, we'd be struggling to have sausages and beer.

And cheese?

I showed them a big Brie from Margaret River. Tom-Tom nodded approval. Asif took it from my hand.

But this is scon-da-lows. You make a ker-pea of our Brie!

Oh, suddenly you're so French! Tom-Tom was taking a risk here with this Monsieur's quicksilver mood-swings but then I thought, oh, why should we pussyfoot around him?

At the pastry shop they chose a couple of large, sumptuous tarts with strawberries, sour cherries and kiwi fruit, arranged in a spiralling pattern.

Ah, thet is egg-zoh-tique, Asif said. In Fraunce we don uv zat, all fruits togethurrgh.

Eh bienvenue en Australie, alors. I managed in my strangled French.

Ah vous parlez un peu, quand-même, he said.

You can call her *tu*, you know, Tom-Tom said.

We went into the Liquorland, which was incorporated in the store. Let's do it all at once.

I chose some very good wines and they caught my enthusiasm in no time: piled into a second trolley were two Limestone Ridges, some Wolf Blass, a couple of top Penfolds. A carton of beer.

No, no, Joe only drinks E.B.

That'll be three hundred and eighty-six dollars.

Putain, what eez zat.

Ne t'en fais pas, Tom-Tom said, don't worry! *Elle est bourrée.* She's loaded.

The checkout girl called after us: You've left a chicken! I realised that all this time Asif had been carrying his briefcase, probably with his papers in it. Used to thefts from cars, I guessed. It was a handsome, capacious one, of the concertinaed classical kind. He caught my eye.

It is how you say … *un cadeau.* From my friend, Basilio. Ee eez vairry kind to me. Ee say now I make *un monsieur sérieux.*

One of his lovers, Tom-Tom whispered. One of his *serious* moonlight lovers, she added, hooking arms with me, brushing my cheek with her lips.

We watched Asif marching back with his briefcase to the checkout counter to claim the orphaned chicken. He ballooned a plastic bag like a spinnaker to snare the yellowish bird, opened his briefcase to receive it, and snapped the lock shut, nodding to the open-mouthed checkout girl and the queue of shoppers. He gave them a ceremonial bow and strode back to us, very pleased with himself. Tom-Tom was marrying a most unpredictable child.

We found the place, staring for some time incredulously at the number on the battered green metal letterbox. It was a squat '40s house, with patches broken away from its stucco and an apology of a tudor gable. Still, there were geraniums making their little claim to optimism in black plastic pots on the balustrade of the little front porch. In the derelict car park in front were a number of prospective spouses, Anglo-Celts, Vietnamese and Nyoongars.

Jesus, there's a queue! Wonder how long we're going to have to wait. Maybe they process us quickly in there. Is this what you call shotgun, eh? There's Millie, Joe and the kids. Their green Commodore was turning in.

Let's knock. We're on time at least.

A little man with comb-marks in his hair — *Brylcreem, a little dab'll do ya* — poked his freckled, ginger face around the screen door. Badaoni and O'Shea? It was a surprising baritone boom.

Zat eez urs, said Asif. The celebrant looked into our faces for confirmation as if Asif were retarded.

That right? You're spot on, then. Come on in.

Hey, we're on! Tom-Tom called to Millie and the others, as if it were a stage show. Millie was looking magnificent in a light woollen suit, a bold black and white print with touches of sienna. She was wearing a heavy gold necklace in a sort of braid formation and several gold bangles. Joe was in a double-breasted, sand-coloured linen suit. His beige and sienna tie echoed Millie's. Josie was in a bronze slim-line dress; Zak in waistcoat, black jeans and Reeboks.

Two great crystal vases filled with orange and lemon gladioli were planted on either side of the electric fire, fake coals aglow. The Mrs Celebrant, her blonde hair teased to a bouffant and a kindly, kindergarten teacher smile, drew out chairs for us. Asif parked his briefcase carefully by the gladioli. Sprawled on the carpet between the glads was a snowy-snouted black Labrador, her tail thudding a welcome from its puckered base, whacking the broken stem of one of the blooms.

Well, if it's all right by you, we may as well get started. Yes, more chairs for your friends. You've brought a couple more witnesses that we expected, but that's fine, that's fine. Now.

Do you, Ez-if Badaoni of Mar-sails, Frence, tike ...

Asif was suddenly earnest, intent on Mr Greg Wilson and mouthed his own name back, mimicking the accent perfectly.

Oi, he said, Ez-if Badaoni tike ...

Fuck, Tom-Tom whispered into my ear. The ring!

You've got them on, remember!

I can't get it off! The one for me! *He's* meant to have it.

Then Asif said. Le chook! *Le poulet va s'abîmer*! The chook will spoil!

I noticed Tom-Tom trembling. A tear stood in her eye and rolled down her cheek. She was biting her lip to repress her laughter. I stiffened against catching it. Then I looked across at Millie who was quite frankly giving way, tears streaming down her cheeks. Joe looked bemused. Zak got up to give the labrador a pat. With all the tension Asif had generated, my stomach muscles seizing up, I wanted to hoot and roll with mirth.

Le poulet, he said again. *Penses-tu qu'il va s'abîmer?*

The Labrador was very stout. She looked at Zak with her benign brown eyes and laughed silently. She stretched slowly, bowing, still laughing, sounded out a yawn and, as if on cue, walked across to sniff the briefcase. Again her tail thwacked the glads. Mrs Wilson moved to save the rocking vase.

Do you have a ring? Mr Wilson asked.

Silence.

Do-you-have-a-ring, Mrs Wilson gave shouted emphasis to get each word across to the slow learner. Her eyes twinkled to reassert kindness.

No I do nert. Bert she … uz-EET!

Tom-Tom, whose face was streaming now, struggled to drag the ring over her knuckle, and passed it to Mr Greg Wilson. She had told me it was one Molly had given her. It was an oval dark jade set in silver, quite lovely in its simplicity.

Mr Greg Wilson passed it to Asif so that he could thread it onto Tom-Tom's finger.

Asif said: Zenk-you-vairry-merch, slipped it on his own

little finger and tucked his right hand under his left armpit, as if that were that, and things could now conclude.

By this time Tom-Tom had pitched into hilarity. The tears were carrying away the kohl from her eyes.

No, excuse me, Mr Badaoni, I think that ring is meant for ... He consulted his notes, for, he swallowed his exasperation, for Thomasina.

Thomasina! I do nert ernderstund.

La bague, tu me la donnes! Tom-Tom managed through spasms of laughter.

And, this one is for you, Asif! The gold band slid off more easily.

Oi neow dee-clare yew men en woif! Yew moi kiss neow — he winked conspiratorially — if yew heven't done this before!

Mrs Wilson tiptoed away to the mantelpiece and returned with a box of tissues in a pink padded cosy: Here, dearie, a lot of us get emotional at times like this!

Hands were clasped and shaken and, bursting through the screen door, we exploded with laughter.

Ze chook, I ev left ze chook!

Mrs Wilson was at the door with the briefcase. It can be nerve-racking, I know, she said.

Beating the Breast

I tell Maurice I need a certain rootlessness. I tell him the romance of the furnished room. The Hotel room with copper-stained basin and the thin towel without pile. I give him the windows rattling as the train passes, hoots.

Incurable romantic, you.

I need that. I'll come back with some drawings, I say.

And it's here, in Bunbury or Albany or Kalgoorlie, it doesn't matter, that I have my encounters. Molly comes back to me. She turns me inside out. I burn, pivot, peak, and then, falling back onto the mattress, can accept the flatness of the scene. Under that bare bulb I can get up and do a charcoal series: just what's available, that basin, that cracked soap with the grime of others in its crevices. I draw the soap-grip. I like ribbing. I like crenellations. Here I don't have to justify a thing. I draw the ribbing as if I have lived my life in ribs. I draw the dust-compacted muslin, veiling the glare. I draw solid the passing cloud. I prepare your return, and this time it's you, Asif, back for another chance, something to erase the father with the fist, something for the dark boy I first knew, rigid with social passion, nerves arcing with that urgency to change the world. I now can be Mother Comfort, even Sweet Miss Oblivion, and take you in. The force of imagining you takes me in, Asif, and you begin to reinvent me.

Many times, I've done it. I close my eyes, stab the map, and take myself to the town closest to the mark to wait. I book into the hotel closest to the railway to begin the vigil: I am holed in for you.

The mildewed poverty of this room strikes home. Of course this is what I want. The mildew gives some sort of presence to the waste of desire. The unnameable is here in the bubbling rust around the tap base, in the fungal culture at the trim, in the tile grout, in the oval of the coir mat — need I go on? — in the wall-to-wall heartlessness of this place. Yeah, I dimly see what I've become, the slow effects of time poisoning me, even as I draw, in this return to descriptive clutter, stroke-stroke-stroke, the exhaustive mania of my strokes, *oh, the fatigue of contingency, oh, the old existential nausea. Why not go for a photo? What redundant gestures*! the voices say. I turn on the TV and I draw very fast to put that moving image in.

The room is literally sealed, I realise, and I begin to panic. I've always been a child of draughts, of moving air. Trying the window, I know I have to draw the line. This has to be the last time I try to bring anything back, to recover from this repetition. Okay, the window is painted in. Let the paint be wrinkled like archaic milk. Let me resist the pressure of the swollen breast to occupy me: oh Karim, my starved baby.

He's projectile vomiting, I said to the doctor.

Your marriage?

My marriage isn't working. Well, not too good. But it's early days.

Yes, it's early days. The doctor wrinkles his forehead. I've never seen this before on a bald man; expected rather the wrinkles to diminish in amplitude as water ripples do, spreading, and to die discreetly but no, the wrinkles stop abruptly just like that, in a skin desert, flat as Formica, as if he's wearing a rubber mask or as if the head, the dome, is in some alien material, grafted so tight there can be no movement. So I think, fuck, I've come all the way to Bunbury to remember that doctor's forehead.

He presses Karim's little stomach. It's hard, he says. He's not getting enough; he's been gulping air. Dr. Roberts takes out a fine-liner from his neat little desk organiser and writes in blue across the card. *Baby starved*.

Look, there are excellent formulae, like S22. You take this to the chemist. Come back and the nurse will show you how to mix it. With a bottle we can measure how much bubby is getting but with the old breast, who knows? So dry your eyes, my dear. Eh, little dark eyes, he says poking Karim's cheek, you've got your mamma's dark eyes, that's a lusty howl! What did I say — he's got a healthy hunger.

A tear-blind mute, I hand over to the chemist the scrawled list.

Bottles, how many? And Milton to sterilise the bottles?

What about boiling water?

Suit yourself but we'd recommend the Milton. Teats? Now we have these new designs in.

They are big, so bulbous you'd think they'd gag a baby.

How many? How many do you need?

I'd advise about four. You can always do with spares. Sometimes the little buggers nip them. When they get teeth.

Back in the surgery the nurses rock him, hand me tissues, prepare the bottle. See what a power sucker! they say. What a champion! He'll be stacking on the weight in no time.

I catch the bus, stroller hooked up on the back, and Karim projectile vomits the wonder mixture over the bus seat. I mop up with tissues as best I can. Asif is coming up from the train as I wheel Karim towards home from Cambridge Street.

Qu'est-ce qu'il t'a dit, le toubib? What did the doctor say?

I can't answer.

What did that doctor say?

I crumple, throat closes.

Come on!

He says I should bottle-feed him, I blubber. I know by Asif's eyes he finds me ugly. He puts down his briefcase and tries to pluck Karim from the stroller. He hasn't undone the security harness. Even through my tears, even in my sleep I can do that. He raises him, studies his upside-down baby under the rolling clouds. You should be glad for him, he says. You're crying for yourself!

I hope Karim spews into his laughing face.

Now your papa can feed you too!

Back in the kitchen he blinks at the tiny instructions. We've got to take a scientific approach. It's all about ratios, see.

Asif, what if …

Uh?

What if that Doctor Roberts is just disgusted by women having milk?

That's crazy. He wouldn't have suggested the mixture if he thought Karim was getting enough.

By the next day my breasts are huge. Massive knots are networking their poker-hot pain. The slightest jolt, even the shifting texture of the sheet on them, makes me want to howl. Look, Asif, you still reckon I had no milk?

That's probably the glands or something.

The glands or something. And the tears well again. I can't tell him I don't think I can stand up. They are so heavy I'll fall on my face. Through the tears I laugh.

What's it now? he says. He is irritated. I would like to punch him.

I'll have to buy a couple of hammocks today.

What for?

For these.

Well. I have to go to work now. Late already for the train. I'm sorry. He strokes my face.

Sorry, why?

Sorry I was harsh, I … I've got to finish that scholarship application or I'm out, man. All that study just to be a button-pusher and instrument-reader.

And he goes to plant his head on my swollen breast so that I bellow.

So-rry!

Stamp, stamp, stamp. The front door slams.

I give way to a luxury of weeping. He wants me free to nurse him.

And sure, I can see now that this is what you've become,

Asif, you've become my child. It's I who have to endure your orphanage. I lost my sense of mothering in you.

So, the sash window is opaque with dust. It's long since been painted into its frame and on the sill there are puddles of paint wrinkled like archaic milk. Outside I try for the sense of the glaringly lit provincial street. Provincial is a word resisting Australian applications. Why do I try for your world outside then? Last time I did this was in a depressed fringe wheatbelt town. Beyond that set I wanted acres of albino stubble, and I'm afraid, beyond those, the simplicity of ruined land, the frozen dance of whitened trees, the craze of saltpan fissures. I've made a desert of your absence.

And now this last time, I've made the town coastal, uneasily spreading towards city status, but retaining the slow time of country town in the main street, a yawn at the centre. I've made it Bunbury. How's that for a heartless name?

Behind the flyblown and insecticidally greased windows I have planted a milk bar, a run down co-op grocery, an uncertain delicatessen, as your French brothers say. I put permanence into the cupcakes with their china-hard caps of icing. I set time in the terrazzo cross-section of brawn, in the jars of lollies, filling them all with Poached Eggs.

There's a street-long queue for *Ghostbusters III*, and further on, a caryard full of '70s Buicks, Chryslers and Cadillacs is still open. The salesman is leaning against a white tail fin, depressed, despite the claims of his shiny suit and the comfort of the coffee mug which he hugs to his chest. He'll want to ask me out. I know this. It's not

. . ..

vanity, or fancy, or the desire for anything to happen; it's as inevitable as breathing. He'll sniff out my old habit of despair, and convert it to his purpose. Despair is not a mood. With me it's become a passivity so accomplished it's indistinguishable from dynamic potential. You see, nothing is a risk anymore. This is what might have made a terrorist of me, Asif.

Beyond all this I can feel the amazing sea. I imagine in my blood its rhythmic scope but will do nothing about getting there. I am still at the window sealed in its frame by the paint. To be truthful, I'd be tricked by the deflected sea-breeze and would walk in the wrong direction. I'm not street-wise, Asif. Unlike you, I can't boast that I've swallowed and metabolised the map. But I remember things. I store all your phrases until I believe they're mine. I almost feel I've made you up.

I can't get out of this sealed room in memory either. If I took a photograph of this room, I'd make sure it was windowless by angling the camera at the skirting boards. Afterwards I'd be glad of the camera's tilt, cocky or drunk, to restore a sense of a mind still there, if awry. Claustrophobia, the photograph might say, is about being forever without a larger frame of reference. And yet, the camera's tilt, cocky, or drunk, also might say I had a chance of breaking out. Later in another town, this image might come to me on a postcard and I'd be crouching in a sealed room eyeing a puddle of paint set like archaic milk on the sill. I'd remember that then I'd been relatively jaunty in my attempts to recapture you. Greetings from Exville, the postmark might say. What a poverty-stricken adventurer I am these days. Is this what happens on the brink of middle-age? But the script would be yours and

I'd see that the miracle had worked. Join me, for old times' sake, for pool?

The *Ghostbusters* queue shuffles its feet — less of them now. The pool players are as quiet and suspenseful as statues: they are fibreglass, pop art statues. They lack the solemnity of, say, granite. Their gestures hang in such a way that I'm not sure anymore from where the cue for them to move will come, in whose gaze they're caught.

Join me for pool, you write, or is that your writing? Why not this last gamble? I will wear Evie's long gloves, the one thing I've kept from her but I'll have them unbuttoned at the wrists, like a woman smoker from the '50s, so that these empty cloth hands dangle beside my own, which, by contrast, become more or less determined. I will wonder if there is any sense in unpacking my cardboard suitcase. It will contain my drawing block, my charcoal, a packet of tampons, a spare pair of jeans, and underpants. I might go into the haberdashery opposite for clothes. From the window I can make out a dummy dressed in a tartan nightie. Each woman in the town will have seen herself inside or out of that nightie, to the point where I'd take on the weight of considerable fantasy in slipping it on. This is a nightie Odette once had. But you wouldn't know that. I'm cruising backwards.

I still resist resolution. I suppose it is what keeps me alive, resisting resolution. While I want this time to believe absolutely in the possibility of our reunion, I must still leave all the options open. I will refuse the brief thrill of the slick twist even as a development, let alone an ending. I will not get caught in any final gesture. I will leave no trail, no hieroglyph dying in the mirror. I will leave the slate clean, an empty register. I will wipe the memory of all that time waiting for you and hiding from them. The aeroplane which took you will be just a silver hyphen. There will be a few dispersed markings in the sky, itself a Giotto blue, as powdery as the skies of failing memory. As far they are concerned, neither of us will have been.

Then I am tempted not to try the pool tables. Anyhow, the time, the day, when? I must learn to inhabit this room at zero-degree desire and to fade to grainy grey along with my sense of its furnishings. The clunking commerce of the streets, the riffs of traffic, the kebabs on roadside braziers, the cool darkness of winebars will not draw me out. That I might have been something, even an effective Webworker beyond the pretension of all that performance, will no longer taunt me. I will become one with my own perduring motif: no development in space or time unless I can count the fading of intensity and the fraying of edges. I will be a motif discharged of any emblematic value.

Like a simile left yawning for its second term I will be ...

Cruising Backwards

In other places they might say hibernate. Well, I have been aestivating. I hide from the heat that draws other people out into air-conditioned cinemas and shopping centres and libraries, or evenings on the beaches. Instead of that boiling little cottage with its ugly striped carpet I'd have given you something like the place Lou and Roly have built, empty except for the light eddying through, green-white, butter-yellow, violet, and then a gallery of frames opening onto the valley with its vertical timber: wandoo, jarrah, marri — and the sense of the stream in the cleft, of its glassy veil over the granite. Then we might have had somewhere to begin. Instead you got locked into the timetable here, and you found a suit that looked, in the '80s way, half-serious, in crumpled cotton, the colour of brown rice, and you waited for buses in desolate streets, asking me every day, where is the street life in this place? Where are the streets? There are only roads here, always between somewhere and somewhere, never being anywhere. In the little research assistant job Maurice strung together with his grant money you became the Errand Boy Friday, *je suis la bonne à tout faire ici*, you complained. And I hated you for your wild resistance because it was my friend's connection that had helped you provide us all with bread and shelter. Look, give me three months, I said, and you can be the house husband, I can bring in the money.

This you told everyone: After three months, Tom-Tom's taking over.

It was having to be the regular father performing the suburban routines, of course, that was the real culture shock. We could move back into Maeve's place, you said. You said it was just a verbal thing, a moral understanding, that I had a right too, that the least I was entitled to was to use a parcel of that land. Ten hectares, after all. We could grow our own stuff, you said. At least we'd subsist away from the shit.

We could, we could, but I'm not about to push my way in. They want Maeve's cottage to be kept empty; for Maeve's sake, anyhow. And to build there we'd have to negotiate that.

Maybe I just forgot you'd had enough of identifying with stinking third class compartments and landlessness yourself. I should've talked it through. Personally I'd get much more out of living with Millie and Joe than in this *petit bourgeois* isolation, you said. You did say that. Maybe you just wanted to live the commune romance, of the disinherited ones together, and in my meanness I twisted that into cupidity.

There's plenty of space there, you said. We wouldn't have

to live on top of anyone. Yet, when we went back to Banksiafold and I fell into their arms and the old ways of taking time and quietly talking and listening with our whole bodies I realised how hooked you'd already become on European time. You were jealous of this bonding we had in silence as much as in our talk.

Yeah, I said, thinking I'm *vache* I'm *veule*. It's maybe something we could do, later. We'd need to save up the money for the building, though.

Tom-Tom, *mon amour*, you said, you forget I have practical skills. I can build us an ergonomic house, low energy, solar-powered, the works, with just the old wood and stuff lying around.

Solar cells must cost something.

There are ways, I'm a *bricoleur*, remember.

Yes, my dear engineer, I quite forgot you have practical skills I said, looking at the dysfunctional machines around us, the TV whose interior had gobbled the on and off switch, the dismantled cassette player, the wobbly leg on the safety cot. Then, remembering your first fervour to make the little house livable for us, I saw how cruel I'd become.

And now the wildness in your eye, the heat of your thighs, the dance of your sentences are so far away. You've become that simplified stranger again and all I can do is the fictions of approach. But even at the beginning, through the maze of performed looks and gestures, it was as if we kept inaugurating the first approach. Not knowing you, not knowing the Spider, gave the pang through all the desiring ducts of my body. Wanting to keep you strange, to maintain that sense of danger, I

271

should have never entered the clotted detail of familiarity with you.

Of course, Lube said, getting into her tutorial mode, by definition, passion feeds on lack of knowledge; passion, she said, is the tension between prolonging the hunger for knowledge and the need to devour the strangeness of the other until you are stretched to the limit, turning strangeness to sameness, glutted, and then, becoming its object, your passion collapses back on itself. There is simply no more space. This is why, she said, my dear Tom-Tom, passion is not a solution.

After you'd left, of course, what was left unsaid between us set inside me like cement. I guess it's what they call depression. I say: Doctor, I feel as if I'm full of cement. Not just bottom of the harbour in cement boots. Like I'm so heavy I'll never be able to move again.

Some Fissures

Some fissures cast shadows as if you could fall forever. I tell myself I have to stop this head-tripping, that I must be in the situation. I feel the cracked vinyl of the seat in front of me. Asif has chosen to sit close by. Sometimes when their questions come too quickly, he turns back to me in an appeal for translation. His confusion shines from his eyes: *What are they saying? Help me!* He has lost weight: he must have been living on fruit and nuts in these past weeks. His hair flashes metallically. Has he discovered the conditioner I left behind, on the edge of the clawed bath? The mice multiplied under it to the point where we didn't dare grope for lost objects. How many cakes of soap that shot from the hand when we showered are still there with toothpaste caps, balls of hair and fluff and old combs?

On his arrival in this country he said: These people speak like Donald Duck. I laughed along with him, then. Now, with the return of my own accent, I've become a Donald Duck for him too. Stop shrieking at me in your ugly accent, he said, when I used my Australian to shock him at the sudden distance between us.

But now it's as if all the work of hatred has to be begun again, this time slowly, through reason. The magistrate keeps probing our memories of that summer day. He has tired little pink-rimmed eyes that flicker, and swim up big to the lenses as he adjusts his glasses.

The weatherboard and iron house with its midget rooms had cooked to the point where we could smell the paint, the exhalations from the acrylic carpet. We had stripped Karim, who was howling red, and bathed him again and again in cool water. The fan staggered through its circuit. Asif's friends from Marseille called by. He served them blackberry syrup. What we called cordial. These grown boys did not find this strange. She is a *bourgeoise*, in the final analysis, I heard him say. Still, what do you expect? She's always had it pretty comfortable, despite, you know, what she likes people to think.

I went back to the washing machine. He was posturing before them: Her grandmother left a 10 hectare property that must be worth quite a bit, well to her and her Aboriginal friends. We might be able to build there later. The land is bound to appreciate pretty quick. It's bordering where the Freeway South is marked for extension. And a new campus of the Institute is being established there. Yeah, if we hang on a few years we'll all be laughing. I'd say in five years it'd be worth a cool ten million.

This was wrong, it banged in my head. This was ridiculous. Now when it suited him, he was able to wear ownership. Like that's what he was, joint-owner. The twin-tub danced on the cement. The load in the spin-dry was unbalanced. It was going to take five loads to get through the nappies. *Bourgeoise, Manic Cleaner, Health Food*

Shopper, Nappy-soaker, Bourgeoise. What would Molly say about me now? We'd had some fun back then. Already it seemed so distant. We never laughed these days. He called out: Couldn't you turn that off, we're trying to talk?

I wrenched out the plug. The old twin-tub danced itself out on the cement.

From the white-anted boards of the front verandah the day opened like a saucer, rimmed with silence, ringing with it. The toy facades of the houses opposite were smugly composed with their colour combinations: violet, ochre, with a touch of olive green, behind their neatly scalloped neo-colonial picket fences. Around me there was mission brown peeling along the cracked grain and underneath, tan, whose chips in turn showed lime green. A cool ten million, my foot. Maybe he was speaking francs. He knew perfectly well that Maeve had wanted it to go to Millie and Joe and the kids. He'd respected that. He was just trying to act important for these friends. The outrage of his words occupied me almost pleasurably, detonating through my blood. With the adrenalin rush I felt my legs could do a kilometre at a sprint, that my hands could hurl projectiles, bring down the axe to cleave rock-hard wood. Yet there they dangled, trembling between my knees. At least it was quiet now. What had I yelled back at him? Not that he would have understood it: Do your own fucking washing then, you posturing bastard. It was pathetic, really. The tree ferns needed watering, frond after frond had coiled up brown. We needed some shade cloth: not expensive; now that would make a difference. We would have room to spread out in the heat, not be so much on top of each another. He was too big for those tiny rooms and when Karim started screaming it became impossible. No wonder, in caravans and trailer houses, once unemployment and booze were stirred in, people exploded. I wished Karim would wake up; I needed to hold him to me against all that other stuff.

The rest tears me from language even now. It is so present, so close, it takes my breath away. I can only do it in a flickering footage, black-and-white, then with the colours brought in from a child's palette. A hand, long-fingered, palm tensed to cement hardness, comes slowly, slowly, with the pace of Sunday padding feet up the hall, through the darkness of the sun-blind house, is paused momentarily at the threshold by the extravagance of the glare. Another hand hardens ready at the sight of the crepe cotton back, the henna-red hair. Blue sky gathers around two fists. Blue air claps on scribbled red, and again, again. Later, after words: What was that you yelled in front of my visitors? Say it again! A tap is turned fully on, a hose snakes and rears. See it shooting white in peripheral vision. Don't turn head because this might stoke his fury ... There's no snaking now; he's grabbed it at the nozzle. The moment stretches for analysis and yet is blindingly fast. The first rush is hot, hot. Lucky he didn't direct it straightaway, or I would have taken the scalding on the neck. The hose has been in the sun for hours: can see its coils scorched ginger into the grass. This branding persists behind my eyes for all the days that follow. Now the jet which strikes my cheek comes cool, is superbly cool, but the tenacity of its aim builds fear, not for what is happening now but that he should apply such manic concentration to the task.

I'm trying to make you see reason, he is bellowing.

A train rushes past. Those commuters will see something like a picnic scene. Tomfoolery! Heatwave brings on this silly behaviour in adults. A window opens up in which I see him linking together ever more improbable episodes, coupling truck after truck, into a killing machine for all that we are have been and might have been.

Now we are both on trial. We can still bolt out of the room, break through the records these people are taking. If you could just bury your head in my arms. But we are already so far apart. The rows of seats between us are infinite. Now you are becoming *him*, someone away from the reach of anything I might say, already on the other side of the glass, bound for the other side of the world.

I am at the fault line now, the slipping edge. I watch his back for clues as he rises to answer their questions. I know that back better than my own, naturally.

Are you contesting your wife's custody?

The voice gurgles in his throat. He is going to win them with his tears: No, she is better for that than me. She will look well after The Baby Karim.

The way he says it gives Karim such dignity, like the Christ Child already an adult, cast in Future Time Sacred on the Madonna's lap.

Here's the great radical standing to attention in their family court. I have to think *enemy*, to let hatred fuel itself. Those beautiful dark hands hanging inert, they hit me, on these cheeks, my cheeks, wet-slapping.

I wonder how much of me has been lost in the shift at the centre of that implacably blue afternoon.

The sky towers above the toy houses in toy street, Leederville. When we signed the deal with the agency I thought something was wrong with the name apart from the *ville* that made me vaguely sick with its hybrid claim, like croissants with bacon. Now it comes to me: I've put myself in Leda's town! The fists come with a roar like those terrible wings beating, a killer bird shadowing my body and all of toytown and beyond, the parks and the skyscraper cluster, shadowing the waters, bearing down huge as buildings, giving Swan River, wide and blue, an awful logic to its name and through this inevitability, destiny taking up residence in potential, it has the stagnancy of death. Out of the blue I taste the toxic sludge.

But here he is, waiting in the foyer of the building after the custody hearing.

I liked your lawyer, he says. She's a strong talker. Pity we couldn't have enlisted someone like her for the *Centre Social*. Eh! What about a drink, Tom-Tom?

His voice is affectionate, softer. What has happened to my hatred? That reservoir of concentrated bile? My head lurches. I see in his offer of a drink the peach colours of the rendered wall through the workshop window when first his outline came into focus.

No I do not contest for her to look after the baby. She is better for that than me, he was saying through his sobs.

Of course he has these resources of charm to draw on, especially now. See, *meek as a lamb*, and modest: with his beauty Caravaggio could make him pose bare-torsoed for an allegory of Remorse. Ah, the black pooling in his eyes. Sackcloth at the loins, ashen tinge to the skin providing the right note of poignancy.

Just a few minutes ago I had said to the magistrate: He

directed the scalding hose on me. Yes punches, slaps. What? How many? About ten.

On a scale of one to ten, how hard would you say these … punches and slaps were?

My God, what do other women cop?

On a scale 1 to 10, if 10 were lethal, I'd say they would have been 2 or 3. But they hurt!

Were stitches necessary?

No. Bruising, yes. Swelling. What? Oh, ten days? And later he swung the bassinette with Karim in it. Yes, he would've been two months at the time and it, yes I mean the bassinette, sailed through the air and slid across the floor. I think that under stress he can't control his violence. That sounded like an apology for him so I added: I'm scared for my baby.

After such a hearing I can hardly go off with the enemy. I am childish enough to glance over my shoulder to see if anyone is watching us.

Now I am back at Banksiafold, washing up, thinking about the bills I have to juggle. At least in Maeve's old cottage, there's no rent to worry about. Like a bad joke from childhood, his face comes in a rush to the window above the sink. His mouth is a wound against the dark.

Leave. Leave me alone.

We share a son, he says. In case you've forgotten. His voice is locked in his throat.

Leave me alone. How can you after what you've done?

He must have been watching for Millie and Joe to go out. I wonder if he's come armed. He's handled guns before, after all, or is that what he said in the performance? I can't think it through. My legs are shaking uncontrollably. Somehow I manage to stab 000 into the phone. The intoxication of betrayal calms me a little; the moment expands around me. Outside is silent: only the crunching of sheoak branches on the roof. I wonder where he could be posted. Outside Karim's room? I foresee a gun poised on the open hopper window. He'd be able to unbutton the flyscreen. The screen is gaping there, anyway. Horror seizes me with the clarity of the vision. I crawl across the kitchen, through the fern room. Somewhere from across the patio his voice comes, shaping the darkness: *I could kill you both. I should, you know, because it's no life for a child without a father. You want to repeat your own story. You want to condemn him to the same. I will not have it.*

The awful measure of his voice. This is the dose of vitriol from what they call passion. Crimes of passion.

Through Karim's window I see the police lights lurch against the trees. There are muffled voices, snatched by the wind. Someone says: Ah fuck, not another ... Was it *wog*, he said? No, he couldn't have. After an age they knock. They look pleasant enough, but exhausted. They sigh: We're not keen on coming to domestics, you know. The best we can do is get this poor fella into the van and take him home. He's hardly dangerous. See: meek as a lamb. He said something about Gandhi. Hunger strike. We told him to go on a diet at his own place, if that's what he wants. Quite a popular method I gather with some of those protesters in Europe. Locking themselves up in churches!

Now in the main street, I turn to him. I have to stop the

tears. They must stand, not spill: No, Asif. I can't take a drink with you. We can't go back there. I can feel him watching without protest as I head for the bus. His pulse beats in my head. You both wear your *farouche*, Choiseuil said. It throbs in my arms, tugs at my back. I have to drag myself out of its influence. We are not yet in our separate landscapes. We could return our lives to the same level, go back to that Sunday afternoon when the horror started and simply miss the cue. Or I could simply turn and catch up with him again.

There is nothing inevitable about the little weatherboard house in Leederville which we settled on; it only seems so now. We'd been house hunting for weeks. Lou took time out Saturday afternoons and Sundays to check out with us terrace houses as cool as cellars, so dark at the height of day that the real estate agent had all electric lights blazing, cottages overgrown with creeper, overrun by rats, judging by the nibbled paper lining cupboards and the size of the black droppings, and blank-facaded sensible houses in which everything was pristine and heartless. We signed for a dilapidated mansion in East Perth, fast-forwarding through renovations, tearing down the metal awnings, restoring the planks of the rotten verandah, gutting the sordid kitchen, ignoring the giant mosquitoes settling on our arms because of the expanse of river from the back, beyond the trotting stadium, the bus depot and the predatory WACA light towers. Asif liked the industrial shapes and I swallowed my misgivings, glad to have that episode rewritten. I decided, yes, I liked the tension between those geometric shapes, the crouching, round-shouldered bushes, and then, the expanse of silver-lilac water, creeping like seersucker in the breeze. For once we were telling the same story, rehearsing changing light and colour, on surfaces, through volumes, as we moved with the rhythm of days together, tearing up carpet, freeing living space by ripping out this partition, or that vinyl bar in the corner. Lou sobered us up that night, scratching at her mosquito bites, reminding us that with rented places, it was even a struggle to apply a lick of paint, to hang a picture, let alone, she said, making structural changes. And if Asif was working, and I was looking after a newborn baby, how were we ever going to do it all? All our money would go fixing up someone else's place, and then, when they saw the improvements, they'd put it on the market and tip us out. Look, I don't want to be a wet blanket, she said, but I can't see a baby doing too well there, with those cracks in the walls, the dust, the mosquitoes. She took it on herself to speak to the agent and by some sort of diplomatic lie, recovered for us our bond and advance rent.

Behind my little frame on the front step of the Leederville cottage, another memory perambulates, taking the broken cement slabs among the tufted buffalo, between the picket fence and the side of the house to the old garage, tucked behind. Outside, it doesn't promise much, except that new hardboard panels have been attached to the front doors, and painted a smoky olive.

In the weeks before Karim's birth, Asif retreated here for hours at a time. He'd set himself up a carpenter's workshop, and though he'd never done woodwork before, he was a driven perfectionist working with the hired tools, the plane, the sanders, the saws. He said it was for some storage shelving. If I came to have a peep, he'd steer me away; it was to be a surprise. I was busy with enamel paints, cobalt, lime yellow, red, and was picking out rungs, panels, and knobs on the nursery furniture: a rocking cradle, to start with, a cot, a chest of drawers, a changing table. Millie and Joe must have fossicked through every swapmeet and garage sale in the metropolitan area to find us these treasures.

I've come to a critical point, he said. I need some advice. He was smiling broadly in his sleeveless shirt, great rings of sweat under his armpits. He smelled of estapol.

Look at you, paint-splattered Mama, he said, stroking my face, fingering my hair.

On my arms, like a fairy confetti, was a myriad of paint droplets.

He made me shut my eyes as he hooked my fingers and led me to the garage. His thudding heart: it was there in his slightest touch. The first thing I saw was the buttery light pouring in from the roof, where he'd replaced a panel of metal by a perspex sheet. He'd finished the interior with gyprock, which he'd painted cream. The roof was lined with silver wadding, cushioning between the rafters: *l'insolation* he said, insulation.

I-I-I-solation, I sang him the John Lennon line.

From floor to ceiling on the left side, he'd installed shelving and racks with huge drawers. He moved across solemnly, and like a conjurer, like the hobo I saw that day at the Préfecture fountain in Marseille, he pulled out a drawer. It was full of my pencil drawings; another, of pastels. He'd inserted sheets of tissue between. On the other side he'd propped paintings I hadn't got around to finishing. Aligned, like numbered exhibits, they detailed my failure. Arrested in their earliest impulse, they were paintings that I knew I couldn't finish. He was showing me the evidence of my aborted energy.

When I saw the work you used to do with Millie, I thought of this, he said, his voice trembling.

Oh Asif, Asif, I said, biting my lip.

It was inadequate. It was all I could say.

Now you will paint.

I couldn't stop the wave of my own desolation even as I saw his pleasure abating.

You don't like it.

I love it. It's the most beautiful thing. It's ...

Well, all you need to say is that you're pleased.

Then I said a terrible thing. I said, hoarsely: I just can't paint on command.

Any retreat, once those words were out, was useless.

I mean, I don't know with the baby coming, and all that.

He took off down the side of the house.

I thought of the way he'd made love to me on the mattress in the front room the night before. So delicate, so fearful of applying any pressure, he had almost telepathically hovered. He had sobbed into my hair as he came, outside me, saying, *mon amour, mon amour,* I don't want to take up any baby space. Now, as I crouched there in my paint-splattered shirt, our baby turned inside me, pushed out an elbow, a knee.

The strawberry Celtic faces above the suits blur past me.

St Georges Terrace is a wind tunnel on this March day. I ache to swing back to him, to see his eyelids working like a speed shutter, to see his sun-black skin, the cutting blaze of his teeth. He has always been quick to soften if I forgive. These men are mice compared with him. These men are scalded mice in their business suits.

Small Prints for a Man

I've worked all day in the sun, clearing the dry grass and my legs are unevenly burnt, radiating still past midnight. I've got used to having them around again and with Joe and Millie and all gone to the funeral in Narrogin the quietness is getting to me. It's having a baby who doesn't talk yet that brings the solitude home, once night settles and the kitchen sink is clear and the broom in its little slot next to the fridge. If only Millie were here. I want hands laid on me, as undemanding as a dream mother's, as cool as cucumbers. Want to be inside a cucumber. And lying here, I want to bring him back. As much as the thought shocks me I yield to its undertow, as if the bad things hadn't happened. I tell myself it's the fact that I see him staring out through Karim's eyes, that I feel Asif's passion in the way my baby clings. I can say our baby no more.

I robbed him of something other than Karim, before Karim: brought him back here like a prize, an exotic, to show off.

The altar of the past.

There's no harm in drawing; like all my desire has retreated into this. If you could see me in my domesticity, Asif! Still I can remind myself that for us here, something like putting paint or charcoal on paper is as simple as breathing or singing. It needs no explanation. Millie says, she's here all right. She'll always be around, old Maeve will. When I try to listen to the bush now, I find it harder to get through the fizzing from the high tension cables and the muted rumble of trucks on Armadale Road.

I leave my legs bare, to yield their heat and stroke the paper with the charcoal, cautious, exploratory, then sometimes, as the rhythm comes, savagely. Again and again the squeaky cylinder breaks into splinters: the black shards stay as part of the drawing. Let the fires break out. Let violence be part of it, too. Marvel at my side maintains her pose. Something bold, determined, is emerging. The cat-woman I am drawing is erect like the sacred cats of Egypt. The cat has the permanent energy of the prowler locked in granite. The power of the drawing makes me afraid. I look at the model: I've tapped something there. I've cast her as my old prowler, outside my time. I reach for her, to reassure her with a pat that she remains outside the drawing. There, after all, is fur, with warm blood circulating, muscles relaxed but ready. But there's instant granitic resistance in the muscles. Viper-quick, she breaks from her pose, sinking teeth into my drawing wrist. She dashes growling to the picture window. I see myself now as I've been framed, in horizontal stripes through the angled venetian slats. Well, both of us: the cat in her black fur and me in my burnt skin.

We're the active things in the picture window for whoever's outside. I must compose myself. I must force myself back into the drawing. It is only my tiredness. It's my tiredness that has hallucinated the prowler. I tell myself that she's a nervous cat at the best of times. Biting me was a reasonable reaction.

Again the charcoal strokes the paper and squeaks, shattering its fires. The hair pricking at the back of my neck, the coldness seizing my blood tell me this composure is mad. I must check other windows. Prowlers prowl, I tell myself and there might be a side door left open. Maybe it's Asif come back! Marvel runs growling ahead of me to the front of the house, to another picture window. This one is firmly masked by the closed venetian blind. Throw the verandah light switch and part the slats are the orders I give myself. The lawn again has the sickly green of algae under the electric light. The rest, I'll be able to tell myself in a second's readjustment, is just imagination, pure and simple. What they said at school: overheated imagination.

For the moment I watch, my skin prickling, the slow side-shuffle of the prowler into the mesh of the Baileyana wattle. This one, I tell myself, just happens to have baggy, iron-shiny serge trousers, low in the crotch with a twisted leather belt, which is knotted rather than buckled. The buckle spike must have broken, I take time to think. The shirt is a North American stevedore's flannel, green-checked, not a real tartan. I have one something like it. The venetian slats snap together and only now the question shakes me: Is it the prowler who has drawn the cat? Has the crochet of shadows, travelling out from the trees like the work of demented spiders, found its channel in my drawing?

The next day I find the footprints. They are small prints for a man. The sandals must have been soled with tyre tread. Hippie artisans used to fashion sandals like this with bits of Michelin tyre to last. I had a pair at some stage. I could take moulds of the prints between the bushes. Durable sandals, durable prints.

Keyhole on Forty

The sky is sped up today: great clouds blossom at the window and are whipped away. I watch them from the couch. I plot my shape like Magritte's keyhole figure against the sky, becoming atmospherically negotiable, fluidly blue. I have to forget the face I saw in the bathroom mirror, between the steam and the canker-eaten silvering, staring back at me, hard-eyed and forty. Forty! Here where no one gives a stuff for history, people celebrate the turn of every decade of their lives, throwing themselves big parties. The big four-O, they say; the big five-O.

Looking at my notebooks scoured with crossings-out, Lou Barb said: Why do you treat all your ideas like inopportune salesmen, selling religion through the screen door? Slam!

Ha, I like the simile, Lube. Well, I laughed, I don't like their suits and their scrubbed faces. Their eagerness embarrasses me.

Seriously, Tom-Tom, what is *wrong* with eager?

I don't like their concerted friendliness, their *intentional* enthusiasm. I feel had in advance. From then on, it's like colouring in.

Oh, she goes, leaning into me, you're the one who's hard to get!

She's right. I need to get out, get challenged, get away from the cling-wrap ghosts, the too-personal smell. Been living in these bedclothes too long.

She's at the door, Destiny, my loud-voiced Havana. It's only struck me now, the downward curve I've marked with those names: first there was Marvel and now there's Destiny. She yells and yells like an old baby recorded on 78. I cling stubbornly to my keyhole self; let me use that aperture. I know the rebuke in the lime eyes of Destiny. Go away. Let me curl up round in my baby fat. Keyhole and cumulus have gone, wind-whipped. I am left with intense cerulean, quite sufficient without me.

Maurice deals with the world. Maurice consults with ministers. Gives them statistics on land degradation, sea grass depletion, carbon-fuel emissions. Every evening he has earned his world-weariness, unlike me.

Those first blood passions are now just a faint echo in the bone. At night, when I could write, I stifle with drink the echo I need to amplify. Now I'm looking at forty, I answer no mail, have forsaken Millie, Joe, Josie, and Zak, and even missed Josie's boy, Little Joe's growing up. Like Chekhov's Grigory in 'Grief' I move into the whiteness, with behind me the whiteness, and what is this dull thud-thud where memory should have been? It is like his dead wife's head banging, banging on the frozen ground. I can't name the source any more or where I lost it, cannot blame it on that stranger, Asif, who wrote his anger into my flesh. I have been — what is it? Ten years with Restorative Maurice. A decade has gone between the scrawled first lines of my story and these aborted fragments, always the same story returning, returning. Tom-Tom, Maurice says, when I chuck my notebook down, why don't you just let go for a bit?

He's exasperated of course. Why don't I do something to pull myself out of this hole, that's what he'd say if kindness didn't prevent him. Kindness!

I've looked into you since, Asif, in those photos Karim brought back and I can tell from your unshaven, slightly jaundiced face and your tufted eyebrows that you're not in my story any more. I felt scandalised, my memory betrayed, to see the white already stringing the blackness of your hair. I sent Karim to you and you gave him a memory of a father with a fist. The fist came down on the table when he wouldn't eat your new wife's cooking. The palm came down on his little eight-year-old shoulder when he let fly a volley of farts. It came down again when he said, two hours away from the village where you'd taken him to lunch, oh-oh I left my coat in that restaurant and your acquiescent wife, who bears it all stoically, said nothing, not a murmur of protest. One must not interfere with the transfer of masculinity, something like that? No, Asif, you have to take leave of my story.

But back in those first days! With the clean lines, the skin lit from inside. Your eyes. Staggeringly white whites. The teeth, like a smile hired for toothpaste ads: *look, all without orthodontistry! Macleans employs me without any touching up.*

Your body was tightly sprung, with that long stride always ready to work itself up. Though work in Perth was for you more of an exile than any of us conjured in Choiseuil's workshop, you found your exuberance again each evening coming back to Karim and me. Sometimes, to escape the heat and watch for your return up from the railway line, I'd sit on the front porch with the little one propped on my lap, laughing at the shivering leaves of the *Ficus benjamina*. Shopping in one hand, briefcase in the other, you'd quicken your pace, lifting your feet, a fluid, cruising run, letting your long hair fly until you were there, with me, cradling Karim with our bodies. Of course I haven't been able to kick you out of my story.

Look at him, you said, when he was still the baby son you claimed: He will be a swimmer, no? There he was, at ten weeks, gurgling in the tub, his black attentive eyes on your face, then my face, his smile flickering, his little hands opening and closing like flowers alongside his head, his toes curling through the suds.

Arreugh, arreugh, he said. Arreugh.

Putain, you said, *il parle deja*! He said *heureux*; he said he's happy! You threw back your head and roared with delight.

And here I am immobilised at forty. Where did I lose it? The will to claim my life? It's like every branch declares itself a support for the noose, every freeway bend with a pole something to drive into. I must stop living posthumously.

Abscess

So how come we don't get to see the Supergnat for ourselves?

Zak's teasing had an edge to it, all the same, that I could connect with. It all sounded too good, like this Nat wanted a ride on what was already happening for Josie's music.

Yeah, I said, what's the matter with the Supergnat? Is his sound sound or does the Gnat just natter?

Does it matter?

If the Gnat has nits or not?

If I give you the wool, Josie, will you knit a Gnat for me?

Ah fuck off, why doncha?

Zak poked his head around the kitchen door to put in one last shot: Knit-Gnat! he laughed and ducked her balled serviette.

Nat had come up to Josie after her gig at the Fly By Night.

He offered himself as her agent, manager, sound engineer, producer — everything to get her launched; he'd help her cut a demo tape, get her a recording contract, secure more gigs for her.

Physically, he looked almost languid: long and skinny; what they call an ectomorph. I had to concede that he seemed attentive, even sensitive. His limpid grey eyes watched us from under an overhang of brow and his ears were like fine bone china. As he listened he'd gather back his straight, ash-blond hair in a ponytail, then let it slide back down in slippery drapes around his face. Often his eyes were in shadow, so it was hard to read his expression. In small talk with adults he gave laconic a new meaning. He was a real miser with words, but he had a way with Karim from the start, a sort of clowning ease, and seemed happy to squat for an hour at a time on the floor making crazy little Lego machines, with levers and pulleys, and multiple trailers. For Karim it didn't matter: four-wheel drives, front-end loaders, bobcats, ditch witches, mobile cranes — all became racing cars for him. He started with spluttering engine noises, gave it the choke, roared it into life, zipped through the gears and reached the high rev zone before relaxing into a sort of overdrive purr as he pushed their mobile crane under the kitchen table, darted between the chair legs, and entered the long stretch to the stove. Nat sat on at the table.

Still, I supposed he didn't need to state his reason for hanging around the kitchen. He picked up Adrienne Rich's *Time's Power*, which I'd left face down on the table. He was leafing through it while I was chopping up parsley and garlic for a marinara. I was raw-nerved and irritable and told myself it was premenstrual tension, nothing to do with Karim's sound effects, or with Nat's lingering. I could have used the knife tip as a fulcrum, a pivot for the blade's dance, taking it through a polite arc and back. I considered this but kept up my routine, alternately chopping, bringing the sharp edge down in a staccato ra-ta-ta, and slapping the blade flat, so that the parsley was bleeding green into the juiced garlic fibre. I paused to concentrate on the crackle of the pages as he glanced through them, letting my nerves amplify the noise, feeding my toxic state. He was relaxed into the shapes of Maeve's kitchen, pelvis to the edge of the chair his skinny legs sprawled out. I don't know where it came from, but when he looked up from the book with his clear, rather beautiful grey eyes, I said: This bothering you?

N-nup. But maybe I'll go and join Josie. He stayed seated, still holding the book. If it's okay by you, he said. He put some weight into those pauses.

Sure, I said. I thought: I can play this game. I can make a big, discomforting pause too. Then I said: Why not … I shrugged my shoulders: Whatever. That relaxed me a little.

I don't think Josie was aware. She was chilling out, listening to something muted and ambient on the CD, but then I picked up the thud of the base seismically through my calf muscles and knew she was playing it for him.

He didn't leave that night. He was there on the verandah of Millie's cottage the next afternoon, and the morning after that. I saw him casting a huge shadow, over the glittering, clodded earth, digging up a vegetable plot. He questioned my using native mulch for the tomatoes; whether I didn't think it might be too acidic. A week or so later he arrived in a panel van full of boxes.

When it came to music he wasn't laconic; he talked at a clipping pace. He was firing off about the sort of material Josie needed to work up in gigs in preparation for the demo. He looked across at me. What we're aiming at, he said, is a cross-over audience. Reggae, country, blues, he said. He was suggesting all sorts of arrangements. He had a tenor saxophonist in mind and a mate on bass. He also knew a good percussionist.

I saw how he managed himself while the rest of us were getting more or less pissed. Josie was looking solemn and blurred and the more blurred she became, the more carefully she looked at him. He was wearing a loose sort of surfer's tank top, Mambo, or something. I could see the silky tuft of ash-coloured hair under his arm. I watched him moulding the contours of his golden biceps as he rested the heels of his hands on the table. I could see by his little smile of complicity that his feet were in contact with Josie's. He was making his every little word count now, as if it was going to be written into history. He was talking tours: he foresaw Europe, the US. He got up and did an imitation of some Dolly Parton wannabe. They were all laughing: Zak, next to him, Josie, opposite, still playing twinkle-toes under the table, Millie; even Joe's clouded eyes were welling with mirth. I could see how practised that act was, but obviously they didn't care. I was biting my nails, I realised, when I ripped one down to the quick. I gathered some plates as an excuse to get away. Knives and forks clattered to the hall floor, but I didn't go back for them. I put the plates in the sink and in the window saw my face like a crude Halloween skull, with huge eye-sockets. I thought *fist*; that face needs a fist in it. I had formed a fist, satisfactory, concentrating my strength and, as I rehearsed its aim, I saw through my reflection Zak's dark blue Falcon waiting. He always left the keys in the ignition.

By the time I swung into Armadale Road, I was gripped by the challenge of the median line, looping like a skipping rope through its parabola, the swooping head-lights, the throbbing red tail-lights of other cars; I wasn't going to be fooled by the outward similarity of blurred objects and their wobbling reflections, or the intermittent erasure of it all as Zak's wipers with their worn rubbers dragged the insect smears across the windscreen. I was delighted with my skill in this very fast guessing game. I realised I was heading for Armadale, that my dull intention must have been to make it to Lou's block in Roleystone. It was Saturday night: they'd be up there. No, the remote voice of reason said, Lou will not be pleased at this hour and nor will Roly. Then I came out of a curve too fast and was slewing into the gravel. By the fierceness of the horn blast as I came back on the road I understood that I had nearly sideswiped another car.

I saw a truck bay and pulled over. I drew my knees under my T-shirt, shaking. I'd rest there a bit, calm down. Later I'd sneak back, be charming, tell them I'd gone for some cigarettes, but I'd say: Do you think I found anything open? I'd help myself to Nat's pouch of aromatic Dutch tobacco and we'd all be mates again. At the same time it was utterly impossible to do these simple things. I had become a *trouble-fête*, and worse, I was furious with all of them. I had left my space behind at the table. I couldn't recover it. I had moved into shame; I had shamed myself and it was his fault.

When I got back, Millie's kitchen light was still on. At the scrubbed wooden table, there she was, waiting: Ah, Tom-Tom, you had us all scared to death. But you're back, that's the main thing. She stood up slowly, slowly, to hug me. I saw that she wasn't young any more.

Bit of rheumatism coming on with the rain, she said. She held me for some time, letting the rain on the roof and our quiet breathing re-establish things.

Then, she whispered, Tom-Tom, he's good for Josie, eh, you *know* that. He's really boosting her confidence.

Yes, I said. Yesss. It was a hiss. Well, like Marvel, when they touched my abscess, I wanted to hiss.

And Tom-Tom, he wants me to do the artwork, when they cut that CD.

Good. That's good, Millie. I just hope he doesn't rip you off, that's all.

Tom-Tom! As if he's going to rip me off. There'll be a contract, a proper legal contract.

Yeah, well, I hope so, Millie.

I had to stop blighting their pleasure with my poisoned state. Almost daily I dragged Karim out with me, in borrowed cars, on trains and buses to the zoo, to swimming pools, to libraries and exhibitions. It was at a graduate show at the Institute, as I wove amongst the clusters of guests toasting the installations with white plonk, that I found myself bawling. I made out that I was transfixed by one called 'Harvest' as I struggled to retrieve a tissue from the pocket of my pants. On the parquet floor were hundreds of little pairs of silver scissors, and at intervals, a thousand tepees of chestnut hair. Karim had moved in to do some rearranging of these elements and I grabbed him, stepping backwards into someone. It was Maurice who steadied me and whose smile of recognition faded as he saw my state. I thought I felt something like shelter in his great big chest.

Adamantine Shine

I needed — well, I have to admit, ways back to the cradle, after Maeve. I felt what I was getting from Lou the other night was reserve, urbanity, lip-service. *Adamantine*, that's the word she'd use instead of simple diamonds: she had an adamantine shine. She was in good form sending up her colleagues but I found her brilliance didn't deliver to me this time. It had been travelling like starlight for millions of years. Old photons. It's the academy. They have an elaborate vocabulary for ethics but beyond that … ? When do they get involved in the muck of life? She's endlessly rehearsing articles to contest the way her colleagues write their stuff. Perhaps it's trying to uphold this sort of critical practice, or whatever they call it, as revolutionary that exhausts their capacity for … What did I want? Passion? Again, was it about boundaries? I'd forgotten that her body was insect-light. I remember talking of her latent plumpness when we were teenagers. Well, the plumpness never really came out. Her spindly hands with their pointed fingers were as fragile as birds' claws. I was afraid hugging her, as if I could crush her bones. She makes me feel my own intensities as vulgar, as indelicate. Perhaps I envy her delicacy.

In any case, nothing much would have happened. Karim came in and sat down with us. He's usually such an introvert but can show an attentive sort of joviality with the dope. And time stretches for him like, like he'd say, something wicked, something intense. All the same, when she's there, I guess I feel time ticking away in my desire. I must say you've got to give her this: she can listen; she seems to have a benign neutrality where kids are concerned which they find very attractive.

Later, we danced a bit. Although I know quite well she doesn't like it much, I put on some hip-hop of Karim's. Okay, I was imposing, stretching my luck a little, but surely that's what exchange is about: stretching, challenging? Then, I couldn't believe it: after flirting furiously, her bronze breasts trembling with her quick brolga-like movements, the high-key sheen in her eyes, her brow glistening with sweat, her voice still breathless with the dance, Lou slipped on her pumps and out into the night with a routine kiss-kiss and some pathetically bland formula like: Don't let it be too long next time, dear T-T. Give Isi a kiss for me.

I stared dizzily at the wrecked kitchen, the scattered CDs, the rolled up carpets and wondered why I'd bothered. The underbelly of the thought was, as usual, the one with the fin poisonous for me: it's I who am mad in my expectations. Her behaviour could just as easily be replayed as devoted, attentive, and entertaining friendship. Well, there she goes, and here I am.

Of Whose Story?

I watch you return as your nephew or cousin. Family ties seemed to puzzle you as well. You used 'nephew' and 'cousin' as if they were synonyms. I've been to this one so often I can play it like a dream. It's the child you might have given the Spider, I see, coming back, a young man. I choose this, not the puffy, jaundiced man with tufted eyebrows you've become. I keep you coming, man-child, for another chance.

I give him, to a certain degree, your ways, and your grace, without the anger. He has a touch of the feminine which enables me to desire you again. I must say that I am shocked to see you bearded.

In this new story we have immediate understanding. No apologies. It's as if we know ahead of ourselves the nasty bits, the flares in the desert, the oases of low-key lyricism, which now I think of as love. I feel an urgent need for a plot, any plot to throw me back into time. Across this distance at the airport my arms are shot with pain. And your difference in this new version I am also ready to love, the signature of that mistress of ceremonies, somewhere between Simone Choiseuil and the Spider. Of whose story has this child been born; on whose wind did he drift to me? Here I take delivery of my own Karim's half-brother, older of course, back-dated but I didn't know this back then. As this love child you speak of her with ritual epithets, my Ridiculous, Extravagant Mother. Always the performer, you would know, Tom-Tom ...

As if I'd lived for years in that amorous alcove, snared by her exotic routine.

A Loopy Detour

It was during the absence of my third husband that the first came back to me in your form, dazzling like an algebraic simplification behind the customs window. The enormity of my experience made me gasp. I watched you nibbling at the inside of your cheek as my first husband had done in anxiety when our tiny house filled with sightseers. They were barely acquaintances. They were blurred figures looking for definition in the exotic beauty I'd torn from his culture to establish him here. In the full sovereignty of his difference, ha. He'd landed in the midst of mutism, in the midst of suburbia. Just think: tongue-tied that way, you taste the feminine. It might have been a chance for us if we hadn't had to live it out in the banality of the day-to-day struggle for bread.

In a glance I found in you, his nephew, the delicacy of his wrists, the length of his fingers, the blazing whites of the eyes against the dark skin, a certain arrogance in the relaxation of the body, in the curve of the lower back, and in the slight reverse-tilt of the head. Any suggestion of disparity between your image and his intoxicated and scandalised me at once.

I wanted to tear my clothes off there and then and without our ever saying a word, to roll with you or him on the hairy industrial airport carpet.

I watched the customs officer turning over the contents of your little suitcase with his big square fingers. I saw that it was full of presents. I thought I saw chagrin glimmer in your eyes as he tore the boutique wrapping. So, you had only brought presents. What about your clothes? Perhaps that's what I wanted: a toy boy to mould, to feed, to clothe. In any case there was at my house a wardrobe full of my third husband's shirts. He'd taken off for New York to think about the baby which I was expecting. Let the customs man keep you there for ever. Let me never know anything more about you than this; let me dream my way backwards to the beginning with him, the first.

And then our eyes met. Our understanding was immediate. In that flash of knowledge we were rid of the boring biographical saga with its genealogical branching, its descriptive departures, its reversals, tangles, and cautionary notes.

At home I helped you unpack. I opened the presents.

It's not me, it's my mother. She's crazy, excessive. She's always been too much. When she laughs everyone in the restaurant turns around. She might well be stunning, a star as you say — she's not my type. She's a prima donna and she's a crook. But for some reason that escapes me she wants to connect with you again.

Your stranger's eyes began to look over my life. With you I lost all sense of the familiar, of family relations. In you I found your mother again and in your eyes, which were, come to think of it more discreet, I found the shimmer of her beauty. Excessive was probably the word for her: she brought to mind the excessive beauty of the Inca princess bound to the consummation of her passion at the same time as her sacrifice. That she was able to function at all in the day-to-day never ceased to astonish me. In fact she had become a successful exporter of North African artefacts. And now, along with all her presents, she had sent me her son.

I'd been right about the clothes. You'd never had to choose them. They chose you. Indifferently you let yourself be picked up by women or men who would sweetly invite you to shower in their bathrooms, eat their pâté, drink their wine, and then watch you settle for the night into their sofas or beanbags. A shirt, a pair of pants lent, while yours were tumbling through their dryers, would assume such distinction on your body that the owners, distressed by their chronic fear of risk, by their invariably classical resolve, would beg you to keep them. Their only reward would be the wild inflection you lent to everything you tried on; the miracle of your body would always elude them.

You didn't suffer from jet-lag. It was not one of the conventions you ran your life by. We took up the discussion where my first husband's fury had cut it short relegating it to the police and the lawyers. So we spent that first night talking and smoking and drinking. My complicity in your adolescent excesses brought on a new febrility in me, who, at forty found myself pregnant again. Already I was getting drunk on infidelity in the absence of my third husband, who from a distance was weighing the pros and cons of this pregnancy as if it were a thing he might regulate without consulting me.

The next evening, when I came back from shopping, I found you downcast on the sofa, a beer in your hand. You had, in fact, put on one of my third husband's shirts. It looked quite good, apart from the collar. Later you would see for yourself the power of his boxer's neck. For the moment, in a voice faint with fatigue, you said:

Tell me. How long does it take to reach the countryside here? I walked for two hours and still more and more suburb.

Maybe ten hours, more or less. It depends on your pace.

But this is scandalous. What kind of place is this then? With that word, *scandalous*, you brought him back. I hated him again with sweet intensity.

How come you people don't die of discouragement? you asked.

There I was, repatriated in that phrase: *you people*, pinned back into the suburbia I deserved.

I told you how I'd spent the summer weekends of my pregnancy listening to the tinkering of the idea of rain on the metal roof and then with the fuse of the full day's heat working through the night, I would await the return of the Banksiamen that used to haunt my childhood.

We live in the certainty of guilt and of the randomness of punishment, a voice said through me. I still expect them to breathe at my window.

In this suburb of retired workers and the generationally unemployed, we're expert listeners to the jazz of traffic on the freeways. We can tell by the gearbox registers as the cars swerve into our side streets, whether it's Porsches, Mercedes or RX7s and when the skidding starts and the cops' sirens join in, we know our boys have come home. Sometimes the stolen cars are driven by two kids, one to work the brakes, clutch and accelerator and the other to do the steering. You know, on account of their size — they can't reach. Some of them Anglo kids, quite a few of them Nyoongar. As you waited with your eyes on me, I felt my pink tongue moving in my face through systematic racism, through government cynicism, through police beatings, through deaths in custody.

You saw this.

Some rosary, you said. Make you feel better, reciting it like that? And what do you do about it? Nothing?

I nodded. Your reproach wreaked havoc through my blood.

Then, in your place I said: Yes. It's scandalous. I do nothing.

Karim came in. It was a strangely stiff, proscenium arch entry. With his open hand, he made a fanning motion in the air. He said with an Australian accent that was exaggerated for him:

So. You're smoking again. And what about ah … your baby?

You looked at him a long while but it was to me you spoke: Be careful. Something's going on there. He's jealous of me?

No.

But I knew very well that he was and that my speaking in French with you exiled him in his own home, making him live out his father's absence like the wake of signification.

From then on I was aware of the depth of our differences

and increasingly giddy with estrangement. You declared yourself a passionate hunter, turning to derision my middle-class green sentimentality. Nibbling your cheek, you pored over the atrocious machinations of the Marquis de Sade. You interrogated me at length about my marriages, incredulous at my masochism. You observed me in intense discussion with my women friends. You said that the marriages had been for me one loopy detour.

You showed me the bush of my country. I felt furious but I had to admit you had delicacy. You demonstrated the subtle, slowed-down gait you used to approach wild animals. From frame to frame, I watched you suspend your gestures and cut the sound track. Kangaroos settled on you and on your camera their gentle gaze. As you neared them, snakes and goannas continued their sun baths, unperturbed.

Sometimes, you'd silently take the tea-towel from my arm, the axe from my hands. Your beautiful, economical gestures! Knotty wood cleaved under your light blow. Shopping together became more and more festive. Just like Asif, at the supermarket you'd drop all sorts of delicacies into my trolley. I enjoyed sharing this recklessness with money. You began to accompany me everywhere. You said that you rather liked people mistaking you for the father of my unborn child.

I continued to operate as an interpreter between you and my son.

What's he saying now? What's he doing that for? What's that sarcastic expression about?

You ended up by conceiving a certain tenderness for one another. In my translations, I suppressed all trace of nastiness. On occasions I manufactured compliments for you to bestow upon one another. In this way I recuperated both of you in the rock-a-bye space of my motherhood.

Because I found my first husband even in the timbre of your voice, I'd let automatic expressions of tenderness slip out: *oui coco*. I caught you rehearsing the gestures of intimacy towards me. Then you began to take your breakfast in your underpants. I wondered if your anecdote about your Parisian friend had been offered as a parable. He put himself through his studies, you said, from the benefits of a single job which involved fifteen minutes a day vacuuming in a G-string while his seventy year-old employer watched from her armchair.

The phone call from my third husband came, of course.

Yes, darling, here I am, back already! But what do you expect? I can't do without you. And our baby, everything all right there? It's wonderful, isn't it? Well, yes, of course. I want to commit myself totally.

I made efforts in ventriloquy. I rifled through my English repertoire to find formulae for him. I put down the receiver.

Our eyes locked for a long time. Without moving, without saying anything, we let ourselves be taken by the tide of blood, by this slow somersault of all the senses.

Violent trembling came afterwards, in our efforts to tidy the house, to empty the ashtrays, take out the garbage. In the end we had to laugh: our teeth were chattering like castanets.

He's on his way, then?

That's right. He's taken a taxi from the airport.

My third husband came in with a smile advertising a whole new policy of largesse. And there I was stammering like a little girl. You whispered your disbelief at my conduct. He, on the other hand, delivered his questionnaire soon enough: But installing his bed in the lounge room, that's a bit much, isn't it? And does he sleep in past midday like that everyday? Has it occurred to him what beer costs? Really, you don't put up with that sort of thing from me or Karim. But I don't believe what I'm seeing! So you've started smoking again? And our baby? You don't give a damn now?

And you said: He's right, you know. You shouldn't smoke. You could damage your baby.

My baby was born a few weeks after your departure.

He marvelled at her resemblance with his paternal aunt, the one with dark skin and a rather Indian look: But she's the spitting image of my Auntie Bertha!

And me? I was grateful that just like punishment, grace seemed to be random. I marvelled to see in this little Inca the loopy detour finally close.

Lou Barb

Exposure

Tom-Tom said: to hell with a book if you can't take it for real. I'll test-drive any story, she said, for torque and handling, wheel base, turning circle, for pick-up when it matters. I was Fou Roux's lover by living his pictures and I let this take me to other spaces within the places of my life. I don't want praise from those wisecracking academics: I say, let them slip down the abyss on their slithery signifiers, or whatever they call them these days. Let them shuffle their surfaces, let them take their thrills in hypertext diving. So, I wondered, what was she really exposing of herself or of her reader in these little stories?

There are many ways to expose a person, of course. Some people feel more exposed if you take a peek at their fridge crisper, see those blue, furry vegetables, future soups and salads collapsed into slime, than if you catch them in naked self-examination. Mabel Grounds, next-door at Roleystone, jumped a foot in the air this morning when I broke her trance at the fridge. She had the door wide open with fridge light haloing her frizzy hair. Her pincer fingers made furtive little dives under the cling-wrap to fetch out the jellied remains of a chicken casserole, her jaws working overtime. *How she gnawed it, how she clawed it when she found herself alone!* So much for Mabel's expressed horror of carnivores! Of course, diary snoopers at once feverishly desire and are sick for this sight of themselves, flattened on a line, skewered by an adjective, skinned by a nickname secreted in the diary space, where loving so easily can fold into loathing.

In opening up the file called 'X-clue' which he had earlier dismissed as some old tax file of his own confection, wondering what fancy had seized him to conjure up such a silly name, Maurice said he was *deeply shocked*. He had never felt his own loss so cruelly exposed. That Tom-Tom could see their reality like that! And I'll have to put myself through contortions explaining Tom-Tom's suppression of him as a person, in the caricatured reduction to third in the series: My Third Husband.

In any case, it's outrageous, he said. I'm the second, not the third, unless she lied to me on that one too. And ... What's more, I wanted Isidore from the beginning. Inca my foot!

It was no use my talking of fictional licence. For him they are all autobiography. In any case, it's true: for Tom-Tom, fables were so intimately tessellated into the real, you couldn't deny that they were there, as part of the same topography, all true. Maurice had come up again to Roleystone with these last print-outs, and an exercise book, whose pages were scrawled in black ink, bristling with paraphs, festooned with arabesques. He was leaning back in the tweed papasan, one from Mother's sunroom, whose Sanderson floral had reminded me too much of our own moment of exposure. Maurice's features were still blurry, slightly pouched; the slanting light from the skinny south-west window further dissolved them. He was wearing an olive green linen jacket, with large, marbled brown buttons and raglan sleeves. The green gave his hazel eyes a seaweedy vividness. I admired the jacket. He opened his hands, wide apart, staring at the vacancy between them, like something irremediable: Tom-Tom chose it, he said. Then there was a long silence.

Lou, he said, his voice catching, there was a different version of the same material in a file called 'Diary' for Christ's sake.

What could I say?

He said that even the idea of her being able to daydream such a thing made him miserable. He still takes me for the guardian of the secret. What was it she so refused in me? he said. There was for a flash so much green intensity in his eyes, that despite his sun-ravaged face, I could see him precisely as a freckled eight-year-old, smarting from some schoolyard humiliation. In any case, he said, it's flagrant: it's written in the first person! For all his mathematical sophistication, when it comes to writing, Maurice is quite naive. I thought here Tom-Tom had probably outsmarted herself. I suspected that using the first person was partly to cover her own traces. A fictional transposition would have been for her too obvious a ploy to disguise its lived reality, that is if, and I doubt it, she had any concern for her reader. Anyhow, now it seems, her words provoke old wounds, which he almost cherishes as if through them he might bring back the voice of the Banksiawoman.

As a child Tom-Tom said she used to play a game she called the Trampolining Romance in which she'd try out versions of her parents in a sort of dysfunctional bouncing exchange. There would be the sad-eyed farmer in his greasy felt hat and the satin-bra'd mother from the South Pacific dressing-room photo. She'd watch them from her bed through the picture window, behind the Banksias, bouncing on Maeve's old rusty trampoline. She would dress them, undress them, make them up, and besmirch them, much as Isi does with her Barbie dolls. Sometimes she would deal her mother's bob a cruel lopping, paint their faces into scowls or give them great bleeding mouths, as fierce cannibals of one another. Sending him up, she'd bring her down, to confront the evidence of the daughter she'd abandoned. After a while she found that it wasn't him anymore, or her, that mattered. The space which she longed to inhabit was between his hat and her conical bra cups, poised ballistically at the window. It was the interval that had the charge for her, that allowed her to possess herself, she said. Of course, I can see now that she transferred this game to Roly and me.

Opening up those files to see himself a punitive Theseus returning, or a plodding Babylonian, numb with number, Maurice then tortured himself with the spaces between Tom-Tom's projections. His own absence from her stories became a betrayal, the quick notation of his presence against the thick libidinousness of her self-portraits, a betrayal, the fictional morphs blending him with other men, once again, provided nothing but figures of betrayal.

Lou Barb

Nevertheless

I begin to understand Maurice's distress. Last night, looking for some sort of compensation, I suppose, I tried the audio-cassette which Maurice had slipped into a plastic envelope at the back of the file. It was a copy of a compilation album by the French singer, Barbara. Tom-Tom had played it to me many times at her place, as if inaugurating each time the experience for me. Still, this was now the Barbara she had left behind and I found myself fumbling to fit the cassette into the cradle.

Ma plus belle histoire d'amour c'est vous. So here again was the voice of seduction she elected, of the older singer returning to the song of her youth. It came harsh at first, hard-edged, as it struck the vein of loss, clawed its way down the scale, struck flint again, flared, fainted, and then, softening, elongated into trance the notes of lament, stalking the figures of desire into some distant recess of darkness. Curled up, died. Memory is folded back and back into this singing. Even the staggering crudity of the synthesised accompaniment is perfect, crying or wheezing its inadequacy. Perhaps that is why it is so poignant as it beseeches through the ear what is lost, calling along the blood canal to the ageing heart. Through the vertiginous glissando I saw the narrow-hipped, black-sheathed singer closing her eyes to the microphone. I saw the light catching the arch of the nose, the flared nostril, its sheen on the vaulting brow, modelling the lids. *Au coeur de vos dédales nous danserons encore*, it reeled, dizzied, slowed again, lowering from the soprano to the contralto moan, to ebb in the break. Oh those hiatuses where death is rehearsed.

Then, there was just the fading pulse. I found my teeth chattering, holding Tom-Tom's absence, my arms around empty dark air. There was something else on the tape now, spoken, which was not Barbara. Urgent, childish almost, the heatwave trawling the chill of realisation: it was her voice, Tom-Tom's. She must have inadvertently recorded over Barbara. She was reverberating in the room, with the big hill she called sacred veiled in rain and black night beyond the window.

It was a whisper, as if she'd been recording in secret.
I dreamed of Asif, she said.
My heart tightened.
I had to turn the volume up.
If only I could have

> *Attendez que ma joie revienne*
> *Et que se meure le souvenir*
> *De cette amour de tant de peine*
> *Qui n'en finit pas de mourir*

Barbara sang and then Tom-Tom's strangled voice, shadowed by another which sounded, I thought, male.

No, but this was mad; it was in English anyhow, but with a slightly French accent into which Tom-Tom drifted at times, reminiscing. It was Tom-Tom talking to herself, once again.

We are on the Catalan Beach outside Marseille. With its coarse sand. With its beige sand. With its oil slicks. And all its changerooms shut. But we like the melancholy of the deserted beach, I tell you pathetically, because it recalls ... maybe Fellini. The changerooms with their aqua-boarded doors are fitted into the limestone cliffs. We note the Man in the Black Leather Jacket and The Two Boxer Bitches held on their short leashes, statue-still. Yes. We recognise these elements as ours. The waves lap in a quick, panicky rhythm. Now we are on the terrace separated by the superb curve of the Corniche from the café itself. The sea's surface has settled into a violet crepe on which the oil slicks have struck a fiesta mode in phosphorescent reds and greens. The waiter, tray shoulder-high, dances amongst the traffic.

He says: No, I don't cross the road to serve you just *un express*.

You say: We'll have an ice-cream as well then, fuckwit.

And he says: I don't cross the road to be called fuckwit either, *connard*!

You smile broadly as you say: No I guess you don't. He returns the smile flirtatiously. You murmur an exchange, your mouths so close. I see that you and he have made your assignation. I feel abandoned. Now our ice-creams drip as we lick, mine *citron givré*, yours pistachio, onto the terrace.

You say: Why is it that you can't connect?

It's you who are elsewhere, I say.

Look at yourself, letting her nurse you like that, you say.

I realise that all the time I have been on Lou Barb's lap, my arm around her neck. I awake from the dream, beached again.

> *Dis quand reviendras-tu,*
> *Dis au moins le sais-tu*

Barbara sang.

And so I nurse Tom-Tom in her last romance of disconnection. Oh, I tried to get back, to nurse her. To resonate with her mother's voice would be rapture, to be inside joy, not yearning for it, she wrote. It would also be to inhabit stillness and silence, finally. Her failure to find in anyone the heat of that dressing-room mirror would blast the sweetest moments with its negativity. Nevertheless, back I'd come, to see her ever more locked into those obsessive patterns and numbing with drink the ability to break through them with any kind of art. Nevertheless, yes, I'd return to her to contemplate the distressed fabric of it all: her face, her talent, her life. The withered crepe of that sea!

Tom-Tom's voice resumed. I gave a yell; I had been lulled back into the music. If you walked in now wordlessly, Lou, and I opened my arms, we'd fall to the floor and in our transport, we'd leave no space for language, accelerating out of ourselves ... Let the demon surfaces multiply; let inside and outside no longer be!

A nurse for her! That, of course, Asif could not be. Until I saw him in the flesh I thought I read clearly between the lines in Tom-Tom's letters. Don't you see what you're getting locked into? I wrote, fearful of rejection, that she'd see it as jealousy: Tom-Tom, how could you, of all people let yourself get bound up with such a man? You're just getting blinded by his picturesque, if you'll forgive me, distrust the seductions of the risk. It's your version of the exotic. This isn't art. It isn't even romance. It's your life, not an imitation of Odette's, for God's sake.

But he was gorgeous to look at all right, her Asif. When I first saw him, it was as if my psyche was impaled on his gaze, and he gave a flattering kind of attention I only later saw as exaggerated. His gaze was outrageous, devouring, like Picasso's. You'd wonder that any object or image survived its passage. In the suffocating lounge room of the tiny corrugated iron and timber house they rented, he strode towards me, arm outstretched for the handshake, and the space hummed with his voltage. Here I am getting caught up in those electrical metaphors of Tom-Tom's. There'd be a high count of those, I'd say.

At other times, perhaps, come to think of it, out of shyness, he'd possess Tom-Tom exclusively in company, lounge on the floor with his head in her lap, veil his eyes and address his visitors from there with an aphoristic authority. And his smile could be shrivelling, silencing in itself. It was a smile of exasperated tolerance approaching its limits. At the same time it offered itself as superior, worked for, a kind of Buddhist removal from the friction of the debates in which others conducted their vicarious living. Nursed, yes. At moments he let himself be nursed by Tom-Tom, but I don't think he was ready to be a nurse for her — and, come to think of it, why should he have been?

Lou Barb

Recovery and Erasure

Karim! Haven't even thought that through. How can I or
Maurice for that matter, claim a right to Tom-Tom's
words, regardless of Karim? Whose are these words, after
all? Did Maurice think to ask Karim, before he passed the
papers over to me? The withheld intensity of the boy.
Where will it go? His solitude seemed absolute,
inviolable, at the funeral. I couldn't find the words to
approach him with. His stiffness made the idea of a hug
seem hopeless. But I tried, baulked, tried again,
awkwardly. Then, how I loved him. He returned the
embrace emphatically, letting his tears flow into my neck.
He cried with the abandon of a baby, his adolescent key-
shifts making it all the more heart-rending.

I didn't even say goodbye! Maurice came and I ... I went
down for a smoke!

Little Isidore rushed to clasp his thigh, fascinated by his
grief. Still at her age, she is only rehearsing the loss she'll
feel later, so terribly, later on.

Maurice made no secret of the difficulty he had, as he said, *with the boy*. Oh if only he'd been able to loosen up, get over his jealousy. He would rarely name Karim, as if the name conferred an autonomy that he was unwilling to give. Never been able to handle adolescents, he said. As if he hadn't been one himself! *Ah, but then, of course, it was different. Times were harder. None of this slouching about. Gangsta rap and ganja. Study was a privilege.* I know the stuff he would have trotted out.

Even with Tom-Tom around, Maurice and Karim gave each other wide berth. Karim would emerge for meals from the shed he'd done up as a bedroom behind the grasstrees at the back of the garden. He'd do the washing-up silently, methodically. His ritualistic slowness would infuriate Maurice. Now, he says, Karim will go back to France, to find his father. At least these days Maurice concedes his own inadequacies. I wish I could find something to console him, he said. His silence worries me. He is quite bereft. His mother was besotted with him. That was always one of our problems.

Tom-Tom said: Sometimes when I look into Karim's face I'm afraid; I'm afraid of my fear and I'm afraid of my passion. At a mere act of thoughtlessness, or a sharp reply from him, I'm wounded like a lover. And I hate him at the same time for locking me back into that. She lived in the thrall of this daily recovery and erasure of Asif, of all that seemed to promise. There was nothing unique in her situation, she must have told herself that. Every mother is and isn't her child. Every child is and isn't an image of the father. She claimed a mythic intensity for her motherhood. Yet she must have settled into some sort of ordinary time: school hours and meals, after all. Even in the guise of finding another life with Maurice she seemed caught in the repetition of loss, obsessive loops outside the petty pace of days. Ageing ever so slightly on the exterior. That took me by surprise. I'd been so much in her sway I never thought time would touch her, but even in that firm olive skin lines of smile and grimace had deepened, and boring through the older face there persisted the direct, unprocessed gaze of a puzzled child, the little girl who fancied herself spied upon by Banksiamen.

In these returns to the child she refused to give up, the child who'd believed in Asif and had clung to that love, perpetrated in her son who looked so like his father, she condemned herself to wipe-out. In permanent anticipation of the marauder, bombarding her with his negativity, she became his mimic.

She's keeping me locked out of my own life. There is Roly, for instance, whose solicitous talk comes to me at times as an alien buzz. Then I have to get away from him. Poor dear Roly. I need to keep for her this space his talk would occupy. When I retreat to the computer, I find death in the whirr of the fan. The desk calendar reminds me of the preparation I should be doing for next semester at the Institute. How can I theorise performance after this? I'll be asking questions like: Do we need the concept of representation? What lies beyond the semiosphere? What lies are in these very formulations for me. In my attempt to mouth them, acid trickles down my throat. So I come back here to The Corner Bar.

Lou Barb

On either Side of the Melody Line

Sometimes I think the anecdotes we exchanged when Tom-Tom was caught at home with little Karim, when we fed off one another with an insatiable hunger, were not from her to me or from me to her; rather they were hatched in a space hallucinated between us, a space that should have been filled otherwise. Here we both were, living out versions of the family, awkward ones, but versions all the same, when perhaps we should have fallen again into each other's arms. Still, had she long given up on me? I remembered her at nineteen or twenty saying that it was my *slow grace* she liked, when I felt so awkward, always too visible. You've got the … you know, the *I'll-maroon-you-Sailor* look. *You'll have to get out fast or just yield to my undertow, forgetting everything else.* I could fall for your womanliness, she said, stretching out on top of me on my little chenille bedspread. Ah your womanliness, and she laughed hot into my ear, so hot that my neck is on fire now as I write it.

Karim went through a period of mumbling recalcitrance in early adolescence. Tom-Tom moaned about this, but at heart I think she knew he had to stake some claims for himself or he'd risk suffocation. Even so, there'd be moments when he'd emerge from that cocoon of mute rebellion and let her take his head on her lap and rock him back into those hummed refrains he hadn't let her sing since childhood. She told me this with tears in her eyes, maudlin after wine, when tipsily regardless of time she'd phoned to ask me over. I remember making the reflection Mother herself might have made, but with a certain thrill of approval: isn't that a bit close to incest, what with that great big boy? I thought of his rough voice and its uncontrollably sliding scales, of the dark hairs on his legs. Somehow there in that space Karim's longing for his father and Tom-Tom's for what Asif barely screened: the woman running around the next corner, hair aflame, eyes magnetic when she'd turned to lure her pursuer, and so on, they had let their voices dance on either side of the melody line. Awkward with their eyes and hands, but delicate in their avowal as in their avoidances, in that searing seam along the old wounds, Tom-Tom might well have tapped a deeper love than she had found anywhere else. This complicity laid to rest her fear of his veiled eyes, the times she'd found him rocking against the hallway wall, banging his head against the skirting, and gave her joy when he scorched his way through his school exams to bring the prizes home. Well, she said, Karim's *stoked*, and so am I.

Until Maurice it was a pact strengthened by earlier poverty, the poverty out of which they'd somehow climbed so that each crusty loaf or wedge of cheese, each bowl of flowers was miraculous and made lovers of them. Of course Tom-Tom had earned little herself; it had been what Maeve had left behind that hitched them out of penury.

Looking at this marvel of the son, she must have seen vividly each time what had attracted her in the father. Her son would reach for the pegs to help her, unquestioning of her eccentricity in night laundry-hanging. Tom-Tom said: Sometimes he shadows me everywhere until it drives me mad. His solicitude strikes me as too honeyed and before I fall for it, I think, wait, he's stoned, or worse, he's after money. And then afterwards, I feel awful because, even if it's sometimes the case, it isn't always. Oh, I guess I'm afraid of getting into this habit of intimacy because I know he'll have to separate …

So, he'd come to share these moments with his mother, out of the reach of Maurice, maybe to ask for money, but happy anyhow to elongate their tacit complicity. He'd pluck the pegs from the bag and watching him, she'd find again the flexion of the Balinese dancer's fingers, his neck rearing from the dark shoulders, the collarbones marked by their sheen in the dying light, the flamboyant darkness of his skin through the T-shirt, displaying more rip than cloth and a certain narcissism in his confidence that, especially in rags, he was the aristocrat. Again she'd see his father, the bulk of his long thighs in that insolent walk.

I can't avoid making them sound like something out of a pulp romance because this is how Tom-Tom seemed to live her motherhood. She enjoyed the torture of his fluctuations between fervour and remoteness, insecurity and arrogance, just as she had with his father. She'd become very adept in reading afterwards Karim's apparent conviviality as a lure, just as she had with Asif. After listening indulgently, with that sexy smile, Asif would cut across her talk, delivering his opinion in a way that brooked no argument.

Lou Barb

Our Perverse Pleasure Now

I had to laugh when Tom-Tom poured out her vitriol about her domestic life with Maurice and Karim. It seemed to be more for performance than for real, although her last words throw a different complexion on that. Maurice was surprised at her, she said, a feminist after all, letting her son manipulate her like that. How's that, Lube, being told by your man you're not a good feminist either? Maurice reckons that I let Karim get away with murder. He fills his shed with marijuana smoke and never changes his sheets till the sight of his bedroom gets too much even for me and then I attack the mess grimly, out of a kind of vengeance, to make him ashamed.

It's true, she said, warming up. I hear him coming in at three a.m. and I realise that my whole body has been listening for this moment and I tiptoe outside, across the freezing lawn, to hiss through the door of the shed: I cleaned your room. My teeth are chattering, I know it's absurd and that I'm waking up the neighbours. But I'm already carried away and I go on: It was disgusting in there and the smell of the piled up socks in the walk-in-robe where you've rigged up that horrible system to grow your plants. You've got such application and tender nurturing when it comes to your plants but you can never scrape the baked beans off your plate. And Pizza packets! I wondered what the vacuum pipe was knocking against and I found all the glasses which were missing from the kitchen amongst the dust balls and discarded jocks under your bed. And, Karim, you gave me such a fright. Under your bed there was also something huge and heavy, and soft and I screamed. I thought it was a body, what with the smell and all. It was Justin's doona! One of the endless, hairy, rough-voiced boys who sleep over. Oh, I suppose he's sweet enough. But his doona wasn't! So I put the socks and jocks into a bowl with Velvet soap powder to treat them, they need Treatment, like sewage, you wouldn't believe it. Socks and jocks cocktail, I said, as I brewed up the horrible organic mix and found myself screeching with laughter like the drover's wife, furious and manic, taking refuge in cleaning with resentment, rather than facing my own vacuum. I taste my venom for this son who is charming and thoughtful to all his friends and who absent-mindedly doormats me.

And again he says: Ah, come off it Mum, what's it to you? You don't have to come here to look at my mess. Give me a break. I thought the whole point of me living out the back was so I wouldn't contaminate you. And you come in search of it! Stop stressing out for once. I was going to clean it in my own time.

And you know Lou, the next day he'll come and put his arm around me, slide the tea-towel from my hand, making sweet talk as he dries up. It does emerge that he wants the car to go to one of his friend's places to smoke their Colombian grass for a change. He puts in: Sorry about last night. The state of the shed and that. You're a wonderful mum, I love you, and he puts his heavy arm around me and jingles my car keys. I really respect you and it's just that things are getting to me at the moment. I can't see the point in anything much, this whole scene in Perth is so fucked and is it okay, you know, if I bring the car back in the morning?

Go on, have a good time, I tell him because you can't send your kids off with your insults festering in their brains, can you? And when he returns the car late Sunday morning the tank is empty. Maurice rolls his eyes and says it's about time he showed some thoughtfulness for something else beyond his own self-massaging little ego.

And I say to him I've folded your clothes and put them into categories. Could you at least put them away in a drawer? And Karim says: Categories, that's cool, I like my clothes in categories! and he laughs. Once again I look into his lovely face, the gleaming teeth, at the light glancing off his gold earring, dancing in his black eyes. I fall for it every time. By now Karim is on the phone and racking up our bill and Maurice says it's time he started looking for a job because this pretending to study is a joke. We should tip him out into the real world. You've got to be cruel to be kind. Let him find out what toilet paper and electricity and long-distance phone calls in the middle of the day cost and what licensing a car and servicing it cost. Then I resent Maurice. Hate myself for not managing a job in the world. Still, Karim's macho way of driving full-bore up to stop signs and then high-revving to be first off again has aged it incredibly. It's true I've spoiled him rotten. But I didn't want to want to squat

333

on his soul, one massive superego, all cement and razor wire and spotlights. His fridge raiding! I cooked for a little dinner party in advance the other night, you know it was something we had to get over, the Minister for the Environment and some heavies from Statistics. The smoked salmon was gone except for the sad bit of cardboard and plastic and there was a telltale spoon left in the half-empty casserole. Maurice says adolescents are not a very likable lot. I think it's better not to even try to like them, he says. Sometimes I wonder what we'd talk about if it weren't for Karim's awfulness. We savour it to the bone, suck out the last bitter bit of its marrow. It's our perverse pleasure now.

Lou Barb

Sleeping on the Space Bar

Roly calls out: Yoo-hoo?

I'm home, base, and anchor for him since I've been on leave. He likes having me to come to. He loops back and forward on this comfortable umbilicus.

I can never think how to answer if not to mirror him. What can you reply to Yoo-hoo?

I have all the notebooks spread out on the sofa in the office.

There's quiet now. The odd creaking board.

Suddenly his voice comes. Since the moment of Yoo-hoo it's as if days have elapsed. Or maybe I was dreaming already. I give an involuntary yell like a wounded animal. He winces into the light. His face is thin and haunted. In his grey eyes I see amber chinks.

Don't answer me then, eh? Anything wrong?

My head must have fallen on the keyboard. Feel the indentation of the keys into my forehead.

What on earth have you done to yourself? Roly can never work out this sort of symptom. As if the most banal domestic event were as mysterious as meteorites. I must have given a start.

How childish I am — as if I should feel guilty. Well, when Mother peeped into my bedroom, she'd say: And there I was tiptoeing around! To think I thought you were working! Lying there listening to pop music! I thought well, if it helps you to work, people are facilitated by stranger things, but sleeping!

Roly puts down his briefcase and, like a child investigating some inscrutable injury the mother has contracted, he fingers the impress of letters on my forehead. I jab Enter and see that I have slept on the space bar: tracts of emptiness have been added.

Nice spare writing, Roly jokes.

I try to grope back towards lucidity.

This falling asleep in the midst of an action. What is happening?

It worries me to see you just living in your grief. What's wrong with The Corner Bar now? At least it got you out.

Oh, I say, Tony's not there anymore. I don't feel comfortable there now. He's started up a new business with his boyfriend. A restaurant just this side of Roleystone. We could try it sometime when we go to the shack. They're off Brookton Highway. What do you mean *just living in my grief*, anyhow? What am I meant to do? I will work through it, working through all this.

How is Maurice coping?

Maurice? Oh dear, yes. Maurice, I'll have to face up to that soon because Maurice's Tom-Tom cannot be mine.

He won't want it published as it is. You'll have to change names, switch the signs.

I'm trying to weave my bits around hers. Some sort of dance around her fragments.

Some sort of posthumous coupling?

Roly!

Sorry. In any case I didn't mean anything obscene by that. But I just can't reach you these days.

I feel raw and sad and slobbery.

I have to work through this I say, tired even before the words come out. I know it mightn't count for you as a grand obsession.

Well you can't say I'm one of them. You could hardly say I'm ... in the grips of a grand obsession.

I know. You're disaffected with it. Like I'm disaffected with mine at the Institute. But I'm not disaffected with this. I just can't face going back to the other stuff.

Do you want to get takeaways? Go out for a meal? Come on, give yourself a break.

He comes back with a beer and heaps the notebooks into a corner of the sofa.

I've only got a month left. I don't know, Roly, if I can face going back to the Institute. So much in me has to be undone, you see, before I find the primitive nerve, you know, of my story in hers. It isn't *posthumous coupling,* Roly. It burns, and matters, like life, for Christ's sake. I can't see how I can get into that commerce of abstraction again, knocking concepts about. And what for? So that I help prepare a few adept theorists and smart critical minds for the advertising industry?

Lou Barb

A Doctorate for Garth

Things have moved so far, beyond the corruption we thought was possible. This morning Roly and I see the front page photo of Garth Hendriks, the orchestrator of the council harassment of Banksiafold, regally robed and topped with mortar board, collecting his Honorary Doctorate in Science from the Institute.

This is the limit. I'm going to resign.

Don't go doing anything impetuous, Roly said. Who would that kind of romantic sacrifice help?

What, you're worried about the mortgage?

There you do me an injustice he said, putting his voice gravely into quotes.

Look, this is as bad as giving science doctorates to the Ceaucescus ... Garth Hendriks was a mate of Red Iron Bill who wanted to poison all the waterholes in one neat act of Aboriginal genocide so he could blow up the North West to mine and export iron. Hendriks led the expedition against Banksiafold to show he was blooded, as hunters say. Ready for bigger territorial disputes.

Take it from me, sweetie, I know how these people work. They'd only be too pleased to get rid of a troublemaker. If you left, rather than fighting it from within, that would just serve the wrong people.

I've never been a troublemaker, that's just it. I've done my job. Well, I'm sick of doing my job for an institution so bent on corruption. Look, they're going to take funding from mining now!

Sweetheart, you'd be better off attending your union meetings instead of having your private little self-destructive romance.

Romance!

Throwing in your job won't help anyone. Are you sure you're not seizing on anything to stoke a passing aversion to cultural theory? You don't have to wear the whole politics of an institution. Where would you stop? Refuse superannuation because it's enmeshed with global capitalism? I don't hear you arguing that. Anyway, coffee's ready!

Letters from Odette

Dear Maurice,

I'm sorry about the news, but somehow, if you'll forgive me for saying it now, Tom-Tom always pushed things to the edge. I am sickened too that my father should have been involved. I can't begin to comment on that. What to say? What can anyone say? What can anyone ever say that makes a difference? My feelings right now are not yours, I know. I suppose we lost our connection years ago, she and I. You see, Tom-Tom cast away our friendship in the name of … well, I suppose she would have called it love but it was her own intensity she wanted to earth. In trying to spread around what she called love, she spread her damage. She was a greedy girl. She always wanted more, beyond what anyone could give her, I think. In my more cynical moments I think she made a conscious decision to write me off, perhaps to convince herself that in rejecting me, the bourgeois connection, she was still somehow radical. I remember her dismay when I suggested her performance work on sites with that Molly Schor would only reach the converted, that it was far too cryptic to carry. Still the truth often shocks. Oh, she was naive about that — and her feverish brand of sexuality, well it's better left unsaid.

I was also sad to see the way she dispatched me to some sort of unproductive afterlife in those pages you sent. You know that these past years I've been working on literacy programs in Lyon. I'm on the senate for a new open university. She might well have dismissed that as social work, as bandaiding, a strain of bourgeois liberalism. I wonder how finally she reflected on her own contribution, taking off with one of the *Maghrébin* youth leaders, de-radicalising him in Australian suburban domesticity, just to cling nostalgically to fuzzy dreams of radical action. I was shocked on your behalf too, reading that extract you sent. The man without a story! Or a story only at the end of number! Yes, Maurice, you've apparently suffered her reductions. Those you say 'cherished' her, to whom she made her avowals, Lou Barb, and this Molly apparently, couldn't compete with that Asif, whose violence she was inclined to gild in memory. As if through violence at least he escaped middle-class blandness! I will look up Asif for you. I must admit I'm rather curious and I don't mind a bit of detective work. And I suppose I could seek out that Molly — although, to be frank, I don't relish the idea of a meeting with that sort of woman. It corresponds with a side of Tom-Tom which, quite frankly, I'd prefer not to have known about. Of course, I can't guarantee they'll talk. Oh dear, in a way it's all too fitting that she chose to go out in a costume drama. Still, I understand your need to understand, if not to rescue anything. Perhaps there's some sort of legacy even in the most abortive acts.

Speaking of legacy, it will be interesting to see their son Karim, if as you say he's still *chez* Asif. And then there is your little Isidore. I'll be sending off a little dress for her as only the French know how to design. As presumptuous as it might sound, Maurice, since I don't even know you, it would be best for you to concentrate on her now. Look to the side of life!

Please give Lou Barb my regards and despite my frankness here, my condolences to you.

      Odette

***

Dear Maurice and Lou Barb

I tracked Asif Badaoni down to a *bastide* north of Gordes. So I took off in the hired Renault, and despite the grimness of the exercise, I was glad to see the walls of Gordes, honeyed in the late afternoon, and the blue light on the limestone of the Little Lubéron range. The chill clarity of the air was invigorating. It gave me a break from the relentless pressure of my work in Lyon. You Australians wouldn't imagine how hard we work here, but that is beside the point.

He ambled down the limestone gravel drive to meet me. His smile was wide, almost showy; immediately I was on the alert. He is good-looking, I suppose, but the lines are set, the curve of the nose more pronounced than I remember from the photo Tom-Tom showed me all those years ago. His eyebrows are infiltrated with white, and his hair is a sort of gunmetal overall. He was in an old blue worker's coat and moss-coloured corduroys. There were cries of children from the walled garden. It looked rather nice in there: a mass of chestnuts and planes; blue smoke floating upwards. It was a far cry from anywhere I had imagined him. The whole place looked like some sort of religious retreat.

He was formal, even punctiliously polite. Of course I'd negotiated it all on the phone, once I'd located him by Telnet. I realised that he would have had the news some time before, since Karim had joined him there. I told him I had agreed to do a bit of work on Tom-Tom's past for the sake of her widower and friends, just piecing things together, said I'd be glad if he could fill me in on what he was doing, how he'd seen his situation, his work, at the time he'd met Tom-Tom. Could he put himself back then?

His long silence was meant to make me feel like an incompetent journalist, at best a cadet.

Of course. I have not moved far, you know.

He shrugged his shoulders. He nodded in the direction of the *bastide*; I followed. It was an old stone building, I'd say eighteenth century, a converted farmhouse, perhaps a *bergerie* in the traditional Provençal rural style, disposed in three wings around a large courtyard. On the fourth side, stables have been converted to a huge dining room. Lunch dishes were being cleared away by some teenagers. Some sort of music was being played, softly, so softly it was almost subliminal, some Malian acid-jazz fusion, he said. The kids smiled as we walked past the windows. The crowns of the huge chestnuts fused above us, dappling the flagstones with green light. The house is flanked by a hill which shelters it from the Mistral. In the courtyard, anyhow, it was another climate. A mob of younger children scattered as we crossed it. Some old men were talking on the bench around the trunk of the tree. There was a group of younger men playing a version of *pétanque*.

He said, so!

I said: so! And gestured at this property around him.

There's a quite a crowd of us here, you know. We teach our children and run summer courses. There's no need to poison ourselves in the city: we do all our stuff electronically, and this is the main way we continue our work. This is our contribution. It's little enough, but it's something.

It was the sort of modesty arrogance assumes. Still, it was hard to reconcile with the muted violence which seemed to bewitch Tom-Tom. If the news of her death had affected him at all I couldn't tell. He certainly wasn't going to show it to me.

He did say: I don't think Australia did much for my son. I couldn't believe how little self-esteem he had when he first arrived here. Of course, he was in pain for his mother too, long before she died. But ... well, there's hope, I think, for him. You'll see him later. He's out pruning the vines, putting some callouses on those soft hands of his.

Inside the dining hall he showed me to a table they had cleared near the big stone fireplace.

He will work with us here until he decides whether he wants to commit himself to the community. He is not very used to work or commitment ... Well, I understand it doesn't crop up much in their vocabulary down there. I am gratified, though, that Millie and Joe's people have held onto Banksiafold. That is something. Something small. But small gains coalesce. That's what Karim will have to learn.

He used the future in a way that discouraged questions. He served us tea. Very hot, very sweet, pungent with mint.

So where I was, back then? I was young and I was angry … I was angry about so much in this society, you know. I think I had expectations which were idealistic, to put it mildly. I was pretty intolerant with the motives of those around me, usually self-serving.

He laughed briefly, rather bitterly.

I remember Tom-Tom, talking about him early on but even more about what they wove between them, that Spider character played by their teacher, for instance, as if she'd also been their fantasy, some sort of screen where they played out contradictions they didn't want to handle themselves. It makes little difference now that you tell me the Spider was probably a sham. In fact it makes a lot of sense: they needed her to be fake to feel genuine.

Then Karim came in. He is quite a handsome young man. More Arab than I had imagined him, tall, raw-boned, with huge hands. He watched me, all the time, with those deep-set black eyes. He kissed me ceremoniously on both cheeks.

Odette! My mother used to take out your photo when she was drunk. She was always saying, I must find out where she's living now. She never got around to it. If she ever wrote letters she never posted them anyhow. I guess there was a lot she never got around to. He shrugged. I wish she had. It might have made a difference. His smile was wide, frankly warm. I didn't disillusion him about these misplaced sentiments.

What do I write to Maurice and Lou Barb? Can I say you are happy, Karim?

You can say that I am happy and that I'm finding myself, as they love to say back there. I hope you will testify that my French is coming on. I'm also learning Arabic from one of the old guys here. In return, I offer my modest bit of muscle.

It's skill-sharing here, Asif said. That's our currency. We have computer programers, musicians, carpenters, masons, *vignerons*, potters. I'm sure with a bit of Tom-Tom's passion for words, and perhaps a few of my mathematical genes — eh? — that Karim will make a contribution here, if he wants to. He gave him a paternal slap on the shoulder. He showed his teeth but the joviality was strained. I remember Tom-Tom being quite smart at maths at school. But I thought better of questioning anything this man said.

As if he picked up my observation, he added: I don't have any idea how Tom-Tom might have depicted our time together in Australia. But you know, that culture ... Well, I didn't translate into it. We had too much pressure on us from the start. I cracked, I'm afraid. Tom-Tom didn't know how to manage my moods any more than I did. She also had too many acquaintances pouring in to check me out night and day. That was a nightmare for me. Also, I have to say, we each stoked the other's fury. We were children.

My mother never grew up, Karim added. I had disappeared for him; he spoke only to Asif. She punished Maurice with her remoteness because of the way you and she failed.

You will send my regards to Maurice, Asif said. Thank him for trying to help my son. But I suppose there are some things a stepfather can't compensate for.

Well, Maurice, and Lou, a meal followed, and quite a

good couscous it was too. Then I hit the road back to Avignon where I was to leave the hire car and catch my train to Marseille. As I cleared the main gate of the property it struck me that no one is indispensable for those who choose the path of survival.

From Avignon I took the train to Marseille. Molly Schor has set up her studio in a warehouse down by the old wharves of La Joliette. She is olive-skinned but untanned, as if she spends little time outdoors. She's on the heavy side, flamboyantly dressed. Still Marseille is not France, if you know what I mean; theirs is a language of overstatement. I noticed a tattoo on her biceps, thought it could have even been a banksia. She was wearing a beaded African necklace and through her hair she'd twisted a scarf in a geometric pattern, a complex of zigzags, in orange, purple and white. The strands left loose, in sickle-shaped bangs in front of the ears, were bright orange. She was on her knees cutting up costumes, her mouth bristling with pins. I gathered from the posters about the place that she was working in musical theatre, in some sort of designer capacity.

Yeah? She said through the pins. The accent was American.

I told her about Tom-Tom. The way it ended, the fragments you said she left. She remained kneeling, leaning forward, the pins still in her mouth, staring at the warehouse wall. Her hands, still gripping the cloth, were tense.

Finally she said, Oh my God. Well, I guess it figures. Oh my God.

Then she looked at me, her eyes hard, stony. Well, come out with it. Why have you come here? I'm sorry, but I wonder why I even have to know this. After ... Then she held herself still for some time, biting into her lip until I thought she might swallow the pins.

I was just wondering if perhaps you could say something about the way you remember her, you know, the work you did together through the *Théâtre des Marges*.

She continued pinning, sizing up fabric samples. I was tempted simply to walk out.

So you're researching her life now?

No, her friend, Lou Barb, and her husband ... her widower, Maurice, are trying to salvage something from the bits and pieces of writing she left.

Salvage something? Surely she could only have done that by living her life. Look, she was an improviser. How can anyone salvage that in writing around her ... bits and pieces?

That's what I've come to ask you.

You want me to tell them how to write it?

Not at all, but they want to respect what your sense of Tom-Tom was.

I never wrapped her up like that. Had a sense of ... Unless you people nail her down.

Look you're busy right now and I can see I'm not welcome. Here's my card if you would be kind enough to talk things through. Lou Barb says she'd like to honour what she was to someone like yourself.

To someone like myself? How come you're so clued in already? What's this about honouring? We can do without honouring. Tom-Tom was my lover if you'd like to know, not that she liked to know it for most of the short time we had together. It was also tied up in our work. That's where we connected to start with. Unfortunately for me I was just an incidental expense along the path of self-improvisation. Something she didn't particularly want to add to her stock of knowledge. Don't ask me how you can use it. I guess they've read her stuff already, raided her files. Seen how she wrote me in or out.

No I haven't, but I gather Maurice has, you know …

That'd be right. That's husbands for you. So you want to spice things up with the ageing lesbian lover on tape too. Yeah, I've got the card.

She kneed her way forward over the mock-up costumes. I was dismissed.

The warehouse floor was immense. It took me an eternity to reach the lock on the door. I found myself on fire with the deadlock mechanism while Molly acted resolutely oblivious. Then she came up beside me, jiggled the key and unhooked the little bar in one neat gesture. Her kohl was blotted.

I'm sorry. What you've said has brought it all back. That stupid, stupid girl threw it all away. She was closing the door on her tear-blurred face. I noticed in the light that her acne scars were concerted into a pattern of pain, like some sort of macabre woodcut.

Well, Maurice and Lou: it's a fairly bitter harvest, but there you are.

On a more positive note, I am delighted that Isidore won't take the dress off! She has good taste. It is a *marque de première crue*, you know, a top rate label? My English is slipping.

Best regards

Odette

True Sons of the Culture

No one wants to make of the dried-out plateau of middle-aged depression their material, I expect. And beyond this petty pathos of the self, there flickers the daily news: the daily drizzle of white lies, the white lies of democracy, the white lies of equality, the white lies of individual rights, the white lies of property and progress and *realpolitik* until we blink, anaesthetised and take it for our natural climate. When I called the cops to the house and they said of Asif: Ah fuck, not another wog; why did I choose not to believe my ears? When I told Karim to walk straight, to ignore them when they told him to go back to his own country, whose side was I on? Some of us have sons too like the ones who make a sport of murder, who drove and reversed and drove again into the sleeping boy, the one they called coon, boong bastard, black cunt.

The boy they drive into as he sleeps will always be alive in his dying, but driven over, backwards and forwards, driven over, still alive, and our eyes flick from image to print, and we think we imagine for a warm moment of blurred sympathy what it's like to be cross-examined by the cops because you are black and are leaning against your father's four-wheel drive, and taunted in streets and in pubs, whether in slum suburbs or river suburbs, you find it makes no difference, because you are black and always looking for trouble and so, for a news flash at breakfast we give into our despair, take a rest on the road side; the grog hasn't killed the pain, and we receive the fading warmth of the bitumen and feel the powdery flow of dune sand under our palms, the faint easterly rising cool on our black skin and the old sickness in our throats with the stillborn promise of half-metabolised booze on our tongues and now there's the roar of our death coming and its rehearsal in burnt rubber and the brute weight of the revved up V-8 comes crushing down, so heavy it may as well be the whole city, pressing with a will to pulverise and we are gone … But we readers are so lucky and so glad to switch with a simple shift of focus to the spot behind the V-8's wheel and we can come alive again to the tang of our murderous sweat and we can make whoopee with the white boys' blood rushing to our balls and we go for it, smash into the sleeper's body at the road side, line him up, we can yell, line up his legs, go for another one, maybe he's still alive, it's not real, it's unreal, it's a sack, an inert sack, a heap of black shit, yeah, man, line it up, go for another, and we are aghast at our own intoxication at crossing these limits so recklessly laughing and our eyes flicker from line to line, his death is alive, his dying is daily, and we are driving it in every day that we read of these things, and yet are silent, and being silent, we also become the ambulance driver who says, *just another glue sniffer eh, drop him off at home*, when he is haemorrhaging from massive injuries, we drive that ambulance, and likewise go home to bed while the Aboriginal boy is dying, *drop him off*, no, don't breathe too close, don't listen too close, we might catch a message there, and our leaders and talkback hosts and columnists say of the car thieves, some of them small children, *I don't care who they are, Nyoongar or white trash, they're rubbish, you dignify them by calling them rubbish,* says the lady caller, *we have a right to shoot on sight to protect our property, send them to boot camps, lock 'em up and throw away the key, good riddance to these glue-sniffing speed-addicted car thieves, rubbish,* say the columnists and we sip our coffee, and nobody says who sells speed and power as part of manhood, nobody asks whose culture runs on speed and power, and we check our watches and drain our coffee and put out the newspapers for recycling.

Lou Barb

A Local Disgrace

Early in their relationship, Maurice said, Tom-Tom
telephoned Millie frequently and sometimes went out
with Josie if Nat weren't around, but it wasn't the same.
Skirting any mention of Nat, they became awkward in
their exchange because music was Josie's life and Nat was
now inextricably bound up with that. Tom-Tom felt she'd
become a stranger, even to Josie. Eventually she also
stopped phoning Millie. We're just breathing into each
other's silence, she said. Anyhow, she'd say out of the
blue, when we'd been talking about something entirely
different, why would they want to see me now? I've let
them all down. I wasn't even there for Josie's babies. I've
done nothing with my life. One night, drunker than
usual, she told him she was ashamed of her jealousy of
Nat yet moved immediately to self-vindication: she'd
been proved right, anyhow, in her instinctive aversion.
One thing I do accurately, she said, is gut feeling. He and
Josie split up three years later and he rarely paid any
maintenance for the two kids. As if that proved anything,

Maurice had wanted to say. He wasn't aware of the wonderful Asif ever paying up for Karim. Tom-Tom was sure, all the same, that the damage had been irrevocably done. She preferred to cling to her misery like some sort of security blanket rather than apologise, and whatever else she needed to do. He found infuriating the vicious circles she invented. He told me he'd been glad to be able to get away to work and even considered leaving her at this stage because she blocked all solutions in advance and refused to get any counselling. To her it was logical, Maurice said, exasperated even now. She'd lost touch because of her shame and then found it impossible to renew contact, ashamed for having lost touch. She settled into a general forgetfulness, numbing out, as even she put it. She became so agoraphobic, he knew it took her immense courage to go to a park with Isidore. Well might she say *loopy detour*: she was wilfully embarked on one long loopy detour away from her own life, he said.

The stories of Bankiafold's problems with the council had been trickling through for some time but Maurice said he was actually relieved she'd missed them. She had become increasingly distressed with the general turn of politics and barely dared scan the headlines. The ostrich syndrome, Maurice said, rather than act, she preferred not to see. But this time, perhaps the word *disgrace* in the headline, perhaps the photographs, spurred her to read on.

The article detailed how the council had passed a rezoning bill sending up residential prices in anticipation of the freeway extension. Banksiafold contested that the council had been infiltrated and that they were trying to put pressure on them to drive them out. In protest they stopped paying their rates. The services were suspended and now even the water had been cut off. The photographs showed the rubbish pile-up as evidence. They included Maeve's old ute, its wheel rims rusted onto collapsed tyres. There was the caption: *Vehicle awaiting repair at Banksiafold*. At that Tom-Tom broke into sobs.

It's all lies and now they've photographed the lies, she cried.

The residents' petition was going to move on Banksiafold the next day, in support of the council order to clean up and pay up or get out. Garth Hendriks would be delivering the order himself; he invoked not just the health threat to the neighbours but to the occupants of Banksiafold. When Tom-Tom saw his name she moaned. The council had been patient, Hendriks said, sending summons to collect arrears in land and water rates to no avail.

Maurice suggested she might be useful as a mediator.

Mediator! she shouted. Mediator! You want me to see the councillors' and residents' point of view?

Soon you'll be accusing me of being a Hendriks supporter, Maurice said.

She tried to ring Millie and Joe but there was no answer.

I'll have to go there, she said. Where are my car keys?

She scurried about, putting frozen kangaroo to thaw in the sink for Destiny, clearing the dish rack, throwing T-shirts and jeans in a bag, knocking over the cat's milk, dragging the squeeze mop inefficiently across the floor, leaving it propped against the cupboard, and then, grabbing a tea-towel instead, she went down on her knees. He saw that she was shaking and almost offered her a beer to placate her.

Instead he said, Just *go*. You'll be better when you see them.

He asked her what she was doing with Isi. It was all very well, making provision for Destiny. What about her own daughter?

Oh, I see. You're saying you won't look after her? At a moment like this?

He thought it useless reminding her that he had work the next day. He could anticipate the response: You don't need to lay it on. You work and I do nothing.

She took Isi in her arms, covering her with kisses. I've got to go see some old friends, Isi, and it might be very boring for you. There's no water there, either. Isi clung tenaciously, tearfully to Tom-Tom's leg. They were rarely separated. In the end, Maurice distracted her by wheeling out her tricycle. Maurice begged Tom-Tom to take his mobile phone, anyhow.

Oh, I dunno. Okay. Can you give me fifty dollars? I'd better pick up some meat and some bottled water.

What's wrong with bottling some tap-water from here?

She closed her eyes as if this were just too hard. She turned back from the front door to kiss him. Thankyou, darling. Sorry.

He still wonders what the sorry meant.

Lou Barb

White Window Shopping

I have been trancing back to these fragments as to a letterbox to see what has happened to me, as well. I begin to be addicted to the oscillation between her excess and my measure. Oh back and forth, *fort da, fort da* goes the reeling spool ...

My own position has its urgencies. I hear the live soundtrack, coming from the white boys of this town and wonder how far our sublimations at the Institute are from this.

Reverse again over this boy, full of grog, yeah, man, line his legs up, go for it, fuckin' boong, ah yeah, another glue sniffer for the glue factory.

Again and again alongside my colleagues at the Institute, I have stepped up to the rostrum to make my position statement, as if to say I've found Jesus: we pledge to critique, resist and disrupt the Discourses of Oppression, of course, so we make of the Oppressed our raw material, drawing our abstractions from their affliction, sacrificing stories of resistance and endurance to the shiny machines of our theory and, stepping down from the rostrum, oh, we are assuaged, the pink rising in our white skins as we soak in the applause; yes! we say, the performance space is always a contested site and we can see that our colleagues approve and that we have used the right words and that we've been saved — kerplunk! — one by one, seminar upon seminar, we faint back into our private ecstasies — another publishable testimony to notch up on our resumés.

At a seminar shortly before my leave I was murmuring in my obeisance the usual weak pieties about divided subjects, about the performance of identity, about identification as performance and all the time I observed the cool protocol of High Theory, a voice in my mind wanted to shout: *Of course we're all split little subjects and what real difference is our verbal finesse going to make to anyone out on the streets.* Then Hal Foster, a poodle-haired colleague, whose shirt is always out of his jeans, rose to deliver his timely paper: Postcolonialism in the Cyberspace. He was talking deterritorialisation as he helped us explore the empire of his own mind, and he was showing us the spaces we should explore if we wanted serious funding. I watched his precise, pleated little pink mouth forming the words I had formed, talking about smooth space and fluid practices, and I watched the tongue press against his cluttered, pearly teeth to talk fictionality and I found myself in a seizure of rage and snarled: *Oh get real, why don't you all get real.* As I walked out I could feel the heat of their looks on my back and I knew that they knew I had lost it.

The next time, without introduction, without explanation or apology, I read them Tom-Tom's 'White Window

Shopping' knowing that I was an exemplary white window shopper for her, just as she might have been for the critics of the *Théâtre des Marges*.

white window shopping
if familiar mirrors peeled
away like skin
could we set our sun-
blind selves out there
on bitumen
to wait for the hit
we identify with?

black memories reverse
against the grain of voices
voices we have tried
without a broken chord
or swollen tongue to show for it
when death strikes dumb
again
again
black memories reverse
and as we cop the muffler's heat
shall we try for street-wise diction,
now, a laid-back line?
how to repeat that squeal of tyres
how to score as metal bites
into our tender bodytexts?

remember times
when we hoped to borrow
for our measured sorrow
a motif from the Nyoongar
Daily News?

sometimes white violence taps
the window of the text
a cry beyond all simulacra
upsets the cool parade
of syllables and blanks
pronouns split like mannequins
bleeding from the neck, the hip, the wrist
of bodies they replace
and then there's something tacky
on that glass we can't dismiss
we try our cloths, our sprays
erase
erase
but still it's there:
these memories conduct their smear
campaign always from the other side

The other day, the teenaged son of a respected white
suburban family was bashed up by the police. He
apparently had a history of small offences. He carried a
knife with him to school. There had been a couple of
break-ins. This was conveniently forgotten in the wider
white community. This particular offence was harmless
enough: smoking a little dope, for goodness sake, they
said; whose kids don't do that? And giving cheek to
police outside a nightclub, well. Elsa at the deli said:
What child doesn't become a bit of bother when the
hormones start? And he comes from such a good family.
Good school. Lovely home. The video of the verballing
records a punch which dislodged a tooth. Dorothy Rich,
at the deli counter, who knows the parents, said they had
just spent thousands on the last stage of those teeth.
Obviously the punches continued to fly because the

soundtrack recorded more slugging noises followed by groans. All the good citizens are up in arms; they demonstrate, they write to the newspapers. They demand that the police sergeant be made to step down. This white adolescent with his concerned and supportive parents holds the front pages for days.

But again and again the cops send their message to the Nyoongars; they routinely mark out the rhythm of the verballing with punches, kicks, head-bashing and, for good measure, the poison pellets of verbal abuse.

And a young Nyoongar lies in a pool of blood and vomit:

Go ahead piss y'rself filth.

This is a banal daily event; it never gets reported unless it ends in death. I know the sound track so well.

O-oh, she's topplin'. What a pity she's gone and gashed herself but what can ya do we're not fuckin' nurses or are we, protectin' them from themselves all the time? Yeah, sure, drunk like all of her tribe, done it to herself. And I look again of those photos of Banksiafold, at the evidence in full-colour, front page spread of the wreckage, uncollected garbage, graffitied walls, bottles, and flagons, flagons.

The eloquence of their fake reporting.

Lou Barb

This Essence

When I went into the Institute to collect my mail I glimpsed the nightmare it has become since I've been living in Tom-Tom's world. The memos accumulating for me while I've been on leave suggest that I'm seen as some sort of regressive, whose research time is being squandered on this dubious material. *We are aware of your personal project but would like more details about its relation to your academic research.* One salacious corridor comment: Still dipping into your friend's life, are you? Since the National Review Committee has made its recommendations to the Federal Department the Institute has accepted increased subsidy from Central Mining in order to maintain Indigenous Studies. There is the added proviso that we rationalise teaching and service students increasingly through hypertext, interactive video, and e-mail. The way I teach performance theory is far too expensive, they say. Why don't I apply for a grant to learn to offer it in electronic mode? Colleagues are outdoing one another for lucrative link-ups with Indonesian and Malaysian universities. No one mentions East Timor these days nor the murderous suppression of pro-democracy protests. We'll have more influence if we collaborate, in any case, they'd say.

More recently: You are not answering your voice mail!

You are not answering your e-mail!

Are you unplugged?

Even when you're on leave it seems you're meant to be wired in, on-line for their surveillance. E-mail gossip bulletin boards are encouraged so the administration can see who is not toeing the line. I certainly don't know who believes what anymore. This has become an old-fashioned question. You're certainly a fool if you think of teaching as a kind of nurture.

I am still unsure whether the visiting Moderator, Shelley Bond, was the maverick she appeared to be or an agent sent to encourage electronic teaching and to recommend disincentives, as they call sacking, revoking tenure, salary drops and other penalties. She was hard to read from the beginning, but I thought for a while she might have been subverting her official role. To look at her you'd never know she represented the new techno-rationalism. She had a good maternal sort of masquerade going: stout, reassuring legs no prosthetics engineer would devise and she wore sensible brogues, which planted those feet firmly on the acrylic carpet. I must say that at first I resisted the lure of the maternal appearance. In nothing she said was there clear identification with the rebels. She let rip a few salvos against them, whose jocular tone made me uneasy: Can't trust those strays: they'd bring back the talk-and-chalk event behind your back, no worries.

Yet, she seemed to be offering a conspiratorial intimacy: she took me aside and through her low, steady, fast delivery in my ear, cautioned me that I was on The List, that I had been identified as resistant to change. She had assured them that in no way was I a Luddite but it was simply a matter of my needing more technical support. I could see in her the symptoms of fatigue, that she too was caught up in these machinations: I thought that with a little effort, I might make of her an ally. There was more than simple cyberpolicing going on behind that vaulted browbone, a bleakness she was confronting in high middle age, a vacuum contemplated beyond the facade of achievement. It wasn't hard to read her symptoms. I began to feel for her — an old-fashioned faculty! I was even on the point of asking her home to dinner; to give her some good nutritious home-cooking, a little genial conversation with Roly. I could see in her skin the incipient signs of kidney illness, of toxicity around her eyes, a look of low vegetable intake, too much of the yellow, nicotine or whisky, the amber irises striking their disconsolate note in old, clouded albumin. Her thankless, lonely work was damaging her. I could read insomnia in the mounting hysteria of her delivery, and found in these things some kind of reassurance.

She began to call me more frequently on the phone, invariably striking a confessional note. When she came right out to denounce the Stalinist self-seriousness of the high-tech teachers I was tempted to open up. They say new graffiti have appeared in the net? Her rising intonation invited comment. I let her voice roll on. I'm sure they're harmless enough; it hardly amounts to a smear campaign against Central Mining, does it? Have you seen any of it? No, of course you haven't, she ventriloquised, *you haven't been reading your e-mail.* By the way, I actually saw one about you on the toilet in the Computer Wing. It was written around a coat-hook inside the door. *Suck on this essence, Lou Barb,* it said!

That's no doubt someone I gave a low grade to last semester?

Well! Naturally I asked the cleaner to wipe that off. I'm sure you wouldn't want it left there for people to snigger at.

No, that's right, I said. I wouldn't.

Then I felt with a panic my body coming back: there was a leak somewhere in my being, as if miasmic fumes were rising, as if she could detect the rebel vapours through the telephone. Could she read me? The image imposed its authority now: yes, I was smeared on a slide for her analysis, as if I had been turned inside out, evacuated, electronically converted, and delivered in clear code straight through her telephone. I breathed away from the mouthpiece.

I recalled Tom-Tom's fish fingers. The call was over. I was becoming unhinged. Then, no: ring! ring! It was her again.

Sorry, but the Director wants a statement about your plans to upgrade as far as electronic teaching is concerned. Now we're getting the Central Mining Union funding, we're expected ... Don't be distressed, my dear, it's just a matter of repackaging what you do. Just say how you'll use electronic teaching. Whether you intend to or not. Your courses are looking far too expensive.

Outside my window there were normal trees, dangling their cat-o'-nine-tails against the blue. Welts came out on my skin as I talked. As if it too were converting to the term of the simile, I was taking these voice lashings literally; I told myself no; that the tree was a weeping caesia, a Silver Princess, white-painted, not a discipline device; that in any case I had to get away from this primitive being-in-my-body; that as my mother's daughter, I could sublimate with the best; that it was just the silly habits of language, coming back to disown me of my own prosthetic power. And, after all, what is the computer, what is the internet but one lovely prosthetic extension? I told myself that I must talk reasonably to this Mother of Sublimations, that I must cyber-cha-cha with her or I was done for.

No, I said, really, I can assure you: there is no smear campaign, whatever the Internet Surveillance might think. And her voice turned through the labyrinth of my ear, performing blindfolds where what I knew and what I didn't know played hide-and-seek.

A phone call was policing me and I couldn't stop talking because of protocol. It was then I had a clear vision of the tape turning at the other end.

Forget it, I said. Forget it.

What, my dear? Is everything all right?

Forget me for your report on cyber-pedagogy or whatever you called it. I'm filing my resignation. I'll pay back my leave from my superannuation.

Oh, my dear you can't be! You are much valued, you know, by all of your colleagues. A quick induction will bring you up to the moment in the electronic stuff, that's all you need!

Tom-Tom O'Shea

This last entry was scribbled when Tom-Tom was holed in at Banksiafold, waiting for the councillors

Okay, I'm sorry if I was harsh, Karim said. But I want to see you around for my little sister. And every single night when I come home you're lining up the empties with Maurice or you give me some incredible serve, go ballistic about all my moral failings. And you never seem to look at yourself, like what you're doing to yourself! I just happen to care about you.

It's true, he does. And I have been so much in myself, I've failed him. I haven't been available. I cry for my love for him when I'm drunk and do nothing about it. I know he's telling the truth, that I've been spreading my damage about. But I hate so much the image of me he sends back, I speak savagely; I speak to hurt. Could you at least break out of your catatonia to put the juice back in the fridge, I say, stalking off to bed, creeping in guiltily, once again, next to the solid wall of Maurice's back. For so long, in trying to kill memory, I've been killing our future. And Maurice, poor Maurice, I've just left him out of the equation. Then, when each new day comes up, it's like a warden's torch in my face.

When the councillors come, I'll stand up to them. This time I'll let no one down. Maybe afterwards I'll be able to go home and actually be there. For Karim and Isidore. Maurice as well. I'll try to connect again with Lou if it's not too late. Like Karim says, we've got to do some chilling out together.

Well, something good's come out of all this trouble if it's brought you back to us, Daughtergirl, Millie said. Josie and Zak were just saying the other day that you didn't seem to want to know us anymore. And the grannies growing up without you! And us not getting a look in on Isi and she's four already. We've got some catching up to do all right! She and Little Joe could be such good mates. But listen, eh? At least you're here now, aren't you?

Last night we made a barbecue with the sausages and kebabs I bought and ate them for old times' sake on Maeve's verandah. Little Joe was careering around on his BMX. Josie's Ephron and Angie whooped under the hurricane lamp, their huge shadows racing over the bush. They took their sausages back to Josie's cottage to watch a video and Josie brought out her guitar, and Zak, Joe's old didge. We tried to sing, but our voices were thin against the enormity of the night. Finally we just sat there watching the clouds loosen and break up. It was weird, an accelerated dissipation. I thought, whoa, what have I got into, some sort of time-warp? Then, wheeling against the ultramarine, there was the old Southern Cross.

Don't you worry, Tom-Tom, Millie said, her voice muffled. We're not about to give in. They're just trying to bully us, to get more bad press for all our people. They've got no legal right to push us off this land. We'll find a way around those rates.

Wouldn't they be trespassing anyhow? We could shoot their tyres, there's the old gun of Maeve's, in the sleep-out. Well, it used to be under the sleep-out wardrobe.

Hey, what are you saying, Daughtergirl, we're not going to gratify that council mob by getting violent.

I'm glad they've left the house as Maeve had it. When I turned down the hallway I saw like for the first time the skinny window Maeve put in where the linen cupboard had been. She knew about looking as an unfolding. I watched the reflected cobs in the red boards twisting, then slashed with black as the birds came down. It was a flock of Mitchell's cockatoos, hilarious and reckless and I thought that the night sky crying rape and broken into bird would sound like this. But then they exploded like keyboards tossed, scattering, reassembling, their white underwing feathers jangling with the black, banking away, stealing the joke, and letting rain down behind them the skeleton cobs emptied of their food. The whole banksia forest moving! Then a bass drone identified itself. For how long had the helicopter been hovering?

I've seen again the fluted chrome trim of the old Laminex kitchen table creasing and buckling the banksia at the window. Even the old scratched surface was amazing, like I was on some sort of potent grass, I couldn't get over the kaleidoscopic proliferation of red straw triangles. On the dresser there was the photo of Maeve in the one skirt she took pride in, a black crepe with licorice allsorts tumbling at cocky angles. In the bathroom I nearly lost it; it was like she only died yesterday. On the big avocado ceramic basin there was a cake of soap, grime in its cracks. It was Maeve's car grease, set in that time trap. I thought I'd wash with the soap in the same old bathtub where she'd float her great breasts. I turned the tap: of course, the water has been cut off.

I tried to use Maurice's mobile. I didn't want to speak to him. He'd lecture me about mediation again. Lou, I thought. I could talk to Lou and reassure her before she saw it all on TV. She'd call Maurice for me; she would know how to placate him. Then Maurice would be hurt not to hear directly, I decided. It had been so long, I had to call Directory Enquiries to find out the Roleystone number. Giving the address, I heard the rattle of broken things in my voice and had to hang up. I decided that for once I had to act on my own.

I found the old Banskiasuit still where I left it on return from Marseille, in the walnut veneer wardrobe. My little contribution: the image brought back home. *You've got to see how it sticks,* how you can wear it. Well, maybe it will stick. Maybe I can wear it. Not in exile any more. The hessian of the Banksiasuit will prickle my stomach and I'll feel like I'm alive with insects again. Molly, if you knew. I've found a length of pipe that'll do, pass for the nozzle of the .22, give them something to make them pause. They can't charge me for that, can they? Oh, Millie said, those pipes, Maeve was going to use them to prop up the grapevines. Saved them from the dump. Never let anything go to waste, would Maeve. A little *bricolage*, eh Lou! They used that word at the Institute ahead of *tinkering*, you said, because of the French cachet. What if they put a tax on those imports, I said, that'd bring in some money, eh, all those boutique words, marking up ordinary old things. Now I think racism's the same, France, or Australia. Nothing is lost really in translation. The helicopter's closer in now. Maybe it's only Channel Nine cruising for a story.

Lou Barb

When the Axe came to the Forest

So he came back all right, to haunt Tom-Tom's story, Garth Hendriks.

Maurice said that Karim had taken the black-and-white shot of Tom-Tom, her face and shoulder obliquely scored with scimitar leaf shadow, her puzzled dark eyes staring childlike straight into the lens. In the paper next to her was a photo of Garth Hendriks. I recall Roly's expression: *some sort of posthumous coupling.* Set up as Hendrik's antagonist, she's forced into a contaminating intimacy with his story. The Turkish proverb came back to me: *When the Axe came to the Forest the trees said: The handle is one of us!* His skin was taut, if a little coarse-pored and florid. He looked surprisingly youthful, his grey eyes darting behind the tortoiseshell frames. His hair was a white soft serve, lavishly brushed to celebrate its thickness. They gave a potted history of his rise, how his vision for Mines and Energy had advanced the state. Predictably enough, Tom-Tom was cast as a white stirrer, with no hint of her deep ties with Millie, Joe, and their family. The petition had been entirely peaceful in its intention and it was only when Garth Hendriks and the councillors and residents' league saw the 'gun' that they called for the police. In Tom-Tom's account, however, the helicopters, which she took to be merely Channel Nine, were already there, anticipating Hendriks, it would seem.

On the phone Maurice's voice had been tremulous, blurred. I'm not sure what he wanted me to do, whether he wanted me to intervene in some way, but I didn't see it as my place. He was telling me of the irrational way Tom-Tom had run from room to room before she left. Instead of advising her to go he wished he'd taken the distributor from the car. She had his mobile but hadn't called him. He was shocked that she had put Isidore so quickly out of mind. Then, My God, he said, my God. Wait, turn on your TV — it's on Channel Nine. And there was Garth Hendriks fronting up to the journalists, his crest of hair shaking in righteous protest. They're armed in there, he said. Who knows how far they'll go! We saw the .22 barrel pointing through the louvres. We could only make out a bear-like shape, some big chap, I'd say.

When they went in, they found her in the Banksiasuit she'd worn in the Marseille performance, cradled in Millie's arms. Some of the bullets were deflected by the carbuncular seed pods. But one had lodged in the right temporal lobe, we found out later.

The police said it was an understandable error. Who was to say it wasn't a gun? She had meant it to be mistaken for a gun. They swore they had heard a bullet fired. On a search of the house they were able to brandish Maeve's old .22 as vindication of their action.

In the next days money poured in to pay the rates and to ensure that there would not be an enforced sale. Volunteers came with trucks to take the garbage the council refused to collect. Now there is a new woman, Elena Something, on the council. She's determined nothing like this will happen again.

At Banksiafold Millie and Josie strung up the suit behind the house, between two Menzies Banksia trees. I hear all those voices of hers through it, Millie said. She told us all about this costume when she came back from Marseille. Said she wondered if she'd ever put it to use here, that it had all seemed like wank back there, you know in that performance thing. But I reckon that her spirit's there all right in that suit. We'll let it go back into this soil.

How I should have stretched myself to you across those tracts. I know now that I'll never again step down from the rostrum, rosy with my own words. *Old photons, my brilliance*, you said, my *adamantine shine* not delivering to you. Now you leave us cherishing even the wounds you inflicted. I have written my resignation, Tom-Tom, in plain English. I wrote it with my old Parker pen, something the computer junkies will have to scan if they want it on their records.

But we must cease calling authentic our acts of severance. Why can't we make our truth the other way, in reaching out, in joining? I have to live the life I denied in you. I remember your coming to me, pregnant with Karim, before Asif arrived in this country. You stood there in your big striped Tunisian tunic, the light outlining your legs. You asleep? Lou, you said. Can I lie down with you?

Maybe I'd contrived, I don't remember, for Roly to be away that night to invite this intimacy. You crouched beside me, stroked my cheek. I felt your lips brush mine, felt the yearning in your breath. I held back, kept still, eyes closed. Why do you do this to me now, you, a pregnant woman?

So, I let categories come down between us.

The storm has come over, pelting the roof.

Maurice brought Isi up here today. That little girl's whole being is one singing Yes. She ran, arms open to the sky, to the magpies wheeling above the wandoo, towards me, her little nut-brown legs cycling on the gravel, slipping and scrambling to where I stood, and leaped to enlace her legs around my hips, her face nestling into my neck, Lou! Lou! She pressed her kisses ecstatically. I wish for her sake Maurice could dislodge his sorrow. It is as if he spent his time detailing the brooding landscape of loss, fetishising every startling detail until its reality is irreducible, permanent.

The walk along the course of Stony Brook seemed to do him good and he needed no urging to stay on for a meal. I managed against the odds to throw together some *pasta al pesto*, rinsed the weevil-invaded pinnuts.

Look, they're fairy nets, Isi said, as the crumby webbing gave way under the water. I chopped the garlic and took Isi down to the herb garden to pick the basil. Then she helped me make a tomato sauce for her, taking great pleasure in grating the cheese, slowly, slowly. I'd forgotten how difficult these small, rhythmic gestures are for little children. After the meal she did a drawing of a huge grasstree, and next to it, arching towards the wind, ready to billow, a multicoloured kite.

It's the spirit of the wind, she said, decisively. The spirit of the wind is making the balga dance.

Balga?

The grasstree. Millie says its real name is balga. You know Lou, it could be Mummy's spirit making it dance.

Yes, I think it is, I said.

It is! Now she was delighted with this new fact.

Maurice was in the armchair, eyes closed.

Daddy's asleep. What's all those questions on the wall?

What questions?

Those. She pointed to the millipedes, dozens of them coiled and clinging.

Those are millipedes, they have many feet. Yes, they're like question marks, all over the wall.

Lou Barb

Raffles

Roly reluctantly accompanied me to the run-down Raffles on the Canning River, wondering, once we were inside, at the perversity of my choice. I just wanted to check it out for old times' sake. Father and I used to drop in once in a while, delaying the threshold reckoning with Mother, having brought Tycho on his routine walk to the Bridge. From the clamour of the bar, Roly and I retreated to a back room. Some man behind me said, Now Keith's new sheila, that Ivy, that's a face for ya, took some talent to dig that one up. Keith always fancies someone's about to steal his Ivy off him. What can you say to him? No guy in his right mind'd touch her with a barge pole. The Willagee Witch is a Marilyn compared to her.

Yeah, well Keef's not exactly a oil painting eiver.

By what machinations of negative design had they construed this lean-to, in mission brown, except for one gyprock partition, doubling as a blackboard for dart scoring? Behind the partition was the Canning River, only offered to the drinkers in little dancing slivers, through the glass panel of the door.

I'm tellin' ya I could of hooked and decked him there and then, a man was saying.

Roly and I sat there contemplating the pitted dartboard, lugubrious over our draught beers as Degas' mates posing as Absinthe Drinkers.

I thought that if we took time out together, you might at least try to climb out of your head, Roly said, his eyes smarting. Make an effort, Lou? he pleaded. I don't seem to be able to reach you at all these days.

I'm nearly through; give me a couple more weeks. Sorry. I'm sorry. I reached for his hand, which retreated.

Outside there were twenty or so miniskirted girls, shrunken tops showing their midriffs, some on folding chairs, some on plastic crates, or eskies, queuing up already, the barman said, for the male stripper. What would Mother have made of that?

Roly nodded at the vacated seat of the Grand Prix video game: I'll give the Grand Pricks a burl, he muttered.

I made off to the Women's toilets. On the floor were puddles of urine already, and misfired balls of toilet paper. I thought of Tom-Tom's aerial pissers — there were plenty in that category here. At the mirror two girls were applying mascara wands, touching up with lip-liner, cheek-gloss. Twittering. As I watched them, the cold white glare of my own contemptuous eye caught me. In the bleaching fluorescent the mirror sent me back Mother's face. Not here, surely, Mother, am I becoming you? I saw as my own my mother's intelligence with nothing but bitter observation to work on, corroding with its own acid, turning ulcerative, blistering my tongue.

Lou Barb

A Garden Fit for Watteau

Not long after Tom-Tom had left for Marseille, Roly and I
had taken our Camparis into the room we always called
the spare. It was a nice retreat, basically part of the
original sleep-out, something between a sunroom and a
nursery caught in a time-trap. It was still full of my
nursery things, including my rocking horse, Clover, his
russet mane the worse for my pruning but the red leather
bridle and the silver stirrups still intact. I still could lock
into this childish adoration and find myself patting his
beautiful satiny chest muscles. Roly sat astride him
awhile, whooping, like Little Lou, he laughed, his
Campari sloping in the glass. The backyard was fit for
Watteau in the dying light, geared for a pantomime, he
said, or an aristocratic lovers' picnic. It was theatrically
pastoral with the great stretch of superfine couch, deeply
reticulated by Father, rolling up to copse-like clumps of
trees, great lemon-scented and spotted gums, and about
them, introduced or exotic plants, hibiscus, the umbrella
trees still fashionable when Mother and Father had

bought into Applecross, and then the omnipresent jacaranda. From the horse, Roly opened his arms to take in the park's span. Behind those tree ferns, I told him, there was a fishpond filled with carp, covered with water lilies. Father's hobby, I said, when he's not writing letters to the Paper.

He laughed softly, endearingly, and cradled my neck in his long skinny arms, nuzzling in under my hair with his warm Campari breath. Lou? He said. You know that you're adorable, don't you?

I saw then what Tom-Tom must have seen when she took a room with him, the night of her farewell party. It was almost as if she had wished this too, as if her voice were in his and I felt so cradled in tenderness, so sheltered from cynicism or reproach, with the last light catching the tree canopy in the garden and the musky warmth breathing in through the window — it was early summer, I remember, because the jacaranda was luxuriantly in flower — that I could almost imagine reciprocity as the global rule. I thought, this man can do no harm. How can this man, so delicate in listening and watching, who smarts before the other feels pain, how can he survive here? We stretched out on the divan, covered in one of my grandma's crocheted rugs. For a long time we kissed, kissed, as if kissing could endlessly reinvent itself and never be exhausted.

The house is so quiet, he whispered, as if it were menacing or surreal — I couldn't tell. His hand had plunged under the band of my skirt, down into my fur. I was delirious, feeling him too, unzipping him awkwardly with my left arm pinned, the right hand fumbling. He assisted laughing. Ah, your silk, your silky, silky, flowing gorgeousness, he said, dipping in and he trawled his kisses down, discarding clothes as he went, popping his own shirt buttons, peeling back my skinny rib halter-neck, the bra I tossed backwards. We both laughed to see it land on the mug of coloured aquarelle pencils. Then, I must say I was slightly surprised, with his pants down around his knees, and without further ceremony, he burrowed in, under my skirt. Apart for my suffocating need and terror of making it with Tom-Tom, I hadn't, as we said then, been *this far before*. Perhaps it was the Campari that made me register the ecstasy and the comedy on distinct planes; just as I was soaring; I saw with my eyes closed his furiously concentrated torso and his small furry buttocks sticking out of my skirt and felt the earnest concentration of this burrower — just as he was sharpening me, like one of my precise aquarelle pencils to an exquisite drawing point and rocking, I was rocking like Clover on my own pivot, sharper and sharper he was making me burn until, pitching, I could have drawn my transport in primary colour on the darkening trees. It was then that the door opened. The hall light came in: a savage wedge on the floorboards, laid down like a mat for her shadow.

Goodness, mother's voice said. What *is* going on in there?

I thought at that flashpoint: it's useless his coming out to answer. I felt like saying: Stay, Roly, stay. As one commands a good dog.

Instead I leaped up leaving his poor head marooned on the bed and answered, just as Tom-Tom's Odette would have had the nerve to do: What do you think is going on here, Mother?

At least my skirt was still on. I slithered into my skinny rib, bra-less, while Roly buttoned up.

Mother shut the door and her high-heeled clicks followed

her down the hall like suspension points. Then we heard a tap being turned on, a fast jet.

Water for the frozen peas I'll bet, I said to Roly.

Oh dear, he said.

We laughed and laughed.

After he left, of course, I had to confront my misery.

Lou Barb

Bypass

I tried to speak to her, of course. I rehearsed aggression. *Mother, you were so disapproving of Tom-Tom and me; are you now going to censor what I do with a man? I am twenty-four and pay my board! Perhaps, Mother, it's time I moved out? But who would drive you about?* I decided to say nothing. I knew that the topic was probably too difficult for her to broach. Not long before she died I thought she was on the verge of expressing sort of remorse for her censorship when I was young. How naive that turned out to be.

Why, dear, do you always have to be in a hurry these days?

I noticed that the sicker she became the more she used terms of endearment.

You seem to take far too much stress on yourself. Surely those students can wait for their results? Roly won't mind if you're half-an-hour late. What about a sherry or would you rather a beer?

Her heart had been already failing for some time. I could barely look at her swollen ankles. She'd always had exquisitely shaped legs with high calf muscles and fine ankles. In fact I think it was the only part of her body she thought was any good. She'd refused the triple bypass they offered. She said: Let others who have more to offer live. I'm too tired now, well past my use-by date. She'd use modern clichés in an awkward way, to cover her embarrassment.

That particular day was over forty degrees Celsius and I took my drink into her bedroom where she'd had the air-conditioner installed. With the venetian blinds closed, it was a shadowy, somewhat morbid retreat. There was a faintly chemical atmosphere from all the drugs. Even the oxygen machine sounded like the rumble of death.

You really going to move totally up to Roleystone, dear?

No Mother, we'll mainly use it for weekends, and of course it's nice to have it as a retreat to work in. There was a plaintive note in her voice that she couldn't put into words. I didn't want to spell out what I thought was her increasing reliance upon me nor the fact that we'd indefinitely postponed this move until the inevitable happened. I listened to her breathing, remembering Tom-Tom's anguish in her Marseille flat, saying that with Maeve on the line, it was like the surf rolling in. Then her matter-of-factness shocked me: Well, dear, you won't have me to worry about for much longer.

Don't say that, Mother. You've rallied plenty of times before.

How's Roland?

Roly's fine.

You're happy with him, aren't you?

Yes, Mother, I'm as happy as I could be, I mean with anyone.

I suppose I didn't value that enough. You know, being happy. I wanted something more. Your father, as you know. He wasn't ...

Lou, I don't know whether there was meant to be a message in it for me, but I couldn't help taking it a bit like that. You know the reading group I've been in? I was a little taken aback about it, actually. The last time Marge seemed determined to have us look at this Thomas Bernhardt book, *Extinction*. Cheery title! Now I hated that narrator's voice at first. So full of spleen! It seemed to me a death-dealing voice, undermining everything with its cynicism, but when he started to talk about parents, killing off in their children all that's not like them, I began to wonder. It's as if the parents in the book made their children into funerary moulds of themselves, cutting away all that was vital, all that was unique, all that escaped them. I thought, what if you thought I'd been like that! No, let me just say this. I wanted so much for you that I didn't have myself. I wanted you to make the most of your university studies. But you're glad now, aren't you? And I was worried about some of those people you mixed with taking up too much of your time, leading you astray, taking advantage of your goodness. Even, I must admit, Roland, I didn't think had the right motives. But before Roland, of course, there had always been that Thomasina.

Oh, Mother, please let's not go into that. My heart cramped.

No dear, I'm not going to go into *that*, as you say. I don't even want to imagine what motives she might have had.

Now of course you are with Roland.

Somehow we had managed to bypass the unspeakable again.

Her hand was tremulously pointing to her Ventolin.

I cast about for a change of subject. I seized on practicalities. Your soup then? Shall I warm it up in the mike?

That would be nice, dear.

Lou Barb

What Escapes

Once he knew that it was done, expedited, received, stamped, and filed, Roly was delighted about my resignation. Now, he said, you can write for yourself, get stuck into your own material. Of course, as they say in funeral services, it's her life I wanted to celebrate, but I wonder whether I have let her emerge or if in my framing I haven't buried her again. All those whose lives touched hers might well find their own versions treacherously inflected.

I don't know, I admitted, if I haven't written my own story there.

How much then did you put yourself on the line? I hope you haven't put me in as well?

Oh, kindly, marginally, I said, as a kind of solicitous, slightly wounded shadow.

Thanks, you make me sound so virile! Yet he laughed softly and held my hand, planting a moth-like kiss on it.

We celebrated by going over to Tony and Eric's new

restaurant, The Hangar, which they've built off Brookton Highway. With its steel-armed glass front and rear, vaulting hangar-style roof, recycled jarrah floors and decks overlooking the cliff face, the restaurant barely interrupts the forest itself: the canopy of mature wandoo and marri was catching the last light, branches sinuously massive, as if siphoning up the essence of granite.

I hope they make a financial go of it, Roly said. How will they attract the clientele all the way up here?

Oh, word of mouth. Let's take a table on the deck. I'm sure they've got quite a network, Tony and Eric. Just look at the menu. It's a sort of Japanese–Australian fusion. I gather Eric trained with a Japanese chef.

So, tell me, Lou, did you find her again, your Banksiasister? Tony asked as he poured our Camparis. His look was warm and intent; he really wanted to know. Happiness had settled his features, clarified his expression. I thought how his attentiveness and delicacy deserved this as climate and location; how happiness, just as much as damage, *wants* to be extended.

You know, this might sound silly, but I find her most in the way she escapes ... She returns to the degree that she escapes my words, her words. It's somewhere in between that we meet, that I guess she'll always haunt me. She said that if you can't dance what you know, then your knowledge is worth nothing. You're in there in a ... minor but important role.

Oh yeah, he said, really? He sounded quite pleased.

You turned up in a dream I had, called yourself Mimesis. You offered your services, you see, as a sort of cross-over spirit for me, a threshold dancer, helping me move through ...

I'm very glad if in some small way ... Mimesis! Did you hear that, Eric? Do you think it suits me? Tony raised his palm to alert us to the thudding nearby. Two grey kangaroos came bounding out of the small stand of jarrah and over the granite outcrop: it was a mother and an adolescent male. They were so superbly confident in their command of this nearly vertical drop, it reduced us to silence for some time.

Lou Barb

She Drives Me Back

She sits low in the seat and positions the mirrors accordingly. When I look at the thighs, alert, contained in faded denim, I think frog. The left index hovers over the gearstick knob, rarely touching it. When it engages the gear, it is by a kind of telepathic enticement, stroking the engine into song, pitching the revs to the limit before sliding into a cruising purr. The thighs stay frog-ready. The dark eyes flick over the neo-Georgian mansion sinking into the wetlands, the emu farm, the blue Soft Serve van in the truck bay, the white dust-storm in the Boral Calsil brickworks, the shade-trapping melaleucas, the blond stubble where the goats graze with the cows, heifers and horses; they check the median line in rear-vision, and flash back to me. As we near the intersection where the flat-roofed cement house stands in front of the battery shed, its reflecting windows denying any possibility of an interior, she says, I bet it's haunted. I only remember this much later, driving past without her. For the moment I am intent on the discipline she imposes on clutch and gears, rarely braking at lights or into curves, but simply shifting down and then up again as she accelerates out of them.

I am ready to put my own life in abeyance, just to abide in this moment.

Her voice whispers along the nerve tracts, mapping, where we might once have been; ardour, candour, a particular light liquefying in me, through which I might move again. Although I don't think these are words she used, she inhabited their aura quite perfectly.

I give myself back her mouth: broad, dark blood blooming in the lip, the upper lip a delicate bow, the lower approaching excess but saving itself. The teeth I feel more than see. They are strong and rectangular, a bright, secure white you get in some enamel car paints. Her smile opens like a bridge, as big as Joplin's was under those feathers, on that couch. I give myself her skin again, like I give myself the skin of any heroine. It is dark olive on which, across the nose, I scatter black freckles, like mica. I can taste her salt. She carries a subtropical climate where it rains; it rains improbably. I imagine now being drenched in it. I have not come back from that summer within all the summers I knew her — the heat simmer of that landscape, the sense of that delicious summer rain.

I can feel its latency in these particular hills. At morning it is beautiful across the valley when the shadows reach up between the trunks and the light picks out upper limbs, rushing them forward into intense focus, like an acu-map of all the pleasure points. As the sun climbs it smears the light up the green-white wandoo until it glows pink. Death is spotlit on the big hill; behind Stony Brook there is some dieback, upper branches intensely white above the foliage and granite outcrops. I move into the green shadows under the canopy. I teach myself how to connect granite, white water gush, tree fern, swooping magpie and the steeped cumulus as she connected them. Then I almost believe that she's here …

Is it a memory or is it a dream that opens up whenever I go back to summers we shared? It is at once precise and mysterious in its precision. When the panic, the spin-out into utter negativity, comes over me, it's the scene I know I'll have to go back to.

The place is marked by the fork in the road. Under a sky with whiteness blazing beyond its cobalt violet, we find ourselves on a mound of granite which some improbable moss stains bright jade. Our silence is intent on the metallic shrilling of the cicadas, fast, so fast, jostling its stuff in the air. We have the bottle of Capel Vale and king prawns on ice in the esky, fresh Portuguese bread, strawberries. Her tongue is twisted out of her mouth, curling against her cheek like a child's. She is drawing the cleft in the rocks as her fingers might slide; with her charcoal, and now the eraser, she insists on the light pulsing in the shadows. Where we meet, of course, there is always a fork, always a cleft. She says: You know, once I was *Fou Roux*'s lover, and her voice wavers between us, a visible fluctuation.

Acknowledgements

I am most grateful to the Literary Fund of the Australia Council for a Project Grant in 1996, which enabled me to do an intensive revision of *Prowler*. Thanks go also to Murdoch University, which supported a stay in Marseille on Outside Studies Leave in 1994–5. In particular, I would like to thank Jenny de Reuck, Horst Ruthrof, Simone Scott and Tim Wright for their encouragement and support during my years at Murdoch. Further thanks go to the Literature Fund of the Australia Council and to Rollins College, Florida, for the funding of a Partnership in 1998, enabling further revision of the manuscript. Special thanks to Hoyt Edge, Doris Lynn and Donna O'Brien, who did so much to help make the Winter Park residency a productive one.

The support of friends and family through some difficult times has been most precious: my boundless gratitude to Joan London and to Morgan Yasbincek for their artistic and intellectual generosity and for their invaluable comments on an earlier draft of the manuscript. Deepest thanks also for their support and inspiration to Bea Ballangarry, Estelle Barrett, Barb Bolt, Margaret Campbell, Morgan Campbell Gasseng, Zoe Campbell Walker, Gail Jones, Sarah Jones, Marguerite Laurence, Julie Lewis, Merle Taylor, Kathryn Trees, Adrienne Walker, Warren Walker and Terri-Ann White. Thanks to Diana Rose also, whose dream story inspired the harvest passage in the chapter 'Nursing Landscapes'.

I am also deeply grateful to Jean-Claude Scotto and Michel Noël in Marseille for their friendship, peerless generosity, and hospitality over the years. My acquaintance with social problems in Marseille owes much to them; thanks also to Annie Dravet, for providing invaluable insight into the situation of migrant workers in France, and to Badra Delhoum for outlining the work and housing problems of *Maghrébin* people in Marseille. I am also grateful to the Municipal Library of Marseille, for permitting me access to numerous works on the situation of migrant workers in France.

The following have been of primary importance in documentation and inspiration: Steve Mickler, *Gambling on the First Race: a comment on Racism and Talk-Back Radio — 6PR, the TAB, and the WA Government*; *Le Nouvel Observateur* (Nos 1389, 1560, 1604, 1616, 1666, 1667); John Berger, *The Seventh Man*; Christian Jelen, *Ils feront de bons francais: Enquête sur l'assimilation des Maghrébins*; Emmanuel Levi, *Le Destin des Immigrés: Emigration et segrégation dans les democraties occidentales*.

Prowler is also indebted to May Gibbs' *The Complete Adventures of Snugglepot and Cuddlepie* and especially to the character of the Banksia man.

Versions of passages in this book have appeared in the following: Helen Daniel (ed), *Expressway*; Helen Daniel (ed), *Millennium*; Helen Daniel and Robert Dessaix (eds), *Picador New Writing*; Wendy Jenkins (ed), *Reading from the Left*; Sybylla Feminist Collective (eds), *Second Degree Tampering: Writings by Women*; Michele Boulos Walker (ed), *Performing Sexualities*; Amanda Nettlebeck and Heather Kerr (eds) *The Space Between: Women Writing Metafiction*; *Australian Book Review*.

I am especially indebted to the editorial finesse and intelligence of Ray Coffey and the infinite care he has taken in guiding me through revisions of the manuscript.

More great fiction from
Australia's finest small publisher

Peter Burke

The Drowning Dream	1 86368 214 7	$16.95

Marion Campbell

Lines Of Flight	1 86368 021 7	$16.95
Not Being Miriam	1 86368 088 8	$16.95

Pat Jacobs

Going Inland	1 86368 206 6	$16.95

Elizabeth Jolley

Milk And Honey	1 86368 017 9	$14.95
Newspaper of Claremont Street	0 949206 59 8	$14.95

Gail Jones

The House Of Breathing	1 86368 030 6	$14.95
Fetish Lives	1 86368 179 5	$16.95

John Kinsella

Genre	1 86368 192 2	$19.95
Grappling Eros	1 86368 219 8	$16.95

Simone Lazaroo

The World Waiting To Be Made	1 86368 089 6	$16.95

Joan London

Sister Ships	0 949206 11 3	$12.95
Letter To Constantine	1 86368 061 6	$14.95

Chris McLeod

The Crying Room	1 86368 127 2	$14.95
River of Snake	1 86368 168 X	$16.95

Deborah Robertson

Proudflesh	1 86368 205 8	$16.95

Bruce L Russell

Jacob's Air	1 86368 152 3	$16.95
The Chelsea Manifesto	1 86368 263 5	$17.95

Tracy Ryan

Vamp	1 86368 172 8	$16.95

Kim Scott

True Country	1 86368 038 1	$16.95
Benang: From the Heart	1 86368 240 6	$17.95

Ken Spillman		
Blue	1 86368 244 9	$17.95
John Tranter		
Different Hands	1 86368 241 4	$16.95
Brenda Walker		
Crush	0 949206 98 9	$14.95
One More River	1 86368 037 3	$14.95
Terri-ann White		
Night and Day	1 86368 099 3	$14.95

FREMANTLE ARTS CENTRE PRESS

PO Box 320 South Fremantle Western Australia 6162
Telephone (08) 9430 6331   Facsimile (08) 9430 5242
Email facp@iinet.net.au   WWW http://www.facp.iinet.net.au

DISTRIBUTED BY PENGUIN